Knight Assassin

The Second Book of Talon

Knight Assassin

The Second Book of Talon

by

James Boschert

www.penmorepress.com

ISBN: 978-1-942756-14-9 (paperback)
ISBN: 978-1-942756-15-6 (Ebook)

BISAC Subject Headings:
FIC014000FICTION / Historical
FIC002000FICTION / Action & Adventure
FIC031000FICTION / Thrillers

Address all correspondence to:
Michael James
920 N Javalina PL
Tucson, AZ 85748
mjames@penmorepress.com

1.0

Contents

This book is dedicated to
My Mother, Pat

Who is as brave a person as I have
ever encountered

ACKNOWLEDGEMENTS

My grateful thanks to my wife Danielle for her everlasting patience in putting up with me while offering good advice as I write. Without her faith and support this book could not have been written.

Sincere thanks to my editor Dorrie O'Brien whose meticulous attention to detail made this a readable book and for the support of my friends who have all had input.

Thanks also to my copy editor, Chris Paige, who tidied up this revised edition for future readers.

Chapter 1

Pirates

Talon stood on the afterdeck of the old Venetian merchant ship and stared out over the sea. Visibility wasn't good in the weak light; there was a haze, almost like a sea mist, that hung low over the oily swell.

His Uncle Philip and the ship's captain stood with him. All three peered over the back rail of the ship, straining their eyes and listening for more news from the masthead.

Behind them the two steersmen, while still holding onto the long arm of the tiller, looked over their shoulders at the trio as they talked, straining to hear what they were saying.

All shouting by the sailors and conversation in the waist of the ship had stopped, as passengers and sailors alike stared up at the quarterdeck or leaned out over the sides of the wallowing ship to stare astern into the mist behind.

Everything was quiet, apart from the low murmur of the voices on the quarterdeck, the creaking of the ship's timbers, the splash and slap of the seas on the round hull and the occasional stamp of a horse below.

The lookout in his basket, high on the cross tree of the mast and the sail boom, had just called down that he had seen something in a gap in the mist. The captain, a barrel-chested, stocky man from Venice, dressed in coarse canvas trousers, a dirty-white linen shirt, and a greasy over-jacket of leather, had looked alarmed, twisted his huge mustache nervously, then had called back to the lookout to keep his eyes open. He motioned for Philip and Talon to come with him to the stern rail.

"It might be pirates, sir," he told Philip in a low voice, looking over his shoulder as though concerned that anyone else might hear. "They prey upon ships that bring the pilgrims to and from the Holy Land." He looked worried. "By the good God, but I wish I had waited for the Templar convoy before I left Acre. God's blood, but it was gold that clouded my judgment." He looked resentfully at Talon. It was because of the bribe the Templars had given him to transport this unusually dressed youth out of the port of Acre that they were now here, vulnerable and in possible danger.

The wind had died during the night to a mere whisper that barely moved the ship and its companion, wallowing off the starboard side a good hundred yards away. The captain had mentioned that there was a change of weather coming, and had told his men to check bindings and stowage.

Now, though, the ships rolled sluggishly in the swell that lifted and dropped the ships in an irregular motion that Talon found uncomfortable. He had not minded the motion of the ship when there had been a fair breeze behind them and the ship lifted and fell in a forward motion. This rolling and twisting made him feel dizzy and although he stood unaided on the deck, he wished the wind would come back.

Turning away from his uncle and the captain murmuring low about the sighting, Talon instinctively took stock of their numbers should there be trouble. There were a dozen ragged, sick-looking pilgrims returning from the Holy Land, who would be less than useful if trouble came.

There were six rough-looking men likely to be handy in a fight. Talon thought they might be mercenaries going home; he had spotted them carrying bows when they'd left port. They spoke a language that Philip had told him was Welsh.

There were no knights besides his Uncle Philip. That left Max, Philip's sergeant, a tough, scar-faced man who had seen his share of fights in Palestine, and the captain with his motley band of sailors who came from a half dozen countries around the inner sea.

He turned back to gaze out over the swell. The mist was beginning to clear as the heat of the mid-morning sun burnt it off. It was going to be another hot afternoon.

Just as Philip was about to say something to the captain, they all heard another call from the lookout swaying high above them.

There followed an exchange between the two that left the captain visibly agitated. He spoke the Venetian patois to his crew so Talon could not understand a word. The captain turned to Philip and then pointed to the southeast. "There are pirate galleys about five miles away," he stated in poor French, angrily grinding his bad teeth and again looking resentfully at Talon. He smacked his fist into his hand several times, glancing about him wildly as though looking for an escape.

Talon and his uncle half turned and stared in the direction indicated. Talon thought he could see something a long way off. A tiny speck of white rose and then disappeared in the distance. He pointed. "Is that what he means?" he asked.

The captain stared hard. "Yes, that's what he means, that's the sail of one of them, may God damn them to hell. We're dead men unless the wind picks up." He turned back to Philip. "They're pirates from Egypt, sir. They plunder ships like ours when they can catch us; we're easy prey. Oh, Lord God, protect us from such scum." He seemed very frightened.

He ran to starboard side and bellowed across to the other ship. From his arm waving and shouts, Talon guessed that he was explaining that they had seen pirate ships coming. He yelled back and forth with the captain of that ship for a few minutes and then turned back to see to his own ship.

The accompanying vessel suddenly came to life. Men ran to the ropes to tighten the large, single sail and turn it to catch the slightest wind, but despite their efforts they could not increase their speed. Men stared aft from the high deck, just as Talon and Philip were doing on their own ship.

The same problem was apparent on Talon's ship: sailors, looking fearful, tightened the ropes that held the sail and managed to edge the ship closer to the wind, but it did not seem to make much difference to the watching Talon.

His stomach, already queasy from the motion of the ship, lurched as he contemplated a fight with pirates. These people would not be deterred easily. To give himself something to do he decided to go below and get his bow and sword. As he walked down the slippery wooden steps he reflected ruefully on the fact that he had been put on this ship in chains as a prisoner at Acre for having killed a man in the Holy Land. Now it was likely that they would be attacked by the newcomers and taken by the pirates as slaves, if not killed immediately. He had no intention of giving them the satisfaction of taking him prisoner without a fight.

Philip lumbered after him with the same intent.

They descended the steep ladder to the lower deck and made their way past the stalls for the horses. While Philip called for Max to arm himself and to prepare for a fight, Talon gave his horse Jabbar a stroke on the nose as he went by, but did not pause. He was too intent upon what might be going to happen. They passed the mercenaries who were jabbering to each other in the middle of the gangway. One of the weather-tanned, stocky men turned to Talon and Philip as they came up.

"M'lord, are there pirates?" he asked Philip in very hesitant French.

Philip stopped and looked at him. "The captain thinks so. Can you fight?"

"We are soldiers from Wales, m'lord. We know how to fight."

Talon stared at the tough, wiry-looking men. "Are you bow-men?" he asked.

"We are, sir." The man turned toward Talon as though to get a better look at him.

Talon said, "Uncle, if we are to survive an attack we have to use bows, to make them keep their distance from us. We might be able to sting them enough to make them wish they had not attacked us."

Philip gave a barking laugh. "You might be right, although if I am not mistaken, it will take more than a few arrows to deter men of that kind. You men, this young man"—he pointed to Talon —"knows about fighting. Work with him."

The Welsh were all older than Talon but they knuckled their foreheads and nodded. They looked skeptically at him, however.

"I'll see you on deck. Bring your bows," Talon said briefly and left them to go and fetch his own. When he came back on deck he saw that their ship was somewhat ahead of the other. Somehow they had gained a small lead. He went to the high afterdeck and joined the Welshmen, who were now clustered at the back railing staring toward the two, small, white triangles that were now more clearly defined against the horizon.

He observed the Welshmen with interest. They were dressed in worn, dirty, tightly woven, heavily patched hose and short, equally well-worn boots—all were down at the heel. They each wore a greasy leather jerkin over filthy, dark, flax-linen shirts that might once have been white; several even had a quilted jacket under the leather that sported the odd ring or plate for protection.

Each carried his long bow and a wicked-looking dagger on his belt. Their quivers were full and their bows looked well cared for, as did the arrows within. They were short, stocky, dark-haired men, one or two with bright blue eyes, and all had weathered, tanned faces. He figured they had to be a tough group to have survived Palestine. He presumed they were on their way home, wherever that was.

No one said anything as they watched. It was clear that the two galleys, for that is what they were, had used their oar power to bring them along that much faster than a sailing ship could move in this light breeze. Their lateen sails were up to catch the smallest breath of air to help them shorten the distance and aid the rowers. The captain and Philip, with Max in tow, joined them.

"Those bastards are going to reach us by noon, God help us," the Captain said angrily. "They will go either side of a ship and board her, and then it's all over. They cannot be stopped." He was almost wringing his hands in his agitation, his bearded face screwed up in anguish.

Talon wondered why men like this went to sea at all, when there was so much danger from pirates. He guessed that they were in the same situation as the caravan masters who crossed the desert sands. This was their only living, and they simply put their faith in God that they might survive one more journey.

Talon turned to the group of Welshmen and at their weapons, and remembered seeing bows of the same kind used by the mercenaries who worked for his father long ago. He knew how deadly these could be in the right hands, with their enormous range. He carried his own bow, which they looked at curiously. Theirs were simple Yew wood and unadorned whereas his was intricately made of laminated wood and bone.

Talon said to the men in French, "We have to be able to force them to keep their distance. If they get aboard we will be unable to drive them off; our numbers are too few. So we need to make it very unappetizing for them to come aboard."

The leader nodded his understanding and pointed back at the other merchantman. "They might go for him first."

Talon nodded, and indicated the other ship with his chin. "I hope they know how to defend themselves, because we cannot look after them, too."

There was a murmur of agreement. They understood him well enough.

The men on the high after-deck watched silently as the sleek, deadly looking boats came closer. Apart from the slap of the sea on the hull and the occasional stamp of a horse's hoof or snort on the lower deck there was no noise. It was becoming clear that the other ship was losing way compared to their ship. It could have been the aged hull, covered in barnacles that could be clearly seen in the water as it rolled from side to side. It was now several hundred yards behind and a quarter of a mile to starboard. There was a lot of activity but Talon could see nothing in the way of armament on the ship. There were no men in armor and he saw no bowmen.

He looked across the water at the other ships moving up. They seemed to be moving very fast. He could now see the single bank of oars along each side rising and falling rapidly. The oars flashed as the sunlight caught the blades coming out of the water.

The galleys' sails were fully set but holding almost no wind, just as their own was, but somehow they seemed to be able to take better advantage of what little wind was available. They were now only half a mile away from the nearer ship and closing in. They reminded Talon of predators moving in on a defenseless prey.

It was by now early afternoon and Talon felt sweat gathering under his arms and dripping down his back under the chain-mail shirt he wore, a suit of fine chain mail he had brought with him from Persia. He looked over at Philip, who was dressed in the heavier chain hauberk the Knights Templar used. Philip looked imposing and business-like with his red cross emblazoned on his white overshirt. His huge, triangular shield leaned against the side rail. Talon could see his uncle was also sweating in the afternoon heat, as was Max, who was standing nearby. It was oppressive to stand there and simply wait.

The captain beat his fists on the wide railing with frustration. "God damn those carrion to hell. Our companion ship is doomed, may the Lord have mercy on their souls, for these pirates will not."

He shouted down to the lower deck for a crewman to bring water. When it came in a bucket he offered it to Philip and the rest. They took a ladleful. The day was hot and everyone was sweating. Even the deck felt hot under foot. The smell of pitch was strong in Talon's nostrils.

Talon looked to the waist of the wallowing ship. There he could see the ragged pilgrims huddled in a tight knot, staring back over the side at the menacing galleys. Some were on their knees praying, while others looked apathetic, just staring off into the distance. They seemed resigned to their fate.

Surely they were the unluckiest of people, he thought, watching them. To have made it so far and then to be taken into slavery or be killed, just before they could get home. Life as a pilgrim was fraught with dangers, but many still made the journey. He smelled smoke rising from the cooking space down in the waist of the ship. The food was foul, and most of the time barely cooked. He started, an idea slowly forming in his head.

He turned to Philip. "Uncle, we have fire on this ship, do we not?"

Philip shrugged. "Of course! How else could we heat that disgusting slop the captain calls stew?"

"Then I have an idea." Talon explained his thoughts to his uncle, who looked at him in doubt at first, but finally nodded vigorously, then clapped him on the shoulder.

"Talon, you have your father's head on your shoulders. It might work; at least it will give them something to think about."

Philip called the captain over and the three of them began to discuss the plan. At first the captain was also very doubtful, for like every sailor he feared fire, but he warmed to the idea that Talon was espousing as he realized that there was nothing else he could do to defend his ship.

He ordered his sailors to bring up a barrel of tar and plenty of spare caulking. Then Talon explained his plan slowly to the Welsh archers. They, too, were skeptical at first, but again he managed to persuade them that if it worked, the pirates would have a nasty surprise. They set to with a will, scooping the soft material out of the bucket, making balls out of the tar and the caulking and putting them aside in several small piles on the deck. They also found some twine that was placed nearby.

A sailor was sent below to bring up an iron pan of coals from the galley fire, which he then presented to Talon. They took Talon's small iron shield, poured the coals into it, then supported it carefully while he blew on it and enticed some flames from the coals, then with more puffs he kept the small fire going. Everyone was fearful of a coal falling onto the dry wood deck. Philip moved the water bucket to be near at hand.

Talon and the Welshmen set about wrapping the balls of tar and caulk onto the points of a dozen arrows, then tying them in place with some twine. It took well over an hour to complete their preparations, but when finished there was a new feeling in the air. The Welshmen were animated, chattering happily among themselves, while those sailors who were nearby seemed less fearful now that they could perceive a plan materializing. The steersmen hanging onto the great steering oar peered back at the activity going on behind them curiously.

As Talon was wiping his filthy hands, he glanced up to find Philip looking closely at him.

"You might have given them some backbone with this plan of yours, my boy," he said with an amused gleam in his eye.

Talon smiled back briefly. He liked his uncle. "I don't know if it will work, Uncle, but anything is better than waiting."

They all turned their attention to the scene unfolding behind them.

Their ship was now almost half a mile ahead of its companion, which was being approached rapidly by the pirate galleys. It was a silent group of men on the aft deck that watched grimly as the galleys pulled up on either side of the luckless ship. They heard the distant roar of boarders swarming over the side and the pathetic attempts of the crew and passengers to defend themselves. Their screams and shrieks came over the still water very clearly; there were splashes as bodies fell overboard, either thrown or as they jumped, trying to escape the savagery of the boarders. The fighting was all over within minutes, and then differently dressed men swarmed the rigging and lowered the sail.

There was a concerted groan from the crew and passengers on Talon's ship as the watchers saw what was destined for them when the enemy had finished with the others.

Philip turned away, his face set in a tight mask. "It will be our turn next. Talon, you and your men stay on this deck. I shall see if

I cannot put some backbone into the sailors on the main deck and repel boarders from there. Come, Max." He led the way down the stairs.

Talon nodded. There was nothing to say; it was their turn now and they needed a lot of luck if they were to survive. He heard chanting in the waist and looked down at the group of pilgrims who were now singing, their thin arms stretched up to the heavens, their rags making them look like a group of scarecrows waving in the breeze. Their gaunt faces were turned heavenward, imploring God to protect them in their hour of need. Talon muttered a prayer to God to ask for help himself. The Welshmen were also crossing themselves and calling on t God to aid them in their own language.

It was becoming late in the day and the sun was a huge red orb above the western horizon. He realized that he was hungry but it was too late for food, and in any case he doubted if he could hold it down. His mouth was dry and there was a knot in his stomach.

Talon wondered if there were just enough time for them to slip away in the dark. He realized that he was hoping for the impossible and rebuked himself for being weak.

He beckoned to the leader of the Welshmen. "What's your name?" he asked.

"Gareth, m'lord," said the man, standing to face him.

Talon was struck by the pride in the man's voice. He was a strong-looking man although not tall. He grinned and Talon noted there were gaps in his teeth. He was unshaven and travel-stained, but he looked friendly enough.

"Well, Gareth, my name is Talon. I want to surprise these people, so we have to have your men on both sides lie down until you and I signal them to get up and begin shooting."

Gareth nodded. "We need to make sure we have the fire going well, m'lord." He knelt and blew on the red heat in the center of the shield. When he had the flames going, he put one of the arrows into the fire and watched carefully as it sizzled and then flared into flame. Before it could take fully he blew it out. "I think it will work, m'lord."

He grinned at Talon, who smiled back grimly, two fighting men ready for whatever fate would throw their way. He felt comforted that these tough men were cheerfully committed to the fight.

He turned his attention back to the tragedy taking place on the water behind them. A tiny gust of wind cooled his cheek.

The captain was quick to notice it, too, and shouted at the sailors, who jumped to the halyards and tightened the sail. The ship seemed to gain speed to the hopeful Talon, but then he saw what he had been dreading. Even at the distance of nearly a mile he could see men pouring down the side of the stricken merchantman into the nearert enemy galley. Very soon after it began to pull away; its sail unfurled and could be seen to fill with the more forceful breeze that had come out of the east. The prow of the galley turned rapidly and pointed toward them, he could even see the wave at its bow, it was moving so fast.

Talon called down to Philip. "They are just leaving the ship and coming our way, Uncle."

Philip waved and went back to bellowing at the sailors and pilgrims, whom he had formed into some kind of pike force to help him should the pirates come aboard. Talon didn't think there was much to be counted on from that motley group.

His archers, clutching their bows, crouched against the sides of the ship out of sight from the sea below. Gareth and another of the men had lined up arrows in readiness to plunge into the fire when it was time. They looked tense, but calm and ready; Talon liked what he saw there. These men could be useful in a fight, he decided. He drew a deep breath and let it out slowly while keeping his back to the men. He did not want them to see how nervous he was at the prospect of the fight to come.

Gareth joined him at the rail where they watched the pursuing galley speed through the swells toward them. There was spray flying from its bow, it moved so quickly. Talon realized that only one was coming and breathed a sigh of relief. He had thought they would both come at the same time, but their easy conquest of the other ship had made them confident that this one would be just as easy to take.

He looked at Gareth and pointed toward the enemy ship. Gareth had realized the same thing and spoke to his men, obviously telling them of the improvement in their chances. Now the question was: On which side would the enemy try to board?

No one spoke as they waited for the other boat to approach. Before long Talon could clearly see the men gathered in the waist of the ship, and he now heard the rhythmic thumping of the oars as they dipped and rose, bringing the sleek ship racing toward him.

It also brought with it a smell that made him wrinkle his nose.

Next to him Gareth did the same, as did those crouching. Gareth spat. "*Dieu Bachan,*" he muttered, "They have slaves rowing the ship."

The prow of the enemy ship was now only several hundred yards back and Talon could make out the men's dress, and that there were many more on that boat than his. They looked familiar with their loose cotton clothing, their weapons, their turbans and round, pointed helmets, but he felt only anger today—they were coming to kill or enslave him, his uncle, and everyone on board.

Their only chance was surprise; he felt the familiar rush that came just before a fight and his pulse heightened as he contemplated the battle to come. Still they waited and watched; the tension on the deck palpable as the men gathered themselves. Talon spotted a bowman on the front of the approaching ship and decided that man would be his first target. The Welshmen could send the fire. The distance closed and then the men on the galley started to shout and wave their swords and spears. The boat was going to come in on the port side, so Talon waved all his men to that side and shouted at Philip to move his men under cover to that side as well.

Gareth must have told his men to start setting fire to their arrows, as several gathered by the shield and blew on the coals, producing a healthy flame. They started to light the balls of pitch and hold them over the iron of the shield. Talon hoped that the smoke from the burning pitch would not send off alarms to the approaching enemy, but they were more interested in catching this easy-looking prize than worrying about some smoke, even if it was unusual. Talon crouched with Gareth, watching carefully for the right moment as the sleek galley full of yelling, screaming men came ever nearer.

Then it was time; the boat was only sixty yards off the port after-deck. Talon knocked an arrow into his bow and stood up. He drew and sighted very quickly, loosing his arrow straight at the man on the prow of the galley. His arrow went true and took the man in the center of his chest. He fell backward, then rolled overboard with a shriek, falling under the fast-moving ship. The Welshmen, with shouted war cries, sprang to their feet and six burning arrows sped for various targets that Gareth had picked out.

Each sped true, some for the sail, others for the cordage piled in the middle of the ship. One went straight into the chest of a huge man standing among the others. He screamed and fell back, leaving a space around him while the others stared up in stunned silence. More flaming arrows followed, aimed at carefully selected targets. Gareth was directing his men, eagerly pointing at this or that object. The space was limited so there was some excited jostling and even laughter from the Welshmen as they pushed forward eagerly to aim and kill with their formidable weapons.

Talon shook his head in bemusement at the laughter but then concentrated on killing the men in the waist of the ship who were beginning to recover from the surprise. Now there were howls of rage, anger, and frustration. They screamed threats and brandished their weapons, promising unspeakable revenge upon the group in the afterdeck, but they were also seeking cover from the deadly barrage of arrows streaming out from their prey.

Suddenly there was shouting of a different kind. Despite the enemy crew's desperate efforts the fires were taking hold. A thin wisp of smoke blew forward of the sail, then a long dark shadow rapidly turning to black sped up its length, followed quickly by a bright orange flame that took hold of the center of the sail. Suddenly the crew of the galley realized that they were in terrible danger. Their shouts turned to panicked yells when they saw what was happening to their own ship.

Abruptly the sail of their ship exploded into flames, shredding into flaming patches that blew forward and fell onto the deck. Fire took hold in other parts of the ship as well.

The Welshmen were cheering and dancing wildly as they continued to pick men off the galley. It sailed right by, only twenty or so yards off; close enough that they could look down into the chaos taking place on its deck. The Welshmen picked off men as they ran about the deck, trying to escape the deadly arrows and the now-searing heat of the flames.

No one had given orders for the rowing to cease, so the oars continued to rise and fall in perfect rhythm, driving it forward. But now the rowers could hear the pandemonium on deck and smell the fire. To the watchers on the merchantman there came a hideous wailing sound that set the hair up on every neck. The rowing became uneven so that the galley slewed to port and then slowed. Even the Welshmen halted their wild victory yells to listen, appalled now at the scene unfolding below them. The smell of the burning ship coupled with the stench of human excrement from the lower rowing decks was enough to make Talon gag. He stepped quickly over to the starboard side and sucked in some clean air, willing himself not to vomit. After a few minutes he returned to the port side and continued to watch what happened on the galley.

The oars became an untidy tangle as those inside fought their locked chains and tried to get out of the death trap, while those on the top deck fought the ever-fiercer flames. Smoke and sparks flew high in the air as the ship burned. Talon and his men watched as the galley come to a stop, wallowing in the choppy seas.

The captain of the merchantman quickly realized his own danger and directed his men to throw canvas buckets of water over the sail to prevent any sparks from the galley taking hold on their ship. The merchantman moved past the galley once more and gradually left it behind. Talon could see bright flames leaping as high as the mast from the deck of the stricken galley; the rigging was on fire. The tarred ropes made a perfect fuel for the greedy flames. A column of black and gray smoke lifted high into the sky over the stricken vessel, pouring out of the small port holes and the holes made for the oars. Talon prayed for the men trapped below decks; they were slaves, men probably just like him who were now doomed to die with the ship, with no one to free them from their chains.

Philip, Max, and the captain, who hurried up to watch, joined the men on the aft deck. No one spoke as they watched the fire consume what had been a deadly weapon and listened to the shrieks of agony and panicked screams of terror. Men began to jump overboard, calling and waving to the men on Talon's ship, shouting something. Talon alone understood their calls to Allah and pleas for help, and turned away. These were not his brothers; they were meeting the kind of fate they had promised his ship and had meted out to so many others. He still said a small prayer for their souls from habit.

Then the captain wanted to congratulate Talon, and Philip shouted with excitement and gave Talon a massive clap on the back that nearly felled him. Max grinned with approval. They were all suddenly shouting with relief and excitement, out of danger now. The crewmen in the waist of the ship cheered and once again the skinny pilgrims were praying their thanks to God. The Welshmen beamed at him and Gareth said something.

Talon looked at him.

"You are a leader of men, m'lord. That was a good fight."

Talon shrugged. "Your men did most of the work, Gareth. I am proud to have fought alongside you." He did not add that he was almost sick with relief that they had escaped a dreadful fate at the hands of the pirates.

Gareth beamed then turned and translated to some of his men. They grinned and clapped and began to sing a wild chant together. They each came to Talon and grasped his hand in their own hard palms, murmuring something he could not understand.

He looked at Gareth who said, "We all thought you were just a boy, but now we know you are a man who leads men."

Talon nodded solemnly, then his gaze went back to the distant wreck of the galley burning bright in the gathering darkness. He hoped that the other galley had too much to do to come after them.

Chapter 2

The Road to Albi

Talon was impressed by the way the captain managed to maneuver his ship among the busy river traffic with only some long sweeps and his cumbersome sail. Finally the wily mariner edged the ship carefully into the main basin of the harbor of Ayga Mortes. It had taken a day and a half to sail and row the ship up the wide, sluggish estuary to the great walled town.

Talon stood at the side of the ship in the waist while Max pointed out the features of the flat marshy country where they were about to land. It was early summer in the region, so the sun was warm on their backs, but there was still a cool wind coming off the land. Talon was not used to the slight chill, and his thin cotton clothes did not keep him warm.

"This port is known for its salt marches as well as being the largest port for both the king of France and the Templars in the south. It was once called Ayga Mortes or 'Dead Waters' and the region is known as the 'Petite Camargue' or the 'little Camargue'; the province of Camargue lies further to the west"

They had to anchor offshore away from the quays, as permission to dock needed to be granted by the master of the port. Philip wanted to go ashore as soon as possible, so they had to be rowed ashore in the ship's boat. Although Ayga Mortes was some way from the sea it was still a thriving hub for commerce and very much a port. Talon noted that the land around the huge city was very flat. The only thing of any height other than the city had been constructed by man. The city itself seemed to be surrounded by marshes.

Talon was struck by the size and extent of the fortifications that encircled the city beyond the port. They looked formidable and very defensible. He began to form an appreciation for the Franks' building skills.

Talon had asked Gareth what route he would be taking to go home. Gareth told him they planned to go into Aquitaine, via Carcassonne, then on up to Nantes, as that would take them to the west of the land of Aquitaine, and from what he knew it was a safer route to take. They at least would be within the domains of the English king for the remainder of their journey. Not that that would guarantee them absolute safety, as the Welsh and the English were often at loggerheads and he was not sure what the situation was at this time. He told Talon the politics changed often and could easily have changed for the worse since he had been away; it had been more than two years.

Talon had had ample time to get to know Gareth and his men by now and had come to like them. Despite the difficulty with the language, they managed to get by with a form of pidgin French. The Welshmen in turn were very curious about where he had been and why he carried such an interesting bow. It resembled the ones the Saracen carried and elicited much comment. Talon was disinclined to talk much about his former life in Persia among the Assassins, and only talked about it guardedly.

He wanted to put aside for the time being the still vivid memories of the years spent in Persia. They were too strong for him to talk about to strangers, the intense training as a young boy to become a killer of men, or *Fida'i,* as the Persians called them. The Franks called them *Assassini.*

He remembered too well the painful lessons of knife, stick, spear, sword, and the stealth mandated by harsh instructors. All this passed through his mind. Then of his parting from Rav'an, the girl he had fallen in love with while they escaped the clutches of her cruel uncle. His sense of loss extended to his brother assassin Reza, who had been through so much with him while they were boys. Everyone on the ship knew that he had been brought aboard in chains by Templar knights and only released when the ship was well on its way out to sea. Few on the ship aside from his uncle and the sergeant, Max, who accompanied him, knew the reason for this.

It had been because of a fight he had had with one of the Templars who had taunted him beyond the point of no return. This same knight had captured Talon while on a patrol that intercepted him, imprisoned him, and despite his entreaties, had prevented him from finding a way back to his friends.

He had slain the man in a knife and stick fight which, though fair, had nearly cost him his own life—the people of the castle had wanted to hang him there and then. It had only been because of the timely intervention of an understanding man, Sir Guy de Veres, who had taken Talon under his protection and sent him back to France with his Uncle Philip, that Talon had escaped the crowd's anger. Sir Guy had admonished Philip to make sure Talon met his parents and stayed there while things cooled down in Palestine.

His Uncle Philip told him, once they were at sea and his chains were removed, that Sir Guy had seen much potential in Talon and expected him to return to Palestine one day. Talon had said nothing then, but this had confirmed his resolve one day to do just that. Right now he wasn't eager to share his personal experiences with anyone, even these newfound companions.

Gareth and his crew were not so reserved about their time in the Holy Land.

"We followed a Norman Marcher Baron, the Devil's curse be on him, in the hopes that we might find plunder in the form of gold and wealth while on crusade," Gareth told Talon. "Instead, we found sickness and disease, harsh conditions and worse. Because we were Welsh, we were treated very badly by the English. Several of our number—we started out as fifteen—died of the bloody flux on one of the sieges, and others from festering wounds."

"Why would the English treat you so badly?" Talon asked.

"Because we are Welshmen! Our land is not governed by the kings of England, although they would like to take our land. King Henry of the English has tried again and again."

"Do you then have a king of your own?"

"Our Princes owe fealty to the King of England, but we are a free people," Gareth said proudly.

Gareth counted himself lucky he and his companions had been able to break away from the English baron's army and come home. Talon wondered if they had deserted. He thought he might have, under the circumstances. He doubted that they had lacked courage; he had seen firsthand how they took to fighting.

Philip, who had been listening on one of the occasions they were talking, had suggested that they all travel together. He needed to go in the direction of Carcassonne in any case, once he had visited one of the main Templar strongholds called Mas Dieu.

Talon had formed an attachment to Max. The sergeant was a scarred, hard-bitten man who had seen many fights in the Holy Land but was now attached to Philip for the duration of their visit to France. He seemed to like Talon.

"Mas-Dieu is one of these places along our route on the other side of Montpellier. It was originally a number of farms that supplied stores and food to the Templar cause, young master, but over time has become much more. They are training establishments and depots for the shipment of supplies to the *Outré Mere*."

"That must be expensive, Max," Talon said.

His education in Persia had included numbers and he was aware of the costs of armor, and the accoutrements of war were expensive in any quantity.

"You're right. The money is often donated by highly placed barons or lords who support the Templars, but also from the Church. Mas Dieu is one of these places."

Philip, who had been listening, said, "There is another near the town of Roussillon. They are well protected places of refuge for Templar and travelers alike, and many have become almost wayside stations for travelers of the poorer kind."

"Are they like castles?" Talon asked. He had in mind the castle of Montfort that was full of Templars.

"No," Max replied. "The Order doesn't have a need for castles in this country, but they're still well protected, and they have churches or chapels. All of the Order's buildings have these, because the Templar Order is very pious. They are often dedicated to Sainte Marie the Virgin," Max said. "But they are centers of more than that, they are places where we can rest and provide news and gain news of events elsewhere."

"I hope to pick up news of events in the region and also to be able to send a letter back to Acre to report our arrival," Philip said.

After some discussion Gareth and his men agreed to come with them. Numbers would always make a difference, and the additional fact that Philip was a Templar was a guarantee of safety in itself; it would ensure that they would not be harassed as much as they would if they traveled without him.

Then it became a matter of the captain obtaining a berth alongside the crowded quay and unloading the horses, while Talon with his uncle and Max obtained supplies and clothes for themselves within the city.

The captain had embraced Philip, Max, and Talon as they left the ship, saying that he owed them his life, and so did his passengers and crew, to Talon's quick thinking. He waved off the remaining fee saying that he had covered his costs and would be glad to forego the profit, as he still had his life.

Talon experienced a sense of excitement as they came ashore; the noise and bustle that went with a busy port town pounded on the senses. The waterfront was a hive of activity beneath the great walls with their numerous towers; the shouts of the sailors and landsmen were joined by the screaming of the gulls that flew in low arcs around the harbor basin, looking for scraps of garbage being tossed off the anchored ships. There were several very large ships lying at anchor in the roads, their sails furled, bearing the distinctive cross of the Order of Templars on their sides.

Talon nudged Max. "There are many ships here, Max; they are huge compared to our ship. Where are they bound for?"

Max, who seemed to be well informed, pointed to those vessels. "This is the main outlet for the Knights Templar to the middle sea and the Holy Land. I came this way several years ago when on route for the Kingdom of Jerusalem," he explained. "They are part of the Templar fleet and will soon be leaving for the Holy Land."

Talon saw many men dressed as was Philip, their cloaks billowing around them in the brisk wind, men who strolled to the side of one of the huge boats and shouted across the water to them. They might have recognized one of their kind, as Philip was dressed in his uniform, but they were too far off to be heard. Philip waved, but they continued rowing toward the quayside.

As they clambered out of the boat onto dry land, Talon found that he had to regain his land legs. Now that they stood on the solid wood timbers of the quay the ground seemed to be moving.

The three of them picked their way along the quay around coils of rope as high as a man's shoulder, along with piles of bales, barrels, and other cargo waiting to be loaded. Large wagons drawn by teams of oxen creaked by. They were full of sacks of wheat, iron, armor, weapons, and bales of leather, among many other supplies.

"This is the Templars' lifeline," Max explained. "They're making their way toward the town harbor to complete the loading of the ships we've just seen."

"I've never seen ships so big," Talon exclaimed.

"These ships, although full of tempting plunder, are rarely attacked, because they sail in small fleets and can well defend themselves against the kind of pirates we encountered," Max said.

"One day I shall sail back from here to Palestine."

Max looked at him. "I do not doubt it, young master, but first you should see your father and mother and let them know you live. After that, it will be God's will as to what path He shows you."

They came to the great gate named Porte De Moulin that comprised two enormous towers with a twenty-foot long passageway which constituted a portal. Talon was impressed with the solid walls of the town. They passed through the tunnel to enter the busy, narrow streets crowded with hawkers of sweetmeats, cheese, and other foods. These people were very aggressive about their selling, pulling at the sleeves of passersby and thrusting baked eel or other pies under their noses. Peddlers, carrying huge packs on their backs, and laborers were going one way or the other. Talon noticed that there was always a respectful space made for Philip as he strode along. Talon thought it was because of the uniform he wore.

Everything was new to Talon. His last days in the Holy Land had not prepared him for the crowded streets, the shouts and curses of stevedores, and the calls of the vendors. He was jostled rudely as men carrying huge loads on their backs, shouting to "clear away," trotted by, often barefooted, heading for the gates that led to the docks. The rancid smell of the people, their dirt-encrusted clothes and the stink of the ditches and other filth on the streets made him want to gag; he did hold his nose. The people were clearly not interested in being clean and there was no evidence that they ever cleared the streets of the offal and other filth that was piled high in corners. This was quite unlike the cities of Persia he had come to know.

They were following an urchin to whom Philip had promised a coin if he would take them to a good clothier. The filthy, ragged child took them to a slightly better-built house along a narrow street that was less crowded than the others and pointed them to a sign hanging out into the street. It showed a crudely painted figure stooped over a cloth, appearing to use a needle and thread. The urchin disappeared the moment he had caught the copper coin Philip flipped to him.

Philip told Talon, "We have to change your appearance somewhat, young man. You still look like a Saracen and some idiot back from the wars might pick on you." Then he laughed. "I would hate to have you kill someone within days of having arrived." He shook his head with amusement. He had by now developed a fine respect for Talon's martial abilities.

Talon smiled at his uncle. "If you say so, Uncle, I'll wear what you suggest, but I want to keep my old clothes all the same."

So it was that Talon came out of the shop accompanied by Philip and Max holding a bundle of his former clothes and wearing the latest in fashion. He still kept his boots, but he now had close-fitting *Chausses,* or hose, of dyed green wool that made his legs feel exposed. He also wore a linen undershirt, and a loose tunic of brown dyed wool with a well-stitched border. He sported a leather jerkin that was well cut, with some leather work decorations on its edges, and a new, green-colored wool cloak over that.

Philip had insisted upon a cloak. He told Talon that the nights in the country were both damp and cold except in mid-summer. Talon felt a lot warmer than previously, his thin cotton clothes had not provided much warmth from the sea breeze as they had come up the river to Ayga Mortes. The wool itched, though, and he yearned for a bath. Philip showed no inclination to find a place to bathe, so he bore the need stoically and hoped that they would be able to find one sometime later.

They returned to the quayside, carrying some supplies in leather satchels that Max had obtained for them, to find the ship had berthed alongside one of the wooden piers. The horses were being unloaded under the watchful eyes of Gareth and his men. The Welshmen looked at Talon's new clothes enviously, their own being ragged and filthy by comparison. Nonetheless they greeted him warmly.

Jabbar nickered as Talon walked over and stroked his horse on the nose; Jabbar was his last contact with his previous life. He had started this journey with Jabbar long ago in the Assassins' castle of Samiran, deep in the Alborz mountains of northern Persia.

But he had little time to dwell upon the past as his uncle wanted to get moving. They mounted up and, followed by the Welsh archers and the friendly calls of farewell from the crew, they joined the crowded street, looking for a way out of the town.

Talon stayed up at the front of the small column with Philip during the early part of the ride to Mas-Dieu. Max rode alongside them. He wore very dark brown clothes, almost black, in direct contrast to the white worn by the Templar Knight he served.

It took two days of steady riding to leave the sand and mud flats of the Camargue behind. They took the coastal route following the shoreline of the Étang de Vacarès to the east of the Rhone River that acted as a frontier dividing the domains of Burgundy and Provence.

They bought food as they needed it from the poor villages they came across and slept in sheltered folds of the ground at night. The nights were cold but Talon liked the salty air and the almost empty region along the coastline where only a few poor fishing villages hugged the higher sandy ground. They continued along the coast, wherever possible, to save time, otherwise they would have had to ride far to the north. Nevertheless, they often had to find a way north anyway; the coast was treacherous and full of creeks and mud flats that were often not safe for man nor horse.

They crossed another branch of the Rhone on a ferry with other travelers and then set out for Montpellier, a small but interesting city, according to Max.

They saw the walls of the city in the distance on the third day.

Max pointed. "You see the two towers, Talon? They are the two main towers of the city, the Tour des Pins and the Tour de la Babotte. We should stay in the city for the night, Master Philip," he said, turning to Talon's uncle. "There is much for young Talon to see here."

They passed a pleasant evening at an inn within the walls where Talon had hoped to get a bath. But no one could help him in that regard and his horrified uncle even told him that he risked getting a cold if he did try to have one. Max smiled sympathetically but could only suggest the water trough for the horses.

This was the first real city in a western kingdom he had been in, other than Ayga Mortes, so he was interested in the defenses and the layout. Their arrival coincided with that of a merchant train.

Talon wondered if they were anything like the merchants of the caravans that he was familiar with. He asked Max.

"These people are much the same, Talon. They go from city to city, and in some cities they make great fairs where they trade with one another and with the lords of the region."

"What do they trade in?"

"Why, silks from the Islamic south where they have brought the silk worms, cotton from the north of Africa, furs from the northern countries where the Danes live, raw wool from England and cloth from Flanders."

Philip decided that he wanted to rest in the inn, so Talon and Max walked around the main square in the middle of the fortified city and watched the merchants, who clearly knew one another and formed tight groups. They stood around engrossed in discussions as they kept a watchful eye on their wares. Donkeys and laden horses stood all around and many bales of wares had seemingly been carelessly tossed on the ground, waiting to be opened.

There was a more varied assortment of people and garb than he had seen even in bustling Acre. Talon saw men among the crowd he took to be Jewish because of their distinctive dress, and he wondered why they were so far from home; these men seemed to follow a different set of rules from those expected from other men

He enjoined Max to sit at a rough wooden table and drink some wine, which they did, sharing one with other men that Max said he thought might be from the other side of the Pyrenees mountains, and watched the hubbub of the merchant train settle in for the evening.

One of the Jewish men, after watching them for a while, asked Talon where he was from.

"I come from the Kingdom of Jerusalem."

The man looked hard at him and then spoke in another tongue than the Frankish patois he had been using.

Talon recognized the words as Yiddish, which he could not speak, so he responded in Arabic. "I do not know that tongue well, good sir. But I do speak the Arabic."

The man, a wiry fellow dressed in long, flowing robes with a prayer cap on his short, curly hair, laughed. His white teeth gleamed in his dark, weathered face. "You do not look like one of us, but you speak the Arabic very well, *Franj*. Just a few of the inflections give you away," he said in a low tone.

"Why are you here, sir?" Talon asked, surprised.

"I am a merchant from the south, the Sultanate of Grenada. We can come here and trade with others as long as we stay with the merchant train and do not stray." He laughed again, showing good white teeth. "I come here to trade but I am always glad to get back to my home and have a bath."

Talon laughed ruefully. "Oh, wise man, I too, long for a bath and have not had one for weeks. I smell myself all the time, and as for my companions it is sometimes too much."

"You will have to build your own. These *Franj* do not like to bathe, but they do like to trade. I earn good silver here; not much gold, but it is a fair trade. At least I can take this money home and keep it. The taxes in Grenada are so high it is difficult to do business there because of the greed of the officials. As it is, I will have to hide my coin with relatives outside the city when I get home, as the guards will search me and take what they will."

Talon and Max stayed with the man for several hours. His name was Joshua and he and his brother were trading silks and silver trinkets and fragrant wood carved in the south from which he had come. Joshua introduced the two to several men, and Talon was struck by the independence and self-confidence of these people. They seemed not to owe fealty to anyone but the master of the merchant train, who was accorded much respect. Joshua told him that the merchant trains were becoming both more numerous and a more powerful entity in the duchies of Languedoc and Burgundy. He pointed with his chin to the west. "The English in Aquitaine are still difficult to work with, but they like our wares so we can trade. Men often put aside their differences when there is trading to do."

Talon decided to buy some small gifts for his parents for when they met up.

By nightfall of the third day they were riding through the small village of Bagard, with its low stone houses clustered almost at the base of the Templar preceptory of Mas-Dieu. According to Max the preceptory was not old, having been awarded to the Templars in 1138. Candles were being lit and there was a bell tolling somewhere in the huge group of buildings as they came up to its entrance. Max pulled on the rope that rang the bell near the door for admission.

A grate opened in the middle of the door and a face peered out at them. Without a word, the wooden door was opened, and Talon's group of men rode into the wide courtyard surrounded by the stone walls and tall stone buildings. It was an imposing place with two tall towers that dominated the approaches. Although he had been informed that it was meant to be a hospital and a farm as well as a recruiting station, to Talon it resembled more a defensible fortress.

Philip called back to Gareth to bring his men in with him, as there would be security within the walls and they would be fed and given places to sleep. Then, as he was expected to go through the formalities when visiting a Templar station, he dismounted and went off with one of the attendant knights to pay his respects to the captain of the post.

While he was going about this duty, Talon, Max, and the bowmen settled the horses. Talon gave Jabbar a good rubbing over his head. It was clear Jabbar enjoyed that; he moved his head up and down while Talon simply held the blanket. After that he made sure Jabbar and the other horses were given good feed and then looked about for some form of accommodation.

A man, a sergeant by his dress, came out into the dusk as they were finishing and told them to follow him. He looked askance at the Welshmen, but when Max told him that they were with their party he shrugged and led the way toward a stone archway. They tramped after him, lugging their baggage while he led them down a long, stone corridor to a doorway at the end. He opened the door and took a rush light from the sconce in the wall and held it high.

They saw a room that held ten basic pallets, each with clean straw upon it. The sergeant indicated that the Welshmen should bed down in this room. The room was quite bare apart from the pallets, but to the Welshmen it was a place out of the weather and a lot better than they might have expected had they been on their own. They made their thanks known.

The sergeant then led the way to individual cells that he offered to Max and Talon. Talon saw a bare cell with a slit for a window higher than he could reach. It reminded him uncomfortably of the cells he had inhabited another time when held in captivity by the Templars while they waited for his uncle to come and identify him. However, it had a truckle bed with clean-looking blankets and looked comfortable after the rough accommodation of the ship and the open-country sleeping they had done for the past three nights.

It was time to eat, so they followed the sergeant back along the corridor toward the smell of food. Talon was hungry, so he was looking forward to a meal of what smelled like stew. His mouth began to water and he realized that he was very hungry. They were led into a bright, candle-lit multi-arched hallway crowded with men. This was where the knights and their sergeants ate their evening meal. It was stuffy and full of men in various stages of dress, some still fully armored in chain mail while others were in leather or woolen tunics. There was not a lot of noise apart from a low murmur of conversation. There were to Talon's eye about forty knights and perhaps twice that number of attendants and Sergeants-at-Arms.

The Welshmen joined him and Max, then they went up to the opening in the wall that led off to the kitchens and took their food from the cooks doling out stew into wooden bowls along with chunks of bread.

Talon was awakened the next morning by a bell in one of the towers, tolling as it called the Knights to prayers for Matins. Despite the chill and severe surroundings of the cell he had slept well and comfortably. He dragged himself out of bed, rubbing his eyes, donned his clothes and sleepily followed the other people in his vicinity to the tall, roofed chapel. There he saw all the knights standing in two rows along the nave fully dressed in their uniforms.

The eldest were nearest the altar. Talon remarked to himself that some seemed really old. Their long, flowing beards, in many cases fully white, gave them the look of great wise men. Those nearest Talon were mostly not much older than his uncle Philip, who was standing among the men in the middle of the group, saying nothing. There was complete silence, punctuated only by the ringing of the bell high above in the tower. Everyone, the knights and the crowd of lesser beings near the door, with Talon among them, waited without speaking.

The bell stopped. In the ensuing silence all that could be heard was the occasional shuffle of feet and the sounds of the pigeons in the rafters. Then the crowd parted and the captain of the post marched in with his adjutant accompanying him. There was a low command and everyone went down on his knees for the first of a long series of prayers.

It was the first time Talon had attended a service by the knights. He was impressed by the simplicity of the ceremony and the apparent devotion of the men who took part.

Talon took the time to remember his old mentor, Jean the priest, who had died at the hands of Rav'an's cruel uncle in faraway Alamut Castle. How brave he had been. Jean had put aside his dread of violence in order to protect the young boy, Talon, whom he considered his ward. His actions had enabled Talon to escape from Alamut while he himself remained and died under torture. Talon said a fervent prayer for Jean's soul, but his thoughts were wandering by the time the service came to an end.

It was time for breakfast; he sought out Philip to find out what he wanted to do. He found Philip engaged in conversation with a tall, thin man dressed in the Templar uniform with a badge of rank on his breast. The man had a long, gray beard and piercing eyes.

Philip turned with a smile to Talon. "My Lord Sir Greves, I would like to present my nephew, Talon de Gilles, who came with me from the Holy Land."

The man held out his bony hand and shook Talon's firmly. "Your uncle was just telling me what a remarkable life you've had." He looked shrewdly at Talon from under his bushy eyebrows. "He tells me that you speak French, Latin, Arabic, and Persian. Is that so?"

Talon nodded. He wondered if Philip had told the knight just how he came to be in France. He hoped not. The knight was speaking again.

"I know your father, Sir Hughes. A good man. We could have done with more of his kind in the Holy Land. Are you seeking a life in the Order, young man? With your language talents we could find good use for you, I am sure of that."

Philip spoke for Talon. "He has come back to this country to show his father that indeed he still lives, Sir Greves. After that, we shall have to see." He laughed and clapped a hand on Talon's shoulder.

"If there is a way to go back to Palestine that lies with the Order, sir, then I might consider it. However, not as a monk, nor am I as yet a knight, sir," Talon said respectfully.

There was a gleam of amusement in the older man's eyes. "For talents of the kind you seem to have we might make some accommodation, Talon. Also you are young; there is time. In the meantime, I wish you a safe journey to your reunion with your father. Please give him my best regards. Sir Philip, I shall ensure that the letter is sent." He bowed slightly to them by way of dismissal and made his way out of the chapel, followed by others who had been waiting on him.

"We should leave soon, as we have a long road to travel to Albi," Philip said. "The Master informed me that it would be quicker to take a route other than the one via Carcassonne. We take the road south to Beziers and then head over the mountain pass at Saint Chinian to Castres by way of St Amans-Soult and Mazamet. It will take at least a week of steady travel and it will be cool up there. Be glad of your cloak, Talon."

The group of travelers set off soon after breakfast, leaving a bustling courtyard behind. Many of the people were junior knights who were grooming their own horses. Others worked their horses in lines out in the fields while still others, in a small area, hacked with their swords at upright poles. Other men from among the retainers went purposefully about the daily chores necessary in an establishment of this kind. To Talon it was a well-ordered society that was dedicated to the cause and seemed to do well.

He asked Philip what kind of men would want to become Knights of the Templar Order.

Philip shrugged. "Some among the knights are raw recruits who, while used to violence, are unused to the strict discipline of the Order; but there are many knights of experience who hear the voice of God and volunteer to come. They bring their own equipment and horses with them. Some of the knights were once thieves and murderers who have come to the Order as the last place on earth where they would be useful in God's work. Their sins are forgiven on the condition that they serve the Templar Order for the rest of their lives. If a man is a knight on arrival at a Templar station, he is given a horse for battle, and armor. If he has his own, he keeps them. He also has full use of the services provided by the Order for his food and upkeep."

"Who provides the horses and armor?"

"The Order will, but a knight may, if lucky or wealthy, have a second horse for travel purposes. In some instances—such as in my case—he would have the services of a sergeant while on some mission, but this is seldom. A knight can have a servant, a sergeant, and a palfrey to ride upon while not in battle, depending upon his seniority. Those men are very senior men and probably need a less fractious horse than a Destriere to ride." He sounded dismissive to Talon's ears.

He began to pay attention to their surroundings. It was a beautiful country, quite different from the rugged dryness of the Palestinian hinterlands, although there were similarities, as both bordered the Mediterranean and shared some similar characteristics, though the country here was more convoluted and heavily forested; these areas became dense pine forests higher up the slopes of the hills to the south. It was very much greener than anything he was used to. The high mountains of the Pyrenees, faraway to the south, maybe three days' ride, formed a barrier to the land of the Catalans, Iberia, and the Muslim lands still held in the peninsula.

They rode through villages, which were often nothing more than a collection of stone hovels set off the road, some going up into the hillsides; some, the larger, more developed ones, boasted a wooden stockade built upon a stone bank and a modest church which stood head and shoulders over the small stone houses. He noted with surprise that some of the towns were perched high on the sides of the steep hills far above the main road. These often huddled behind formidable stone walls. Max told him they were well protected from the incursions of robber bands—led as often as not by a renegade knight who had a small castle to retreat to—and the depredations of roaming landless knights with a bent for booty.

There were small castles perched either alongside the towns or higher still on some peak where they dominated the surrounding countryside. People built with stone in this country, Talon observed, just as they did in the mountains of the Alborz, in distant Persia. He noted the many crude stone shrines along the route. The inhabitants of this country seemed very devout in their faith.

He noted that they used white limestone that was easily dressed for walls and buildings, either around their villages or to construct the low, Romanesque churches. The color of the stone reminded him of the color of the walls of his father's old castle in the Kingdom of Jerusalem.

It was a mixed assembly of people in their now larger group of travelers that proceeded along the main highway in the direction of Carcassonne. They had left the Templar stronghold of Mas-Dieu in the company of only their own Welshmen, but a party of monks and several men easily identified as peddlers with huge packs on their backs had joined them along the route. Talon suspected that many of them had slept rough last night, and were thankful that they had Philip to take care of them.

There were even a couple of wealthier merchants, better dressed than the peddlers, riding on donkeys and leading other donkeys loaded with their merchandise. Talon was informed by one of the monks who had joined the group that the road they were traveling had once been a Roman road. Talon, remembering his history lessons from Isfahan, asked if the Romans who built the roads had been prisoners and slaves.

Somewhat surprised at his question, the monk, who introduced himself as Claude, gave him a short history lesson. "Young master, the Romans legions built the roads themselves in order to reach distant lands, and while they used prisoners, for sure these prisoners were not Romans. The Romans were the engineers who did the design of the roads and bridges, and more often than not it was the Gauls who were the slaves who built them."

He pointed out to Talon on several occasions the work performed by these men as they walked along. They even went beneath the great arches of a structure that Claude called an aqueduct. Talon was awed by its size; it seemed to have been constructed almost entirely of stone and spanned the entire valley, completely dominating the surrounding countryside.

Their conversation continued in this vein for a while. Claude pointed out landmarks to Talon as they moved at a brisk walking pace along the road. Talon could not help but see that there were many vineyards over the cleared hills that looked well established. Claude assured him that the same people who had made the roads and the now distant aqueduct had also established the vineyards, which had been around almost as long as the buildings. Talon was impressed; he had seen signs of order and cultivation in Palestine and in Persia, but nothing as well cultivated as this land. He was interested in what Claude had to say and asked many questions.

He had dropped back to where Claude and his companions walked, dismounted, and was leading Jabbar, leaving his uncle and Max at the head of the convoy as it moved along the dusty road. The monks were dressed almost all the same way in simple, coarse-woven habits of dyed brown wool, much patched and threadbare in places. Their heads were crudely shaved at the top and all carried a staff and a bag of leather hung off their shoulders on wide straps to carry their effects. Claude and one or two of the others wore small wooden crosses hung on a length of twine around their necks.

Claude in his turn was pleased to provide answers when he could about the people of the land they were crossing. He told Talon the region was known as Languedoc, that it was a duchy belonging to the powerful Viscount of the Trenceval family. Most of the people traveling with them spoke the dialect of Languedoc, which was hard to follow. Talon's mother had spoken it to him as a child. Talon had to concentrate on what people were saying, as he had not heard it spoken since he had been a very young boy.

He did surprise Claude when he inadvertently reverted to Latin to ask one meaning. The surprised monk stared at him with his mouth open for a moment before responding in kind.

They conversed in Latin for awhile and Claude complimented Talon upon his mastery of it. Although it was clear he was rusty, the monk told him that it was correct for the most part.

"Few people of the knight's class," he told Talon dryly, "can speak even a few words of Latin."

On being asked his destination, Claude told Talon that he was going to an abbey very close to the town of Albi. He asked the same of Talon and received the response that Albi was near where Talon's father held a small castle. Claude knew of the castle, more of a manor or fortress, and something about the family even though it was over twenty miles away. Claude looked speculatively at Talon when he said this as though about to ask him a question, but held back and continued instead to describe the land and its people to the inquisitive young man.

The morning passed quickly while they talked, and midday arrived. They came to one of the small towns which marked the commencement of the mountain route. The whole party gratefully passed in through the wooden gateway to head for the market place and seek out food and refreshment.

Philip was accorded considerable respect when he came into a town or village. It was clear the overskirt with its red cross sewn onto the left breast that Philip wore over his mail hauberk attracted attention. People would sidle up to the mounted man and touch his stirrup or his foot and then cross themselves as they moved off. Philip seemed unconcerned at this. Talon was disconcerted by it, but he got used to it as time passed because it was simply a gesture of respect for one the people deemed to be a fighter for God's great cause in the Holy Land.

They arrived in the small square of the town to be greeted respectfully by vendors who offered them food. They refused to take money in Philip's case, although he tried to pay, telling him that a soldier of God was entitled to food without payment.

Their horses were taken to the pond to water. Talon paid for Gareth and his men to eat, which drew smiles and thanks from the

Welshmen. It was becoming clear to him that he had inherited them for the time being and would now have to pay their board. He didn't mind. They interested him and he felt that it could do no harm to keep them with him for the time being.

Talon walked around for a while, stretching his legs, then found himself alone holding a loaf of bread that would have fed a family of three, some hard cheese that smelled very much like the rear end of a cow, and a wooden bowl of rich, steaming stew. He looked around and saw that the monk Claude was sitting with his three companions on a grassy knoll close to the graveyard of the town church. The Welshmen were sitting some way off, chattering in their own language as they ate.

The monks, however, looked tired and hot as the sun was high and the day warm. They were not eating, which puzzled Talon, so he walked over to them carrying the food with him. As he came up they greeted him politely, looking at the food wistfully, but obviously not able to bring themselves to ask for any. Talon realized that they had so little money they had to starve once in a while and could not ask for alms.

He sat down next to Claude and said carefully, "My Uncle Philip and I have more food than we know what to do with. I would not like to waste it nor insult the good people of this town by throwing it to the chickens. Will you share with me?"

He was rewarded with a chuckle of appreciation from Claude and the others. Claude said gravely. "Young sir, you are very generous. We will be happy to help you save the honor of the people of this town."

His companions smiled with him and Talon carved the bread loaf up into five pieces and then held the stew out for people to dip into.

The stew was a mixture of vegetables and meat pieces and made his mouth water as he dipped his bread into it. He was not familiar with the taste, however, and asked Claude, "What meat is this? I do not know it."

Claude looked surprised. "Why it is pork, young master. Surely you know of pork?"

He seemed even more surprised at the expression on Talon's face. Talon wore a look of shock and alarm that would have been comical except that Claude and his companions could see it was not a laughing matter. Talon spat the piece of pork out on the grass in front of him.

"Why, young master, what ails you? Why do you look so alarmed?" Claude asked.

"I-I have not known of pork for so long, I do not know if I can eat it," Talon stammered, looking sheepish and worried. He was in fact appalled that he had made the mistake of eating pork, but also for having betrayed his feelings.

Claude looked at him. "Where have you lived that they do not eat pork?" he asked, puzzled.

Talon took a chance. "My uncle and I have come back from Palestine. We do not have pigs there, or at least very few. I am more used to mutton or goat," he finished lamely.

There was a surprised silence while the monks digested this, even as they themselves tucked into the remains of the stew.

"I am content with the bread and the cheese," Talon said, as though to reassure them, and motioned them to continue.

"I do not think the pork will harm you, young master," Claude said slowly. "It is very common food here in this part of the world, but we also eat many other types of meat. You must tell us about the Holy Land. We are men of God but we hear almost nothing of the one place in the world where the forces of good are fighting a great battle with those of evil."

Talon nodded a bit reluctantly, but he said firmly, "This I can do, as can my uncle, but I will want payment in kind from you, good Friars. I do not know this country, for I grew up in the *Outré Mere*, which is the name of the Crusader states that were formed after the First Crusade."

"We know of the Holy Land, but what do people like you who have lived there call it?" Claude asked.

"The Christians govern four main counties: the County of Edessa, the Principality of Antioch, the County of Tripoli, and especially the Kingdom of Jerusalem. That is the only one ruled by a king that I know about."

Claude smiled happily. "Yes, we, too, have heard the names but you have explained it more clearly to me, as I did not know which counties were in the *Outre Mere*, other than the Kingdom of Jerusalem. Firstly, I will thank you for your kindness to us humble monks, young sir; then I must ask your name?"

"It is Talon de Gilles."

"Ah, now a puzzle is about to be solved," Claude said. "I have heard the rumor that tells of a young boy who disappeared from his father's castle in the Holy Land."

One of his companions, Pierre, nodded vigorously. "Claude, that's right. They had an extraordinary tale of how their eldest son had been taken by the Saracen and never seen again."

Talon looked at him, saying nothing. His blood surged in his temples. He was nervous for some reason he could not explain.

"The rumor goes on to say that Sir Hughes lost his son to the Saracen many years ago. He then returned to his wife's property here in this land, as her father and family had died of the plague, but they came without the boy. Are you, then, that young man, Talon?" Claude asked, peering up at him from under bushy eyebrows.

Talon nodded, still looking at the monk. His heart beat fast. He was not sure where this might be going.

"We shall enjoy telling you of this land, young master Talon, but I do beg that you tell us of your life and where you have been, as I suspect that there are few from Christendom who have been where you have gone." Claude smiled at him.

Talon gave an inward sigh of relief; he felt that some kind of unspoken agreement now existed between him and the monks. Perhaps they were destined to be friends; he was not sure.

It was time to leave so he stood up, as did the monks, and they waved him off as he strode back to Philip, who was looking around for him. Max was holding his horse, looking impatient.

Talon trotted up and grinned at his uncle, then at Max, who gruffly asked him where he had been. Didn't he know better than to run off to wherever without telling them first?

"Uncle Philip, Max, I can look after myself as you well know. I was talking to the monks over there. They are good men," he said, without being irked by his uncle's fussing.

His uncle responded with a grunt of agreement and smiled down at him from his horse. "Mount up, Talon. We are keeping them waiting," he said kindly.

Talon sprang into the saddle and kneed Jabbar alongside his uncle's larger horse and they joined the group that was about to leave the town. Although now dressed as a young man of means, his accoutrements were the same as they had been at his departure from Palestine. He retained his bow in a sheath along the back of his left thigh and his quiver hung from his cantle. His sword was of the slightly curved, well-tempered steel used by the Seljuk cavalrymen and hung in a battered leather sheath from his waist.

Talon found the clothes he was wearing to be warm for this season and now longed for the cotton pantaloons and long cotton shirt he had become used to. The climate alternated between sticky and warm during the day, and cold and damp at night. It had not rained since the one time just after they had left Ayga Mortes. Fine weather had followed them since then, but he had felt the chill, for they had been on an exposed beach with nowhere to take shelter.

He no longer had the loose turban he had become used to. Instead, he wore a velvet cap that his uncle had insisted upon. The tailor in Ayga Mortes had sworn it was the latest fashion. Talon was not convinced and felt that he looked ridiculous wearing it. His hair was much shorter than formerly, now cut in the style of the times, just down to his shoulders, trimmed straight across the front.

He rode next to his uncle, wishing that he had been allowed to wear his chain mail shirt rather than this irksome clothing. Talon was still self-conscious in his thick linen undershirt with its wide collar over which he wore a doublet of leather with much fine stitching along its edges and hems. He found the woolen pair of pants much too tight and because of the short doublet he felt very exposed. The hose was tucked into his worn horsehide boots that he would not throw away despite the admonishments from his uncle, who thought he should wear more ornamental footwear.

As they were leaving the gates they were joined by a small party consisting of a well-dressed horseman who seemed to be about the same age as Talon, accompanying a lady a few years younger, riding side saddle. Talon was not so much interested in her as the way she rode. He recalled how Rav'an had ridden and how easily she had guided a horse and wondered how on earth the woman could ride this way. It appeared to be that she rode on one side of the saddle only, with her right leg hooked over a horn of some kind, but because the skirts hid her knees he wasn't sure. She seemed comfortable enough despite this and controlled the pony well.

He paid them no attention after his initial inspection, although they came quite close to Philip and himself, riding almost alongside for a while, after assuming the position at the head of the column by virtue of their rank as people of the knightly class.

The party was now composed of the rough group of Welshmen on foot, the four monks, a few pilgrims, the merchants and peddlers who had latched onto the group, a priest on a mule who kept to himself, and now the newcomers, who numbered five. These last were composed of the young woman and her fine-looking escort, and three well armed but rough looking retainers who appeared to be their guards.

They rode out of the gates, watched dourly by the men-at-arms on the parapet of the walls as they left. The gate slammed shut behind them almost as a rebuke. The road headed north toward Cartagan, which they hoped to be able to reach that night. No one wanted to be out in the country after sunset, even if they were as well armed as was this group.

Talon took the time to assess his companions. He rode with Philip, who maintained a slight aloofness due in part to his role as a Knight Templar, hence he seemed to others as somewhat exotic. Talon watched the people around him.

The young lady wore a loose *chape,* or overcoat of heavy wool, with the hood thrown back. Her hair was covered by a fashionable *guimple*, a fine white linen veil that covered her hair and came down past her shoulders, but it was still easy to tell that she was fair-haired.

The young man who commanded the small group was dressed to Talon's mind rather foppishly—a new word for Talon, learned from Philip—in elaborate clothes of fine wool and other material in a wild mix of colors, red and yellow being predominant. His hose—Talon had learned at the tailor's shop that the tight leggings all young men wore were called hose—was of wool, dyed yellow. His boots were calf-length and had an impossible length of toe. Talon smiled when he considered how difficult it must be for the man to walk when not on his horse.

His shirt of white linen, with its long sleeves tied at the wrists under a spectacular doublet of heavy but fine wool, was decorated in intricately sewn patterns. Talon noted the long, slim dagger on a thin leather belt that hung to the right and the heavier sword that the youthful man carried hanging off a wider silver-studded belt. He noted, too, the shoulders and neck of the man and decided that although he was foppish, he could probably take care of himself.

As though he had read something in the scrutiny that Talon had subjected him to, the young man spurred his horse to where Talon and Philip were riding, a frown on his young, shaven face.

"You stare. sir. Is there something you wish to ask of me?" he demanded as he came abreast of the two.

Philip glanced round and down at him from the great height of his own destriere and asked, "What do you mean, sir?'

The young man indicated the silent Talon with his hand and repeated himself. "He is staring at me, sir. Does he have something to ask of me? I find his staring offensive."

Philip considered the young man carefully, then said, "Young man, we have come from the *Outré Mere* and are new to this land; if my nephew stares he is only doing so because all this is new to him. I would ask that you forgive his impertinence."

Talon and the young man were eye-to-eye by now. Talon did not feel the need to add to what Philip had said, so he simply looked straight into the man's eyes.

Something in Talon's gaze might have unsettled the young man, for his eyes shifted. "Staring is improper and bad manners, but I shall not take it further this time." He allowed his horse to drop back to his female companion without further words. She leaned over to ask him what had happened.

"What is it, Marcel? What did you say to them, my brother?" To which he gave an irritated shake of his head. She gave a look forward to where Talon and Philip were riding, their backs to her. But her words came clearly to the two nonetheless. "Why, Marcel, I find the young man ahead to be very attractive. I wonder where he got that scar on his face." She laughed, seemingly at her brother's discomfort.

"Probably from some man like me who objected to his manners," her brother retorted.

In the front, Philip gave a comment out of the side of his mouth to Talon, "Don't start any trouble with that jape, Talon. I don't want to witness another incident where you carve someone up."

Max overheard and chuckled. He cocked an amused eye at Talon.

Talon smiled, equally amused at his uncle's blunt assessment of the young man. "I am sorry, Uncle; but I am curious, that's all. Everything is new, including the way people dress. I swear that if he tried to fight on his feet I would have to do nothing but dodge about nimbly while he fell over his long toes. I doubt he could do me any harm," he answered, *sotto voce*.

Philip and Max gave snorts of barely suppressed laughter, their shoulders shaking.

"There is much that is new to both of us, in this land, my boy. We are strangers in our own country; we'll have to feel our way."

Talon nodded.

The party continued on, staying within its separate groups for the rest of the day. The groom they had hired came along at the back with the monks and the servants belonging to the young couple. Simon, who was leading a packhorse with the Templar's baggage, was questioned by the others who were curious about the knight, his sergeant, and his young squire in the front of the cavalcade. He could provide almost nothing in the way of information as he had only just been hired. He told his companions that the three had come off a Venetian ship a few days before; and that most likely they had come from Palestine.

Simon was in awe of the Templar who looked as though he had seen a good deal of life. The young man, Talon, simply didn't seem to fit any kind of type he had met before. Simon was a little afraid of him, although Talon was polite and did not bully him. There was something there that Simon could not fathom and it gave him cause to step carefully when in Talon's presence.

They came that night to the small town called Cartagan. It boasted a high wooden stockade built on a low stone wall around its perimeter. No walled town of note this, but nonetheless well guarded. The party with their horses and donkeys came within its safe enclosure well before dusk, which gave them ample time to seek out the two inns and the stables nearby.

Philip, with Max and Talon, as well as Marcel and his female companion, went to the larger, more prosperous-looking inn by unspoken agreement, and the Welshmen and the servants made for the smaller, less well-maintained one down the street. The stables were nearby so Talon walked with Simon and Max to ensure the horses were taken care of. The grooms for the others came with them, leading the horses.

Without any sense of being out of step, Talon saw to Jabbar personally, much to the approval of Max and the confusion of Simon, who thought he should be doing the necessary work.

The other grooms gave Talon curious looks as he talked in Farsi to Jabbar like an old friend and rubbed his head with a blanket. It was clear to him that Jabbar was having as much difficulty with the climate as he was, so he covered the horse with a light blanket over his sleek flanks and then left the chattering men to talk about him while he walked the short distance to the inn.

Candles and oil lamps had been lit in the houses nearby, the glow shining through the more wealthy owners' oilskin windows or through the shutters of the less wealthy. He remarked to himself that although this was a town of limited size, its equivalent in Persia would have been no more than a collection of hovels. He had yet to see a city, he told himself, and then he could make real comparisons.

As he walked down the unpaved street, Talon wondered at the land he was now traveling through. The town was going to supper, and the smell of cooking encouraged him to increase his pace; he was hungry. The air was cooling and the smoke from the fire holes and some chimneys hung in the air. There was the sound of subdued voices from doorways. In some entrances old men were enjoying the last of the warmth of sunset while in others women were taking advantage of the remaining light to sew and mend clothes. It was a new experience for him to be in a town at peace and seemingly not threatened by war.

He pushed open the heavy wooden door to the entrance of the inn and stepped inside to a blaze of candlelight. The innkeeper wanted to give a good impression to his unexpected guests. He would burn candles otherwise destined for the church this night. The cloying warmth of a crowded room greeted him as well as the light, but the wood fire was welcoming, as was his uncle who greeted him with a loud, "Talon, there you are. Are the horses settled in to your satisfaction?"

Talon smiled at his uncle's teasing. "They will be fine, Uncle. Max will see to it that the new man, Simon, does what he should."

He noted that his uncle had company. The young man, Marcel, was seated on the bench across the wooden table from his uncle. Next to him was the young lady, his companion.

Talon bowed briefly, sufficient to be polite to them, and moved round to seat himself on the same side of the table as his uncle. This placed him opposite the young lady, who smiled at him.

Philip said, "I should introduce our companions, Talon. Meet Marcel De Guillabert, and his sister, Petrona. They are cousins on your mother's side. What a chance that we should meet them, and they are going our way."

Talon looked at them with new eyes and some of his surprise must have shown. He nodded to them both and received a cool nod from Marcel but a friendly smile from Petrona.

He took stock of them. Marcel would have been handsome except for a certain petulance to his mouth and unfriendliness in his demeanor. He was fair-haired and clean-shaven, unlike Talon who wore a short beard.

His sister had discarded the *chape* and now he could see she wore a *pelice,* an outer dress, with fur at the arms and neckline. He noticed that she had a good complexion and clear blue eyes that regarded him with interest. He remarked to himself that apart from an *afiche*, a broach, she wore no jewelry, unlike the eastern women who wore much on their necks and wrist, even their ankles.

He studied them overtly and did not lower his eyes. Marcel dropped his eyes after a brief glare as once again he sensed something in Talon that did not brook a challenge. Petrona, on the other hand, gazed right back and Talon felt his pulse quicken. This young woman was not afraid of him, that was clear. Yet he did not detect any overt invitation.

"Before you came, your uncle was telling us of your life in the Holy Land. He said that you had been taken by the Saracen and lived among them for several years. Is that so?" Petrona asked, her voice a little high, but otherwise pleasant to hear.

The accent was still something Talon was getting used to so he had to listen carefully, but he evaded the question with a demand. "Uncle, is there anything to drink here? I am right thirsty."

Philip laughed. "I shall call them over; I am not only thirsty, but hungry, too. Marcel, I trust you will drink some mead, but my Lady, will you have some wine?"

Both nodded acceptance and there was a brief silence among the three younger ones as Philip bellowed for service. The innkeeper himself came hurrying over to serve such a distinguished guest. He bowed clumsily to them and stood to take the order, wiping his hands on his greasy, flax-linen apron. He promised to bring them the food prepared for the day, which he told them they would not find disappointing.

Petrona would not be put off any longer. "Monsieur Talon, I am still waiting for your answer. Do you wish to keep me in suspense?'

It was asked mildly enough but Talon sensed something there, as though she was used to getting her way, which made him cautious. "I was captured by the Saracen and taken to Persia, where I grew up. There is really nothing else to add. Uncle Philip, on the other hand, has been fighting the Saracen most of his life and can tell you many more stories about his adventures."

"Are they not heathens in all these countries and this Persia you talk about?" Marcel asked, sounding truculent.

"They do not consider themselves heathen," Talon replied mildly.

"But they do worship another God, do they not?" Petrona asked.

The last thing Talon wanted at this moment was to discuss the differences between the Christians and the Muslims. He cleared this throat. "I would like to talk about this some other time; perhaps we should hear about my uncle's adventures?" He said this firmly enough to silence the discussion for a moment and then nudged his uncle. "Uncle Philip, tell our guests about your life as a Knight Templar." He turned to the others. "The Templars are the true defenders of the faith in the Holy Land. My uncle has fought for them the length and breadth of the country."

His uncle laughed, but before he could respond the drinks arrived and then the food. Before they had even started on the food, Max walked into the room and made for their table. Introductions began again and a thankful Talon was able to sit quietly while the young man Marcel plied Philip with questions about his life as a soldier in Palestine. He was particularly interested in the battles that had been fought and, to Talon's ears, not interested in the country at all. Talon ate his food in silence while the talk went over his head and let his thoughts wander again. They almost always came back to his time in Persia and his worry for Rav'an.

He became aware that he was being watched. Petrona was watching him with frank appraisal as though assessing him with her blue eyes. He looked up and stared straight into hers. He smiled and was amused to see first surprise, then something else. It amused him to see a flush begin to rise at her throat. She smiled back almost tentatively; now he thought he saw an invitation there.

He decided that the over-protective Marcel was not worth provoking, so he finished off his drink and stood up. Bidding the party goodnight, he pleaded the need for some fresh air before bed. He walked out of the room and onto the street and took a deep breath once he was outside the stuffy, smoky atmosphere of the inn. He felt restless, so he walked along the darkened street. The moon was just beginning to rise over the trees to the east, shedding its bright silver light on the deeply rutted road. His ears caught the sound of singing; it came from the second inn where the archers and the servants were billeted.

He opened the rough wooden door and was confronted by the thick air and noise of a busy, crowded inn. At the back of the long room were the Welshmen, well into their cups and one of them, Anwl, was standing up, singing. The crowd of peasants, monks, and soldiers seated at rough-hewn tables all around sat quietly as he sang. The notes were clear and pure. They resonated off the low ceiling and reached clearly to the door where Talon stood watching.

He walked in and shut the door. The sharp-eyed Gareth seated among the Welshmen stood up and beckoned him over. Anwl finished his song and there was loud applause. No one in the room had understood a single word, but they all appreciated a good singing voice. They banged their earthen mugs on the tables and demanded more wine—this was wine country after all. They also demanded more songs from these foreign men. Happy to oblige, the Welshmen gave them all they had.

They greeted Talon as a friend and bade him join them in their drinking, and he did so. The entertainment continued as this man or that sang of his native land. The crowd loved the Welshmen most, however, and made the men stand up and sing, plying them with wine until they were gasping for air and too drunk to stand up. Talon found the wine to his liking and spent his time with Gareth and the couple who were sober, talking about their native land.

Gareth could not get him to talk about himself, so instead he talked about his own homeland. He told Talon about the high, misty hills they came from. There were virtually no towns in Wales, he said. It was a forested, mountain world that few outsiders could find their way through. He talked about the wild tribes and the freedom they shared, although he remarked wryly they seemed to spend a lot of time quarreling amongst themselves.

"We are true Christians these days," he said, "not like those damned Saxons and Normans who swear by God and then break their word the very next day."

"Why did you go to Palestine?" Talon asked.

"Because we are men of war and hoped to be able to gain much booty while there," Gareth answered reluctantly. He took a long drink as though to wash the memories away.

"We wanted to be soldiers of God, but we ended up as robbers and beggars," Anwl, who was well into his cups by now, slurred.

They all laughed uneasily, but it was clear that all they wanted to do now was to just go home. Palestine had not been a good experience for them.

"I must come to your land one day," Talon said, "but from what you say it is cold and very wet there. I'm used to the dry land and the heat. I might drown."

There was another roar of laughter at that.

"You would be welcome to our land, young sir. We would be your host and take you to meet the prince."

"Are you then nobility that you can introduce me to your prince?" Talon asked skeptically.

"In Wales any man can go up to the prince and demand audience, even be he a cattle-herder," bragged another.

"Then I would be honored," Talon told them.

The drinking continued and the songs became bawdy. The Welshmen were now the ones who did not understand anything. Talon had to admit to them that the language of the locals was impossible to understand and most of the jokes and songs went right over his head.

He kept a clear head as he did not know the people in the inn and wanted to make sure the Welshmen were not going to be robbed. He saw Simon with the other servants over the other side of the room and signaled him to come over. "Watch that they do not get robbed tonight, Simon."

The man nodded and grinned. "I'll keep an eye on them for thee, m'lord."

By this time hardly any of the Welshmen were able to sit upright so he told the servants to help them to bed while he paid the innkeeper. He warned the innkeeper not to rob the drunken men while they slept or he would be paying him a visit. The man looked into his eyes and nodded his understanding.

He walked back in the moonlight to his own inn and found it quiet. Obviously the night life did not extend to this upper-class locale. There were still a few peddlers and merchants sitting at tables, but his party seemed to have all gone to bed. He made his way up to the room he was sharing with Philip. His uncle was fast asleep and snoring loud enough to shake the rafters. Talon lay down on his pallet, pulled the blanket over his head to shut out the noise, and went to sleep.

Chapter 3

The Homecoming

Their party came the next day to the village named Ville de Moulle—which they had been told belonged to Sir Hughes—just as dusk was beginning to close in around them. They rode down the muddy, rutted road that ran between the low stone houses with their thatched roofs.

There were the usual smells of a farming village. The stink of cow mingled with that of sheep and other stinks from the midden nearby. Talon was surprised to see no activity around the shuttered cottages and hovels that made up the bulk of the village. Dogs were not much in evidence either. The doors of all the houses were closed, which in itself was unusual for this time of year. People in these parts, Talon had already discovered, were wont to spend the summer's evening light sitting at their doorways or standing around in small groups discussing the day's events.

Here no one greeted them and those few who saw them moved hurriedly out of sight as soon as they became aware of the horses and the footmen coming down the street. Even the sound of the farm animals seemed to be muted this still, warm evening. Talon had noticed that the further inland they travelled the warmer it seemed to become. Talon's hand strayed to his sword belt and he adjusted it to make the handle of his weapon more accessible. He didn't like what he was seeing; all his senses were awake. There was no welcome here.

He glanced at Philip and Max, whose training as fighting men was also telling them something was not right and they were both looking sharply to left and right, alert for trouble.

He looked back over Jabbar's haunches at the Welshmen and caught Gareth's eye. They understood each other; Gareth muttered something to his comrades. Without saying anything the archers took arrows out of their quivers and knocked them in their bows in readiness for trouble. Everyone became very watchful.

They rode cautiously through the length of the village and out the other side without a single greeting. Philip looked back at Talon, who was riding just behind him, with a question on his face but Talon could only shrug and look around as they went out. He was glad that his uncle and Max, too, were worried about the reception they had received in the village; it wasn't just his imagination.

They rode another few hundred yards north, where tall trees towered over them, closing in on the track for a few dozen yards, then abruptly gave way to a rough pasture. Low, heavily wooded hills loomed over them in the dusk on the far side of a wide swath of grassland.

Then they saw the walls of the fortress that Talon's father owned. It was situated on a low rise in the middle of a large field with plenty of space between the walls and the surrounding forest; he estimated a good arrow-shot distance with a bow like those the Welshmen carried. Talon noted in the gathering dusk the base of stone with the high, wooden palisade on top. The structure was for the most part a mixture of stone for strength at the base, and thick wood for towers and overhangs. The walls were about fourteen feet high in total, and, as far as he could see, enclosed about an acre and a half of land. There were four high emplacements, like rough towers, on each corner. The gates that faced the village had a protected walkway above them that was higher than the surrounding wall and there were wooden buttresses on either side of the gates. It looked solidly built, but Talon had difficultly in making a firm judgment in the failing light.

They had been seen, that was clear by the activity they saw on the walls. Talon could just see the dark shapes of men gathering on the ramparts and pointing at them. They rode closer, heading for the wooden gate. As they rode up there was a shout.

"Halt where you are! Who travels at night? Name yourselves."

"It is Philip de Gilles and Talon, son of Hughes de Gilles. What kind of greeting is this?" Philip bellowed. He had not expected this kind of reception at all, and it showed in his tone.

There was a startled silence and then a muttered conference on the wall. A short while later a man leaned over the wooden rampart.

"Philip, is that really you? Who did you say was with you?"

"Yes it is I, brother, and yes, I have your son with me. Open this confounded gate and let us in. I am right tired and could do with something to wash the dust from my throat."

There was an incredulous chuckle followed by a sharp command. The gate was opened slowly by two spearmen in patched leather jerkins and dented iron helmets, who knuckled their foreheads as Philip led the way into the bailey. He ignored them completely.

They were surrounded by men holding torches on high that flickered and guttered in the now darkened evening. Talon dismounted from Jabbar and gave the reins to a complete stranger, who was about to lead him away, so he quickly snatched his bow out of the sheath as his long-standing habit of self-preservation took hold.

Men peered at him from all sides, and then he was facing his father. He remembered him well, but was not prepared for the emotion that came with the greeting. Sir Hughes had just finished embracing his brother, shouting with delight, and then turned to look long and hard at his long-lost son. He seized a torch from one of the men and raised it high so that he could see more clearly. Like Philip had done those many weeks ago, he, too, peered at his son, looking for some feature that might tell him this was the boy he had known.

He shook his head and gave a tentative growl. "Talon, is this really you?"

Talon nodded, too overcome to speak, then cleared his throat. "Yes, Father, it is I, Talon."

His father faced him and tears began to pour down his bearded face. "My boy! My long-lost boy! It's been so long. We thought those heathens had taken you forever."

He handed off the torch and stumbled forward and the next thing Talon knew, his father was giving him a bear hug. To his surprise, he was as tall as his father. He returned the embrace with fervor, the emotion of the moment threatening to overwhelm him. They stood for a long moment, father and son, in front of the gathering crowd of servants and men-at-arms, while Sir Hughes wept unashamedly in front of everyone, his hands still gripping Talon by the shoulders.

"Ah, my son," he said, wiping the tears from his eyes with his sleeve as he stood back and looked at him. "You've become a man. Just look at you! We must tell your mother this instant or she will not forgive me for being so slow."

"Being so slow at what, my husband?"

Talon had never expected to hear those gentle tones again. Then he was standing next to his father, facing his mother, who simply stood in place, staring back.

She went white and seemed almost ready to faint. She murmured as though to herself, "Dear God, it's Talon," with a certainty that surprised him. She swayed.

Without thinking, Talon stepped forward and took her by the elbows to steady her. "Mother, I've come home," he said gently, tears welling in his eyes.

She gasped and continued to stare up at him. He stood, silently gazing back down at her. None spoke in the entire courtyard as they witnessed this extraordinary event.

His mother came into his arms and he held her gently as though afraid to break her. But she clutched at him as though she was drowning. There was a cheer as the people gathered around gave vent to their emotions. They clapped and shouted greetings to Philip, while he and Sir Hughes gripped each other's arms, happy beyond words to see one another.

Both turned and watched the oasis of quiet where Talon and his mother, Marguerite, stood, oblivious of the noise around them. She was weeping into his chest while he murmured words of endearment; tears now flowed freely down his cheeks. They stood that way for long minutes, and then Marguerite collected herself and pushed herself away, but still held onto him with a hand on his tunic. She wiped her tear-stained face with the hem of her apron and then took his hand in hers.

"Hughes, we forget our manners." She sniffed. "We have to remember ourselves and provide food and drink for these travelers. Your brother and our son have come back to us. The Dear Lord God in his mercy has given my son and Philip back to us, from so far away."

That said she led the way, still holding Talon by the hand, to the main buildings where at the doorway he saw a girl and two small children standing somewhat shyly, watching the events taking place in front of them.

Sir Hughes shouted orders for meat, cheese, and drink to be brought to the main hall, and for all to come and take part. Philip introduced Max as his sergeant and then the Welsh archers, who bowed to Sir Hughes politely, remaining silent. He regarded them with interest, bade them welcome and to take part in the feast. Then he followed his wife and Talon with Philip, arms around each other.

Talon's mother stopped in front of the three figures at the main door to the hall. There was a girl of about eighteen years standing with a young boy of perhaps five years and girl who was about three, hiding just behind her, holding onto her dress. As they came up she looked Talon over curiously and patted the boy on the shoulder with her free hand as though to reassure him. Marguerite stopped in front of her.

"Talon, this is your distant cousin, Aicelina, and the boy hiding behind her skirts is your younger brother, Guillaume. He is now five. Say hello to your elder brother, Guillaume. God be praised, he is back with us."

Talon nodded politely to Aicelina and smiled, which brought a dimple in response and a bobbed curtsey from the girl. He knelt on one knee and put out his hand to his new brother.

Guillaume hid his head in Aicelina's skirts shyly, peering out at this stranger who had suddenly come into his life. Talon smiled and kept his hand out. Guillaume reached out tentatively and touched the proffered hand, and then, as though ashamed of his shyness, stepped out of the shelter of the skirts and solemnly clasped Talon's hand.

"We have much to talk about, my brother," Talon said quietly. "I have much to tell you."

"The baby is your little sister, Talon. Her name is Ermessenda and she is two years younger than Guillaume," his mother said.

Talon turned and gazed back at the wide-eyed child partly hidden behind Aicelina's skirts. Still kneeling, he once again held out his hand and waited for the shy child to touch his and then smiled at her. She continued to look at him solemnly without smiling.

"She is afraid of you," Aicelina said quietly. "She will be better in the morning."

He nodded and stood up. His mother reached for his arm and held him tightly, as though to prevent him from disappearing, and led them all into the hall. The bright fire in the middle of the smoky building was surrounded by a low wall of stones to contain it and put out a welcoming glow for the visitors. The light gleamed off the few iron shields hanging on the walls and flickered off the great black beams that held the roof together, creating huge dark shadows.

Sir Hughes was in a joyful mood. The arrival of both his brother and his son was an occasion for great celebration. It was too late to prepare much of a meal for them tonight but his father promised them that on the morrow there would be a great feast for all and they would honor their arrival as custom dictated. In the meantime, they should drink some good wine and eat from the already prepared cheeses and meats that were available.

It was inevitable that Talon should be the guest of honor. He would much rather Philip had been placed in that position, but his uncle was eager to ensure that Talon was accorded the honors due. The questions from his father and mother were continuous and probing.

The questions came thick and fast that evening. By the light of the flickering torches and dancing black shadows along the wooden walls of the great hall the people of the fort crowded near to hear the tale of the long lost son. There was silence as they waited.

Talon's mother and father, impatient to know what had happened to him, barely touched their supper while he, tense with the newness and sudden demands made upon him, ate sparingly.

"The last we heard of you was when Philip came back to the castle and told us of the ambush," Sir Hughes said. "I went back the next day to investigate, but there were no clues as to whether you were alive or dead."

"The Templars," his mother said. "Remember, Hughes? They came and told us that you had been taken by the Assassins for reasons we shall never know to far off Persia and not to expect to see you ever again, Talon. It was cruel news for me and I fear that I did not believe them at first. I could not believe them. Dear Lord be praised, He has delivered you back to us safe and sound." She wiped another tear from her eyes with the hem of her apron.

"Talon, tell us what happened to you."

"I will, Mother, but it is a long tale to tell."

"I don't care," Sir Hughes growled. "Tell us what happened to you in that barbarous place."

"They first took me to Castle Samiran, which is deep in the mountains of Persia. The journey was long and took months. They did not treat any of us well and several died along the way," Talon started. "But for Jean, I do not think I could have survived."

"Jean de Loche? The priest? What happened to him?" Sir Hughes asked.

"Later, some years later, he helped me to escape from their main castle, Alamut, which is the secret lair of the Agha Khan and is even deeper into the Alborz mountains, a sinister place and bad for him, but he stayed behind and they killed him for it," Talon said harshly, looking down at the table.

"God have mercy on his soul. The poor man to die so far from home in that barbarian country," Marguerite exclaimed.

"He was my friend and mentor, Mother. I miss him sorely even now. Mother, Father, in that country the mountains scrape the heavens and the plains are so vast that it takes weeks to go from one end to the other with barely a tree to be seen. I have seen cities that glow in the sunlight! Isfahan is a sight so beautiful that the people there call it 'Half of the World.' I was placed in this great castle called Samiran, first. They trained us to kill with stealth, quickly and suddenly, by night or day. Some boys could not do well enough and they, too, died."

"Why? Why did they do this?" his mother asked, looking horrified.

"These are the Ismaili, the Hashashini, or, as you know them, the Assassins, who are feared across the Moslem world. Their master, the Agha Khan, is feared by all and hated by sultan and prince alike. He uses the trained young men to kill his enemies by stealth, often in public places, and no man is safe from him. They made me into a *fida'i*, a member of the brotherhood, and prepared me to kill someone, any enemy that the Agha Khan might command me to slay, either at night or in front of many people."

"Yes, these are the people that that Templar knight, Sir Guy, told us about," Sir Hughes exclaimed.

"It was Sir Guy, brother, who knew of these people and understood what they were about," Philip said. "He told us then that these people were creatures of darkness and were to be feared by all men, and that they could be invisible to their enemies before they slew them."

"Did they make you as one of them?" Sir Hughes asked, somewhat apprehensively.

"Yes, and more; it was the only way I could survive, and Jean told me that I needed to make sure that I came back to my people one day."

"So you lived among them for all these years? Were you not afraid that they would kill you?" Marguerite asked.

"They nearly did, both on the way there and once there; they were not kind to me. There were many other boys of my age all being trained to kill with the knife and other weapons. My friend, Reza, who was one of the boys in training, and I became among the best. It was sometimes very painful to practice with him; he is a ferocious fighter." Talon grinned ruefully at the memory.

There was hesitant laughter at that from the listeners. Even the Welshmen were listening, trying to follow the language, sitting in the dark behind the others in the crowd.

"So how did you escape, Talon? The Templar told us that few if any ever came back. You were not then a slave?" Sir Hugh asked.

"No, I was a *fida'i*, a full member of the brotherhood and therefore I belonged to them just like any other. I eventually had to escape because while I was in the castle called Alamut, I and my broth... friend, Reza—who became like a brother to me over time as we shared many dangers and hardships together—discovered a plot to kill the Agha Khan. All the same, we were not allowed to move around the country freely, especially as he and I were the guards of the Agha Khan's sister. She was a virtual prisoner in the castle because her uncle was plotting to kill the Agha Khan and did not want her to be free to move about in case she suspected something. Which we did in the end, and then we had to get away as we discovered that she was in mortal danger, too. We escaped and made our way back to Palestine where the Agha Khan was staying, to warn him of the danger."

"Did you succeed?" his mother asked.

"We did. Uncle Philip, you might remember me telling you about it when you came to release me from the chains the Templars put on me."

"I do, indeed," Philip mumbled, speaking with his mouth full after tearing a piece of meat off a bone. "You should have seen him, brother; he was so changed and the Templar had beaten him badly. I was hard put to recognize him."

"What do you mean, Philip? The Templars beat him and chained him?" Sir Hughes asked incredulously. "Why in God's name would they do that?"

"Because he looked like a Saracen when they captured him and his story was so incredible that no one believed him," Philip replied, wiping his mouth on his sleeve. "They locked him up and waited for me to come and clear his name. Talon, for the life of me, if you had not spoken up I would not have recognized you."

"I'm glad that you came, Uncle Philip, but it was too late for my friends." He turned to his mother. "We, my friend Reza, Rav'an his sister and I did save the life of the Khan. For which he released me to go back to the Franks. I had wanted to bring Rav'an with me despite the dangers and was trying to get to her when the Templars captured me. Their lives were in danger but the Templars refused to believe me and locked me up until Uncle Philip came with Sir Guy."

"I pray to God that your friends still live, Talon," his mother said kindly, putting her hand on his arm.

"Yes. So that's the story, and here I am with you today."

He had left much out, but gave a good enough story to his impatient parents to satisfy them for the evening. Indeed, it was very late when he had finished. The fire was low and the hounds were quiet but not a soul in the great hall was asleep. They were spellbound by his story and talked among themselves late into the night about his miraculous return. His mother wept again and gave thanks to God often while his father nodded vigorously at the tale of Talon's adventures and frequently wiped tears from his eyes, too.

"Not so fast, Master Talon, you have not finished your tale, for there is more to tell of the journey here," Max said, wagging a finger at him and laughing. He looked around at the company.

"This young man was indeed well trained. I and Sir Philip here have seen him at work." He paused for effect, glancing at Philip, who nodded with a grim smile. "The knight who imprisoned Talon was too eager to teach the 'boy' a lesson. They fought with knife and stick and the knight died. I have never seen such a display of skill. The man never stood a chance! Talon danced rings around him and then slew him in front of everyone! For that they put Talon back in chains.

"Sir Guy had to get us all onto a ship before we were allowed to release him again so that he could not get into more trouble." He smiled at the silent Talon. "I have rarely seen such a thing, Talon, and then you saved us from the pirates. Sir Hughes, your son is already a knight in all but name."

"Pirates?" Marguerite and Hughes exclaimed together.

Philip thumped the table gleefully. "We were attacked by *pirates,* brother, and this young scamp burned them out before they could set foot on our ship."

After that there was much loud talk back and forth about the event at sea; even the Welshmen were brought into the discussion and Talon was able to relax while everyone else talked. He felt he was being watched and turned his head to see Aicelina looking at him appraisingly. He attempted a smile and received a cool dimple in return. She turned away and then got up and bustled his young brother off to bed.

Finally it was time for everyone to retire for the night. Talon was shown to his lodgings by his mother, who held the candle high for him to see by. It was nothing more than a closed off area with a pallet and some warm furs. There were rough cowhide skins on the floor, along with the rushes. A far cry from Isfahan, he decided, but he was too tired to care or to quibble over the sleeping conditions by then. He was exhausted from the day's ride and the emotional reception and he went to sleep quickly.

Talon woke to the sound of bustle and activity outside. A cock was crowing and hens clucking, while people rattled metal pans and gossiped. He lay there listening to the new sounds of the fort waking up and starting the day's business. There were all the sounds of a farm community, cows lowing, and horses stamping and snorting into their food, while people chattered and bustled about in the cool of the morning.

He wondered again at the ominous atmosphere they had experienced on their arrival at the village. He was puzzled but decided that his father could probably shed light upon that. He got up and, only wearing his breeches and his linen shirt, looked about for some water to wash with. There was none.

He gave a resigned shrug, pulled the leather curtain aside, then walked out into the short corridor toward the Hall. Three maids were clearing the old rushes off the floor and brushing at the dirt floor. They all greeted him politely with a curtsey but they whispered and giggled as he walked by. Servants were bringing logs inside and stacking them for the night fire and there was his mother just coming through the main doorway carrying some linen.

She stopped halfway into the hall about ten feet away and looked at him. Then she beamed, laid aside the linen and came forward to embrace him. He opened his arms and once again they held one another without words. Then she stood back to look at him in the poor light of the hall. He was wearing his shirt loosely over his shoulders. She gave an exclamation and stared at him. The long scars of the old lion wounds drew her attention.

"Talon, what happened to you? Did they torture you?"

"No, Mother, I won a battle with a lion. It happened a long time ago, but it left its mark on me. I would not have lived but for the skills of the doctor who came and looked after me. He later became like an uncle to me. There are good people in those lands, despite our enmity."

"Praise be to God that you survived, my son. This is a story that you must tell tonight at the hearthside. Your father will want to hear all about it. But you look as though you could do with some breakfast. I shall get Aicelina to provide you with some food. You are not dressed for company," she said reprovingly.

"I want to wash. Is there no water I can bathe in? I have not bathed since I left Palestine and I swear I am getting fleas."

She looked at him in some surprise. "There is well water and there is water from the small river nearby." Then it dawned on her. "Ah, you want to bathe. Well, I shall have to arrange for some water to be heated, I suppose." She looked at him curiously. "I remember the times in Palestine. It was a rare event when we got you bathed then, you were such a restless boy."

"I learned to bathe, Mother," he said simply, smiling at her.

"Very well, I shall have the maids heat some water for you. Perhaps you can teach that brother of yours to like bathing, too, some day. He smells worse than a badger even for this rude place." She chuckled dryly.

She bustled off and he made his leisurely way out of the front door of the hall and out into the yard, where a flock of woolly sheep were being driven out of the gates. There was much bleating and scrambling as they all tried to get out of the narrow gateway at the same time, driven by two small boys dressed in very ragged clothes of homespun wool. Talon assumed they were being driven out to graze in the pasture that surrounded the fort.

He had a chance to look around and see the layout of the fort. That was all it could be called to his now-practiced eye. His father used to run a castle, but now he owned this small fortress of wood pilings deep in a valley of the Languedoc. Talon was unimpressed with what he saw; this was a far cry from the castle of Montfort in Palestine.

The smells of the yard struck his nostrils like a blow. He was quite unused to the odor of cattle and pigs, which was predominant. The smell of horses and goats and sheep in small wattle corrals mingled with the stink of the dung heap. This was not just a fort; it was a farm as well with all that went with it. He noticed the crude living quarters, stables, and barns arranged around the inside of the defensive timber walls. Their roofs provided a broad walkway along the battlements. He looked hard at the walls themselves. They were more of a palisade with platforms along the inner wall upon which men could stand and watch over the fields beyond. The high wall of timber would not stop him should he wish to enter. He recalled how he and Reza, his *fida'i* brother, had climbed rock walls twice as high in the dark and managed to get into people's rooms undetected. Nonetheless, it offered space inside and protection for the village folk to take refuge in bad times from marauding bands of men.

The hall where he had slept the night was a thatch-roofed, wattle-and-brick-walled structure located almost in the center of the yard. Now that it was daylight he could tell that it was a large building with huge wooden beams supporting another story above the one he had slept in. He assumed that his parents slept there with Aicelina and his brother and sister. He had noticed some crude wooden steps toward the back behind the alcove where he slept. Behind the hall were the sleeping quarters of the maid servants and the butteries—the place where the cooks carried out their work—and the storerooms where there seemed to be a lot of activity this morning. The steep roof of the huge wooden structure was covered with a thick layer of thatch that looked well maintained.

He was absorbed in the inspection of the fortress when his father walked up.

"Talon, good morning. I trust you slept well?" Then he exclaimed, "My Good Lord God! Where did you get those scars? Did they torture you?"

"Good morning, Father. No, I had to kill a lion to get these," he said dismissively, grinning.

"I want to hear about that tonight. In the meantime, I want breakfast and I don't doubt that you do, too. It is almost Terce and still no food. What is that good woman doing that I must always wait when I am hungry?" he growled, but it was with good humor.

Talon noticed that his father's hair and beard were streaked with gray, but he still seemed fit and strong, carrying himself as though still on military business. There were a few more lines etched into his face, however; he looked careworn.

He put his arm over Talon's shoulder and led the way to the kitchens where he harangued the cooks to make a meal of eggs and meat for them both. Talon realized that he enjoyed the casual closeness his father was bestowing on him. He had not felt this kind of feeling with another for some time now. He ignored the curious looks from the cooks and the maids as they hurried by on various errands. There were several appraising looks from the maids.

They sat at a rough table outside near the back of the hall where the kitchens and pantries were located. They tore pieces of bread off a huge loaf and dipped them in fresh, cool milk while they waited for the cooks to complete their work. While they were so occupied Philip sauntered up and then Max. They both had slept well and were hungry. Talon looked around for the archers. They were squatting in a corner over by the gate as though waiting for instructions; they looked somewhat lost.

Talon excused himself, got up and hastily went back to his room, donned an over jerkin, then walked to the archers and bade them good morning. "Have you eaten yet?"

"Not yet, young master. We did not know who to ask," Gareth said, standing up politely.

"Come with me," Talon said. He led them to the table where Sir Hughes and the others sat. "Father, I want you to meet some men from Pays de Gaul whom I have grown to respect," Talon said. "You met them last night, but you were not thinking of them then." He introduced the men by name to Sir Hughes.

Philip concurred with Talon when Hughes looked at him with a question in his eyes. "They know how to fight. They helped us ward off the pirates. Now they cling to Talon as though he is their leader. I hope he can afford to pay them," he said cheerfully.

Hughes smiled but glanced sharply at Talon while doing so, as though already re-evaluating him. He then bade the men to go to the cooks and get breakfast. Food was beginning to arrive on their table so there was almost no talking while hungry men ate the plentiful meal of eggs, meat, and bread with slices of cheese.

To Talon, unused to the produce of cows, the cheese was rank and tasted of the back end of the cow, but the milk he decided was good. And while the bread was coarse, it tasted delicious; its crusty outside was particularly enjoyable having only just been baked. He was still wary of the meat, but despite that he liked the reddish meat that Max told him was smoked ham.

Philip asked the question that was on his and Talon's minds. "Brother, we came through the village just across the fields last night and there was not a good feeling to it. No greetings, all the people were inside with doors shut and bolted. I wouldn't mind betting but that they watched us go by. This is the first time we have encountered this in all the journey since Ayga Mortes. What's happening there?"

Hughes hesitated but then shrugged and seemed to make up his mind to talk about it. "There is fear about in the land, Philip. I have an enemy who is causing me trouble, and we have had raids from marauders. I can't prove anything, but I am sure it's this man. He is Marguerite's cousin."

"What's the reason for the enmity, Hughes? Why should a man, especially the cousin of your wife, have a grudge against you?" Philip asked with a surprised glance at Talon.

"You will recall that we received a letter from the secretary of the Count of Carcassonne, telling Marguerite that her father and brother had died of the plague. This made us the inheritors of a very large estate, along with this village."

Hughes took a long draught of milk and wiped his mouth with the back of his hand. "It was true enough that the estate belonged to Marguerite's father and, as her husband, I am therefore the male inheritor of the estate. We came back because we had had enough of the heat and the fighting that took you, Talon. Your mother just wanted to come home.

"However, when we arrived it was to find there was a dispute from her cousin who owns lands north, some ten miles away. He is laying claim to the land and the estate; he can't claim it legally as there is not enough proof on his side. After several years of agitated talking to and fro and nothing being resolved, he has stopped talking, but I suspect that he is responsible for our dead cattle, stolen sheep, and the death of several of my villagers."

Philip glowered. "We spent time on the road here with a Marcel and his sister, Petrona. They are his whelps?"

"Yes, that's right, they are, and I have no grudge against them, but it changes not the fact that there have been killings, and I suspect my wife's cousin, Guillabert."

"That is an accusation of murder, brother. Have you proof?"

Hughes shifted on the bench and frowned, his normally open face revealing both frustration and anger. "None, Philip, there is never a witness to be found; those who could be are usually dead, nor will anyone speak out."

"Not even the priest? Philip exclaimed.

"He is but a simple soul who is afraid of the dark. He would rather tell the poor peasants to repent their sins than help me, an outsider, investigate. I find it somewhat curious that he has not complained to the bishop on my behalf, though." Sir Hughes snorted contemptuously.

Talon was reminded of Jean and how fearful he had been. Yet that man had martyred himself to save Talon's life.

"Is there no place where this can be resolved for you, Father? No court of law to decide this issue?"

Philip and Hughes stared at him. "There is the man-against-man combat to settle the dispute if we resort to ancient law. Or the court of the Count that is convened on occasion in Albi for matters of this kind," Sir Hughes told him reluctantly.

"Would it not be a good thing to have done and resolve it there, then, Father?"

"It would if I knew for sure that your mother was the true inheritor and had the documents to prove it to the world." Sir Hughes looked at Talon. "Talon, it is a complicated situation. I came with good faith to Marguerite's inheritance, but we have not found papers to confirm it was her father's land. She is adamant that there were clear papers to this estate but we have not found them as yet, and it's not for lack of hunting, including in the town of Albi. Hence, I am reluctant to go to court without them. All the same, I am sure of it, why else would the Count's secretary himself inform me that indeed she is the only inheritor of this land? That's what brought us back after all. Nevertheless, there are no deeds to be found."

Talon understood now the dilemma his father faced. To rush to court could in fact place him in a precarious position and, if the judgment went against him, leave him landless. However, the current situation was not a very tenable one, either.

Hughes obviously didn't want to dwell upon the discussion any longer and stood up. "We can go hunting today if you wish, Philip, Talon. I can take you to some good forests where we might start a deer for the feast tonight."

Everyone became interested and began discussing the chance for a successful hunt. Talon gave scant attention to the conversation, resolving to have a discussion with his mother when the opportunity presented itself. Perhaps she could shed some more light upon the situation.

Talon noticed his younger brother playing in the courtyard with another boy. They were playing with wooden swords and shouting fierce battle cries at one another as they attacked each other recklessly. He smiled at the sight. It did not seem too long ago that he had done the same with another boy in another place. He recalled how he had played at knights with the other young boys of the same age who were the offspring of the men-at-arms.

Then, too, they had emulated their elders by charging ferociously at one another with sticks shouting shrill war cries, the one being always the Saracen, the other the legendary Templars. He decided that he wanted to spend some time with his brother when he got the chance. In the meantime there was a hunt to take part in and in spite of himself he was excited at the thought.

Turning to his father he asked, "Father, may Gareth and his men come with us? If it is forests we are to hunt in, then these men tell me they know that kind of thing well. Are we to go on horses?"

"Yes, Talon, they may," Sir Hughes said. He looked at the wiry men. "Can they keep up with horses?"

"Gareth!" Talon called out.

Gareth got up from the table he was sharing with his companions and came over with cream still on his chin. He wiped at it with the back of his hand. "M'lord?" he asked politely.

Talon smiled at him. "My father wants to take us on a hunt, Gareth. Do you want to come? My father asked if you could keep up with horses in the woods."

Gareth grinned his broken-toothed smile. "Yes, we would like to come, sirs; and yes, we can keep up with horses in the forest." He turned to his men and called to them in their language. They laughed with excitement and nodded vigorously, their faces beaming.

Sir Hughes shrugged. "Then it's settled. We leave in an hour." He said to Talon, "I think you are now their leader, Talon. We shall have to get you knighted as soon as we are able. We can't have a common squire leading men all over the place. It isn't proper."

"And calling you 'm'lord'! It isn't proper!" Philip laughed.

Max grinned at Talon and winked. Talon punched his uncle on the shoulder lightly and laughed away his embarrassment.

"I would say he has already earned his spurs, Sir Hughes. It was Talon who defeated the pirates with his cunning and with the help of those men over there." Max indicated the Welshmen with his thumb.

Sir Hughes looked at Philip. "Yes, I heard last night. Is that really so, brother?"

"Indeed, it is. And Max is right, he's a born leader of men. Takes after his father!" Philip clapped Talon on the shoulder, further embarrassing him.

"I think there is much to tell that has not yet been told, my boy," Sir Hughes said, staring at his son thoughtfully. "Now let us prepare to hunt for the feast tonight."

Talon made his way to the well where he hauled a leather bucket out, dipped his head into the water and scrubbed the sleep and dust of several days' travel off his face. He was just standing up to start on his torso when he felt a nudge and a linen cloth was handed to him. Dashing the water out of his eyes he turned to see Aicelina standing there. He muttered an apology, and stepped back from her. He caught a faint scent of herbs and then he could see her better. She was dressed in a light-brown woolen dress with green sleeves that came down to her bare feet. The wide sleeves turned back to reveal slim, nut-brown arms carrying a stack of cloths.

"Good morning, cousin," she said in a low but clear voice. "Did you sleep well?"

"Good morning, Aicelina. I did, indeed. I trust you did, too?" He regarded her in the bright morning light. She was a good-looking girl, he decided, and well formed. Her dress could not hide her figure entirely. Her dark blue eyes were direct and coolly regarded him. Her auburn hair was swept back and pinned with a wood comb under the veil that covered her hair at the back, that left her smooth, well-formed features clear.

She stood silently under the scrutiny, but her eyes widened as they were drawn to the scars on his chest. She said nothing, however; instead, she dipped her head and walked past him to one of the huts against the walls. He paused for a second, watching her as she moved away. Then he shook his head and made for the hall, and beyond to the dark alcove, which was now his sleeping room.

He pulled on his shirt that was to his mind now quite dirty from the days of riding it had taken to get to the fort. Once he was fully dressed, he collected his bow and went to tell his mother that the bath would have to wait until he came back from the hunt, then outside to attend to Jabbar and prepare for the hunt. His ears caught the ring of a hammer striking an anvil and somehow this sound made a connection with his past. He resolved to make the acquaintance of the blacksmith later.

Within the hour they were riding out of the front gates. Talon had been given a heavy javelin-like spear with a long, iron shaft and a small, wicked-looking head that his father told him was for killing boar. Had Talon ever see a boar? He shook his head. "Well, then, stay close, if we find one we will hunt it." was the terse answer from his father.

His father and six retainers, including a heavy-set man with a hard face, whom Sir Hughes introduced as the chief huntsman named Domerc, led the way out through the gates. Talon and Philip followed with the Welshmen trotting alongside their stirrups. Feeling the excitement, Talon leaned down and patted Jabber on the neck. His horse pranced acknowledgement, happy that they were out and about.

The troop moved across the green swath that surrounded the fort, now dotted with grazing cattle, then down the village street which was much more alive than the previous night. They disturbed chickens and goats that ran in all directions while grubby children stared at the assembly as it went by. They came to some tracks that led north toward some dense-looking woods.

Chapter 4

The Hunt

The hunting party included four large hunting hounds. They were very excited at the prospect of the outing and started grunting and yelping as the men and horses made their way out through the gates.

Talon was familiar with hounds from his youth, but these were huge, gray, brindled, and fierce-looking. Their massive jaws looked capable of crushing a man's forearm. He was glad they belonged to his father. Domerc the huntsman led the way, with Sir Hughes alongside. The rest of the horsemen comprising Philip, Talon, Max, and four other house retainers on horses who followed behind. The Welshmen brought up the rear on foot with several other men from the village who wanted to come for the sport and to beat the woods for game.

The hunt was to be for deer but, as Sir Hughes put it, "If a boar runs onto my spear, so be it."

Talon had asked about game earlier and Sir Hughes told him that this far south there were no bears except up in the highlands farther to the north. But there could still be found good-sized boar and of course the deer were plentiful. Talon had asked about lions and received a puzzled look. He settled comfortably in the saddle and set out to enjoy the day. It was a warm morning of mid-summer with a cool breeze coming in from the west. The ride promised to be enjoyable and Jabbar was keen to fly along the wooded trails they soon found themselves negotiating.

Very quickly they were among the tall trees and the canopy closed overhead. The thud of the horses' hooves became muted on the thick carpet of old leaves and loamy soil. The hounds were staying well up in Domerc's charge, who held them with an iron hand, calling them sharply to heel whenever they began to drift off. He carried a long leather whip that he cracked regularly or lashed at them to keep the huge animals in place. The hounds were clearly cowed by the man and his whip.

The party trotted along at a good pace with the Welshmen keeping up effortlessly. Talon was impressed with their ability to run with almost no interruption in their chatter as they did so.

Then the hounds abruptly picked up some kind of scent as there was a short-choked howl from one of them which turned into a full-throated baying. It was one of the female hounds. She started to lope off into the deeper woods. Then the others caught it and they too began to bay. Their excitement was infectious. Sir Hughes gave a shout, then turned back to wave at Philip and Talon, beckoning them on impatiently.

Talon and the Welshmen had dropped back a short distance from his father, but he could still clearly see Domerc lift his hunting horn—made from the horn of a cow—to his lips and blow. The long, low tone carried well in the air. Then Sir Hughes and Domerc were cantering after the hounds that had vanished into the woods. Everyone could clearly hear their baying, however, as the horsemen hastened to follow.

Talon put Jabbar into a fast canter and turned him in the direction his father and Philip had followed. The chase had begun. He had no idea what the hounds had scented, but it didn't matter, they were now involved in a chase and the thrill of the hunt took over. Calling to Gareth and his men to follow as quickly as they could, he cantered after the others.

Although the forest canopy was dense and allowed only limited light to fall onto the ground, the trees were well spaced and this made it easy to move quickly through them on a horse, although low branches still posed a serious hazard to the unwary. Talon kept a keen eye open for the lead riders who were moving very fast in and out of the trees some distance ahead.

Even when he could not see clearly he could hear them shouting and crashing through the occasional stand of undergrowth. Only one of the horsemen who belonged to Sir Hughes' entourage was visible. Talon decided to watch him and follow closely, even if it meant the occasional clod of earth flying by from the leading horse's hooves.

He glanced back at the Welshmen and to his surprise found them running hard over the hillocks and in and out of the trees, well able to keep up with him. They had left the other footmen behind. It was likely that those men would take shortcuts or simply stop and wait for the hunt to come back.

He had dropped back farther than he'd intended and found it difficult to keep an eye on the rapidly disappearing men in front. He could still hear the hounds baying clearly so he used that as his compass.

They were now several miles deep into the woods. The undergrowth in places was very thick. Talon avoided it as much as he could, making detours for Jabbar's sake while trying to keep up the pace.

It was at one of the denser thickets that Jabbar suddenly swerved sharply to the left and almost unseated the surprised Talon. He spent several seconds regaining his seat and settling Jabbar down. He talked to the nervous horse, trying to understand what had made him shy when he saw that the man in front had fallen and was still lying on the ground. Talon could see no sign of his horse.

The man was struggling to get up but had difficulty as his arm seemed to be broken. Talon tried to settle Jabbar down but he seemed to be unusually disturbed and reluctant to remain calm. Talon slipped off Jabbar's back and called to Gareth while watching the man on the ground. He was groaning and sat back holding his arm, a grimace of pain on his face.

"Gareth, take Jabbar, there is something worrying him and a man is down with a broken arm," Talon said as Gareth came running up to him.

Gareth, barely breathing hard from the demanding run, nodded agreement and took the reins. Talon began to stride toward the man who was half lying in a wide, leafy dip in the ground. There was a dense thicket of bushes and small saplings to the right of Talon. As he walked forward he watched the man, but at the same time he was puzzled by the behavior of Jabbar, who was watching the thicket to his right intently, ears pricked forward and his whole body tensed. Talon glanced at the thicket as he walked down the slope toward the man.

Just as he did, the bushes parted and he saw the reason Jabbar had been so frightened and very likely the reason the man had been tossed off his horse: it was a boar, a huge one, much larger than those he had occasionally seen in the north of Persia while with the Ismaili. From where he stood it seemed massive. It stood slightly above Talon as he made his way down into the dip toward the man. The boar was about twenty yards away and facing the man on the ground, who saw the boar at the same time as Talon and yelled with fear, starting to scramble back from the glowering beast.

Talon could only really see the huge head from where he was. Most of the dark, hairy body was still hidden in the thick bushes it had emerged from. He was stunned by its size and ugliness. He saw only too clearly the huge tusks protruding from its lower jaws and the long, long snout that rose sharply into the massive head. He could barely see the two small, reddened eyes set wide apart in the black forehead. The hairs on the back of his neck felt as though they'd raised and he had a cold feeling of dread. This was a monster. Talon felt a trickle of fear as he stared at the huge creature.

The beast was clearly enraged at being disturbed and was glaring shortsightedly at the man directly to its front. It shook its head, tossing streams of saliva from side to side, then suddenly, without any warning, charged.

The man screamed and tried to run, but it seemed the pain in his arm slowed him down and he was dizzy from the shock so he stumbled and fell again.

His mouth dry and his heart pumping wildly, Talon started fast toward the man, his javelin held in both hands, hoping with some desperate kind of luck to strike the boar in the side as it came at him. He had barely covered two paces when an arrow whispered by him and struck the boar in the side with an audible thump. One of the quick-thinking Welshmen had loosed an arrow if only to distract the animal from its intended victim.

It certainly did that, but not as had been hoped. The arrow struck well behind the beast's heart and while it might become a mortal wound it did nothing to arrest the speed of the charging animal. The boar gave an agonized squeal and spun on its four short legs. It sprayed dead leaves and dirt into the air with its hooves as it spun around.

Then it charged directly at Talon, who stopped dead in his tracks and sized up the situation. He had no time; the animal was almost on him. He could see the malevolent look in its red eyes, and he watched the huge tusks lower until they seemed to be almost waist high. Talon decided to try to dodge the charging animal and pierce it with the javelin as it went by. This proved harder to do as the huge creature was moving very fast. Then it was almost on him and he stepped quickly aside, but quick as he had been, the animal was quicker. Talon had to throw himself out of the way as the head came up and the tusk grazed his thigh, tearing easily through the fabric of his trews. He felt the sting of a cut, then he caught the rank smell and even felt the stiff hairs on its side brush him as it hurled past.

Talon rolled and leapt to his feet, knowing that if he tarried he would be ripped to pieces. The trees nearby looked very appealing suddenly, but he knew with a certainty that should he climb one the boar would turn on the wounded man and kill him.

Squealing with rage and pain from the arrow embedded in its side, the boar spun completely around within a few yards of where Talon was. Another arrow struck the ground behind it and another went over its body. The animal was incredibly fast. The bowmen could not hit it and now, as it charged Talon again, they could not shoot or they risked hitting him. Talon braced himself for another encounter; he was afraid. He had never had to deal with an animal like this before. This beast was monstrous and incredibly fast.

They were now right in the middle of the dip where the man had fallen. He had dragged himself off to the side and rested against the roots of a tree, watching the battle unfold.

Once again the animal dipped its huge head, snorted loudly, then charged. Talon hefted the javelin and this time very quickly leaned aside then threw the heavy weapon as hard as he could at the racing animal's shoulder. His aim was true. Although the boar changed direction and came directly at him, the spear was embedded deep in the animal. It staggered, but still came on. Once again Talon had to leap out of the way. This time he tumbled to the right, rolling hard to get out of the way. As he came to his feet he heard shouts from the man by the tree. He glanced up and saw the man pointing at his feet. He looked down and saw the man's javelin lying among the leaves less than a yard away.

Talon snatched it up, barely in time to dodge out of the way yet again. This time the animal was hurting and could not move so fast. Talon struck hard as it went by, burying the iron tip deep into its chest cavity. It gave an agonized squeal of pain and staggered a few yards farther on. Talon was dragged along for a couple of yards, and then was thrown to his knees. He let go as the dying animal tore the haft of the spear from his hands. Talon clambered groggily to his feet and stood panting, feet apart, watching as the beast turned slowly back toward him. He dragged out his knife and waited, braced. This creature seemed invincible. An arrow whispered past him and embedded itself deep in the animal's back with a thump on the solid flesh, then another and another.

The boar, now bristling with arrows and two javelins and pouring blood from its wounds, stared at him with pain-filled eyes and started to run at him. But it was done. The massive animal ran four paces and fell on its front, almost at Talon's feet, its snout buried in the deep loam of the ground.

Talon remained where he was, bent over, his hands on his knees, gasping for breath. He barely heard the shouts and cheers from the Welshmen and the wounded man who staggered down to slap him on the back with his good arm, grinning and yelling praise. Then Gareth and the others were clustered about him, shouting and clapping him on the back as well.

"M'lord Talon, what a battle! What a great battle! That is a noble beast you have slain. We shall sing of this."

"You mean *we* slew, Gareth! I could not have killed that monster on my own. Your arrows did good work!" Talon gasped.

They all stared at the dead animal. Once he had caught his breath, Talon had time to examine it. It was an enormous animal, even in death. He estimated that it had stood a good four feet at the shoulder. All of them clustered in awe about the creature, the spears and the arrows still protruding from its body.

They exclaimed at its size and the length of its tusks. Talon remembered the feel of the razor edge as it tore his trews. He glanced down and noticed with some surprise that there was a trickle of blood down his leg.

Gareth noticed as well. "M'lord Talon, are you hurt?"

"No, Gareth. It is only a scratch. He could have done much worse."

"Thank the Lord that he did not, sir."

The man who had broken his arm was sitting down again, attended by Anwl, who was talking to him. He said something in Welsh.

The man told him his name, Cervin, in his native language of Languedoc. They were both babbling in their own language, quite unaware, it seemed, that neither could understand the other. Nevertheless, Anwl had fashioned a respectable sling for Cervin within minutes.

Cervin thanked him and then came to kneel in front of Talon. "My Lord, you saved my life. I shall always be grateful. May the Lord God protect and bless you."

Talon was embarrassed and helped him up. "You should thank the Welshmen here; they killed it as surely as did I. We should get you back home to rest and try to set the arm. Perhaps I can help when we get there."

Gareth called Drudwas, the archer who had held Jabbar, to bring him over, then handed the nervous horse over to Talon.

"Forgive me that we could not hit the animal during most of the fight, m'lord, but he was so fast and we were afraid to strike you."

"I realized that, Gareth. But it was a close thing, I will admit," Talon said with a relieved grin. One of the other Welshmen pulled the javelin out of the carcass and showed it to them. The long, slim, iron shaft covered with the blood of the animal was bent well out of true. Talon recalled how much force it had taken to ram it in and then he had hung onto it. No wonder it had bent.

"We can get the blacksmith to straighten it out for us when we get back," he said.

Talon noted that two of the archers who seemed to be arguing over which arrow belonged to which archer, and which had done the most harm. They would examine each arrow carefully, and then point to features that indicated it's ownership.

Gareth noticed Talon's attention directed at the two men and grinned.

"Pay no attention to them, m'lord; Belth and Devonalt argue all the time. They're cousins," he said, as if that explained it.

He sharply called over to the two, whereupon they looked sheepishly at him, then stopped arguing to come over and work with the others.

"If you will take our bows as well, m'lord, we will carry the animal back with us to the fort." Gareth suggested politely.

Talon agreed willingly, whereupon the Welshmen quickly and efficiently set about cutting long poles and hoisted the boar onto their shoulders. It took four of them to carry the huge animal hanging from the two poles.

As they set off through of the forest with Talon in the lead they heard the distant sound of the horn. They all paused to listen. In the silence that followed Talon was struck by how quiet the forest could be. The light was soft and tinged with a light green reflected from the high canopy with only stray beams of light coming through to illuminate the leafy floor.

They had all forgotten the main hunt in the excitement of the kill. They decided they should find their way out of the forest and wait on the edge for his father to show up. Which they did, thanks to Gareth and Belth, who seemed to be able to find their way back out of the labyrinth with ease. They emerged almost where they had entered the woods and here they rested thankfully, as the load was very heavy. While they were resting they heard the horn again, much closer, and soon after the other horsemen came out of the woods farther off, sweating and ruffled but excited from their success. They came galloping along the edge of the woods shouting and hallowing toward Talon, who was still mounted.

"What happened, Talon?" Sir Hughes shouted cheerfully. "Did you get lost?"

Talon said nothing. He pointed to the archers, who were now standing respectfully for Sir Hughes.

His father glanced at them and then stopped. His eyes widened. "My saints be praised, Philip, they have killed a boar!"

After that there was much calling and exclaiming as the rest of the hunt came up with their trophy and men exchanged stories about each kill. Sir Hughes was enormously pleased that Talon had so distinguished himself. The pride in his son was clear in his eyes as he clapped Talon on the shoulder. Philip did the same, but with loud and exuberant praise. Max grinned and lifted his hand in a half salute. Talon grinned back at him.

"Father, Philip, this was only done with the help of the Welshmen. Without their arrows I truly think I would have become its prey, along with Cervin here."

They moved off back to the fort, a joyful party of men with the Welshmen singing at the top of their lungs as they carried the boar between them. It was a triumphant party of disheveled men who arrived back at the fort and paraded through the gates, followed by half the village eager to see the kills and share in the excitement.

People from inside the fort came running from their tasks to witness the great carcass of the boar and to exclaim at its size. Children ran up and gawked, touched its coarse hide and then ran off to stare wide-eyed while the grown-ups discussed the last time they had ever seen one so large. Women folk who were there cast admiring glances at Talon, who quickly made himself scarce and set about putting Jabbar up in a stall and making sure he was well fed.

Having done that, he made his way toward the main hall, where this time he was determined to ask his mother for a place to have a bath, where he could sit and wash weeks of grime away. He had barely crossed the yard when his younger brother came running up and without preamble stood in front of him, feet planted apart and his arms crossed, demanding to know if indeed it was he who had killed the boar.

"Yes, Guillaume, I did, but I had help from the Welshmen too," he confessed.

"I want to hear the whole thing from you, Talon. Were you not afraid?" His eyes widened as he saw the blood on Talon's right leg. "You're wounded!" he exclaimed in awe.

Talon laughed and, squatting down, he faced Guillaume. "I was frightened out of my wits. It was so fast I could hardly stay in front of it. The Welshmen and I ran about in circles all the time until it was so tired it died right behind us."

Guillaume looked hard at the man squatting in front of him; he was sure that he was being teased. "I do not think you would run from it," he said gravely and then he laughed happily at the twinkle in Talon's eye.

"Now, Guillaume, I need your help. I have to have a bath and I want to ask Mother where I can get one."

Guillaume looked appalled. "A bath! Talon, those are bad for you. You can catch your death from the grippe that way." The boy spoke with authority as though he had learned this lore from others. There was a snort of derisive laughter behind them. Aicelina was standing by the well and heard the exchange.

Talon turned and smiled at her. "Perhaps you can help me obtain some hot water, Aicelina? I would truly have a bath, but I do not know where to get one."

She smiled, showing good teeth. "I shall talk to your mother. I see you are wounded. Do you need help to address that?"

"Thank you. I am fine, but we should help Cervin. He has a broken arm that will need to be set." He saw a hesitation and hurriedly said, "I know how to set a broken arm if it's not too badly damaged. We should do this before I take my bath. Can you help?"

She nodded. "I have helped to set bones before."

They found Cervin sitting on a pile of hay still telling the story of the battle. He was surrounded by villagers and children listening raptly to the tale.

He saw Talon and Aicelina coming up and hastily got to his feet. "I would thank you again for my life, m'lord," he stated respectfully.

"You might not thank me when I have finished with you, Cervin, but we have to set your arm or you will never hold a tool again. Have you the courage to go through with it?"

Cervin blanched, but then set his chin. "You have shown me your courage, m'lord. I shall show you mine."

Talon nodded approval. By this time Gareth and a couple of the archers had sauntered over.

"Gareth, Aicelina will need your help," Talon said. He was relying on his memory and the instructions he had learned from his mentor and friend, Dr Farj'an. "I shall need four sticks about the width of your thumb, and then some leather straps and a width of linen. We will have to replace the sling that Anwl made when we are finished."

They took the white and nervous Cervin into the hall and shut the doors on the curious. Talon made him sit with his forearm on the table. It was now quite swollen and red. He gave the sweating man a strip of leather and told him to bite down on it, and then asked Gareth and the other archers to hold him while he and Aicelina examined the break.

To his relief it seemed like a straight break and there was no puncture. Aicelina saw this, too, and agreed with him that it was less serious. Then, with Gareth's help, he held the trembling man's upper arm rigid and they pulled the wrist as hard as they could. Cervin promptly fainted.

After that it was easy for Aicelina to locate the bones and with Talon's help fit them together. In his opinion, it was a good effort and it seemed that the bones went together where they should. After that it was a matter of wrapping and splinting with the sticks and leather. By the time Cervin woke up, his forearm was well and truly trussed and they were preparing to put it in a sling. He gasped with the pain but Aicelina gave him some mulled wine with some herbs that seemed to alleviate the worst of it.

He wiped his pallid sweating brow and thanked them all. The archers, thankful that it was over, were rewarded with some of the same wine by Aicelina and settled in to do some drinking.

"All we need is a good bard with his harp well tuned and we will have a Welsh feast," said Gareth to Talon.

Talon was puzzled, "A bard? A harp? What do you mean, Gareth?"

"Ah, Talon! In Wales we make the best music in the world with our bards—minstrels as you call them. Our bards can make stones weep with their music. Are you going to join us Talon, Bach?"

Talon looked at the ragged group of grinning archers doubtfully then smiled and shook his head. "I am away to clean the mud off."

Talon went after Aicelina, who was walking away. He smiled at her with a new respect and asked again for a bath. She nodded and smiled back. It seemed a bond of sorts had grown between them.

His mother had been watching from the background and now bustled up and took charge of organizing the bath. She clucked at the torn hose and the bloody leg, but didn't insist when Talon told her not to fuss. Aicelina gave him a small pottery jar of smelly ointment that she told him to put on the cut when he had finished his ablutions and told him to bring the garment to her for repair later.

He luxuriated in an old trough full of hot water that his mother had commandeered for him. Aicelina even provided him with some coarse soap she told him she used on the linen. He took it gingerly, realizing that this was the best he could expect.

Chapter 5

The Feast

The rest of the day was devoted to preparations for the feast. Sir Hughes and Sir Philip were to be found near the fire pits with Max and other men from the fortress. The deer and boar carcasses were gutted and skinned. The great boar's head was cleaned and then given pride of place on a long table in the hall.

The skins were quickly placed on stretch frames for drying and scraping. Nothing was going to waste. The vital organs of both animals would be served that evening, including the lungs; the belly would be boiled down as tripe and the intestines would be cleaned and used for sausages.

The hounds seemed to be everywhere, trying to snatch a piece of meat when people were not paying attention, and were often kicked or beaten out of the way for their pains. Then they'd take to snarling at each other, and at the person who might have delivered the kick. They would not bite, however, as that meant fearsome punishment at the hands of the huntsman and they knew better.

Talon, fresh from his bath, had time now to seek out the black-smith. He found the man working in a crude, open-walled hut. There was a dirty urchin pumping some leather bellows while the blacksmith, a tall rangy man with strong arms, beat some iron into a tool of sorts. He was bare-chested, wearing only trews and a leather apron.

He saw Talon watching him and looked up. His face was long, but strong-featured. His dark-gray eyes were deep-set under bee-tling brows that gave him a permanent frown. He wore a huge beard but it seemed well cared for. His hair was very long and braided in two tails that fell down his back. He paused in his work, then knuckled his sweating forehead to Talon in salute, leaving a smudge where his knuckle had been.

Talon smiled and lifted the javelin up and pointed to the bend. "This needs to be straightened."

The man took the spear and held it balanced in his hand and then said dismissively, "I did not make this; it is not well-tempered."

"Will you repair it?"

"Yes, it will be repaired and it will be better when I am done."

"What are you making?" Talon asked, pointing at the metal in the tongs.

The man turned the still red piece of iron over in his tongs and looked at it reflectively. "It's just a farm tool, m'lord," he said po-litely, without being servile.

"Do you make chain mail?"

"I can... do you need some?"

"No, but it is good for a blacksmith to know how."

"We have no need of it here, m'lord."

"There is always a need for men who make weapons and ar-mor," Talon said.

"I have made axes and spears, but not a sword, and I have yet to make more than a few hauberks, m'lord."

"What is your name?"

"It is Feremundus. I am from the north."

"Well, Feremundus, I might come to you one day for weapons. I hope you can make them."

"I shall make them for you, m'lord," the man said, obviously eager to get back to work. The man seemed taciturn and unwilling to talk much.

Talon left him to his work and went to find the archers.

Talon enjoyed the rest of the daylight hours spent with the Welshmen. They practiced with some makeshift butts they had rigged out on the grassy field in front of the fortress. He impressed them with the accuracy of his strikes, but they in turn impressed him with the power of their bows.

They could send an arrow one hundred paces and strike the straw target every time. They gave derisive hoots when one of their number failed to make a "killing strike" as they called it. He had never used one of these yew bows and at first found it hard to draw the full amount. He understood now the reason for their big chests and huge arms. But he soon got the hang of it and then began to match them for placement in the target.

They in turn were curious about his bow but he was at pains to point out that it was designed to be used from a horse at a gallop, which they appreciated as they were well familiar with the Seljuk cavalry of Syria, having fought them.

He even rode Jabbar out onto the grass and demonstrated how it was done. He put Jabbar into a tight canter, guiding the horse with his legs and back, leaving his arms and hands free. Then he cantered past the target, loosing arrows off from the front, and then turned completely around in the saddle and again hit the target with well-aimed arrows. Then he did the same thing at a full gallop.

Gareth pointed up at Talon when he came back to the gathered archers. "That, M'lord, is how we saw them Turks doing it! They was very dangerous if they could get close enough, but we could keep them away with our arrows."

They spent the rest of the day in companionable discussion as to the various merits of weaponry they had encountered while in the Holy Land.

Soon it was evening and time for the feast. Rush and oil torches were lit and placed on the walls and at the gates to show guests from the village the way in, and all along the walls of the Great Hall. Their smoke was soon curling up to the rafters, creating a dense cloud among the beams. Clean cut rushes had been strewn about the floor of the Hall, and enough benches and tables put out for everyone to be seated.

Talon's mother glanced at the oil lamps and muttered about the cost to Sir Hughes, but he hugged her and told her, "The cost of oil is high, that's true, my dear, but the arrival of our son is worth much more!"

She nodded contentedly in the circle of his arm. "You are right for once, my husband. God be praised for his deliverance and for that bear of a brother of yours."

Sir Hughes grinned but said nothing; he knew when to stay his words.

The precious copper plates used for carrying food were polished until they shone. Baskets of bread appeared on tables and leather mugs were distributed, while at the high table rough pottery mugs were placed on a flax-linen cloth at the place where Sir Hughes and his lady would sit. There was an abundance of olives, garlic and cheeses in other baskets. Large trenchers were cut for the family at the high table and laid out, ready for the meat.

The baker and cooks under Marguerite's eagle eye had labored the entire day to produce pies and cooked vegetables. The two carcasses were becoming well roasted in the main yard by the fire pits. The tantalizing smell of roasted meat wafted in through the doors, making everyone suddenly very hungry.

People from all over the countryside came to the fort that night. They came on foot for the most part, some bringing modest gifts of food to add to the collection.

Talon had the place of honor at the high table, between his father and his uncle. His mother and Aicelina sat to Sir Hughes' left side, as did his younger brother. His baby sister was put to bed screaming, well before the feast began.

He had time to observe the womenfolk and the way they dressed as compared to the women of the East. His mother was dressed severely in a long, forest-green dress that came down to the floor and even dragged in the newly strewn rushes. The sleeves were long, down to the wrist, where they became huge and draped wide. The dress came up to her neck, leaving only her throat exposed.

At her waist was a thin, loose belt of leather known as the *ceinture* that hung low off her hips and came to a silver ring in front from which dangled some attractively knotted cords of silk. On her head she wore a small tapestry hat of some red material with a white linen veil that covered most of her hair behind.

Aicelina had a similar dress of a light-brown color that set off her hair well, but its cut was less conservative and did not completely conceal the rise of her full breasts under the material. Instead of a tapestry hat, she wore a *guimple* of thin linen, with a light, thin crown of embroidered cloth that was held in place with a copper pin. It left much of her hair and her whole face and throat exposed for the men's admiring eyes. As with his mother, the thin red belt with small silver studs was of well-worked leather that rested on her hips and drew the eye to her waist.

Several of the village women, although not as finely dressed as his mother and Aicelina, had attempted to imitate them; while their men folk, for the most part cleaner than usual, were dressed in whatever they had available.

Talon's archers were as badly dressed in patched coarse cloth as the peasants who sat with them. Talon resolved to try to do something about that. He was beginning to like the idea that they served him, so he now felt responsible for their attire.

Only his father, Philip, and Max were dressed in clothes that could be even vaguely defined as fine. Philip wore his Templar dress, as did Max. Sir Hughes, however, dressed in hose and practical calf boots, scorning the modern fad of pointed toes, and his overcoat was of good, although plain, dyed-brown wool. He wore no armor and only carried a dagger to the table, which he used on his meat.

From where he was sitting, Talon could look directly across the fire in the middle of the hall to the main entrance. There were benches and tables on either side of the hall for the retainers and villagers and other guests who had been made welcome. He saw the priest for the first time. He was a plump man with a badly cut tonsure and a habit that had known better days. He stood up to bless the assembly, and then Sir Hughes and his family. The priest didn't seem to be able to look at Talon, which puzzled him and he resolved to find out why.

The wine and ale was passed about in earthenware jugs for the family and skins for the people in the hall. A festive air permeated the room, and there was a lot of curiosity about this newfound son of Sir Hughes, who had already distinguished himself at the hunt. Many an eye was cast toward the huge boar head which had been placed on a bench just below the high table for all to admire.

There was an excited hum of conversation among the crowd which became a loud murmur of approval as the house churls began to bring the first slabs of cooked meat into the hall. The meat was quickly distributed and people began to eat. Sir Hughes told Talon that meat was not common fare for the villagers, so this was quite an occasion.

Talon could see how much the people enjoyed their food. Men and women tore at the meat and the bread as though this was to be their last meal; at the same time, their faces went red with the wine and ale. He began to understand what his father meant. There was an almost complete lack of spices and although salt was available, it was offered by the servants with restraint. A man could take a pinch, but could not take a spoonful. He told himself firmly this was a lot better than the dreadful fare they had been subjected to on the ship.

As the food was enjoyed so too was the wine, and before long the noise level under the steep rafters of the hall was so high that conversation at the high table was difficult without shouting. Sir Hughes was beaming at one and all, raising his cup to people who wanted to toast him. Talon heard his name called and noticed Gareth standing with his mug in his hand raised to him. He raised his mug in salute.

Then the people of Languedoc called to Sir Hughes to speak to them. They called in their language, but he understood and got up from his seat. He raised his beaker unsteadily and shouted to the assembly, "Welcome all, my people, villagers, and guests. May you all leave with full bellies and a skin full of wine!"

There was loud, raucous laughter at this sally, followed by cheering.

"I and my wife Marguerite have been blessed by God today. My long lost son is returned from the far lands of the Saracen to the bosom of his family. I wish that you would all welcome him."

The crowd cheered and stood to its feet, all hands raised to Talon. He stood up and bowed to his father and mother and then the assembly.

Sir Hughes continued in this vein for a while longer while the villagers on the benches cheered and applauded him. It was clear to Talon that his father had made himself popular with the people in this area.

Sir Hughes finally settled down into his seat. His face was flushed. He turned to Talon and said loudly, "Talon, I want to hear about the fight with the boar, and then the lion!"

There was an interested murmur from the crowd who had heard him. But then Cervin got up. "M'lord, I was there. Lord Talon saved my life."

Sir Hughes nodded for him to continue. So in the language of Languedoc, Cervin told the assembly of Talon's courage and how the battle had been fought. In spite of his broken arm he mimed the Welsh shooting their arrows and then Talon striking so well that he had the full attention of the crowded hall. No one moved during the tale and at the end an acutely embarrassed Talon found that once again he was the center of attention.

The story had just ended when there was a disturbance at the entrance to the hall. A guard from the gatehouse came rushing in.

"We have visitors, m'lord—Lord Guillabert d'Albi and his men." He appeared nervous.

There was consternation at the name. Sir Hughes stood up, suddenly sober. "How many men, Bermon?"

"Eight, Sire."

"I shall come and welcome him, then. We have guests, my people; we should not keep them waiting."

He stood down from the table, motioning for Philip and Talon to follow. As he got up Talon caught Max and Gareth's eyes. They both nodded and with their men got up and moved off from the crowd. Talon thanked them silently. They would arm themselves and be ready if there was any trouble. The sentry's behavior had told him all was not well with this visitor.

The three men walked down the center of the hall. Servants lead the way, with torches held high, into the warm evening to meet the visitors who, still mounted, walked their horses in through the gates. Their dark forms were muffled in cloaks and hard to make out, other than the rounded helmets on the riders following the three leading men.

"Well met, Sir Guillabert," Sir Hughes called. "I had not expected the honor of a visit this night. It has been many a month since we last talked."

The lead rider halted in front of him and allowed his cloak to fall aside. "I expected an invitation, Sir Hughes," Guillabert stated sharply. "When none came I decided to come anyway. I hear you have some special guests?"

Sir Hughes hesitated. Then, as if he had not noticed the tone, he said, "Indeed, I do, sir. Will you not join us? You are welcome to my Hall."

The bulky man got off his horse. He tossed the reins to one of the servants and came into the torchlight. He was a heavy man with a full gray beard. He pulled aside the cape of his cloak and revealed short gray hair, cut short to enable him to wear the tight helmet of the fighting man. He was richly dressed, far better than Sir Hughes, whose clothes looked threadbare by comparison.

He turned to the other two riders and called out. "Get off your horses, Marcel, Roger; we are bid to sup with the Gilles family."

The two dark shapes dismounted and walked toward them. Marcel barely acknowledged Talon, although he greeted Sir Philip in a friendly manner.

Sir Hughes made the introductions. "Sir Guillabert, Marcel, Roger, this is my brother Sir Philip de Gilles, and this is my son, Talon de Gilles."

Sir Guillabert gave a short bow to Philip. "It is always an honor to meet a Templar, sir."

"I am honored to meet you, Sir Guillabert," said Sir Philip stiffly.

The man turned to Talon, who bowed politely.

Sir Guillabert nodded. "So you are the long-lost son of Sir Hughes. My son informs me that you have lived with the Saracen long enough to become as they are."

Talon gave him a cool look. "That depends upon what it is you think they are, sir."

Sir Guillabert gave a short bark of a laugh and walked past him, ignoring him. Marcel again barely even acknowledged Talon as he, too, strode past him. The other man in chain mail and helmet followed them. His eyes glowered from behind the nose piece of the helmet. He took his helmet off and shook his head. Greasy locks flew round his sharp features. He had a scarred face and was tall with very strong shoulders. As he strode past Talon he stared at him as though sizing him up, then grinned nastily through bad teeth, after which he followed his father and brother into the hall.

Philip gripped Talon's arm hard. "Hold onto your temper, boy. This is not the time to rip his gullet open," he growled.

Talon smiled at his uncle. "I shall be as sweet as one of the pies Mother has prepared tonight, Uncle. But Marcel should tread carefully about me in future."

Philip grinned in the darkness. The torchbearers were well ahead, leading the guests and Sir Hughes into the Hall. The other men, who had dismounted, remained outside under the watchful looks of the fort guards. Talon watched to make sure the gates were shut and a sentry was again standing on the walls, then walked over to talk to Gareth, whom he saw standing discreetly in the shadows.

"Gareth, I need a reliable man to watch for trouble. Will you stay for me?"

Gareth knuckled his forehead. "I shall be here, as will the others, m'lord."

Talon touched the man on the shoulder by way of thanks as he passed.

He followed the others into the hall where he saw that Sir Guillabert had been placed at the high table. He was provided with wine and meat and began to eat without more ado. Marcel sullenly watched the crowded hall while he tore at the meat and bread and his brother Roger slouched nearby, drinking and glowering about him at the crowded hall.

Sir Hughes and Marguerite made polite talk and slowly the silence that had greeted the newcomers was replaced with a low murmur and then talk resumed as people began to relax. As the evening wore on Talon noticed that Sir Guillabert and Marcel and Roger were drinking heavily. Neither of the sons spoke to Talon; indeed, they ignored him as though he were not there.

Sir Guillabert finished his wine and gestured for more, then he turned to Hughes, pointed to Talon. "This boy has come back from the Saracen side, I hear. Does that make him an unbeliever? Has he seen a priest to confess his sins, Sir Hughes? What foul things has he picked up from the unbelievers?" His eyes fell on the priest who was clearly trying to make himself scarce. "You, Priest. Have you heard his confession as yet? What sins does he bring from the Saracen lands?"

Sir Hughes visibly restrained himself. "My son has come back from the dead just yesterday, Sir Guillabert. We will see the priest and, of course, he shall hear confession all in good time. However I believe that is between Talon, the priest, and God. Not of our concern," he said levelly.

Sir Guillabert shrugged. He was into another cup by now. "In any case, he should not count on an inheritance. Is that not right, Hughes?"

"Cousin, I forbid talk of this nature at such a gathering." The hitherto silent Marguerite spoke up sharply. "Did you only come here to taunt and insult us at our own hearth?"

Talon glanced down at the crowded benches. People were becoming aware that all was not well at the high table and conversation was slowing again.

"It is I who should feel insulted," Sir Guillabert said truculently. "I was not invited to a feast of this nature, even when you are my cousin."

"I did not ask for you because you do not bring good will, Cousin."

"You have been made welcome at my hearth, sir. If you cannot restrain your quarrels at a time like this, then you should not be here," Sir Hughes said sharply.

But Sir Guillabert was not to be put off. "The secretary of his Lordship made a mistake when he wrote to you. This land and all about is mine. My uncle left it to me by his word when he died."

Marguerite said in an exasperated tone, "Cousin, we have been up and down this path many times. My father left it to me, by right of being direct descendant. Why then did the secretary of his Lordship the Count of Carcassonne call upon us to come here if that were not true?"

"Because you were not in this land and hence forfeit at the time. He should have known about the law. There is a law that provides for that, my dear." He sounded very patronizing. "We both understand that your tenure of this land is only temporary," he returned sarcastically.

"What law is that, sir?" Talon asked

Sir Guillabert glowered at him. "Stay out of this conversation, young pup."

"Why, sir, I may be a 'young pup,' but I can think for myself, and so I ask again, where did this law appear from, sir?" Talon appeared calm but he sensed that he was treading on dangerous ground with this bucolic man who called himself cousin to his mother.

Guillabert reared up, his anger surfacing. It was clear to all that he disliked the confidence of the unknown youth talking to him. "Have a care, boy. Your impudence can get you sorely hurt. Hughes, bring the whelp to heel or I shall."

"Or I shall. The very thought of having this dirty Saracen in my vicinity is disgusting," came another voice.

Everyone turned to see a flushed Marcel staring belligerently at Talon. His brother was grinning nastily next to him.

Sir Hughes had had enough. He stood up, his face red with anger. "I have to ask you to leave, sir. All three of you! You may be my wife's cousin, Sir Guillabert, and you are protected by rules of hospitality while here, but you do not insult my family or anyone else in this house with impunity."

Sir Guillabert stood up, unfazed. He wiped gravy off his chin with his sleeve. He was a heavy man, powerful and in an ugly mood. "Very well, sir. You need to know that the church itself is on my side, so beware that you do not overstep their good will. Come along, Marcel, Roger; we do not need to stay in this midden heap any longer."

He stalked out of the hall with the two brothers in tow. The family watched him go. There was complete silence in the hall after he had left. Talon hastily walked down the length of the Hall, listening to the whispers all around. He wanted to make sure that Gareth had everything under control. He need not have worried. Max and Gareth were just turning back from the shut gates.

"What happened, sir?" Max asked.

"Come inside and we can talk, both of you. Thank you for keeping watch."

They shrugged aside his thanks and followed him in.

Sir Hughes was trying to calm Philip. "Don't be a hothead, Philip. It is just what he wants, some impetuous idiot to ride after them and provoke a fight in the dark."

Philip noticed Talon. "Do you see that 'boy' over there, Hughes? He could kill all three of them in the dark and they would not even know who did it. I have never seen anyone kill as easily as your son!" His tone was loud and carried the length of the hall.

People stared at Talon from all sides. He felt suddenly very uncomfortable. Philip was flushed with rage.

Talon came up to his uncle. "Calm yourself now, Uncle. You know I will not be provoked."

His mother and Aicelina were looking at him oddly.

"Hughes, we should find out what the law has to say and then take a petition to his Lordship the Viscount of Albi, Count of Carcassonne," Philip growled.

"He talked about the church being on his side, Father. What did he mean?" Talon asked.

"I don't know. I think he means the Bishop of Albi. But why should he be interested in this land? The church has more land than anyone else in the region as it is."

"Is there no one to whom we can turn for advice, Father?"

"I don't know of anyone who can help us. It is rumored that the abbot at the monastery near to Albi knows law as it pertains to the church, but I don't know for sure. For all I know, he'll side with the bishop. He is of the church after all."

"Then I shall ride out there and see if I can talk to him, Father. We must try something. Sir Guillabert seems so certain of himself. I do not understand how the church can be involved in men's affairs so much. Land disputes are usually the province of a vizier—uh, a lord," he corrected himself.

"My cousin ever was a hard-headed man with a spiteful will," Marguerite said ruefully.

"Mama, are those then his sons?"

"Yes. Their mother died giving birth to Petrona. Sir Guillabert has raised them since."

Abruptly Sir Hughes turned to the assembled company who were still there talking in low voices, not wanting to disturb the family at the high table. "Friends and companions, it is late. I beg your forgiveness for the unfortunate incident. It's time to go to your homes and rest. I thank you for coming to the feast to honor my son."

Slowly, as if reluctant to leave them, the villagers and other guests filed out. They bade the Knight and Marguerite good night, and to a man wished Talon good fortune. Many a married woman and her daughter fluttered their eyes at him as they curtseyed.

"It's time for us all to go to bed as well," Sir Hughes said glumly. "Talon, I regret this ever happened, especially for your homecoming."

"Father, I've had a good welcome from all who are here. I thank you and Mother for your kindness. I shall stay with my men for a while longer and then go to bed."

His glance caught Aicelina, who was still sitting next to his brother, who was trying to stay awake, but failing.

On impulse Talon reached down and picked Guillaume up in his arms. He asked Aicelina to show him the way and took his younger brother out of the hall. He followed her as she took a candle and showed him to the alcove where his brother slept. He lay the boy down on the pallet and covered him gently with a blanket.

Turning, he saw that she was watching him with a thoughtful look on her face. "What is it Aicelina?" he asked.

"Uncle Philip said that he had never seen a man kill as easily as you. Yet I see you now with your brother . . ."

"That is only for show," he said gruffly, wishing his uncle would shut up about what had happened in Montfort, and left her staring after him.

He went down to the hall and found some of the men from the fort sitting comfortably with Max and the Welshmen at one of the long tables. Sir Hughes, Philip, and Marguerite were seated near the fire and Aicelina came to sit next to them. Talon walked over to the Welshmen. They made space for him companionably alongside, and a mug was planted in front of him without ceremony. He took a long gulp of the good, dry red wine.

"So, m'lord Talon, what's going on?" Gareth asked.

"It is simply Talon to my friends, and I am among friends tonight. I understand little of what is happening other than that man who was here tonight, although my uncle, is our enemy, and we should be alert and very careful. I don't trust him at all. He covets my father and mother's property and my guess is that he will stop at nothing to take it one way or the other."

It was a long speech for Talon and it got their attention. He turned to Gareth.

"I can't ask you to stay in harm's way, for I am sure that there is a feud developing here. You must soon leave for your Wales."

Gareth looked down at the table and then glanced up at his men. "Well, Talon, we don't quite see it that way. Me and the men have been talking, see; what with all the hospitality we've received we feel that we owe something, too. How can a few weeks or a month or two make any difference right now, as long as we make it back to our land before the winter?" The others nodded solemnly.

"We would like to stay for a while, if you would have us. Can you pay us just a little?" wheedled big Drudwas plaintively. There were suppressed, nervous chuckles from the other archers.

Talon gave a snort of laughter. "I might just be able to pay for your breakfasts once in a while, you rascals."

Max laughed out loud. "Talon, Gareth has given you a small army," he said accusingly.

"I know, Max. I am grateful for your offer, you men from Wales. Of course I shall pay you, and pay you well, but be aware that we have trouble to come."

They all quieted at that but soon they were happily drinking again. Belth and Devonalt started to argue about something in Welsh, but then the impulsive Welshmen began singing. Later in the evening Gareth got up from his seat and, weaving about, shouted in his dreadful French. "I would demonstrate how well m'lord Talon fought the boar."

Talon laughed lightly as did his father and mother.

"Well Gareth, do so, this should be entertaining."

Thereupon Big Drudwas stood up and slurred, "I will be the boar."

Gareth crouched and waved a stick threateningly at Drudwas, who stamped and lowered his head. He had placed two chicken bones in his mouth that stuck out of either side of his large mustaches to resemble tusks. He charged and Gareth dodged and struck at him with the stick as he went by, shouting abuse.

The men sitting at the benches joined in shouting at the boar to gore Gareth or else. Everyone was roaring with laughter at their antics. Even Talon was laughing at the two clowns entertaining everyone. Sir Hughes was shaking with merriment, wiping tears of laughter from his eyes while Marguerite and Aicelina were hiding their faces behind their hands shaking with laughter with him.

Then during one of the charges Gareth tripped and fell over backward into the rushes. Drudwas promptly followed him down and gored him ferociously with his makeshift tusks. Then the hounds were tempted to join in and take bites out of the struggling, yelling Gareth, who was eventually saved by the other men who pulled both the hounds and Drudwas off him.

The two men staggered drunkenly back to their benches to more applause.

So the rest of the night passed with jokes, tales of valor, and songs. They went to bed as the first light of dawn was streaking the eastern sky.

Chapter 6

The Monastery

Talon woke with a terrible headache. He made his way shakily out to the well and found Max looking equally sick, trying to wash away the cobwebs by scooping water out of a leather bucket and throwing it over his head with cupped hands.

"Good morning, Talon."

"Good morning Max. Ah, my head. Is that what wine does to you?"

"Yes, sir, it does. My mouth tastes like a Saracen's loincloth."

Talon grinned through his pain. "How would you know?"

He sloshed cold water from the bucket over his head to shake away the pain between his eyes. He took a long drought of water and immediately felt nauseous all over again. Stumbling over to the midden heap he heaved the last of the sour wine out of his stomach. Then he headed back to the well where a sympathetic Max was holding the bucket of water for him to rinse out his mouth.

They were breakfasting gingerly on fresh bread and milk when the Welshmen surfaced and came over to join them, one by one. They did not look as badly off as Talon felt. It must have shown as Ap-Maddock gave a wry grin when he saw Talon's haggard face.

"Ah, Talon, m'lord. How do you feel, Bach? You look terrible."

"I feel terrible. You poisoned the wine. And there is an awful banging going on in my head." Talon winced as his head pounded.

They all laughed at his discomfort.

"The noise in your head might be the blacksmith. Feremundus is already busy," Max said.

Some of the others looked just as hungover but they joined in the fun at his expense anyway.

Breakfast was almost done when Hughes sauntered over with Philip. The two of them seemed none the worse for wear. Both looked unsympathetically at the huddled Talon and called for lots of food which they ate with gusto in front of him.

"You need to eat, Talon, especially after a long night with wine," Philip said in his tactless manner, his mouth full.

His father nodded wisely, an amused expression on his lined face. "It is always a good idea to eat a lot when you look like you do, my son."

Talon glowered; he hated them both for being so smug. "When I am wounded and dying on the battlefield I shall call upon you, Uncle, for help and comfort in my last moments," he grunted.

All he got for that was a grin as Philip stuffed more food into his already full mouth.

"You should have a hair of the dog, m'lord," Gareth advised him, grinning.

Talon looked up sharply. "The hair of a dog? Why?"

"It helps get over the hangover," Philip said.

"How can dog's hair help me in my condition?"

Max roared with laughter. "No, a hair of the dog that bit you, Talon. It means another drink of wine. It settles the stomach."

They were all laughing now, including a rueful Talon who was holding his head with both hands.

"I don't think so, Max. I forsake wine for all time. Never again! Not ever!" More laughter.

Later in the day when he felt somewhat better Talon joined the Welshmen at the butts and practiced his weapons skills until he was sweating. Initially he felt tired, but felt better when he had spent several hours working the poison out of his system.

He made his way back to the hall and ran into his mother. She obviously wanted to talk to him, so he allowed her to guide him toward the small garden which was situated on the south side of the compound.

The garden was small and protected by a stout wattle fence from the incursions of the pigs that wandered the yard. They sat together on a rough oak bench near the well-tended soil where she grew plants. It was a quiet place where his mother had lavished time on several neat rows of herbs and vegetables. She had even planted a cherry tree which she showed him when they arrived in the garden. It had survived three winters and was now about four feet high. Nearby was the pond in which ducks were busily swimming, looking for tidbits. The day was bright with only a few clouds in the sky, and the sun overhead warmed them as they sat together.

"There is a great deal that has happened to you since the Saracen took you, Talon. I want to hear more about it. What did they do to you? You have changed so very much."

"I hope that you do not disapprove of me, Mother?"

"No my son! I thank God every minute that he brought you back to me. But you are so different. I can't place my finger on it but there is something there you certainly would not have if you had not been taken."

One of the hounds came over and nudged his knee insistently, wanting its ears to be rubbed.

"It is probably true, Mother. I don't see it in myself, but they did train me well and it was very hard at first. Jean the priest helped me so much. But now I feel as though I've come back to a world that I don't know. I felt at home there with the Persians. It is hard to explain."

"Will you try to explain to me how this came to be? How you came to become one of them?"

"I'll try, but I would ask you be patient with me and try to understand."

So while he played with the ears of the hound he sat with his mother and told her of his time in Persia, the affection he had formed for Isfahan and the people he still loved there.

"You lived in the Kingdom of Jerusalem and know something of the world I was taken to. But I find it hard to describe even to you how utterly different life in Alamut was, compared to our castle in the Kingdom. It was harsh, mountains are all around, and there is nowhere to which you can escape. Jean and I lived at their whim. We were free to go where we pleased within the castle, but where could we go if we had tried to escape? We would have been caught and killed immediately.

"They trained me well, and it was only when I was trapped by the lion on a hunting expedition that life changed for me. I met Rav'an. I was wounded and recovering in the Khan's garden when she came and we met. She was like a wraith from a fairy tale. So beautiful, Mother! I fell in love with her and later she with me. We grew up and then went to Alamut, which is the castle of the Great Agha Khan. It is deeper still within the mountains and impregnable. 'Alamut' means 'the Eagle's Nest.' It is perched on a high rock overlooking a deep valley.

"I became a *fida'i* and my brother Reza did too. We were among the best that they had." Talon paused and smiled at his mother. "Can you imagine me being proud of that? But, yes, I am."

He looked up to the sky. "But I am prouder of the love I gained from Rav'an. A forbidden love, though, as her brother, the Agha Khan, would have had me killed had he known. We became lovers while we were in Isfahan, after our escape from Alamut, and after a tragedy there—which I will tell you of some time—we came back to Banyas Castle. There she told me she was pregnant.

"I could not save her! I wanted to bring her with me, but the Templars apprehended me before I could and I lost her forever. When she is discovered, her brother the Khan will have her killed. There is no mercy for her crime. She is most likely dead as I speak." He stopped, his throat too constricted to continue.

How could he explain how he had lost it all when he had been captured by the Knights Templar and they had refused to listen to his pleas to release him? That he blamed himself for having lost Rav'an and that he believed her to be dead because that was how it must be for a girl in her world who had loved a man out of wedlock, and then been exposed.

His mother sat quietly and listened as her son poured his heart out to her. She wept when he told her of his aching love for the beautiful girl left behind in Persia. Eventually, he stopped. It had been a long tale through which his mother for the most part had sat quietly listening.

The shadows had grown long by the time he stopped and the hound slept at their feet, and he could go on no longer. The dreadful pain of the parting and his utter despair at having lost Rav'an had come to the surface and now it hurt too much. His mother quickly sensed his state of mind. She reached up, cupped his face in both her hands, gently shaking his head and stared up at him. He was surprised at how small she seemed to have become.

"The Lord works in strange ways. I see the great pain in you and would that it were not so. If God wills it then you may find her again one day. Although I would pray that you could live out your days here in Languedoc with us."

"I cannot lie to you. One day I have to go back and find out what has become of her or I shall never rest; I'll never know peace until then. I will avenge her, if she is truly dead, for the reasons I have told you," he said with tears in his eyes.

His mother knew then with bitter certainty that while her son had returned to her it was not ordained that he should stay. She could not comprehend the world that her son knew so well; it terrified her and she dreaded the thought of him going back to the dangers there. She resolved to keep him as long as God permitted. She kissed his cheek again, stood up, and with a heavy heart, put her hand on his arm for him to escort her to the Hall. The hound woke and slowly getting to its feet, followed at their heels.

Three days later as Talon and Max were finished working on the leather of the saddles and making good some repairs on some of the other bridles there was a commotion at the gates. One of the sentries shouted down that there was a party of horsemen coming to the fort.

Talon walked toward the hall where he met his mother and stood with her. They looked at one another and then she tapped his forearm.

"I know, Talon. Go and get ready if you have to."

He kissed her cheek. "I shall wait here with you to find out who it is."

The Welshmen were not going to be caught unawares; they came jogging up to stand with their new master, their bows strung.

His mother looked at them with a question in her eyes.

"They are my men now." He smiled at her, then at the men, who grinned back self-consciously, only half understanding the meaning of the interchange.

"I see," she said doubtfully.

Sir Hughes and Sir Philip came striding out of the hall to hear what the sentries on the gate platform were saying of the visitors.

"Who is it?" Sir Hughes asked as he straightened his tunic and tightened his sword belt.

"M'lord, it looks like the Church," said the sentry up on the walkway. He sounded awed.

"Then open the gates, man!" Sir Hughes bellowed. He and Sir Philip walked forward to a point where they could greet whoever came through.

The gates were opened ponderously and in rode a man dressed in fine clothes followed by a small retinue of horsemen. He was mounted on a spirited horse which he seemed well able to ride.

The horseman's clothing was plain, but of rich blue material and had all the symbols of the church. A cross was sewn into the cloak in silver thread and the great velvet cap he wore denoted a man of the Church on business. The priest, for that was what Talon thought he must be, was a middle-aged man not much older than Sir Hughes and obviously enjoyed riding good horses to the hunt.

There were hunting hounds on leashes held by a man striding behind him. He rode into the yard as though he owned it and doffed his huge felt cap to Hughes and Philip as they bowed to him.

"Well met, Sir Hughes. I was not aware that a member of the Order of the Templars was your guest? I am honored to make your acquaintance, sir," he said to Philip.

Talon heard the remark but somehow he didn't believe the man was very sincere.

"You are welcome, Father. May I introduce my brother Sir Philip of the Order of Templars. He is just arrived from Palestine this short while."

"I had heard that you had visitors from the *Outré Mere*, Sir Hughes." He bowed briefly from the saddle to Marguerite. "Madame."

"Will you not dismount and take refreshment with us, Father?" Sir Hughes asked politely.

"My thanks, I think I will," the man said.

"It is the Secretary to the Bishop Bohemond," Marguerite whispered to Talon. The priest dismounted and handed the reins off to one of his retainers, who remained mounted.

He strode to the two men, shaking the dust from his cloak, and bowed again. He was fit-looking for a man of the church. He had a stern look on his clean-shaven face, with a fleshy mouth overlooked by a beak of a nose and restless, darting eyes that did not seem to miss anything. Talon was unused to seeing men completely shaven and so he regarded the man curiously.

Then the priest was coming toward them.

"May I also present my wife and my son, Talon, Father."

The priest stood in front of Talon. He was almost the same height although much older. He looked Talon over and then said, "I was not aware that you had an elder son until quite recently, sir. Is this the boy who has come back to us from the side of the unbelievers?"

"This is my boy who was lost to the Saracen as a captive long ago, my Lord," Marguerite said levelly.

The Secretary of Bishop Bohemond ignored her and stared at Talon. "I shall be glad to hear your confession, young man. I do not doubt but that it must be a long one. We shall welcome you back to the fold with a suitable penance and forgive your unfortunate regression over the time you were away."

"I do not feel that I did anything that should make me feel like a sinner, Father," Talon said bluntly.

The Priest smiled thinly. "You may not realize it in your ignorance, young man, but we have a responsibility to God to ensure that one who has been sullied is cleansed and then taken back into the bosom of God."

Marguerite tightened her grip on Talon's arm so he held his peace.

A cup of wine was handed to the priest and other mugs were passed around to the family as they stood.

The priest toasted them then turned to Sir Hughes. "I came here on other business, Sir Hughes."

"What might that be, Father?'

"My Lord the Bishop understands that you continue to disregard the will of your Lady wife's father, which was that the land should go to his nephew."

He held up a hand to forestall the indignant words about to come from either Hughes or Philip. "One way or the other, sir, you should not disregard the words of a dying man. If he did indeed say that the land was his nephew's on his deathbed, then it must be so. It has been many years since the untimely death of your wife's father, but it is now time for the law to be observed and God's will be done."

"Why then did the Secretary of My Lord the Count of Carcassonne send us the letter recalling us to this land?" Marguerite asked, disregarding the protocols of the moment.

It was clear to all the priest was annoyed by her impertinence, but he answered patiently, if somewhat patronizingly. "My lady, it is the Church's law that protects the last wishes of a dying man. The secretary was wrong; he should and will be chastised for the confusion he has caused. You have no proof of the written kind to present that can counter the claim, is that not true?" He looked keenly at Sir Hughes as he said this.

Talon's antennae went up. Why was he so interested in the lack of proof?

The priest continued without waiting for an answer. "I am sent here by my Lord the Bishop to warn you that you will run counter to the laws of the church should you continue to refuse to honor your father's wishes. He is gravely concerned that you shall sin against the Church and God in this. I pray you will find reason in your hearts and allow due process to take place."

Talon felt that the priest was beginning to sound just a bit too sanctimonious for his liking. He was about to say something, but his father got in first.

"Father, we have only the word of my wife's cousin, and that word is suspect to my mind. I have no faith whatsoever in our cousin. I shall, however, be glad to take this to a court that will settle the issue," Sir Hughes said irritably.

The priest looked at Sir Hughes for a long moment then shrugged. "Then so be it. My Lord Bishop will be disappointed that you will not see reason, Sir Hughes. I shall mention this to him. If you will answer to a court appointed to review this case, then I cannot stop you. We shall make arrangements to make this so. I regret but I must leave as I have a long ride to Albi before sunset. Thank you for your hospitality, sir. My lady."

"From where have you come, Father?" Talon asked innocently.

"From your... from the forest where we have hunted today," the priest answered.

Talon noted that the man's face flushed for some reason.

The man bowed shortly to them and then turned and mounted his horse. After a brief salute he wheeled his horse and led his party out of the gates and down the dusty road toward Albi.

There was silence as everyone watched his departure.

Then Sir Hughes slapped his hand on his thigh. "What is the Bishop of Albi doing sending his lackey here to warn me to comply with the wishes of your cousin, Marguerite?"

"It comes too closely to the quarrel of three days ago, Hughes." she said bitterly. "Somehow my cousin has reached the bishop and he has decided to force us to agree to his terms. I wish I knew what was going on."

"I think he has just come from the Guillabert's home. Did you hear him when Talon asked him outright?" Max, who had been listening, said.

Talon looked at Max. "Yes, I agree, I think we caught him in a lie, Max."

"Maybe, Talon, but it doesn't change our situation. I still don't know what they're up to," Sir Hughes growled.

Talon thought he might know but he was silent. His parents' agitation was concern enough. He recalled that the monk Claude was at the Abbey of Saint Marc; he decided he needed to talk to him. Perhaps he could help bring some kind of reason to this situation.

It was a subdued group of people at dinner that evening as they discussed the new twist to the situation. There were no conclusions to be drawn; they were all nervous because the Church had seemingly weighed in on the side of Sir Guillabert. He obviously had a very powerful ally in the bishop. Talon went to bed wondering why a powerful bishop would be so interested in this kind of land dispute.

The next day he told Sir Hughes of his decision to visit the monastery and see what he could find out from the monks. Being a well established monastery there might be some clues as to the status of the land.

He took with him Anwl, Belth, and Drudwas, and one man Sir Hughes gave him to show them the way. It was almost a full day's ride according to Hughes. He asked Gareth to stay at the fortress with the other two men and ensure that his father and Sir Philip were well protected. He did not think that there would be any trouble at this point, particularly now as there was every likelihood that the bishop would convene a court to hear the case.

Just before they set off that morning, Aicelina came up to him and gave him a leather bag which she told him held bread and cheese for the journey. He thanked her solemnly and took the food gratefully. Mounting Jabbar, he looked down at her.

She was squinting up at him, one hand protecting her eyes from the sun. Her look was quizzical but all she said was, "God speed, Talon. Come home safe."

He murmured his thanks, a little surprised at the attention. She had seemed to have avoided him since their last encounter.

He thought about the food he was eating in this foreign land. In many ways it was completely different from that which he had become used to in Persia. He had already eaten hare stew with root vegetables and herbs. He had taken a liking to this soft matter that they called butter and spread all over the bread which he had also come to like very much. He had watched butter being made once. The maid had poured cream from the milk of the cows into a long wooden barrel and then closed the lid and then beat a long stick with a flat end up and down inside it making a loud sloshing sound. He had been very surprised to come back within the hour to find this slick, fatty-tasting stuff sitting on a board instead of the cream. Talon remembered the way yogurt had been made in Persia. There they used a skin full of goat's milk that they shook back and forth on ropes for some time until it separated and then they took the cream and hung it in cloths from beams, after which they shook the skin until its contents became a soft, very sharp cheese.

He had come to love cream, too, and had once gone with his mischievous brother Guillaume to steal some from the cool of the pantry near the kitchens. They had been caught by Aicelina with the white stuff all over their chins. She had laughed at their guilty looks, scolded them and then chased Guillaume off while she took a cloth and wiped Talon's face for him. It had been a curiously intimate gesture and he had felt himself getting hot. She simply smiled at him and then left wagging an admonishing finger at him at the doorway, while he had grinned guiltily after her.

With a bright summer's day ahead of them, the small troop of riders were on their way along the well-worn tracks that led to Albi, but which would eventually take them north into the foothills where the old abbey was located. The journey passed uneventfully along forest tracks where the trees towered over them. Talon was still getting used to trees that made a man on horse seem insignificant; the lack of a distant horizon still bothered him and he felt enclosed. They would come out of the forest and ride across open country, avoiding the cultivated fields where peasants worked the ground. He enjoyed the warmth of the sun on his back, and the men with him seemed to enjoy it too. The Welsh chattered incessantly, leaving Talon to his thoughts, which revolved mainly around the predicament his family found itself in.

His thoughts also drifted for the hundredth time to the Holy Land and what might have happened to Rav'an and Reza, his Persian brother. If anyone could keep them alive, he thought it had to be the resourceful Reza.

He was deep in these not-so-cheerful thoughts when they came within sight of the buildings just before sunset. Talon was impressed with the layout of the monastery. Situated on the crest of a lightly wooded hill, the abbey was walled and seemed defensible. It was composed of a large, rectangular building surrounded by stables and barns. On one of the sides of the stone building was a square tower with red tiles on its roof and long windows, giving it the look of a watch tower. Talon noted many fields surrounding the abbey, some of them vineyards. There was an air of careful cultivation and quiet wealth about the place.

Their presence had been noted as they came up the gentle slope toward the buildings where they were met by a monk in a gray-brown habit. Much patched, as were, it seemed to Talon, everyone's clothes in this region.

The monk politely asked them what their business would be, and when Talon said that he had come to visit Brother Claude and perhaps talk to the abbot, the monk hesitated, but then asked his name.

"I am Talon, son of Hughes de Gilles."

"Please come with me and we shall look to the horses, Sir. I think Brother Claude is in the fields nearby."

"I would like to go and meet him, if you have no objection, Brother," Talon said politely. He dismounted, gave Jabbar's reins to Drudwas, and got directions as to where the field might be. In fact it was one of the vineyards on the slope to the south of the buildings; as he made his way there, he saw Claude and several of the monks who had come with them from Mas-Dieu, working along the rows.

Someone saw him coming and nudged Claude, who stood upright from his hoeing. He straightened his back painfully and stared at Talon. Then recognition dawned and he beamed and called a welcome. He leaned his hoe against one of the dense vines, and, calling to Pierre who was also there, he hurried up the slope toward Talon.

"Well met, young sir," he said as he came up, panting and wiping his brow with his sleeve. "I had not expected a visit so soon. I hope you are well and found your family in good health?" He beamed his pleasure at seeing Talon.

Talon smiled. "Indeed, Brother Claude, it is a pleasure to see you again, and you Pierre," he said as he clasped their hands firmly. "This monastery is far larger than I had imagined," he said as he gazed about.

"It is founded upon an old Roman villa that existed hundreds of years ago," Pierre said proudly.

"It was in ruins many, many years ago when the order bought it and rebuilt it along much the same lines as formerly. You will note it is situated on this hillock. That was to provide some means of defense, as in those days life was even more precarious I think than it is today."

"I just wish we did not have to work so hard in the fields," Claude said with a rueful grin on his round, sweating face. "My back aches more each time we have to go out there; I think I am getting too old to do that all the time. I much prefer to spend time in the Scriptorium where I can hunch over a book and read."

"It is all God's work to be done and you know that you are one of the slowest at the hoeing in any case, Claude. You came along just in time, Talon—he was about to fall over from exertion," Pierre said, with a laugh.

Talon smiled at the friendly banter.

Brother Claude stood back and looked at him carefully. "What brings you to this place, Talon?" he asked quietly.

"Much and perhaps nothing, good sirs. It will take some time to explain however."

"Then we must take you to meet the Abbot Matthias. I have told him of you and he would be very keen to meet with you. Later when it's dinner time we shall eat together and also I hope Audric, our vintner, is feeling generous so we can have some of the better wine tonight." Claude said hopefully. Talon shuddered.

They left the other monks in the field and made their way up to the abbey. They walked through the gates into the courtyard that surrounded the larger building and saw that Talon's companions were busy taking the horses to the stables. He paused to tell his men that he would be spending time with the monks and that they should find a place to sleep and eat for the night. Pierre left them briefly to take charge of the sleeping arrangements and told them he would follow them in later.

Claude called greetings to men as they passed and led the way to the entrance below the tower. They went up some stone stairs and then along a short veranda that opened out onto the yard. Claude took him to a large wooden door and knocked. A voice called and they entered a medium-sized room with rough-hewn wooden beams supporting the roof.

It looked comfortable and cluttered. There were rolls of papers, and books in piles on the floor and all over a table. Behind that table sat a thin man, well into his old age, attested to by the halo of pure white hair that stood out around his balding head. He was dressed in an almost-white woolen habit and, despite the warmth of the day, he wore a heavy cloak over his shoulders. He regarded them with a calm expression on his long, lined features.

"Ah, Brother Claude, what brings you this evening? Is the work in the fields not to your liking?" he asked without malice and smiled gently to take the sting out of the comment.

Claude smiled back unabashed, and then said diffidently, "I would always prefer the Scriptorium, my Lord; the exercise of the mind suits me better. I ask your pardon, sir, Pierre and I have brought the interesting young man named Talon to meet you."

Abbot Matthias' reaction was instant. He stood up and came round the table to greet Talon. He was a lot taller than he had seemed behind the table. He extended a bony hand to Talon and said warmly, "Ah, so you are the Talon I've heard all about from Claude and his companion, Pierre. They are very impressed with you, young sir."

"I have done nothing that I can think of to impress them, my Lord Abbot," Talon said politely.

"Perhaps it's in the lack of what you have said that impresses them," returned the abbot. "I hope that you will partake of our poor hospitality while you're with us."

"Willingly, Sir. I came to ask questions to which I hope you might be able to provide answers."

"Then I shall charge you, Brother Claude, to see to his needs and to take him to evening supper after vespers—which is almost upon us—after which we can discuss your needs."

"Yes my Lord Abbot, gladly."

Claude led the way out and took Talon to a small but clean cell where he told Talon he would sleep for the night. He assured Talon that his men would be taken well care of and not to worry about them. He excused himself with the explanation that he had to go to vespers, after which they could go to dinner. The bell at the top of the tower was ringing by this time, calling the monks in from the fields to prayers.

Talon listened to the silence of the abbey as the monks congregated somewhere within the complex and then very faintly he heard the murmur of many voices at prayer.

Within half an hour Claude came and collected Talon, they then went and found Pierre, who told them that the horses were being taken care of and the men were being fed as they spoke.

Talon would be a guest of honor at the high table with the abbot and some senior monks. Claude and Pierre, by virtue of the fact that they knew Talon, would be nearby.

The tables were filling up quickly as they entered the main hall although for the most part there was not a lot of talking. The rule of silence, while not fully enforced, was encouraged. Talon was shown to his place at a table that faced the monks. Talon estimated that the company assembled here must have numbered at least thirty. They all stood up when the abbot made his entrance, then continued to stand as one of the senior monks at the high table read a short lesson. When the lesson was over the abbot blessed the company and they all sat down.

They were served by young novices who hurried about with water, bread, and even wine for the company. Talon allowed wine to be poured into a jug for him but after his indulgence at home he was wary of taking more than a sip. But it turned out to be very good wine and he realized that he liked it. This was a far better vintage than the poor stuff at his father's hearth, he decided ruefully.

The meal was simple, but good. There was plenty of crisp bread available and even some salt for all to enjoy. The meal was a rich stew of vegetables and some threads of meat.

Talon sat quietly, enjoying the company of the monks. The conversation was muted in most part as tired and hungry men consumed their basic food. The abbot gave him a welcoming smile when he saw him, but did not speak to him during the meal.

When it was over everyone stood up and waited until the abbot and the elder monks had left. He signaled Brother Claude and Pierre to bring Talon with them as he left. They arrived back at the abbot's office in time to see the candles lit. He offered Talon some more wine, which he accepted, surprised that he should do so but it was a good, heavy vintage that he could enjoy.

The abbot settled into this chair and addressed him. "My Brothers here told me that you were a hostage of the Saracen for many years, young man. Once we have dispensed with the other business of yours, I would like to hear more of this."

"I shall be pleased to tell you more of that once I have discussed my other business," Talon said politely.

The abbot indicated that he should go on.

Talon went on to outline the situation he had found his father facing when he came home. He described the visit of his uncle Sir Guillabert and his sons and then the visit by the priest on behalf of the bishop. When he got to the part about the bishop, the abbot looked surprised and then somewhat alarmed.

He interrupted Talon. "This priest came to your father's house and threatened him?" he asked incredulously.

"I can only see it that way, sir." replied Talon. "We are to take this to a court the bishop wishes to convene that will decide the issue once and for all."

"Why have you come here? To tell us of this story?"

"I came because I thought you might be able to interpret the law and help us understand why everyone is so interested in taking the land from my father. There must be some papers somewhere to prove that it is rightfully the land willed to my mother." He tried not to sound exasperated but it was difficult.

The abbot leaned his elbows on the desk and steepled his fingers thoughtfully in front of him."We do read law here, that is true; but it is Church law and not feudal law. For the most part, it only applies to our own brethren. We also hold in trust those wills of the commoners and knights, indeed, lords, too, who wish to leave their papers in our care. With the lack of some written evidence, this is going to be a difficult interpretation. To my mind, though, it sounds suspicious that your uncle should have been at the bedside of your grandfather if he died of the plague."

"Even a priest was unlikely to be present at the death of someone with the plague," Claude agreed. "It raged through here like a wild fire and then was gone, almost as quickly as it came, but it left many dead. Those who survived fled the region completely or hid themselves away in the forests until it was over."

"We were ourselves very frightened of the pestilence that swept over the land at that time," Pierre added. "People would not go back to their villages but lived in caves and shelters in the forest where many died of starvation rather than risk the plague they thought might linger in their homes."

The abbot nodded. "That is the first part that I do not like about the tale. The second part is that there seems to be no written document proving your uncle's claims, either. This means that the dispute can be settled by armed combat as is the old way, or must be settled in a court. However..." He trailed off.

"What are you saying, sir?" Talon asked, looking at him curiously.

"I am disturbed that the bishop has shown such interest on the side of your uncle. This is not a good sign, especially as he will be one of the presiding officials at the court. The Count or his secretary will be one of the others, and there will be one other appointed officer of the State who has good knowledge of the laws of the land, namely Languedoc, as we are ruled by the Count of Carcassonne."

Talon's heart sank. "Does this mean that the bishop could influence the case against my father from the start?"

The other two men looked at one another, then nodded reluctantly.

"It is very unusual and I think irregular for a bishop to become involved in a land dispute, which makes me wonder why this should be so," said the abbot thoughtfully, "If we could understand this, perhaps we could solve this riddle."

"Can we not challenge the case as only hearsay?" Claude asked.

"Without papers of his own, your father is not very much better off. The whole thing would not even be in dispute if his mother had been the first-born son," the abbot remarked with a wry smile at Talon. "Does your mother know if there were papers of any kind to be had?"

"She is certain that there were, sir. But they cannot be found and all the people who might have known have died, so we now do not know where to look."

"Pierre, we hold papers of a legal sort for people; where would we hold such a document of this kind should it exist?" the abbot asked.

"We do, indeed, my Lord. I shall see if there is anything in our own records."

The abbot hesitated, and then said carefully, "Talon, you need to understand that despite the honor attached to men of the crusades who go to the Holy Land to fight for the Lord, the kind of thing we are seeing here is not uncommon. Man is a lowly creature for the most part, and more often than not his greed will shut out matters of principle and many will not scruple to distort or cheat the law, or their own kin for that matter."

"I am not sure what you mean, sir," Talon said, although he thought he might. Was the abbot warning him in some manner?

"There have been many examples of theft and greed visited upon people who have either left for the crusades or, often as not, visited upon those unfortunates left behind who are too weak to defend their rights. Women have been dispossessed by the very families of those who left on God's Holy errand. In other cases, the land is simply stolen and never returned as there is no one to dispute it. This has happened from peasant rank on up to that of knights and beyond, despite stern admonishments from the Church that this is terribly wrong. We are vehemently opposed to this kind of thing. It is an affront to God." He looked sternly at Talon, then changed the subject. "It is almost sunset. The bells will ring for Compline prayers and then it is bedtime. We monks have to rise and go to chapel for the midnight Vigil mass. Will you permit me to say goodnight? We shall talk again in the morning about this, and I hope about your life in the world of the Saracen."

Talon rose and bowed. "Thank you for your patience with me, sir. Of course I should retire; it is late. We shall talk on the morrow."

He left with Claude and Pierre close by. As they walked, Claude touched Talon on the arm.

"Talon, you need to understand one thing."

"What is that, Brother Claude? That even the church is corrupt and trying to steal my father's land?"

"What I wish to say about the abbot is this," Claude said calmly, ignoring the jibe, "he's as honest a man as I have ever met, and that's why I stay here. I can assure you that if he can help you, he will."

"I am with Claude on this, Talon. Our abbot is one of those rare men of the Lord's class who has renounced worldly goods and placed his life in the hands of God. You have come to the right place to hear wise words and good council. He will tell you the truth as he sees it."Pierre said.

Talon paused. "I understand Brother Claude, Pierre. I apologize as I, too, feel that he's a good man and I didn't mean to include him in my comment. But I had not expected to come home to this kind of strife and intrigue. Is it truly as he has stated?"

"Yes and worse, my young friend," Pierre answered. "The things men do to men is horrifying often enough, but to steal from those who have taken up the Cross and gone to fight in a holy war is despicable. Many are the examples we know of, and not in this region alone. We try to intercede where we can, but it is the responsibility of the parish priests to at least observe and report, which sadly few do."

They made their way down the stairs to the yard; there Claude turned to Talon. "Be of good heart, Talon. If we can, we will help. I have heard that your father is a good man and looks after his people. He should not be cast out of the inheritance."

He clasped hands with both the monks and they went their separate ways. The bell in the high tower began to toll the time for prayers. It filled the evening with a sound that carried far. When it stopped there was a long silence, almost as though the birds themselves were contemplating the night to come. As it was still dusk and Talon was too restless to go to sleep, he went to the stables. He had always found comfort in being around horses, so he walked along the short row to where he had heard Jabbar whicker. Jabbar was standing with his head poking out over the rail that kept him enclosed, looking for him.

"We have come a long way together, you and I," Talon said unconsciously using Farsi. The horse nuzzled his hand, looking for a tidbit. His master did not disappoint him. Jabbar slurped the tiny sugar cake happily and then allowed Talon to stroke his muzzle and chin. They stood this way for a few minutes while Talon reflected on what the abbot had said.

Could it really be possible that the bishop was involved in some kind of scheme to disinherit his mother of her rightful inheritance? If so, why?

He resolved to ask his father to take him around the property when he got back. He heard a slight sound and instantly faded into the shadows. Someone was coming down the length of the stables cautiously: Drudwas. He held a large stick in his hands and seemed to be looking for someone. Talon waited for him to pass, so close that they could have touched, and then stepped out behind him and tapped him on the shoulder. Drudwas was quick; he spun round and slashed at Talon with his stick. Talon was faster and ducked and then stepped well inside Drudwas' guard and tripped him. Talon followed him down with his knife out.

He leaned over the surprised man. "What were you doing, Drudwas?"

Drudwas gasped out, "No! No, don't use the knife. Oh, it's you, m'lord! I thought I heard some person speaking a strange language and I wanted to make sure no one was about to hurt the horses. I did not know it was you."

"Up you go, man. I was talking to my horse. He doesn't understand French."

Drudwas clambered to his feet. "I did not even sense that you were there, m'lord. I did not mean to attack you. I love horses and cannot abide them being hurt, you see. I am the guard for the next few hours."

"You're a good man, Drudwas. I thank you for your concern. I was simply thinking out loud and talking to my horse, Jabbar. He is from Persia."

"Magnificent animal too, if I may say so, sor. I shall leave you alone then, m'lord."

Talon smiled in the dusk. He would not be able to get them to call him by his name. These men were going to insist that he be called sir or m'lord no matter what. He bade Drudwas goodnight and left the man looking after Jabbar.

The next day dawned bright and sunny; a few clouds could be seen in the western sky but otherwise the sky was clear and blue. Talon ate a frugal breakfast in the company of Brothers Claude and Pierre, who had more or less adopted him for the duration of his stay. They asked him if he could stay one more day and he willingly agreed after making sure the men were comfortable. He need not have concerned himself; the men were intent upon lounging in the sun as much as they could after tending to the horses. Talon went back to Claude and Pierre.

The abbot was engaged for the time being so the two monks decided they would take Talon on a guided tour. It was a fascination for Talon as he could not compare the monastery with anything other than the castles of his boyhood in both Palestine and Persia. This monastery was every bit as well run as the Templar station of Mas-Dieu, where they had stayed the one night. There were many similarities and then some differences.

First, this was not a military order, Brother Claude informed Talon proudly. "Although this monastery has a very long history with the Benedictine Order, we are an order known as Cluny. We are especially fortunate as we are immune from both lay and Episcopal interference; hence, we owe nothing to the bishopric that rules in Albi. We do, however, owe much of our patronage to the Count of Carcassonne, who is one of our greatest benefactors."

"So he protects you and pays you?"

"Not quite. We have to pay our way, but we observe the full Benedictine Rules."

"What does that mean?"

"It means that as a result our liturgical devotions are among the most beautiful. Therefore many lords, and even counts will come to us to say prayers for their relatives and give us money for doing so," Pierre answered.

"Also, our abbot is of a very aristocratic family and can see more clearly than most the state of the governance of the country, and to some extent affect it. This means that he might be able to exert some influence upon the bishop in his cause," Claude told Talon.

Claude and Pierre took him on tour of the winery, which contained many barrels of aging wine. Dates written on the casks went back at least ten years in some cases. Then they toured the olive press, where a couple of sweating monks were walking around, pushing a long pole ahead of them. Attached to the other end, rotating about a short axis, was a wide and deep, circular stone with rough grooves emanating out from its center. The stone crushed the olives as it went, the oil being captured in a crude drain where they showed him it could be filtered. There was some joking between the monks at Claude's expense as the two monks offered him their workload and he laughingly refused.

Talon smiled as they teased his newfound friend; it seemed common knowledge that Claude hated hard physical work. Claude bantered good naturally with them and it was clear to Talon that despite his aversion to work, Claude was respected and liked, as was Pierre.

"We receive our olives from Provence and farther south. The olive tree cannot grow here, Talon. It is too cold. It is easier to bring the olives to the press than to trust the oil that comes by way of the merchants who sell it." Pierre laughed.

Talon came away from the machinery of the monastery impressed, noting that the monks did most of the hard labor; there were few work animals about that he could see. The Templars had had no such inhibitions about using whatever animals they could.

He asked Claude about slaves and received a very odd look. "There have not been slaves in this country for generations, Talon. Are they then plentiful in the *Outré Mere*?"

"Yes, they are, mostly taken from battle or successful sieges. They are then put to work on building castles for the Christians. The Saracen does the same thing with our people. It's a very hard life."

"I see," Claude said, shaking his head. "It would seem that there is much for us to understand about that part of the world. Slavery goes against the tenets of our religion, but castles have to be built." He shook his head again.

Soon they were told that the abbot wanted to see them and they hurried up the stairs again to meet him. He greeted Talon cordially and then after bidding them to be seated he plied him with questions as to how he had lived in Persia and how he had survived. Talon had learned to keep certain things to himself so he bypassed the fact that he had been well trained by the Assassins in Persia. He told them about the Saracen castles and the time on the way to and from Isfahan. He described the huge caravans of camels with the merchants and talked about Al Tayyib the caravan leader and made them laugh at the manner in which he controlled the caravan and its many differing peoples.

He could tell that they were almost disbelieving when he described the opulence and advanced state of medicine in the College of Isfahan, but they held their peace politely, not wanting to be rude. He told them how the Persian water ways and systems worked, borrowed from both the Romans and their own ancestors. How water was made to travel vast distances underground from mountain springs to cities. He spoke of baths, fountains, and gardens.

The abbot was a keen listener and Brother Claude and Pierre were awed by what Talon had to tell. When he spoke of the great city of Baghdad past which he and his friends had ridden they shook their heads in wonder.

He bemused them with tales of the vast spaces and the impossibly high mountains. He told them of Jean the Priest and how he had been martyred. By the time he had finished telling them about Jean's sacrifice of death, Claude was in tears and promised to make a devotional prayer especially for him at the chapel. They fell silent when Talon told them about his adopted uncle and aunt, Farj'an and Fariba, who had given him so much. How they had educated him and his companions in the art of music, medicine and other sciences and made them think for themselves instead of blindly following the words of others.

The abbot nodded his head and said kindly, "You have been blessed to have known people such as these, my son."

The abbot called for refreshments and then continued to ask him questions and listened raptly to his replies.

Finally Talon came to a halt; they had passed most of the day talking. Talon was tired but also realized that he had made some friends. They had shared something of his life.

Finally it was time to go to dinner. The abbot came around to Talon. "You are a remarkable young man, Talon. I shall do all in my power to help you and your father to solve this mystery."

"Father, I have one more request of you."

"Speak, my son."

"I was told I had to go to confession by the priest who came to our house the other day. He implied that I needed to come to him to confess. Should I do this? I would rather not."

The abbot's eyes gleamed with amusement. "I have already heard what I could call a confession. Indeed, it would take a book to tell it all. Let us say that I have heard the first part. I absolve you, my son." He made the sign of the cross over Talon's bowed head. "The penance is that you have to visit us regularly to tell us more of your time in those far-off lands."

Claude and Pierre chuckled at that and they all left for dinner, smiling.

That night Talon woke to the sound of the Midnight mass. The tolling bell calling the monks to Vigils reverberated in the silence of the night. He lay awake. Listening, until it finally stopped and the night was quiet again. Then he heard the faint sound of the monks singing in the chapel. For some reason the tone of the bell had made his heart heavy and he felt a deep loneliness within him.

He got up, pulled on his trews and walked quietly out of the cell into the balmy night. He paused by the courtyard and sat on the stone wall of the well. Somewhere in the distance across the fields a fox barked but otherwise the night was silent. The monks were finished and gone to bed.

Despite his earlier sense of aloneness, Talon found the buildings and smells of the monastery comforting. This was a very different land and in many ways threatening to him, but at the same time he felt a certain kinship to the monks.

He heard the slap of sandals coming across the yard.

It was Claude, who had noticed him and recognized him despite the darkness. "I saw you walking and assumed it was you, master Talon."

"Are the prayers over now?"

"They are, and we should all be abed but the night is warm and I am restless, too. You have told me so much of this Persia that I cannot sleep for thinking of it."

"It was my home," Talon said simply.

"And yet you were a prisoner there and it killed your friend."

"That world and this are not so different when it comes to men fighting other men for unclear reasons."

"I hope that you do not feel that this cannot be your home."

"The ghosts and demons within me are quiet for the first time in many a month, Claude. Perhaps this is possible." He took a deep breath and bade the monk goodnight then went back to bed where he slept well.

The next day Talon and his men bade Brothers Claude and Pierre goodbye and waved to the Abbot Matthias, who stood on the second floor of the building, looking down on them. He waved back and then turned away to deal with other business.

Talon thanked the two monks sincerely. "I have been fortunate to meet you, brothers. I hope to come back soon to share time with you."

"As my Lord Abbot said yesterday, Talon, you are always a welcome guest at his humble house and we would welcome another visit. God go with you and may He be your guide in all things."

Talon wheeled Jabbar and led his retinue out along the old Roman road toward his father's fort.

They arrived late that evening to find the place a hive of activity. After having been greeted by his father and mother and everyone else who saw him, Talon asked what was going on.

Sir Philip told him that there were two pieces of news. First, a cottage up river from the fort had been burned and the peasant who lived there killed. "Right in front of his wife and children," Philip said in disgust. "His cottage was on Hughes' land."

The second thing was that there was to be a fair at Albi and did Talon want to go?

Talon shook his head in dismay. "Uncle Philip, you have just told me that we have been attacked by someone, and then in the same breath you invite me to a fair?" he asked incredulously.

Philip looked confused. "So I did, Talon. So I did. We are riding out to the cottage in the morning. The news only came this evening just before you arrived, so we're getting ready to leave early. Do you want to come?"

Talon smiled grimly. "Of course. Why would I not?"

"But don't forget that there is a fair in three days at Albi," Philip added.

Talon shook his head. His uncle sometimes seemed to think in two places at once. He made sure that Jabbar was taken care of, then found Gareth and Max, who seemed to have become inseparable, and greeted them. They were pleased to see him back and told him the news much as Philip had, omitting the news of the fair.

"Who do you think did this Max?" Talon asked.

Before Max could answer Sir Hughes came over and joined them. "Ah, there you are Talon. I did not know when you would be back. Did you find out anything useful from the monks?"

"Perhaps, Father." He told them about his discussion with the abbot and mentioned the hint given that the abbot distrusted the fact that the bishop was involved. They discussed the issue over dinner that night, but as before the talk went round and round without any conclusions being reached.

That night Talon went out to the well, stripped down to his trews and tried to scrub himself clean. The water was cold and he did more to get himself wet than clean but he felt better as he shook his long hair to get rid of as much water as possible. He heard light footsteps in the dark and knew without being told that it was Aicelina. He half turned and watched her form coming toward him in the darkness.

"Do you always come to save me from the water?" he asked quietly.

"I heard you were back, Talon. Here is a cloth to dry yourself with," she said, equally quietly.

The men standing guard on the gates could easily have heard them talking if they had raised their voices.

He felt her eyes on him, but was not able to construe their meaning. "I thank you, Aicelina. How are you?"

"I am well, but you have to spend some time with your little brother, he has been pining for you. What did you do to have him believe you were his hero?" she said this with amusement in her voice.

Talon smiled in the dark as he dried himself in front of her. "I don't know, but we must change that point of view."

He heard a low laugh and saw the gleam of her teeth. He could smell the light scent of herbs, dried in the sun, slightly sharp, but clean and fresh. He wondered how she could remain clean in this place. He yearned for a hot bath and resolved to have one the next day.

Aicelina stepped back and then turned to leave. "Goodnight, Talon," she said as she walked away.

He would have liked to spend some more time with her, but he was not yet ready to call her back. "Goodnight, Aicelina," he said.

Chapter 7

Guillabert's Lair

The next day Sir Hughes led a group of armed men out of his gates. In attendance were Talon and his archers, who ran easily alongside the riders. Sir Philip and Max along with five of Hughes' retainers rode with them; all were armed with swords, bows, or lances.

They headed for the river Tarn, where Sir Hughes' land ended. There they turned their horses north along the banks of one of the tributaries that flowed into the larger river and rode upstream for about two miles to where the river narrowed between steeper banks and the water flowed faster. There they came up to a water mill that was on the property.

Talon was impressed with the size of the building and curious about how the water was used to drive the machinery inside. He could see that a part of the river had been diverted into a channel that could be shut off by dropping a long wedge of wood into slots.

Right now it was open and the water boiled down the channel to fall upon the huge wooden wheel placed in its path. The wheel was being turned by the force of the water and a shaft from the wheel led into the dark interior of the building. Talon, who had never seen a mill before, dismounted and with Sir Hughes and Philip went up to the miller, who was standing, waiting for them. He bowed low as they came up. He was covered with flour from the filthy leather cap on his head to the apron held round his waist with a wide leather belt. Even the leggings he wore were gray with flour dust.

He was surprised when Talon told him that he wanted to have a look inside. Begging their forgiveness for the state of the building, he edged backward and then bowed them into the main room. It was noisy inside. The water wheel was turning outside with a loud growling sound while inside there was a lot of machinery in action, and, as the miller explained in a shout, the wheel was now connected to the system inside. Looking up, Talon saw long and wide leather belts moving over huge wooden wheels that in turn drove long wood shafts.

Finally, the miller, who had regained some of his composure as he proudly showed off his technical knowledge, pointed out the great granite wheel itself seated in a wooden frame that enclosed it all around. Talon estimated the wheel to be at least four feet across. It rested upon another that did not move. There was an urchin, Talon assumed he was one of the miller's children, also covered in flour dust, stooped over the slowly turning wheel, trickling grain into a small hole on its exterior. The miller then showed them where the powder came out in a grayish-white stream into a sack being held by another child standing below.

The noise of the outside water wheel turning on its bearings, the slap and whirr of the wide leather straps and the creaking of the wooden wheels combined with the slow grinding sound made by the mill stone on its anvil made talking difficult.

The miller, now well into his stride, took some of the powder and sifted it between his fingers. He showed them how soft it was and free of stones or husks. Talon took a pinch and agreed. He put a little on his tongue and was impressed at how fine the powder was. The miller grinned and pointed to the stone.

"These stones are granite, m'lord. They come from Brittany and are the finest in the world. Even the English buy these. You will not break your teeth on this powder like some of the lesser stones."

Talon, who had only seen grain crushed in the crudest fashion up to now, was impressed.

They were remounting when he asked about this mill and was surprised to hear that there was another, both situated along tributaries of the Tarn. That river, his father told him, gave him fishing and boating rights, although it had been some time since he had collected any real revenue, he said glumly.

"I have been unable to enforce the law regarding my rights as yet because I don't have the manpower to do so." He then cheered up. "But we're realizing some revenue from these two mills. The people from Albi even come here and the miller is supposed to take a coin for a bag and two-thirds of that coin is mine."

Talon thought about that. He agreed the mills were substantial and represented a considerable value. He wondered if his father appreciated that fact. "So, how much do we take in earnings from the mills, Father?" he asked as they trotted their horses by the building.

"Why, I shall have to ask my huntsman, Domerc, that question, as he's the man who collects for me," said Hughes vaguely.

Talon looked at him. Did his father really not know the sum of the revenue that two mills could give him if carefully managed? His instinctive dislike of the dour huntsman made him skeptical that the man was as honest as his father thought. He knew that he was not a great calculator of figures, but at least he had had the basics of arithmetic taught to him in Isfahan and could recognize that there was some real potential in these mills. He decided to ask his mother about this.

They rode along the banks of the river, enjoying the morning and the view. Here the land was spectacular. The river flowed past slowly as though content to be within its banks for the moment. Then the trees closed in again and they were forced away from the river into single file on a crude track that headed toward the hills.

The relaxed mood of the riders changed when they came at last to the cottage of the man named Brunhild who had been murdered. It was more of a hut with low stone walls which supported a badly burned roof that had caved in as the fire consumed the thatch. This had not been a tiled roof. That was for wealthier men. The hut had been built against the bank on the rise of a low, wooded hill. The trees gave some shelter from the north, and the door opened toward the west.

Hughes and Philip were enraged at the ravaged property.

Philip said loudly, "It is easy to guess who did this foul deed, Hughes. We should ride over there and confront Guillabert in his nest and demand reparation. I am surprised he did not burn the mill while he was at it."

Hughes nodded. "I agree with you, but I don't think that a confrontation will work in our favor. I'll ride over there today and let him know that if I catch any man doing this again on my property he shall hang where he stands." His face set in anger as he wheeled his horse and galloped hard along the track toward the east. His men followed him.

They arrived at the stone fort of Sir Guillabert early that afternoon. It was substantially larger than Sir Hughes property, and the walls were of coarsely dressed stone. The gates were of heavy log, studded with iron nails and bands. To Talon's eye it looked as though it might withstand a short siege. But his eyes were on the walls. They were only twenty feet high and looked badly maintained. There was a ramp held up at the gates by stout ropes that could be dropped across a moat only half-filled with stinking water and the rest offal.

They were challenged as they rode up by men on the walkway above the gate.

Sir Hughes bellowed his name and then they waited.

Before too long a man came onto the walls and called down. "Sir Guillabert will see you, Sir Hughes."

"About time, too," Sir Hughes grumped, who didn't like to be kept waiting.

They heard the winches inside being turned and the ramp was lowered slowly to land with a thump on their side, then the gates were opened inward equally slowly. They rode across the ramp with a clatter then on into the courtyard. Talon searched the untidy yard and the large keep situated almost in the center, which was actually a small cluster of crudely joined towers. This was a substantial keep. He wanted to know how many men were housed and turned to Gareth, standing at his side, and whispered to him to get his men to count everyone they saw. Max heard him and nodded his head.

"I shall look for weapons, too, Master Talon."

Talon looked around the inner yard. It was dirty and untidy. The stables looked as though they had rarely been cleaned and there was manure all over the yard and several noisome-looking puddles. There were eight or ten big and vicious-looking hounds snarling over some bones in a corner and several tough-looking, dirty, and unkempt men lounging about. These men, who were well armed, watched the new arrivals with hard eyes.

Sir Hughes and his brother dismounted and were met by Sir Guillabert and his son Marcel. They were both in hunting garb and, other than the standard long dagger they carried at their belts, were not armed.

"What brings you to my humble house, Sir Hughes? You are not as welcome as you might have thought after your behavior toward me the last time we met," Sir Guillabert growled

Hughes ignored the jibe and came straight to the point. "Guillabert, I have just come across one of my landsman's huts. It is burnt, and he is dead. Men came out of the forests and committed a heinous crime."

Guillabert glared at him. "What is this to do with me? God's trews! What do I care if brigands decide they do not like your landsmen? Why come here to tell me?"

"Because we think you know who did it!" Philip shouted. He wore his Templar uniform. It gave him an air of authority and he was using it.

Sir Guillabert's face grew crimson with anger. "How dare you come here to my house, accepting my hospitality and accusing me of complicity in some imagined charge or other!" he roared.

Marcel glowered angrily. Roger strode over from the stables having heard the exchange, a menacing glare on his bearded features. The men who were standing idle started to saunter purposefully toward the Sir Hughes' group, looking as though they were preparing for trouble.

Talon thought Guillabert's display of temper looked feigned, but he did not like the fact that his men were coming together. They would be completely outnumbered here.

His father stood his ground but put a hand on Philip's arm to restrain him. "My brother is quick of temper, Sir Guillabert, but you have to allow that a grievous harm has been done to my people and that means to me. I came here to ask you to pass along a warning to others. If I should find the men who have done this, I shall hang them out of hand. I shall furthermore track down the man who gave them the orders to do so."

He said all this in a matter-of-fact tone. Talon admired his ability to control his anger. Then he added, "As to your hospitality, why, I see no wine being offered, so I shall leave you now." He gave a perfunctory bow, climbed back into the saddle and steered the angry Philip on his horse back toward the gates.

"Take your scabby men with you and know this, Hughes, neither you nor your family is welcome in this house!" Guillabert shouted.

"And take the Saracen whelp of yours with you. May God rot his heathen soul!" Marcel shouted. There was a nasty laugh from Roger standing nearby.

Talon bit his lip when he heard this but he did not need Max's restraining hand to keep his temper. Sir Philip, however, had no such inhibitions. "Marcel, you ignorant pup. Do not test this man's temper too far. Or you will regret it as others have."

Marcel gave a contemptuous laugh and waved them off dismissively. For a moment Talon thought his uncle would ride the young man down, but he held onto his fiery temper just enough to leave with the others.

As they rode away, Talon watched the men on the ground for any indication that they were about to commit some treachery. Instead, they looked balefully after the group as it filed out of the castle and onto the wide swath of grassland in front. He breathed a lot easier when they were out of crossbow range. He decided to leave his father and uncle in the lead, talking animatedly to one another while he collected the information he wanted.

Gareth strode alongside and Max sidled his horse alongside. "What numbers did you count?"

Gareth, who could only just count, grinned his gap-toothed smile and raised his right hand fingers spread three times. "That is how many men-at-arms I saw, Talon."

Max nodded agreement. "I saw that number and more loafing in corners, and there had to be some in the keep itself. There are crossbow men and spearmen, as well as a couple of knights who have sold themselves to Sir Guillabert."

"That makes it nearer thirty or more," Talon mused. He was silent while he digested this information. His father's men barely numbered twenty-five in total and only then if they included the Welshmen. He was thankful that he had asked them to join him.

Actually, he told himself, they had volunteered. He made a note to pay them an advance to sweeten the taste. He trusted Gareth and the other men now, so he had few worries that they would sneak off in the middle of the night. All the same, it was not their quarrel.

After thanking the two men he rode forward to where his father and uncle were still debating the events just past. They stopped when he came up and both querried him almost at once.

"Do you think Guillabert is a party to the burning?"

Talon shrugged. "If he is not then I cannot think who could be. However, we have no proof, so we could only do what you did. You warned him."

"I think we have passed a point of no return with my wife's cousin," Sir Hughes growled.

Talon had to agree.

They rode into the fort in late afternoon, the sun a red orb over the trees to the west. It promised to be a balmy evening. Talon and Philip, after seeing to the horses, went to sit in the one place with the last vestiges of sunlight they could find and talk together. Talon liked his uncle and he realized that Philip valued his opinion.

They sat in silence for a while and then Philip said, "Talon, I am impressed that you did not attack and kill Marcel for what he said today. I, more than most, have no doubt as to your courage."

"One day, Uncle, if he continues in that vein he surely will regret it," Talon said calmly.

Philip nodded. "Talon, you have been thinking?"

Talon gave a short laugh. "My brother Reza used to say that! Uncle, there is much to think on. Yes, I have been thinking about the burning and what we can do about it. Do you think they will attempt to burn the mills?"

The female hunting hound came over and demanded attention from them both. They obliged, absent-mindedly scratching her behind the head and along her back.

Philip thought about it. "That's a good question and perhaps one for your father. But I don't think so, as that would destroy a large part of the wealth of your father's estate. If they are after it, they would lose it, too."

Talon nodded. "I think so, too, Uncle. If that's the case, we should ask father's opinion. However, that means that we can narrow down some of the targets. There are a few of father's landsmen who do not live in or near the village. We should try to keep an eye on their houses after we have brought the people in. I think I might have a plan."

He outlined his idea to Philip who, although he had some reservations, agreed in principle with the idea.

They went in to supper where Talon was greeted by his brother, who now wanted attention. Aicelina smiled at him as he knelt before the boy and discussed the day's events. Then it was time for Guillaume to go to bed, so Talon had to take him there, followed by Aicelina.

"Tell me a story from the far lands that you lived in, Talon," Guillaume demanded.

Talon smiled at him. "I shall tell you of a great warrior named Rostam. He was a great Persian hero."

"Oh, yes!" Guillaume squeaked in excitement. "Did he kill lots of warriors and become king?"

"Patience, young lord, I have to tell the story as it should be told, and perhaps he did win great battles. Settle down and I shall tell you." So Talon told him of the great Persian hero named Rostam and how he conquered the lands of the gods in distant times. "Once long, long ago there was a great hero who lived in the vast eastern lands of the Persians. His name was Rostam and he was the son of Zal and Kaboli. Zal was his father who had magical powers and the protection of a great bird called Simorg."

"A bird?!" Guillaume exclaimed. "I would have preferred to have a bear or wolf!"

"If you would let me continue I shall explain that Simorg was a huge bird and probably ate bears for dinner and wolves for breakfast. Besides, it had magical powers, too.

"Rostam, too, was protected while he grew up by Simorg. I shall tell you of only one of the legends of Rostam tonight because there are so many. He lived for five hundred years and when he was a younger man he underwent seven trials of strength, cunning, and endurance which tempered him like a sword and made him the greatest warrior in the world.

"He spent most of his life fighting for the kings of Persia and he defeated and killed many of the king's enemies, but also dragons and demons. He served as the champion of no less than five Persian Shahs and lived through much of the reigns of two more.

"The tale I shall tell you tonight is about his battle with the demon Akvān, According to the *Šāh-nāma,* which is the great book written by Ferdowsi and is therefore the book of truth; the story goes like this:

"The Persians are superb horsemen and therefore they kept great herds of fine horses in the distant land of Fars—"

"All these strange names! I shall never remember them," Guillaume grumbled.

"If you would only listen you might be able to learn them, now be quiet and let Talon tell the tale!" Aicelina said a little sharply. She patted Guillaume on the arm to take the sting out of the comment. "Please go on, Talon; we are both listening." She smiled at Talon, obviously eager for him to continue.

Talon grinned. "Messengers came from the land of Fars and told the Shah—and before you ask, a Shah is a king—that a demon was eating the horses which lived in the plains and was destroying his herds. The Shah—I cannot remember his name—was upset and called all his warriors together.

"'Who among you will rid me of this demon?' he asked. Many a brave warrior stepped forward and then set off for Fars, but still the messengers came with the news that the demon was killing and eating the warriors as well as the horses, and nothing was being resolved."

"He ate the warriors! Yech!" Guillaume said, pulling a face.

"Even demons have to eat something!"

"Be quiet, Guillaume," said an exasperated Aicelina.

Talon struggled to suppress a laugh. "Finally, in desperation, the Shah sent for Rostam, who he then asked to help him. Rostam agreed and set off for Fars.

"Akvān, the demon that was eating everyone, knew that Rostam was coming and knew, too, that here came not only a great warrior, but one famous for his cunning and even magic powers. Akvān was afraid, so he resorted to cunning and first confronted Rostam in the shape of a wild ass, huge, powerful, with a yellow hide and a black stripe from mane to tail. Akvān had a head like an elephant, long hair, a mouth filled with tusks, blue eyes, black lips, and an extremely ugly body, so turning himself into a wild ass was a big improvement.

"Rostam knew immediately that this was Akvān in disguise and chased him on horseback for three days and three nights, but whenever Akvān was in danger, he concealed himself by magic. Rostam tried every trick he knew to find him but the demon was invisible. Rostam got little sleep during these three days because he knew that if he let his guard down he would become vulnerable to the demon.

"In the end, however, he became very tired and could not stay awake, so he fell asleep. Akvān, who had been watching him from a distance, approached warily, creeping in stealthily and cutting away the earth around him with his tusks. When he had done this he gave a great shout and lifted Rostam high into the sky. Akvān changed back into his normal shape and shook Rostam awake.

"Because he was a nice demon, he asked Rostam how he wanted to die, and whether he should throw him upon a mountain or into the sea."

"He was a nice demon! That can't be!" Guillaume said skeptically, and even Aicelina smiled.

"Hmm, well anyway, Rostam preferred the sea because he knew he might live if he were thrown into the water; but he was cunning, too, and knew that the demon's mind was perverse and would probably do the opposite of his request.

"'I would prefer to be thrown into a mountain because I cannot swim,' he said.

"Just as he thought, Akvān gave a nasty laugh, bade him goodbye and threw him into the sea.

"It was not good to be thrown into the sea, but much better than the mountains, so Rostam swam back to the shore. When he had filled several new lakes with all the sea water he had swallowed, he set off to find his horse. It took a little while to find his horse, Raš, who had thought that his master was dead, and joined a herd of horses out on the plains of Fars. When Rostram found Raš, he set out after the demon again.

"This time he was the one who was the more cunning, and captured the demon with a long rope that he threw around his neck as they galloped across the plain, and then, with a great swipe of his sword, beheaded him.

"He took the head back to the Shah and showed him in front of all his court. Of course the Shah was pleased and gave him much treasure for which he had little use, so then Rostam went back to his lands in the great mountains of the eastern kingdoms.

"And that is enough for tonight, my brother."

"That was not a romantic tale, Talon. Where are the lovers? Is there no love to be had in this Persia of yours?"

"I am sure there is, Aicelina, but the legends do not talk of it very much."

Guillaume had listened to the exchange. "I don't want any of that silly love stuff; I want to hear about heroes and be a great hero myself when I grow up!"

"I am sure you will be, Guillaume, but now it's time for sleep," Aicelina said.

Talon got up and patted his brother on the hand. "Goodnight, my brother."

Aicelina smiled at him and took over while Talon went back to the hall where people were already eating. His mother called him over and he gave her a peck on the cheek then sat down beside Philip, who was already into his second helping of meat pie.

There was no talk, for the men were hungry. When the meal was over the wine and mead came out and the men sat on benches around the hall fire and discussed the day.

Talon and Philip had agreed that they would not discuss his plan in front of the entire group as Talon had reservations about this. But nothing stopped them from talking about other aspects of the situation. Everyone suspected Guillabert of some treachery; he was generally hated.

He was unloved for his rough ways and frequent abuse of his own and other landsmen, even on one occasion for whipping someone who did not get out of the way of his horse fast enough. The man had almost died from the beating. He had hung men for almost no reason. But still no one could put anything against him with certainty.

The attack on the villain's house had come at night and the survivor, the landsman's wife, was now in the village living with relatives. All she had been able to say was that men came out of the dark, threw torches onto the roof, and when her husband went to the door he had been killed with bolts from crossbows.

Crossbows were common enough and much used nowadays so it could have been anyone.

Sir Hughes liked the idea that people who lived outside the village should be brought into the immediate area and housed temporarily until they could find the culprits and punish them.

Talon spent the next few days training. Philip and Hughes agreed that while he might be very adept at using the weapons of his choice, he had had no training with the weapons of the knights. The conventional battle, as fought by members of the feudal knighthood, involved the heavy sword, axe, lance, and shield. The shield of the day was almost universally a long, triangular object, sometimes with a slightly rounded top, made of heavy wood. There were often metal studs or a thin beaten layer of iron wrapped over its external side and it was quite heavy. Talon soon discovered that its stout design was for a good reason—it had to withstand a blow from a heavy, two-edged sword and the terrific impact of a ball and chain, or an axe. When Philip wielded the axe it almost brought him to his knees.

His uncle had insisted that he practice with the lance because that was the way all Knights Templar commenced their battles. It became very clear to all that once he was mounted, Talon could point his lance at a small ring suspended from the battlements on a string and stick and nearly always run his lance point through it. It was another matter when he was on the ground in front of his larger uncle, fighting with the sword and axe.

Talon endured the punishment as he realized that he was in a new world and might need to fight like this some time. He would have preferred to use the methods he excelled at, but it was clear that he would be at some disadvantage against a well-armored man brandishing a weapon like the ball or an axe. His own shield could not have taken such punishment. After a day or two of training and after yet another bruising bout with his uncle that left him black and blue, he rested, sweating copiously on a bench alongside Gareth and the archers, who enjoyed watching and had offered worthless advice while Philip pounded on him.

They had cheered him on while he staggered about in the heavy chain mail—his borrowed helmet too tight on his head, the nose guard too wide so that it impeded his vision—trying to avoid being decapitated by his enthusiastic uncle. Still they were impressed, because in spite of the blows from his uncle he had managed to get in some telling blows of his own and Philip was nursing some badly bruised ribs.

"You will do well at this before too long, Talon," Philip told him with a sweaty grin as they rested, panting. Keep that shield up more and you will be able to stab more easily."

Talon nodded. He received a clap on the shoulder that made him wince and drew a dry chuckle from Gareth.

"I would not like to have to stand in front of your uncle and fight him, Talon, Bach. I am surprised there are any Saracen left after watching him at work."

Talon grinned ruefully. "He is an artist with the axe, I can tell you, Gareth." They all laughed at that. Then it was time to set to again. Talon staggered to his feet and prepared himself for the next onslaught. They went at it for a few minutes, the clang of sword blade on shield or other blade, ringing around the yard. Then Talon thought it was time to use some guile of his own. As Philip came at him with his axe raised high, Talon stepped well into his uncle's guard and stabbed him hard in the midriff with the blunt blade. Although the chain mail protected him, Philip's breath went out with a whoosh. Then Talon tripped him up and Philip crashed to the ground, the axe leaving his hand. Before he could recover Talon was on him, sword point at his throat.

"Yield, Uncle! I have you fair and square!" he shouted loudly.

The archers laughed and clapped while Philip lay gasping. "You rogue, Talon. You tricked me. That was no fair fight." But he was grinning behind his nose piece.

"Begging your pardon, Sir Philip, but it was as fair as anything I have seen before."

Max had joined the spectators and was laughing with them at Philip's demise.

"Quiet, Max. You are supposed to be on my side," Philip growled good-naturedly.

Everyone laughed at that and Talon extended his arm and pulled his uncle back up onto his feet. They stood eying each other warily then Philip chuckled happily.

"Talon, you are wilier than a fox. You are a worthy adversary in any guise. Well done. Want some more?"

Talon shook his head. "No thank you, Uncle. Please, let's close the lesson for today. I am so tired I can't hold my shield up anymore."

Talon left the men talking and made his way toward the well. He wanted a bath more than anything. Searching out his mother he asked her for the trough and hot water then waited for her to arrange for a space in one of the back rooms of the building to be made ready. Sitting near the entrance on a bench he was surprised to see Aicelina coming toward him.

They had not had much time to talk during the last few days other than to greet one another and to share time with his brother. This time she came to stand in front of him. He looked up to find her observing him. He had divested himself of the heavy hauberk and was now clad just in his trews and a loose linen shirt that clung damply to his body. His hair was tousled and loose. He swept it back with his hand to see her better.

"Aicelina, how are you?"

"I am well, Talon. Have you been fighting your uncle again?"

"He means to teach me how to use the Frankish weapons or kill me in the process."

She sat next to him on the bench. "Did you fight a lot in the Saracen Land?"

He thought about it. "Yes, I suppose so. It's a land at war, so men fight, all the time it would seem."

"Men should fight less and respect the scriptures more," she stated, looking across the yard.

"I once knew a man who would have agreed with you. But others killed him, nonetheless. A man has to learn to defend himself and what belongs to him."

She sighed. "The world is full of contradictions. The scriptures and the priests say one thing and men mostly do another. This is a world in turmoil and womenfolk have to keep some peace for themselves, for men will not provide it."

"Do you wish then to become a nun and serve God alone?" he asked teasingly.

She turned to him almost sharply. "No, I serve God my way and am in no need of a nunnery. We people of this region are not as other Christians. We believe in a wider way."

Talon was intrigued. "Are you then really Christians?" he asked.

"Of course we are, but we do not owe allegiance to the Pope, for his place is not ordained by God as he would claim. He is only seeking power over men and this is not what God intended."

"Is everyone here then of your persuasion?"

"Many are, within this region. We Albiginians do not talk about it very much as the Holy See in Albi condemns us as heretics for our free thought." Then, almost as though she had decided they were on uncertain ground, she asked him, "I am going to the fair next week. I had hoped to be able to take Guillaume. Will you escort us?"

"Yes, with pleasure. Is mother going, too?"

"Your mother cannot go, as Ermessenda has the grippe again, so I have asked if I can go, but she told me that I should have an escort as times are dangerous."

"I would be honored to escort you."

She smiled at him and then, as though satisfied that she had achieved her objective, got up and left him to go about her work. He sat pondering this quiet girl who said little but was still pleasant to be with. He realized that he liked her smile. It seemed to light up her normally solemn features. He wondered if there was a man in her life.

He went off to find his mother and get the promised bath. He considered what his brother would do if he threw him into the water and scrubbed him. The urchin was grubby and if it were not for Aicelina's stern ministrations he would have been filthy most of the time. To Talon the total absence of cleanliness about the yard was irksome, but no one seemed to care. His father and mother managed somehow to stay reasonably clean and of course Aicelina did, too, how he could only guess.

For the most part outer clothes were washed reasonably regularly although he could have done with having his under linen washed more often. He had noticed that people smelled of the work they did. He decided that the town people must smell even worse if the country people only smelt of cow or goat or pig.

Talon spent most of the following three weeks with his archers. His father and Philip were about the business of the estate and often included him, but he wanted to learn something from his new-found army.

It was apparent to Talon that the Welshmen loved nothing better than to be in the forests. Gareth explained that his entire country was forested and that they had all grown up in the woods. He went with them on more than one occasion and found it hard to keep up. They were approving of his ability to do even that, and it was not long before he began to enjoy the dense and closed feeling of the forest. These tough men of Wales had come to like and respect him and now enjoyed showing him their ways.

They showed him how to walk quietly in a wooded environment and were surprised at how good he was already.

They showed him how to recognize the new animals he had never seen in Palestine or Persia, the badgers, stoats and weasels, the mark of the boar, a female or male. He came to understand the calls of the forest animals and birds and to know that when it was quiet a large animal or other men were nearby. Together they hunted deer on foot and brought home venison for the hearth. They taught him how to trap rabbits. It became a very enjoyable and absorbing sport for Talon and took his mind off the darker thoughts that were always just beneath the surface—his mind worked on how to deal with the cabin arson and slowly a plan began taking shape.

Soon he was well able to keep up with them and then he in turn began to improve upon what he had learned, drawing upon his earlier training in Persia with the Assassins. More than once he came upon one or two of his men so quietly that they were visibly disturbed when he revealed himself. Their respect grew. Gareth asked him once how he had learned these skills. Talon responded that he had grown up in a place where to be noticed meant punishment or death.

He enjoyed being with his young brother and sister, although Ermessenda was too small to go anywhere as yet without being held by Aicelina. She liked to accompany Talon and Guillaume when they went fishing, carrying Ermessenda with her.

There was a small brook that tumbled down a hill not far from the fort where Talon took his brother and demonstrated his skill at tickling trout out of the pools. They spent lazy afternoons on the banks of the stream, enjoying the late summer sun. Talon wove goose down onto a line and then tied a small hook on the line below with a wriggling worm and let it float on the top of the pool. Guillaume would shriek with excitement if the feather started to bob. Talon would have to tease the trout out of the water on these occasions, careful not to let it break the fine thread and escape. He earned his bother's approval most of the time, but when the line did break, his brother would be scathing and demand another attempt at once.

On the occasions Aicelina would come with them the two would converse while watching the children playing in the shallows. Sometimes they sat silently, enjoying the sound of the water rippling over the rocks and splashing into the small pools. Aicelina would wander off and pick small flowers while Talon lay back and dozed in the sun. When she came back, she'd sit nearby and show Guillaume and Ermessenda how to make garlands. Talon came to enjoy the company of the girl, but although she quickened his pulse when they were together he made no move to change their relationship. She in turn seemed content to simply be with him and the children.

Once she asked him about his life in the other world. "How did you live, Talon? Do the women marry like we do? You have talked about great cities. I cannot imagine a great city for I have never been to more than a town like Albi."

Talon lifted himself onto one elbow and squinted up at her in the afternoon sunlight. "Persia is vast. Cities like Isfahan are huge and full of many people. These cities exist in the plains near to a desert and are supplied by camel caravans."

"What are camels? Are they like horses?" she asked curiously.

He took a stick and drew a crude outline of a camel.

Aicelina burst out laughing. "That cannot be, Talon. You mock me. That is a strange creature, indeed. What is that on its back? How can a man ride a creature like that? It looks as though God made a mistake when he created it."

"No, He did not make a mistake. These animals can walk across the deserts without water longer than any other creature, and that includes horses. Their feet are flat and softly padded underneath and this allows them to walk on sand that a horse would fall into and die of exhaustion if it tried to keep up. "But"—he smiled at her—"God forgot to give the camel a good nature. They have an unpleasant disposition and spit at people."

They both laughed at that and he realized that the light tone of her laughter was a very pleasant thing to hear.

Her interest piqued, she continued to ask him about the places he had seen and he in turn was glad to tell her of them. One area that he had tried to stay away from was talk of Rav'an and Reza, but something told him that she knew a little and he guessed that his mother had talked to her. He had noticed how fond of Aicelina his mother was, so it did not really surprise him. She did ask him only once if he thought of going back to Persia.

He hesitated, but then said, "Aicelina I have two friends in Persia, and I need to know if they are alive. We were parted by force and I have not been able to divine what may have happened to them. I need to know... so one day, yes, it's very possible I shall go back there."

She surprised him. "Is one of them the princess?"

He stared at her for some moments then looked down at the grass. "Yes... one of them is the Princess."

She had nodded but said nothing further and soon the awkwardness of the moment had passed and they were distracted by Guillaume, demanding their attention again.

At other times Talon accompanied his brother and Aicelina for walks in the fields along the hedgerows where Aicelina pointed out various wild herbs and berries they would be picking when autumn came, which Talon realized with some surprise was not that far off.

His mother exclaimed that they had never had so much fish nor venison since Talon and the Welshmen had come. Sir Hughes laughed and said that he would employ them when his son's money ran out, which had to be soon. Talon's mother responded that if the Welshmen stayed his father would not have any fish left in his streams nor deer in his woods, they were such good providers. The archers grinned at the backhanded praise.

The Welshmen were now better clothed than they had been. Marguerite had agreed with Talon that they were a sorely ragged group of men and had, with the willing help of the maids, produced new outfits for them. They were given clean linen to wear with woolen hose and outer shirts sewn by the maids. They had made up for the lack of outer wear and boots with skins of animals they had hunted. They were now also speaking French mixed with Languedoc passably well. Guillaume shadowed them constantly; he could not get enough of them and wanted a bow of his own. Gareth cut him a small one with which he practiced under the supervision of one or other of the archers while the others were out foraging.

There was even a hint that one or two of the serving girls might be showing too much interest in the tough stocky men from Wales. There was much speculation as to who might be sweet on whom. Talon did not pay much attention to it until his mother brought it to his attention one day by remarking that his mercenaries were showing a disturbing ability to draw the girls away from their duties. He smiled. They seemed to be irrepressible and were well liked, but this could lead to complications over and above what they faced at present. He resolved to talk to Gareth about it, but somehow he kept putting it off and then forgetting to say anything.

But one cloudy day as he and Gareth were striding past the hay barn, Gareth held up his hand and signaled Talon to stop. He listened and then whispered. "Can you hear something, Talon Bach?"

Talon nodded. He had caught the sound of some rustling in the upper part of the barn where the hay was kept. They listened carefully and then both of them walked quietly toward the doorway of the barn.

The noise became more pronounced as they stood at the bottom of a ladder that led to the attic above. The sounds coming from above were now distinct. There was a stealthy coupling going on and it was clearly not at the point where restraint mattered anymore. There came a gasp and then a moan and then the slap of flesh and another squeak and more moans and gasps.

Talon left a grinning Gareth at the bottom of the ladder and climbed up carefully, not wanting to make too much noise. The sight that greeted him confirmed his mother's worst fears. One of the maids was lying in the hay with her skirts up around her waist while one of the Welsh archers was lying between her thighs, his buttocks, white in the gloom, pumping away lustily. Talon could not see in the poor light as to who it might be. They were totally oblivious of Talon peering over the edge of the frame. He withdrew carefully and descended the ladder, shaking his head.

He and Gareth left the barn and walked off some way. "I could not tell who it was, just an arse was all I could see, Gareth."

They both grinned and then Gareth laughed outright and slapped his thigh.

"But I am sure it was one of our men; whoever it was, he is going to get one of the maids in the family way. I fear my mother will have a lot to say if that happens," Talon said carefully.

Gareth chuckled again. "So it's one of us Welsh playing bury-me-peg, is it?"

They waited to see who it might be and before long they were not disappointed. A disheveled Drudwas came furtively out of the barn still brushing hay off his doublet, and walked off toward the Hall, trying to look nonchalant.

"I'll have to talk to him, I suppose, m'lord?" Gareth said reluctantly.

"If he does get one of the maids pregnant, he is going to stay here, Gareth."

So we'll dance round the tree, and merry we will be,
Every year we'll agree the fair for to see;
And we'll booze it away, dull care we'll defy,
And be happy on the first Friday in July.
- The Fairlop Fair song

Chapter 8

The Fair

The time came for Talon to take Aicelina and his brother Guillaume to the fair. Albi was four full hours away by cart. It was probably much less on horseback by Talon's estimation. One of the Welshmen, Anwl, offered to drive the cart. He had hurt his foot while trying to run down a deer in the forest. The others ribbed him mercilessly, and then disappeared back into the woods to hunt more game.

The group left at dawn just as the first streaks of light glowed in the eastern horizon. It was going to be a fine day without many clouds in the sky.

Talon rode Jabbar, who wanted to run and gave some small pops to indicate that he wanted to be paid much more attention than he had been recently. Talon grinned and patted his neck, chiding him for being rude. He received a snort in reply and they were on their way. Almost four hours later, after much singing and playing of guessing games, the little party arrived at the thick wooden gates to the town of Albi. They joined others with the same intent and were granted entry by the guards at the gates, who eyed Aicelina appreciatively.

Albi provided a market place for the country all around and as such boasted several inns and a newly cobbled space in the center where the market was located. The keep towered over the market square, in company with the stone Roman church nearby. The houses gathered around the market place belonged for the most part to the wealthier personages of the town, including the three-storied building that was known as the bishop's house. Talon noted the extensive use of red brick in between the solid wood frames of the houses around the town. He had seen more stone in use elsewhere, particularly to the east of the country. The combined effect of brick and stone gave the town a warm orange glow in the sunshine.

They parked the wagon and the horses at one of the inns where Talon impressed the innkeeper with the show of a little silver coin. Then they were walking together along the main street of the town. This street, as well as the market, was already crowded and full of bustle. Shopkeepers and farmers from the outlying areas were presenting their wares, laid out on bare planks in an area of crowded stalls, shouting cheerfully at the passers by. Fishmongers displayed pike, succulent trout, and baked eels from the nearby river, the flies already taking an interest in the fish.

They passed by the bakers and their huge loaves of bread stacked on trestle tables. The bread looked like big flat, rounded stones, the flour dusting the gray of the bread crusts. The very smell was mouthwatering. Nearby there were huge, strong-smelling cheeses that were stacked carelessly on the ground, and then the three of them walked slowly by the olive sellers who came from faraway Provence, offering the passersby a taste of their plump wares coated in olive oil and even dipped in crushed garlic or herbs. None of them could resist that temptation, so Aicelina bought some for the midday meal.

She pointed to the bluish balls in several stalls and told Talon that these were woad. The raw dye powder was taken from the plant that the area was famous for. The plant was dried, then ground into powder and made into balls to be sold down the river to cities like Toulouse as a cloth dye.

There were game birds still with all their feathers hanging from stall beams, some already rank from days of hanging. There were ducks, pheasants, and some fowl Talon did not recognize. Aicelina told him they were ground birds from up in the hills. The nearby cooking stalls gave off mouth-watering scents of baked pies, cooked meats, and stewed eels that followed them down the road.

To Guillaume's delight, Talon bought them all a small, hot, sweetmeat pie each, which they ate as they walked. The appetizing smells of cooking were intermixed with the not-so-pleasant stinks of a market day: goats and other animals being run through the streets, and of course the open drains down the middle of the street, which made them all wrinkle their noses and Guillaume to pull a comical face of disgust.

There was the constant risk of stepping in the dung of some animal or something worse, so they picked their way carefully. Aicelina lifted her long skirts away from the mud, displaying a very elegant pair of ankles to Talon's approving glance.

"Fortunately, it has not rained recently or we would be sloshing though ankle-deep mud," she remarked to Talon then she smiled at him as she observed where his eyes were looking.

He looked away hastily, feeling the blood go to his face. But then she put her hand on his forearm and left it there, so he knew he was forgiven.

They came to the peddlers and merchants' stalls farther along the street away from the food vendors. There were utensils of carved wood or beaten copper, beads, threads of many colors, and much in the way of cloth. There were foreign fabrics in rolls, and the wool from England woven into fine cloth in the Lowlands to the far north. On enquiry, the merchant gave them a price and Aicelina shook her head. It was very expensive. She pointed to some colorful, finer cloths and he said they came from the south, from the Saracen lands, and even perhaps from the Holy Land.

Talon was reminded of the merchants he had met in Montpellier and wondered if that group might have come to Albi, as it was not an insignificant town. Aicelina was not there to buy the silks, but she had come to the market to buy some coarse woolen cloth for clothing. They spent some time there fingering the wools, so while she bargained with the peddler, Talon, Anwl, and Guillaume looked around.

His interest quickened when he heard the clink and ring of hammers and recognized the sounds of a smithy at work. It evoked memories of another time for him. Sure enough there was an armourer hard at work with his bellows, a blackened, skinny urchin pumping furiously on the bellows to keep the fires burning hot as the smith beat out some spear heads. The owners of the weapons in for repair were lounging nearby, drinking wine and making lewd remarks about the young maidens as they went by.

Peddlers were to be seen from all over the region and beyond, from Aquitaine and even farther north, as this was a well-known market. Aicelina told him it was second only to the great markets of Carcassonne and Toulouse. They were selling pottery and bijou, knives and utensils, combs of bone and ivory, crudely carved. Talon on impulse bought a small ivory comb for Aicelina. She protested when he bought it and almost refused it when he presented it to her. But he persisted, so with a blush she accepted the small gift. It disappeared into the pocket of her dress quickly. He smiled as she recomposed herself.

Talon was reminded how he felt long ago when Rav'an, Reza, and he had been in Hamadan in distant Persia, and had enjoyed the noise and smells of the market there. He pulled himself back to the present and guided Guillaume along the crowded streets with a hand on his shoulder.

He was unaware that he drew interested looks from the young maidens who were part of the crowd. But their glances did not escape Aicelina, who kept close to Talon while they wended their way toward the center where the main trading would be taking place. There was a friendly festival feel in the air as the jostling crowd of men and women, freedmen and villain alike, rubbed shoulders with each other. Children were everywhere, running in and out of the crowds, playing tag and getting underfoot. No one seemed to mind unless they tangled with a stall and threatened to upset it. Then the stall keeper would shout and wave a threatening fist at them while they ran off cheekily thumbing their noses.

Wine appeared to be flowing freely as men strolled about refreshing themselves with full jugs or leather sacks, and there were already a couple of drunks lying senseless against the walls of the houses.

Talon could not help but notice the way the maidens and young men interacted. There was none of the restraint he had observed in Persia. Here a kiss was given and taken without retribution or embarrassment. Many of the couples embraced publicly in a quiet corner here or there. On one occasion a bold, well-endowed young woman came up to Talon and would have slipped into his arms if Aicelina had not stepped adroitly into her path and, using a smile and a wagged forefinger, informed her that he was off limits. Anwl behind Talon gave a quiet chuckle while Talon grinned with embarrassment and ruffled Guillaume's head before the boy could say anything.

At one street corner the young maids and men were standing in couples listening to a man in colorful yellow, brown, and red clothing playing a mandolin. He sang with a clear voice, his fingers dancing over the instrument, the music rippling off the strings, bringing what seemed to be a well-known tune to the gathered crowd.

They paused to listen and watch the rapport between the troubadour, as Aicelina called him, and the people gathered around. Even Talon could understand some of the words he sang, although it was in broad Languedoc. There were many bawdy references to love that drew laughter from the young men and giggles from the maidens. He was cheerful and light with his notes and his next song was obviously very popular.

The Troubadour's voice took on a high note as though imitating a lady's voice.

"I was plunged into deep distress

By a knight who wooed me,"

"And I wish to confess for all time

How passionately I loved him;"

"Now I feel myself betrayed

For I did not tell him of my love."

"Therefore I suffer great distress

In bed and when I am fully dressed."

The crowd cheered and hooted. He continued.

"Would that my knight, might one night

Lie naked in my arms."

This drew guffaws from the young men and blushes from the maidens.

"And find myself in ecstasy

With me as his pillow

"For I am more in love with him

Than Flores was with Blanchefleur."

"To him I give my heart and love

My reason, eyes and life.

The Troubadour gave a flourish on his strings and continued the last verse.

"Handsome friend, tender and good

When will you be mine?"

"Oh, to spend with you but one night

To impart the kiss of love"

"Know that with passion I cherish

The hope of you in my husband's place.

The young people cheered and clapped.

The troubadour finished his song with a flourish of notes and the final lines of the song.

"As soon as you have sworn to me

That you will fulfill my every wish."

The troubadour put heavy emphasis upon the last line and received a cheer and much clapping from the gathering. He closed with some energetic plucking of his strings, bringing the song to a close amid applause.

Small coins were thrown into his hat that lay nearby. He bowed sardonically to all, winking at the ladies.

Talon smiled. He had enjoyed the interaction and noticed that Aicelina had been laughing at the words of the song; obviously she knew it well.

They moved on but then had to step out to the sides of the street among the stalls as a party of dignitaries went by. The young man at the head of the procession was obviously a very important person, for everyone bowed and doffed their hats, and the ladies along his path curtsied. He was richly dressed and his coat of arms was woven into his doublet. He wore a huge cap that sported a large feather, wore no armor but had a fine sword at his side. His men-at-arms were well armored in chain hauberks.

Talon noted their hauberks were well maintained and smart, each with a coat of arms emblazoned upon the shield. He was not aware that he'd been staring until the young man rode by and his gaze landed on Talon. Their eyes met and held for a moment. Then the man had ridden by and all Talon saw was his back. His retinue of knights, pages, and ladies followed in a light cloud of incense and heavy perfume.

"Who is that?" Talon asked.

"That is the son of the Count of Carcassonne. His name is Roger." Aicelina used the expression *Com de Carcassonna*. "We are honored today. Talon, do you not know about the counts?"

He shook his head.

"Your father is the Count's vassal, as are all the landed knights of this area. You are distantly related because of the name 'Gilles' of the line of Tranceval. As is my family line, but we are even more distant, I think. My father came from Provence, near the city of St Gilles, east of here."

They continued their interrupted way, joining the noisy crowd as it headed for the jousting arena.

At one point Aicelina was knocked about accidentally by a farmer dragging a reluctant sheep. She almost fell but Talon seized her around the waist and held her, pulling her back upright. Their faces were inches apart at that moment. He looked briefly straight into her eyes. He liked the small quirk of her lips as she thanked him and then he released her. She linked her arm with his again and then took Guillaume's hand, and with Anwl behind protectively they pushed on. Talon realized with a twinge of guilt that he enjoyed having this girl on his arm.

They arrived with the noisy crowd to witness the beginning of the auctions. The auctioneer was from the south and spoke the fastest Occitan Talon had ever heard, and of which he understood not a word, as he rattled off the bidding for the group of animals for sale. Bidders would raise their hands or staffs as the price went up, guided by the cunning man. He joked, encouraged, and goaded the bidders to pay just that little more than they had intended. His fee depended on it.

Talon glanced about him while they waited for another group of animals to be brought in. There was a commotion as a pig escaped and ran squealing into the crowd. There were shouts of worthless advice and joking encouragement as the poor man herding the animals tried to get it back. Boys ran in front of the pig, playing at being matadors while young girls screamed and clutched their parents.

Talon made sure that Guillaume was safe, even to placing him on his shoulders so that the excited boy could see over the crowd. All the same they had to make way hurriedly for the fleeing pig and his by now very irate herder as they rushed past. They all laughed, enjoying the excitement. The mood of the crowd all about them was infectious. Aicelina pointed toward a street that led off the marketplace and said over the noise, "Let's go down to the river; they will hold the tournament on the other side. Would you like to see that, Talon?"

He nodded, the noise of people shouting was too great to speak easily to one another, and they pushed their way along the side of the square. They were able to move with more ease down the steep street that led to the Albi bridge known as the Pont Vieux. It was quieter here, so Talon put Guillaume down and Aicelina took his hand firmly to ensure that he stayed with them. Once again she casually put her hand on Talon's arm and they moved along the street for all the watchers to think they were man and wife, Talon thought, bemused.

The town was built on both sides of the river Tarn, which at this point was about fifty paces wide, and Talon could see that there seemed to be a lot of trade as it was well frequented by barges and other vessels. Aicelina told him that these barges took the dye to cities like Toulouse by way of the river. The main part of the town was built on the hillside on the north side of the river. The houses, densely packed in places, seeming to be pushing against one another as they vied for space down the slopes of the hillside toward the water, some even leaning out precariously over the river itself.

As they came to the bridge, meaning to cross it, they heard the clatter of horses' hooves behind them and a group of horsemen came boiling down the street behind them. There was a shouted "Way there! Get out of the way! Stop blocking the road!" from one of the riders.

The people in front rushed to get off the road and into door-ways and side alleys. Talon pulled Aicelina and Guillaume out of the way as several horses trotted by. The foot of one of the riders almost kicked his shoulder. The man looked down and growled at him to make way.

Their eyes met. It was Marcel. He was accompanied by four men-at-arms and his sister. She had not noticed Talon but Marcel gave a start, then the group was by. They clattered over the bridge, and as they did so Marcel gave a backward glance at Talon. It was a baleful look that boded no good. Petrona had not noticed them.

Still, Talon felt that here in this crowded place with many of the town's pike men in evidence if Marcel wanted to pick a quarrel it would not be a good place to do so.

They crossed over the river after paying the small coin re-quired to use the bridge, but Aicelina noticed that Talon was tense and asked why.

"The people who went by just now were Marcel and his sister, Petrona. He has made it very clear that he does not like me."

"Do you think we should go back?" she asked.

"No, I do not think he will do anything stupid while here," Talon said with more conviction than he felt.

They had a pleasant surprise when they had crossed the bridge over the slow-moving river. Talon spied a stall with several monks standing nearby. He thought he recognized Claude. He looked again. It was Claude. He was with some of his fellow monks and it appeared they were selling honey and cakes.

Talon squeezed Aicelina's hand. "I know these people; we should go up and say hello."

Claude gave a great whoop when he spied Talon coming toward him. He embraced him and turned to his brothers. "Remember Talon of Persia, my Brothers?" he asked them.

They all nodded and smiled. There were introductions and curious looks at Aicelina. It had not gone unnoticed that she had been close to Talon when they came up. He introduced her as his cousin; that she was looking after Guillaume, who was his brother.

The monks were pleased to see Talon and made them all welcome. Claude even brought out a small leather beaker of wine that he offered them. Aicelina refused politely, but Talon took a sip and enjoyed it. Something told him, however, that he should be alert now that he had seen Marcel, so he gave it back with a compliment. It was good wine. They left the brothers with promises to visit. Talon wanted very much to ride out to the abbey again as he had enjoyed the calm atmosphere while there. Claude shouted after them to beware of pickpockets.

"They will even pick that of a poor monk," he called after them.

Talon had spotted on the other side of the main arena a place where competitions would take place later in the day. He wanted to see this, but it depended upon how much time they might have left before they had to leave for home.

There were some men in chain mail lounging against the crudely marked-off arenas where swordsmanship and single combat duels for a prize would take place. The men looked rough and unkempt, mostly men-at-arms for hire, trying their luck for a small purse, he supposed.

They moved on to the area where the ground was laid out for jousting. Although he had heard of this relatively new sport, Talon was curious how it worked. Aicelina explained that men would fight for the honor of a Lady's kerchief or some other emblem of love. Guillaume snorted and made a face in disgust, clearly annoying Aicelina but making Talon and Anwl grin.

They joined the noisy, cheerful crowd that was beginning to assemble in some of the stands around the main arena.

As none of them had ever been to one of these events before they were completely in ignorance about what to expect. Guillaume was agog at everything.

They settled near the barricades to watch. There was a blast on a horn, inexpertly blown but enough to hush the crowd. A man dressed in some colorful cloth stalked out into the grassy space and began to announce the coming event. He spoke slowly and with much ceremony as he described the men who were to face one another in the arena. They were to fight with lances, on horseback. Then with the sword until one was struck off his horse. If he rose to fight after the fall then the battle would take place on foot until one asked for *Paix* or was downed by the other and forced to submit. The tournament went to the last man standing or the last men of that group standing.

The crowd enjoyed his flowery prose. Finally he finished with a flourish and left the field to raucous applause.

The men were fighting for a purse of some small silver money but that did not seem to matter. The two groups of eight walked their heavy horses forward from opposite corners of the arena toward the middle where they saluted the stands.

Some dignitaries were seated in a tiered stand and Talon supposed it to be the young Count of Carcassonne who would be the guest of honor. When he looked, indeed, he was in the center of the group of colorfully clad people. Talon's sharp eye noticed that Marcel and his sister were seated some distance away from the center of the stands among other people. He hoped his small group was inconspicuous enough that Marcel would not notice it. He didn't want the day spoiled.

The combatants shouted their names and hereditary history to the stands, then the two groups rode off to opposite ends of the arena where they turned and faced each other.

The banner came down and the two bands of men lumbered heavily toward one another at a ponderous gallop. They came together with a crash as lance met shield and lance splintered or slid past a shield and struck a telling blow to a man's body. Men went down immediately and it was clear from the start that some would not rise for the remainder of the tournament.

A freedman nearby gave a running commentary to Talon and his group as the fight progressed. There were not many rules as such in a mêlée of this kind, he told them with satisfaction. A man could even be killed, but woe betide a rider who struck a horse deliberately.

The remaining riders, still horsed, took out their swords or maces and began to hammer at each other—driving their horses into one another, looking for an advantage. Talon noticed that the unwary often got a blow from behind, which in one case at least finished the rider and he tumbled to the ground senseless from the cowardly blow. The crowd booed happily and yelled abuse at this un-knightly display.

Finally there were only two men still on their horses. Both were dressed in heavy hauberks and leather boots with the standard helmet and nose guard. Their overshirts were torn and on one of them bloody. There were other horses trotting about but they were riderless and grooms were trying to capture them without being ridden down. Talon could see a couple of unconscious men lying on the grass. There was blood on tunics and streaming down horses' flanks from careless blows with sharp objects. The crowd was screaming itself hoarse as the two riders made some distance between one another in readiness for the final bout.

Both were wielding maces that they swung menacingly around their heads in an attempt to intimidate one another as they cantered closer. They came together with a metallic crash, their maces swung almost at the same time, and the heavy balls smashed into each other's shields simultaneously. It was clear from the start that one rider was the more powerful, as the other was rocked deep back into his saddle by the terrific blow. He lost a stirrup and it was while he was trying to regain his balance that the other man leveled another terrific blow to his shield. It was enough. The man toppled out of the saddle and landed heavily on the grass. He lay there, stunned for a few seconds, while his opponent halted his horse, then dismounted ponderously, preparing to finish him off.

However, the grounded man managed to get up, albeit groggily, and drew his sword with a shout of defiance. He hurriedly regained his shield, then stood waiting for his opponent to come to him. Then they were at it, belaboring each other with their swords. The crowd loved the bout; they shouted abuse and encouragement to their respective champions, wincing at a blow landed on their man and cheering whenever he was able to deliver a cut or blow to his opponent.

For a time it looked as though the larger man was going to knock his opponent to the ground again. That is, until his less heavy opponent managed to get in a couple of swift and sure jabs at his chest and stomach. It seemed to take the wind out of the big man. The chain mail did a poor job of protecting from a direct stab which could bruise badly, whereas it deflected a side blow quite well.

Following up on his advantage, the lighter man smashed his shield ridge into the other's nosepiece then struck hard with a downward blow to the side of his opponent's head with the pommel of the heavy sword. Down went the man to lie on his face, semi-conscious. His opponent stooped over him, hauled him over onto his back, then jabbed the point of his sword into his mailed throat shouting hoarsely for his surrender.

The crowd cheered and booed the victor, who nonetheless gallantly helped his opponent to his feet. They stood, arms around each other's shoulders, and saluted the stands. Then they staggered off out of the arena, holding onto one another as though afraid they might both fall over.

Talon found the whole thing riveting, aware that it was this kind of fighter that had defeated the lighter-armed and lighter-horsed people of the East. It had to count for something, he thought; but it seemed so clumsy.

He turned to find Aicelina watching him. He looked his inquiry, but she tossed her head and said nothing. They settled down to watch several more bouts.

Before long it was late afternoon and time to leave. They began to make their way back to the Inn where Jabbar and the cart were waiting. Talon and Anwl discussed the fights. Anwl told him that only lords in Wales wore this much chain mail, as it was expensive. Talon refrained from telling him that the much patched and worn chain mail he had seen hitherto in Languedoc was pretty poor stuff compared to the elegant, rippling mail used by Templar and Saracen alike in the Holy Land. Most of what he had seen on both the jousters and the other men at the jousting arena, who could afford a chain mail suit at all, was either rent or badly patched together. Few people in this country dressed in any kind of cloth that Talon would have considered rich and attractive to the eye. He ruefully listed himself among them.

He glanced at Aicelina walking near them, holding Guillaume's hand. She somehow managed to look attractive even in her simple dress of dyed green wool. She glanced up at him just as he did so and they looked each other in the eye. She seemed cool and collected until he noticed the beginnings of a blush. He was the first to avert his eyes.

The interchange unsettled him so he set a slightly faster pace, thinking of the hours they would be on the road. He wanted to make sure they came back in time for supper.

He had not noticed that Marcel had left the stands and was talking to his men and pointing at Talon as he crossed the bridge with his wards.

The little party drove down to the edge of town at a brisk pace that allowed them to make good progress. Guillaume bounced up and down on the front seat alongside Anwl, recounting to all the details of the battles he had witnessed. Aicelina was looking pensive as she sat on the other side of Anwl.

Talon was listening to his brother, amused at his excitement, as he rode alongside, not paying much attention to the road ahead when Jabbar skittered his ears back, giving him a hint that there were others on the road. Talon turned in the saddle and saw a group of men on horses coming at a fast trot along the road behind them. He was sure he had seen them before. There were four of them and they were armed. He called over to Anwl to drive off the track and allow the men space while he reined Jabbar in and turned to watch them.

An instinct told him that there was something wrong, but he could not tell as yet what it might be. The men were rough-looking, bearded, and unkempt. Their chain mail hauberks were patched and soiled. Their horses were not a lot better and their tack was badly maintained. All this Talon could observe as he watched them warily while they came toward him.

"Anwl, get your bow out and be quick about it." he called softly. He heard a grunt of surprise from Anwl and a quick movement. "Aicelina, take Guillaume and get out of the cart and near to a tree or behind a hedge. Be quick," he ordered.

Aicelina said nothing, but he saw her out of the corner of his eye as she grabbed a startled Guillaume, helped down by Anwl, and hurried over to the dense shrubs nearby.

"Anwl, are you ready?" Talon asked.

"Aye, m'lord," Anwl responded from behind him.

Talon watched as the men on horseback came closer, scattering other people off the road as they rode.

He reined Jabbar back so that he could sense Anwl to his right. He hoped that Aicelina was well back and protected. He drew his own bow out of the scabbard under his left leg and drew an arrow from the quiver at the cantle and settled it onto the bowstring. Then he waited and watched as the men came closer.

They were now about sixty yards away and well within bow shot, but he stayed Anwl with a murmured, "Don't shoot unless it's clear that they are coming right at me."

There was a grunt of acknowledgement.

It became clear that the men were coming for him—their eyes were fixed on Talon. He tensed up and his pulse pounded: there was trouble here. They were all in heavy hauberks with round, pointed helmets with long nose pieces. It gave them a sinister, intent, look. They held their shields close; Talon thought this could present a problem if they all came at him at the same time.

He drew his bow and aimed it straight at the men. "If you are looking for me, then I would tell you to stop where you are," he called to them when they were about forty yards distant. They barely paused; there was a muttered command, and they put spur to their horses.

Talon loosed his arrow at the lead horse. The arrow struck it in the chest, going deep. The animal screamed and stumbled and fell forward. Its rider was toppled over its head to crash hard to the ground. The other three were momentarily caught short by the obstruction of the animal and rider on the ground, but not for long. An arrow whispered past Talon from behind him that buried itself deep in the chest of another man who gave a choking cry and toppled backward off his animal, which ran on a few yards and stopped.

That left two men still on horses and one picking himself up off the ground. The odds were still significantly against Talon and Anwl. Relying on surprise, Talon danced Jabbar forward, using his knees, riding hard into the pair, his sword drawn. He feinted high and then stabbed past the rising shield of the lead man who was quite unready for the maneuver. Talon's sword pierced deep into the man's right arm at the join of the hauberk to the sleeve. His fine steel was more than a match for the badly linked chain-mail shirt. The man gave a shocked cry and was taken away by his horse, clutching his arm and swearing loudly with the pain.

Talon turned and parried a wicked downward blow from the other man, but just then an arrow from Anwl hammered into that man's thigh. He, too, gave out with a surprised yell and, clutching his saddle, allowed his horse to take him away from Talon.

Talon watched the two wounded men as they fled from the battlefield and decided they were not going to get involved again. He quickly dismounted and, letting Jabbar go, ran straight at the first man. The man barely had time to draw his sword. His shield lay off to the side where it had fallen. He was stooping to pick it up when Talon ran up and planted his foot firmly in his backside, kicking him off balance. He fell forward in an undignified position onto his hands and knees with Talon standing over him. Talon reached down, jerked his helmet off, then placed the point of his sword against the side of the man's throat.

"Who do you belong to?" he asked harshly, aware that his anger was rising and that he could quite easily kill the man if he made one wrong move.

The man shook his long greasy hair out of his eyes and wordlessly looked up with bloodshot eyes. It was obvious he had been drinking.

Talon applied more pressure. "Who sent you here and why did you attack me? Answer, you pig." He pressed even harder with the razor-sharp point and drew blood. "Anwl, keep an eye on those other men."

"Aye, m'lord, I've got them in my sight. They don't look eager for more."

Perhaps realizing that Talon meant what he said, the kneeling man turned his head and muttered, "We were told to chase you out of the town."

"We were already leaving the town, you lump of sheep's dung. Answer my question: Who sent you?"

"Marcel, son of Guillabert d'Albi."

"Tell my cousin that he failed to achieve his ends and the next time we meet he had better be ready for a fight. Tell him he is a coward. I have no time for his sort, or for you," Talon spat out. "Count yourself lucky that I do not kill you here and now."

He stepped forward and gave the man a savage strike on the top of his bare head with the pommel of his sword. The man went down without a sound. Talon looked around and saw that the other two men were nowhere to be seen, but there was one man lying in the grass, an arrow protruding from his chest, along with the downed horse that was still struggling on its side and another loose, grazing on the grass nearby. Talon reluctantly walked over to the horse and slit its jugular, standing back as the animal went into its death throes. Anwl instinctively ran and retrieved his arrow from the dead man. Good arrows were hard to make.

People were beginning to gather and shout. Worse, the guards on the walls were taking an interest, pointing and shouting down behind them to others. He realized that they could be in a lot of trouble if they did not leave at once and it could not be with the cart. He ran over to Jabbar, then collected the other horse while telling Anwl to fetch Aicelina and Guillaume. They came running from their cover by the dense hedge off to the side of the green area where the fight had taken place. She was white but looked determined; Guillaume was frightened, but it was also clear from the set of his jaw that he was not going to cry.

"Aicelina, we have to ride out of here quickly, the cart is far too slow. I do not know what will happen if we stay. Pick up the wool, you will ride with me, and Guillaume will ride with Anwl," Talon commanded.

She nodded mutely and they mounted. Talon drew her up behind him on the now excited Jabbar, knowing that his mount could only take their combined weight for a limited time. The other horse, although a nag by comparison with Jabbar, was a larger animal and could take the combined weight of Anwl and Guillaume easily. By now a crowd was beginning to gather and there was much shouting and gesturing. Although they did not seem to be hostile, the incident occasioning much excitement, but they would for sure bring the sheriff and others to the scene very soon. Talon did not want to be there when they came.

They set off at a brisk trot but Talon knew better than to head directly to his father's fort. This would be fatal as, even if the men of the city did not give chase, then there was a good likelihood that Marcel would try to intercept them. He felt Aicelina's arms firmly round his waist and turned his head.

"Do you know the way to the abbey from here, Aicelina?" he asked her.

"Yes, but we are going the wrong way for that, Talon. We should go east, not west."

"Good, then we shall go west for a few miles, then change direction and pass the town to the north to pick up the route to the abbey. How far is it from here?"

"I think it is about ten miles."

"Anwl, follow me as fast as you can," Talon called. "Guillaume, are you all right?"

"Yes, Talon." His brother looked worried but not terrified. Talon nodded approvingly.

Talon put Jabbar into a fast canter and they were off. They covered a good two miles before they were well out of sight of the town. Talon stopped and found a place where they could turn off the track into the sparsely wooded area that led into the low hills to the north. Talon made sure that their path from the road would not betray their exit.

He looked back along the road and could perceive no indication of any chase, but he wanted to put as much distance between himself and the town as he could. They wove their way in between the trees, moving quickly, keeping the sun to their left and then when they thought they were well above the town, they headed directly east.

The horses were working well even with their extra loads and had they not been fleeing from trouble it would have been a pleasant ride.

Apart from asking Aicelina from time to time if she were still all right, there was not much conversation between them. He was worried that when they did not arrive at the fort that night there would be a lot of concern, even to the point where a rescue party might rush off into the night and start hunting for them. He wondered how to send a message. Despite his worry, however, he found that he rather enjoyed having Aicelina with her arms around him as they rode. Her body pressed against his back was disconcerting. Despite his resolve to stay aloof from her, her proximity made him uncomfortably aware of her as a woman.

They continued on into the evening, making the miles count. Talon began to recognize the terrain and knew they were not far from the abbey. They came up the hill and into the main yard of the abbey just as the sun was beginning to set. At this time there were few people about; the monks were all eating supper; it was between Vespers and Compline. The economy of daylight was used frugally here.

They were nonetheless noticed and a lay brother came running toward them as they came up to the gates. He recognized Talon with some surprise. "Master Talon de Gilles," he exclaimed, "you are not expected. Is there anything wrong?'

Talon let Aicelina slip off the back of Jabbar before he replied. "Brother, we came here as I wish to seek refuge for this girl and my brother for the night. I also wish to speak to the abbot, please."

The lay brother stared, surprised at Aicelina, then averted his eyes. "Er, yes, Master Talon, I shall go at once to speak with him. Do you take the horses to the stables and we shall look after them."

He ran off with the news of their arrival while Talon dismounted. They took Guillaume off the horse he had shared with Anwl. Guillaume was very tired now and all but fell into Talon's arms; all the excitement had worn him out.

Talon smiled fondly down on his brother and brushed the tousled hair back from his forehead. While he carried Guillaume, Anwl took the horses to the stables where they were met by other equally surprised lay brothers whose work it was to see to the livestock. Talon led the way toward the main building, not certain as to how he would be received. Not only was he uninvited but he had a woman in tow.

He need not have worried. The Abbot Matthias himself came bustling along the cloisters, followed by his secretary and others of the brothers whose curiosity had overcome their hunger.

"Master Talon de Gilles," he exclaimed. "To what do we owe the honor of this visit?" He stopped talking when he noted Aicelina and Guillaume. "Ah, I take it this is not quite a social visit."

Talon quickly explained what had happened and why he had come to the monastery rather than going directly home.

The abbot looked concerned but nodded his agreement. "I think it might have been a wise decision. You could not afford to be intercepted. You will stay here the night and I shall send a messenger to your father to inform him that you are safe and not to worry. I am sure that they will send an escort by noon tomorrow."

Talon breathed a sigh of relief. "Thank you, Father. I would not have indisposed you but I did not know where else to go."

The abbot smiled his warm smile that crinkled his eyes. "You are always welcome here, but there is a price to pay."

Talon gave an exaggerated sigh. "You mean that I have to discuss my time in Persia some more, Father?"

The abbot laughed gently. "Just so, but only after you have supped and we have provided for the young lady here, and of course the child."

He gave quick orders to his secretary, then Aicelina and a sleepy Guillaume clutching her hand were guided off by one of the older Brothers to an area reserved for visiting ladies and gentry. The abbot assured Talon they would be well looked after.

Aicelina touched Talon's arm lightly with her fingers as she left. "Thank you, Talon. It was very brave of you." Her look said more.

Talon mumbled that he could not have done anything without Anwl to help and got an equally embarrassed mumble back from that man who felt totally out of place in this high company.

The abbot, considerate above all, asked one of the brothers standing around them to look to Anwl's needs and provide him with a cell to sleep in. Anwl left after ducking his head to Talon, who grinned at him and told him to sleep well.

Then taking Talon by the elbow, the abbot returned with him to the main dining hall to continue his interrupted meal, and to spend time with him over some wine.

That night was one that Talon would remember.

The abbot was a learned man who had lived beyond much of life's pettiness and went directly to the point of most issues. Talon was reminded of another man he had known in another life who had been very wise in the ways of men. The doctor Farj'an, physician to the Khan, had taught him much about the gentler side of life, and had imparted his own understandings of existence to a half-savage youth new from the Valley of the Assassins.

The two retired to the abbot's rooms where candles were lit and they settled into comfortable chairs and sipped the good wine. The abbot talked to Talon as an equal while the light breeze coming through the open windows made the candles flicker and their shadows move around the stone walls.

They talked much of Talon's boyhood experiences as well as the issues of the day here in Languedoc. Talon now had questions of his own about the land in which he was now living, and this man could answer many of them.

One big question Talon finally posed although he was uncertain as to its reception. "Who are the Albiginians, my Lord?"

The abbot gave him a sharp look but nonetheless after a pause answered, albeit reluctantly. "They are Christians, Talon, otherwise known as Cathars. But they go very much their own way. They do not accept the Church of Rome or the Pope for their leader. This much complicates their position alongside the Catholic faith."

"What is it that is so different? Are they then considered to be heretics?" Talon asked, very much aware of his own precarious position within the Christian community.

"There is a risk that they might one day be considered so," the abbot observed. "They claim to be of a more fundamental faith than that founded on the Rock of Saint Peter. This some find disturbing."

"Do you, sir?"

The abbot smiled wryly at his directness. "In fact I do not, but I would not say it abroad too loudly." He paused, looking at Talon thoughtfully. "Talon, I have lived a long life, most of it devoted to God and the Church. I am here because I shun politics and the pursuit of power. I do not claim to be wiser than other men, but I have had the time to contemplate much of what I see around me."

He looked up at Talon with a wry smile that crinkled the corners of his eyes and then took a sip of the fine wine they were sharing. "I know that the people of Occitania, those who speak Languedoc, are free-thinkers. You could say that our neighbors in Aquitaine are somewhat to blame for that. There is much ado about the troubadours and their songs and the freedom of the expression of love. Our Lady of Aquitaine, Eleanor, now married to Henry of England, is the most ardent purveyor of this kind of thing. Her songs of love are seductive and allow many freedoms to the ladies of the realm. That is all very well, but when it comes into contact with the Church of Rome—which would prefer that all people simply bow to the church's rule and abandon song and dance—then there is the making of conflict."

"What is so wrong in songs and dancing?" Talon asked naively.

His host smiled. "Very little in moderation, but the church cannot abide that people should find the time to enjoy life without they pay homage to God and observe the rules of the Church with all."

"This sounds like the Mullahs of Persia," Talon said. "They do not encourage life's enjoyments. But the Ismaili did," he observed.

"So they were heretics, too?" the abbot asked.

"I suppose so. But they also bring terror to everyone. They are hated and feared by all."

"Hmm, well, in the case of the Cathars it presents a conundrum because although they are Christians they claim to be from a more distant source than the Rock of St Peter. They are not, as far as I know, violent people, however."

"I don't understand," Talon said, puzzled.

"Nor should you be expected to. But I can assure you that the Church in these parts has played the game of power and politics to the point where I fear it might have lost its way; small wonder then that a group of 'free-thinkers' should look for other paths. They will pay a price for that, as the Church of Rome will treat them badly should they confront it too loudly. The Church has only just completed its subjugation of the kings of England, Germany, and France. It will not tolerate independence from such as the Cathars."

The conversation drifted to other things and then on to Talon's time in Isfahan. The abbot wanted to know all about the city and the curious game of Chess. Although known, it was not a commonplace game, more to be found in palaces of the kings of France and other kings than anywhere else.

Talon was in the middle of describing the game when there was a disturbance at the main entrance to the monastery. They listened intently while the gates were opened and men talked to one another. They were relieved to hear that it was the group of monks returning from the fair who had arrived late.

Within minutes Claude was at the door to the abbot's office, greeting them. He glanced at Talon and then said, "You have left the town of Albi in an uproar, Talon. They say you attacked innocent men with a band of archers and slew three of them before running off." He chuckled at Talon's bewildered look. "It is clear that was not what happened, but indeed you have left the town of Albi on its head. What did happen?"

Talon told the story again of how they had to defend themselves against the four men and then their flight.

When he had finished, the abbot said, "Brother Claude, I have already heard the story and I believe Talon's version of it. I have also sent a layman off to Sir Hughes' fortress to inform Talon's people that they are safe with me for the night."

Claude looked relieved. "I was so worried, my Lord Abbot. We met Talon and his companions at the fair and then later we heard these wild stories. I did not know what to think."

"Well, calm yourself, Brother Claude. I shall even offer you a beaker of wine to assist you to do so," the abbot remarked dryly, "then we can continue our discussion. I was hearing about that interesting game called Chess and more of that splendid city named Isfahan. Talon, pray continue."

Chapter 9

The Reckoning

Sir Hughes was at the gates to greet Talon and the escort sent to fetch them when they arrived home the following afternoon.

There were many questions and angry exclamations that Talon hastened to calm, saying that they were perfectly safe and that the damage had been done to Marcel, not him. The only thing missing was the cart but that was easily replaced.

Philip, his beard bristling with rage, wanted to ride out straight away and confront Guillabert at his castle gates. Hughes and Talon persuaded him to relent and discuss the situation first. Aicelina and Anwl added to his story so that between the three a clear picture was painted of the events.

There was an impromptu council of war between Talon, his father, mother, and uncle, and it was here that Talon outlined his plan. By now three of Sir Hughes' villains had been burned out and killed, their families were within the confines of the fort where they were wards of Sir Hughes.

There was now a genuine fear in the land, which had consequences as the fields were only being worked in the immediate area of the fort and village. No one dared to work the outlying farms and could not be persuaded to. This meant a poor harvest in the coming autumn, and a lean winter. Even the millers were fearful and wanted to know if there was going to be any protection for them.

Talon told Sir Hughes and Sir Philip of how impressed he had been with the Welshmen and their ability to live in the forest. Most men could hunt in the forest; but these men, he pointed out, were able to live comfortably.

He wanted to send them out to watch the remaining houses, patrolling the forest and taking note of men who should not be there and might be up to mischief. He wanted to go with them. Both his father and his uncle looked at him as though he had lost his senses.

"Why would you want to go and live in the forest? Why do you not stay here and go out every day?" his puzzled father asked.

"Because there may be a spy within these walls or even watching our activities from the village, Father, and I do not wish to advertise my movements. Let me take the Welshmen out into the forests and see what we can do."

"Very well, but I doubt very much that we have a spy in our midst and I am not at all sure what to think of this; but you have proved to have a good head on your shoulders. Go with them, but not for too long, and let me know your movements."

"Thank you. I shall report... when I am able to."

Talon went out to talk to Gareth about his plan. It was well received and the Welshmen all enthusiastically signed up for the work. He had to disappoint three of them by telling them they would have to stay at the fort; but he told them he would rotate the duty, which mollified them somewhat. When he had explained that he wanted men who could shoot a long bow in the vicinity of the fort in case a problem developed here, they were quick to agree.

Talon, Gareth, and two other archers, Drudwas and Ap-Maddock, slipped out of the fort two nights later as though on a simple hunting expedition and headed for the extreme edge of Sir Hughes' land where it abutted that of Sir Guillabert. Talon reasoned that whoever was raiding his father's land was not taking much in the way of precautions so it would not hurt to be right in the area if they did come.

Gareth was enjoying the whole adventure. He told Talon that he thought it was a great idea, but if they wanted to remain inconspicuous they should have a camp deep in the forests where there would be no possibility of discovery by others. After all, these were ruffians who most likely rode the trails and were more interested in reaching their objectives quickly than probing the depths of the forest. Sir Hughes' landholdings, while not extensive, were nonetheless large. They were a good hour's march from the castle when they set up a very basic camp with only a bank and a crude branch shelter for them to sleep under. They kept a fire alight for warmth on the cold nights and to cook what they had trapped or killed for food. Their supply of bread and cheese, some olives and herbs that Aicelina had slipped into Talon's leather satchel, were to last a week.

They patrolled the boundaries and checked the hovels and huts of the villeins during the following days and evenings. Some had refused to leave and hence were considered good targets, while others had left and their stone-walled huts were deserted. Talon and Gareth resolved to stay as near as they could to the occupied huts.

Talon and Gareth were taking their ease at the camp on the fifth night, making shafts for more arrows to pass the time. Both were unshaven, dirty, bored, and about ready to go home when Drudwas came running into the camp to tell them that he had heard the sound of horses out on the edge of the woods. This was a good mile away. Gareth immediately interrogated Drudwas in rapid Welsh as to where he thought the horses were going.

The response excited Gareth. "Talon, we have to hurry, they are probably headed for the house of that man we visited yesterday. Remember he refused to leave his house, in spite of our asking him to."

"You're right. Gareth, come on. Where is Ap-Maddock.?"

"He is following them on foot," Drudwas said.

It was a sticky evening when they set out. Although he could barely see the sky, Talon could sense that there were dark storm clouds gathering with a good chance of rain. They ran as fast as they were able through the dense woods over soft loamy ground, which allowed them to make almost no sound as they hastened toward the edge of the forest. They then headed in the direction that Drudwas had indicated. They ran silently along the dimly lit track, tall trees on either side of them. So quiet were they that they disturbed a fox crossing the path. He barked with surprise and sped off into the undergrowth at the edge of the wood.

The running men did not pause. They heard the rumble of thunder and several drops of rain landed on Talon's shoulder. Then it began to rain harder. Lightning flashed and lit up the track they were running down, throwing the nearby trees into sharp relief, pale and ghostly. They were a quarter of a mile away when they saw a glow ahead that lit the sky.

"We're too late," Gareth said angrily.

"Hurry, we have to catch the murdering pigs," Talon replied.

They each took out an arrow and notched it in readiness. It was not long before they heard the sound of men shouting ahead. Talon hoped that they were not too late to at least kill some of them; he, too, was angry now. He remembered that the man had three skinny children and a wisp of a wife who had looked worn out and very frightened when they had appeared at the door asking to speak with him.

Suddenly a dark figure ran out in front of them and they came to an abrupt halt. It was Ap-Maddock, who whispered that they were going to be too late for the house, but there was no time to lose as the men on horses were about to ride away.

They ran hard the last few hundred yards along the trail toward the opening in the forest where the hut stood. The hut was on fire, the roof exploding upward in a stream of sparks and flames. The now fierce wind was tossing the black tops of the trees about and blowing the sparks in all directions. The flames cast an ominous light on the dark horsemen who were milling about, preparing to leave, their dirty work done. Talon spied a form lying on the ground near the door but no sign of the woman or the children.

He had told Gareth that they should attack immediately. So it was that a shower of arrows flew with deadly accuracy at the group of six mounted men. They were well silhouetted against the flaming hut. Three men cried out in pain and surprise and fell off their horses, arrows deeply embedded, while another clutched his arm and yelled with pain before another arrow silenced him forever. He, too, fell off his horse with a thud. The remaining two, although taken by surprise, were quick to react. One of them jerked his horse toward the gap in the trees and, jamming his spurs into its sides, fled down the darkened trail. An arrow whispered after him but missed and fell to the ground to the side of the trail.

The other turned his horse the wrong way. He quickly realized his mistake but still tried desperately to run the group of archers down. They all had to dodge out of the way as he thundered by, but another arrow from the quick-acting Gareth felled him before he had made twenty yards. It was over within seconds. There were two men groaning and writhing on the ground while another three were untidy bundles lying on the ground, very dead.

Walking carefully over to one of the men lying clutching his chest where an arrow protruded, Talon knelt and placed his dagger on the man's throat then told him, "You will tell me who sent you and then I shall send you to your maker. Otherwise, you shall be left to die in agony in the forest where the animals shall eat you as you die."

The terrified man groaned in pain, the light of the fire illuminated his sweating face, pallid with agony. He rolled his eyes up at Talon, wide with fear. "Save me, do not kill me. I beg you, do not kill me."

"You are already dead. You can confess to the forest before you die. Tell me who sent you?"

As he said this there was a flash of lightning and huge crash of thunder overhead. The rain that had been only a steady shower up to now started to come down in earnest.

The dying man seemed to come to a realization. He sobbed as he felt his life ebbing away. "Will you confess me if I tell you?"

"Yes," Talon said.

"It was Sir Guillabert. He wants to burn all the huts and houses to destroy the crops and put fear into the people who belong to Sir Hughes," he gasped. "Please, I need water. This hurts so much."

Talon cupped his hands and caught some of the rain as it hurled down. He poured some into the man's open mouth. He need not have bothered; the man gave a gasp, blood trickled from his open mouth, he kicked his legs in the mud, and was still, his eyes staring up to the dark sky, oblivious of the rain.

Talon straightened up and turned to the others, who now gathered round. "It seems we were right about one thing: this was done on Sir Guillabert's orders."

He had to shout over the noise of the pouring rain. They were already all soaked to the skin but they had work to do before they could take shelter.

Gareth had looked at the other wounded man and pronounced him fit to ride, but there was no fight left in him. Talon had an idea, now that he knew for sure who had given the orders.

First they had to find the woman and the children, which eventually they did, hiding in the overhang of a bank deeper in the woods. They persuaded the terrified and sobbing woman to come out with her three fearful, crying children. Talon told them who they were; he was angry that they had not arrived in time to save her husband but it was no use worrying about that now. They had to get her away.

He told Drudwas and Ap-Maddock to take them back at once to the fort where the woman and her children would be given shelter. He told the men he would follow with Gareth when they were done.

Early the next morning the guard at Sir Guillaberts' castle's gate house gave a start. He peered hard into the misty area about a quarter mile away where the track led into the forest. Coming toward him was an unusual procession. Soon he was able to make out more clearly what it was. He shouted urgently for his companions to get up on the rampart with him. There was a yell from below as Marcel splashed through some puddles and came running up the wooden stairs to join the small group staring out to the edge of the forest. What they saw was not something they had anticipated.

The only man to survive the raiding party had ridden in just after midnight, frightened and confused. He told a story of goblins and devils who came out of the night with the storm and bewitched their party. There had been no warning, he said. They just appeared with the storm, their huge figures had completely petrified everyone, or so he had claimed. They slew all in their path, he babbled, there were so many of them.

Neither Guillabert nor his sons had believed him for a minute, but they realized that they were not going to get any sense out of him at that time so they sent him packing to his billet.

Now here were the remnants of the group coming toward the gates. There was a man slumped in the saddle of the lead horse. He looked exhausted and there was a red stain on his shoulder. He lacked his hauberk and any arms.

Behind him were three other horses, one of which was carrying two dead men slung over its back, the other two carried one man each. The men were naked except for their undershirts, tied face down on the horses' backs. As the sorry procession made its way to the gates everyone on the platform looked at one another.

Marcel's face was pale. He looked more worried than angry. He turned and stamped his way down the stairs to tell his father while Roger looked after him with a sneer and then continued to stare at the group now clustered on the grass before the gates, waiting. The gate had still not been opened. A shouted order from Roger and the men standing below began to open the wooden gates and to lower the drawbridge to let the party in.

Marcel, Roger, and Sir Guillabert were there when the horses came into the courtyard. They looked up at the lead man and it was Roger who shouted at him.

"What happened man? Don't tell me it was goblins and demons that attacked you. We heard that nonsense last night when Jacob came back."

The wounded man looked as though he would rather fall off the horse than answer the question. "I know not of demons, but these men were not of us, m'lord. They spoke in tongues and were very fierce. They were enormous and made me sore afraid. They came out of nowhere; we were completely surprised." He shifted in the saddle uncomfortably. "One of them, a taller one, spoke our language. He told me to tell you to stay away from the forests of Sir Hughes. He said he would send the heads of anyone of us who ventured there back to you on stakes."

Sir Guillabert and his sons looked at one another.

"What else did he say?" Marcel snarled with false bravado. He tried to look as though he were not concerned about the situation, but to the crowd gathering it was clear that he, his brother, and his father were unsettled. The man slumped in his saddle had no more to say.

Sir Guillabert's face was red with anger. "Take this mess out of my sight," he roared. "I know who did this and I shall be revenged, do you hear?" He rounded on Marcel and Roger. "Find out how many there were and get back to me. I want to plan against this. They will not thwart me." He turned and stalked back to the main keep where he disappeared into the hall.

Marcel and Roger had the difficult work of getting the dead taken off their horses and interrogating the survivor. They came back to their father in the main living hall on the second floor to find him drinking from a flagon of wine.

"Well, what did you discover, more goblins and demons?' Guillabert demanded sarcastically.

"The two men who survived said there were at least twenty people who attacked them," Marcel said uncomfortably, shifting from foot to foot. Roger stood next to him with his habitual scowl on his face.

Marcel was remembering the incident at Albi and wondering if this was not Talon's work. That boy used a bow. All the dead had been killed with arrows, although the shafts had been retrieved by their killers.

Sir Guillabert snorted from his chair by the fireplace. "My guess is that it was probably no more than ten at the most. These lying dogs are useless to me. I shall have to find replacements and that costs money. I would to God that I knew where in hell that uncle of mine left all his ill-gotten gains. He did not die without he had a lot of silver. Where is it?!" he shouted at the rafters.

Marcel flinched and then turned as he heard a movement coming down the stone stairs from the floor above. His sister Petrona appeared at the doorway.

"Why all the shouting, Father?" she asked timidly, looking her question at her brothers.

Her father shook his head and shoulders as though to shake off the question and refused to answer. It was left to Marcel to respond.

"We have had an unpleasant surprise this morning, Sister. It seems that honest men cannot ride abroad these days without they are ambushed and killed on the road."

Petrona stared. "What are you talking about?" she asked, bewildered.

"Do you not remember the lout who came with the Templar, Sir Philip from the Holy Land? The youth named Talon? Well, it seems that he is engaged upon robbery and killing on the roads hereabouts," her brother said angrily.

"He is a man of the devil and needs to be taken down," rasped her other brother.

Petrona gasped. "You cannot mean the young man Talon? Why should he be engaged upon such a horrible adventure? What harm have we done him that he should do this?"

"We have done no harm to him!" Guillabert roared. "He is Godless and worships the devil. We know this as he told Marcel that he had lived among the Saracens for many years. He shall be made to pay for this, by God."

Petrona now looked fearful, "What could have happened to make him do these things? How has he harmed us?"

"He has only killed five of my finest fighting men in ambush, no fair fight, mind you. All were killed from behind. There were many more of them, dozens of them. That wretch shall burn for this," her father raged. "I shall impeach Sir Hughes at the Court of Albi for this dispute and make him forfeit all his land and that hovel of a fort to boot, and then I shall have the pleasure of taking his life."

He suddenly got up as though he had decided something. "Have my horse saddled, Roger; we are going to Albi. I want to find replacements. You, Marcel, ride with some men to the area of the village next to the fort and see what they are about. Do not be seen, d'you hear?"

The two brothers hurried off glad to be able to get away from their father. Both feared the consequences of their father's rages, having been on the receiving end of them for most of their lives. It did not matter that both were now grown men, the fear was still there, particularly with Marcel, who did not have the backbone of his older brother.

Petrona watched them leave the castle. After waiting for an hour she told the groom to saddle up her pony and left quietly on her own, telling the indifferent guards at the gates she was only riding down to the village by the river for a few hours to see widow Flamert, who was sick.

She rode carefully along the track fearful of what her brothers had told her but sure in her mind that the Talon she had briefly met could not have done the things he was accused of. She had some vague plan about going to Sir Hughes' fortress and confronting them as to the truth. So it was that a couple of hours later she came to the gates of Sir Hughes' fort, where she was admitted by a very surprised guard and met by an equally surprised Marguerite.

Sir Hughes and Sir Philip were away, looking over the fields as it was not far from harvest time and they had been concerned about the power of the storm and any damage the rain may have caused to the fields.

"What brings you here, Petrona? I have not seen you since you were a child. You have grown into a splendid young lady," Marguerite said, squinting up at her against the sunlight.

Petrona blushed and dismounted, handing the reins to a groom. "My Lady Marguerite. I hope I find you well?"

They exchanged a kiss on either cheek as greeting and Marguerite studied the young lady in front of her while still holding her hands. She saw a pretty young maiden of seventeen, blue eyes and fair complexion with light brown hair held together under a wide straw hat. She dressed well although not extravagantly and looked reasonably clean and fairly well groomed. Marguerite was particular about young women keeping themselves clean even if she lost the battle with her men folk, especially Guillaume.

"Is Talon here, Marguerite?"

"Talon? Why no, he is not. He is out hunting with his archers, I believe. Why do you ask, child?"

Petrona was now uncomfortably aware that what she sought was going to be harder than she had imagined. "I simply wondered, Marguerite. Did you know that men from my father's guards were attacked last night while on the road and several were killed? They are blaming Talon for this."

Marguerite gave a start. "What is this, my child? I know of no such incident as you have described. But I forget myself. You must be tired and thirsty. Come into the garden and we shall talk some more. Aicelina, my dear, please go and get us some wine and water."

Marguerite took Petrona across the muddy yard to a sunny patch of grass near a pond and made her sit on the wooden bench nearby.

"Now, you need to know something important, my child," she said firmly to a tense Petrona. "Late last night one of the families from among our villeins, a mother and three children, were brought into this castle. It was raining and they were soaked to the skin. Their father was dead and they are now homeless."

Petrona looked puzzled. "What has this to do with Talon, my lady?"

"Much, I have to tell you." There was a pause while Marguerite collected her thoughts. "Talon and his men came across the men in the act of burning the house, but too late to save her husband."

Petrona looked stunned, but before she could respond the girl Aicelina arrived with a beaker of watered wine for them both. She regarded Petrona with cool eyes that Petrona found unsettling. However, she was more concerned about what she had just heard to pay much attention.

Marguerite continued, "I believe the men who carried out this horrible deed paid for it with their lives, Petrona. Were these the men you were asking about?"

Petrona could only stare at her. Her eyes wide and her mouth open. "Then... then my brothers and father lied to me," she whispered. She looked at Marguerite with haunted eyes. "Oh, Marguerite, what shall I do? I didn't know this, and my brothers told a very different story."

Aicelina interrupted her with a snort. "Did your brother Marcel tell you that he sent his ruffians to kill Talon at the fair in Albi?"

Petrona had the grace to look embarrassed. "I heard that there had been a brawl and that Talon had provoked some men," she said, sounding to her own ears somewhat lame.

"I was there with his little brother, Guillaume; we watched the 'brawl,' as you call it, while it took place," Aicelina said scornfully. "If Talon and his archer had not been so able, they would have been killed by the hired mercenaries your brother set upon him. It was no brawl. It was an unprovoked attack."

Petrona looked as though she had been struck in the stomach. She was white and trembling. "Marguerite, my lady, I did not know," she whispered.

Marguerite patted her on the hand. "I understand your not knowing, but I am disturbed about the lies that are coming from your family, Petrona. I think you should be careful not to discuss this with them when you get back. Your father will not be pleased to know you've been here. But know this; Talon is innocent of all they accuse him of. Your brother Marcel evidently does not like him, and there it is."

Petrona nodded. "He disliked him from the onset, even while we were on the road to Carcassonne and Albi, while he was traveling with his uncle the Templar," she said ruefully, remembering how taken she had been with Talon at first sight.

Marguerite took pains thereafter to make her more comfortable and before long they were talking of other things.

Petrona did not have the luxury of the company of other women of her rank so she was inclined to tarry. After a couple of hours of pleasant conversation, however, she looked up at the sun and exclaimed. "Oh, my lady, I have forgotten the time. I must be home before my father and brothers or they will ask too many questions as to where I have gone."

Aicelina was looking at her intently but Petrona thought nothing of it as she got up.

"I have intruded upon you enough, my lady." She gave a small curtsey to Marguerite and nodded distantly to Aicelina. They followed her to the pony and waved her out of the gates.

No one paid any attention to Devonalt, one of the Welch archers, as he slipped out of the gates just before she left.

Petrona rode home as though in a dream. She had been badly shaken by the news. She had been quite taken with Talon when they first met. Indeed she had thought of him often during the long evenings at her father's castle while sewing or darning and doing all the other work that she was expected to carry out for the untidy men folk of the family. His manner had been quite different from that which she had become used to.

Her mother had died of the vomiting sickness, a lingering lonely death with no one to confess her when she was close to her end. Not even her father had found the courage to attend his wife and comfort her. Petrona had been left with loutish brothers and a father whose temper often left her frightened and crying. Now they were working themselves into fits about Talon for no other reason than he was a stranger in their midst.

While she had only a sketchy understanding of the feud developing between her father and Sir Hughes she had not until this moment felt involved, hence she had paid no attention whenever Marcel or Roger and her father talked about the land dispute taking place. Petrona didn't like complicated things in her life and thus shut her ears to the heated discussions, keeping to her tasks, not wanting to incur the ire of her father for some triviality.

She awoke from her reverie abruptly, as suddenly there were men standing around her and her pony was skittering with fright. Petrona had to rein the pony in and keep her own seat while she tried to comprehend the situation. The men were dirty, armed with bows, and wore hoods of rough cloth that hid most of their faces from her. They looked very frightening. Petrona felt fear deep in the pit of her stomach and regretted not having taken an escort.

One of the men took her reins and calmed the pony in a foreign language while another came up to her. Her first reaction to the surprise was to raise her whip and start to bring it down upon the head of the man holding her reins but a strong arm came up and a hand stopped her and clasped her wrist. The man threw back his hood and she saw Talon. His hair was long and tousled. He looked none too clean and his cloths were common and rough, but the smile he gave her was disarming and genuine.

"I believe we have met before, my lady," he said politely as he released her hand.

"T-Talon! I did not know you were in this area," stammered Petrona. Her heart was beating furiously as she tried to bring herself under control.

"One of my men came and told me we would meet you on this road, my Lady," he said calmly. "I was concerned enough to come and offer myself and my men as escort to you for the rest of the way home. These are uneasy times and a lady should not be on the road alone."

"I have heard that there are bandits who attack people without warning." said Petrona tartly. She instantly regretted her words.

Talon frowned. "Indeed, my lady, there have been reports of bandits who burn other people's houses and leave them for dead. I wish only to make sure that you are not harmed. Will you allow us to escort you to within sight of the castle? I do not think we will be welcomed at the gates."

Petrona looked down at him. What she saw was pleasing in spite of the peasant guise and the grime. She was struck again by his piercing gaze; those green eyes were penetrating. In spite of her attempt to be calm she felt weak. She nodded dumbly and Talon released the pony and fell in alongside her as she led the way. The grassy track was thick with long grass so it was quiet, other than the swish of the men's leggings in the grass, and she suddenly felt a lot safer with these silent men as they walked alongside with all of the forest to either side.

They did not say very much. Petrona could see that her escort was very alert and watched the trail ahead and behind carefully. She did ask Talon to tell his version of the "brawl" in Albi, which he did. He told the story in a matter-of-fact manner that she found very believable. She was unwilling to judge him as she had few illusions as to her brother Marcel's temper nor Roger's ability to adjust the truth to suit his needs. She engaged him in other matters willingly after that, enjoying his company.

It seemed but a short while before the castle came into sight. Petrona gave a small inward sigh as she saw it, knowing that the interlude had ended. Then she noticed that there were men coming out of the gates and trotting across the drawbridge. She wondered who it could be, unsure at this distance. She turned to say something to Talon but he had vanished. She was quite alone. Petrona shivered; she had heard nothing of their departure. She was still wondering about this when her brother Roger came cantering up.

"Where have you been, Petrona? We have been waiting for you."

"I was out riding, Brother; I went to the village to obtain some unguents for burns."

"The village is that way," Roger said sharply, pointed away from the direction she had come in. "Also, I thought there were people with you? Were there? Where have they gone?" He looked very puzzled.

"Roger, have you had too much wine? I took a ride and came back the long way. If there are people with me then please thank them for their company as I have not noticed them," Petrona had the wit to say.

Roger scowled. "Sister, I do not want you to ride alone anymore. These are dangerous times and I am worried about your safety. That rogue Talon and his murderers are abroad and could harm you."

He did not sound convincing. Petrona knew her brother well enough to know that concern for her was not in the forefront of his mind. "I shall remember that, my Brother," Petrona said, trying to sound contrite.

"Good. Now come back to the castle and tell the cooks to prepare a good meal. We have visitors and they need entertaining."

"Who is here?"

"The Bishop of Albi," he said proudly. "He has come to talk to father about the land dispute."

They rode together back toward the castle; their escort of two men fell in behind them.

Talon and his men watched them leave from their hidden positions inside the edge of the forest. Talon looked thoughtful. The others asked him what had been said.

"Nothing of importance except for one thing," he replied. "The Bishop of Albi is staying the night." He turned to Gareth. "This is the man who is one of the judges for the land dispute. Why should he be here in this castle? How can he be a judge and be thick with Sir Guillabert at the same time?"

Gareth shrugged. "I do not know, Talon, Bach. But it does not sound as though he is being impartial."

"No, indeed. I think I heard Roger say the bishop was here for the purpose of discussing the land dispute. Why then has he not visited my father?"

The four men were crouched a good five yards back inside the woods, well concealed from the road. Talon stood up and began to pace in agitation. "I must know more, but how?"

They were about to leave when Devonalt seized Talon by the shoulder, forced him down with his great strength and put his finger to his lips. Talon gave him a startled look. Devonalt pointed out onto the track. They all crouched down and listened. Talon was impressed with the man's keen ears—it was some seconds before he saw what Devonalt had been talking about.

A party of horsemen was coming down the track, moving quickly and quietly, almost furtively. They were well armed and very alert, watching the sides of the road intently as they rode by. But it was not the men themselves that caught Talon's attention most—Aicelina was seated at the front of the party on one of the men's horses, her hands bound. Behind him came another horse and on this was Guillaume, looking small and frightened, and also held by a burly man to prevent him escaping.

Talon flicked his gaze back to Aicelina and saw that she was limp, with her head lolled back; there was a lived bruise on her cheek.

Marcel was riding close to both and looking very pleased with himself.

Talon looked hurriedly about at the men with him and realized that they were too late to do anything but watch. Neither of the prisoners would survive if he charged in at this late moment, although he saw the anger and willingness to do so in his companions.

They were too few and all they would do would be to alert the men of the castle that they were in the vicinity. He put his finger to his lips and cautioned his men to do nothing. He was thinking furiously as to how he could get into the castle. Marcel was a dead man once he got close to him.

They watched enraged as the party came to the gates and after an exchange of shouts the drawbridge was lowered. Marcel led the way over and the drawbridge was withdrawn.

Chapter 10

The Bishop

Talon gained entry to the castle the hard way. Late that evening, when it was quite dark they gathered at the base of the walls near a corner where there was no activity. While they were all looking up at the dark walls Talon whispered to Gareth that he would go up at that point. Gareth stifled a startled exclamation when he realized what Talon was going to attempt.

Talon then astonished the archers by climbing the rough stone walls using only his fingers and toes in the crevices just as he had been taught. For him it was relatively easy even in the dark but as he reached the top he heard the muttered exclamations of relief from the archers.

He had Gareth toss up a rope end which they'd stolen from the village nearby, which was a lot closer than the de Guilles' fort. It took two tries but he finally had the end in his hand, then pulled the rope up. He estimated the length and then dropped the loose ends down so that he had just the loop at the top which he dropped over one of the stone emplacements. He didn't want to leave any clues as to how they had departed if he could help it.

Talon and his men had correctly deduced that the visit of a bishop to the castle of Sir Guillabert would probably take a lot of attention away from the walls. No one was threatening to attack, so there was only a lone sentry walking the battlements near the gateway, his attention more on what was going on inside the castle than without, which suited them well.

Talon could see all the way along the walkway; there was no one there so he jerked the rope and instantly felt a tug back. The Welshmen were waiting for his return. Not for the first time he gave thanks for these tough men from a distant country who seemed to revel in this kind of thing. He had to firmly refuse to allow any of them to come with him, even when Gareth vehemently begged him.

"Gareth, this is what I was trained to do when I was with the 'Assassins. Please wait here and cover me if I have to make a quick escape."

Gareth, Belth, and Ap-Maddock gave way with ill grace, but he knew they would be there with Drudwas, bow strings taut, when he came back.

Talon was wearing his forest rags which were of dark brown material and blended well with the dark, but he needed to find a change of clothes if he was to walk freely among the company below. He quickly got off the exposed walkway and descended the wooden stairs to the main courtyard, keeping to the shadows. His plan was sketchy but he hoped that he could masquerade as one of the visitors and find his way into the main keep that way.

His first objective was to find Aicelina and Guillaume. He had been greatly angered to see them taken prisoners and wondered how it could have happened. Were his parents safe? Had Marcel taken the fort by surprise while he was away? The questions rattled around in his head as he moved cautiously down the steps from the ramparts. He remembered that there had been some nasty-looking hounds in the yard the last time he'd visited and wondered where they might be. He knew he'd be no match for them if they came for him while he was creeping about in the darkness.

There was a lot of activity. The entire population of the castle was occupied in the business of making sure that the bishop and his men were taken care of. The cooking pits were alight with burning wood that cast a deep red glow over the sweating men who turned the spits. The carcass of a bullock was being basted and huge chunks of cooked meat were being sliced off. Talon's mouth watered at the smell of it. It had been some time since he had eaten a piece of beef, since he was thirteen when in his father's castle. It was not a meat commonly eaten in Persia and they had been eating venison at this father's fort. The cattle would be killed for the winter but for now they were left to eat their fill when let out onto the common ground near to the fort.

Servants ran about bringing jugs of beer or wine to thirsty throats within. There were shouts from the cooks as they prepared the pies and tarts for the honored guests and called for the servants to hurry up and take them away.

Talon crouched in the shadows, watching the activity, waiting for an opportunity to present itself. When it came he found it almost too easy. The man was clearly one of the visitors as he wore a livery that Talon guessed belonged to the bishop. He had not seen any livery on the men in the castle the last time he had visited with his father and uncle. The man came to the corner of the wall and the stairs near Talon to relieve himself.

Talon came up to his victim without a sound and slipped his blade into the man's back, exactly placed to reach the heart. His victim died with a huge convulsion, but Talon had a hand was over his mouth to prevent any scream. He held up the corpse for a few more moments and listened tensely in the dark for any indication that the man might have been expecting company.

After lowering the dead man to the ground, Talon went through the gruesome task of changing clothes with his victim. When he had finished he pulled the heavy body up the stairs as quietly as possible to the battlements and dropped him to the ground on the other side. He was sure the archers would dispose of the body after they had heard its fall. It would be late in the following day when anyone discovered him.

The next thing he had to do was disguise his face. Talon went down the stairs quickly and headed for the pits. He stood back from the group of Sir Guillabert's men and when the opportunity presented itself he moved forward casually and took one of the burning brands from the fire. It was not an unusual thing to do—people needed to light torches so they used a brand from the fire.

He retired to the shadows, dowsed the coals and waited until they were cool. Then, reaching down, he used the dust to change the color of his beard and rubbed it into his hair. He wore a cap that he had taken from his victim but all the same he rubbed it in hard. He hoped fervently that no one would notice. Then he pulled the cap down over his eyes. When satisfied that he was reasonably well disguised, he sauntered out into the main throng of people, adjusting his clothing as though he had just been relieving himself.

He made his way with the jostling servants toward the doorway of the hall. There he was greeted by a wave of warm air. The hall was full of people. Mostly men-at-arms and some few favored villagers who belonged to Sir Guillabert, but it was quickly clear to Talon that the bishop had come with a sizeable retinue as well. They were seated on benches along either side of the hall mixed in with Sir Guillabert's men. The high table drew his attention.

He quickly found Sir Guillabert, Marcel, and Roger. Seated in the place of honor was a man Talon had not seen before; he assumed the man was the bishop. Talon watched him intently. He wanted to recognize the bishop another time. The man obviously enjoyed eating. There was gravy on his chin and he ate the meat like Sir Guillabert, without ceremony, tearing at it with his teeth, using his hands and a knife to cut the meat off in front of his munching jaws. The bishop had a look of arrogance to his features that Talon recognized well. It was clear that this man wielded power and knew how to use it.

Talon was well shielded from the table by the throng at the main entrance so he could pause and watch. The bishop, seated in the center, was engaged in an intense conversation with Sir Guillabert to his right; Marcel listened intently from his left side. Roger was staring vacantly off into the distance and looked drunk.

Petrona was seated to the left with the priest who had offered to confess him. She looked distracted and unhappy, although the priest was paying her a lot of attention.

Talon realized that if she looked up he could be discovered if he lingered at the doorway. He noticed that servants were coming in from behind the trio at the table.

He moved back into the press at the doorway and then walked purposefully around to the back of the building. There he found what he was looking for, steps led up to a door that in turn led to the kitchens and the living area of the castle. He eased his way in past the sweating men-at-arms and the irritable servants who shouted for way while they carried the food to and fro. It was easy to become lost in this confusion so Talon decided to take the first set of stairs he found and see where it led. He seized a jug of wine that was standing waiting to be taken into the hall and moved out of the main throng.

Looking purposeful, he searched for and found some stone stairs that led up into the gloom of the upper stories of the keep.

Checking that he was not being watched or followed, he edged in that direction and then took the stairs. His exploration took him to the first floor where he discovered another chamber from which led short passages. This chamber looked lived in, so he assumed it might be where the family would retire when they had eaten. He looked it over carefully and then took one of the passages to see where it led.

He was thorough. When he came back he knew exactly where Sir Guillabert, Marcel, and Roger slept. Their chambers were filthy, particularly Roger's, which stank of sour ale and other un-pleasant things. He also knew which was Petrona's apartment. The rooms prepared for the bishop were adjoining to those of Sir Guil-labert. He hadn't discovered where Aicelina or Guillaume were, and this worried him. He continued looking in the immediate area, hoping that they might have simply locked the two in a room nearby, but no chamber offered them up.

Talon reasoned that when the meal was over the men, and perhaps Petrona, would come to this anteroom and settle by the merrily glowing fire to talk some more before retiring. He hoped that he could perhaps get close to Petrona and ask her where the prisoners might be. He looked around for some hiding place.

There were a few rough, moth-eaten tapestries hanging on the stone walls, and a chest nearby. The tapestries presented just enough space to stand behind, although he found he could crouch near the chest that was close by. This afforded him a limited view of the room, but he would hear any conversation well. Near the fire was rough furniture, unadorned wood that would not be very comfortable for a long talk. He found a good place to hide himself that allowed escape if discovered and settled down to wait. He was tense and hoped that they would be sufficiently in their cups not to be too alert; although crowded with furniture, the room was not large and there was the real possibility of discovery.

If that happened he would be lucky to escape with his life, let alone Aicelina and his brother. He tried to control his breathing and waited. The fire crackled and spat, sounding loud in the silence of the room. He could hear the noise downstairs abating somewhat as the night drew on, while outside the slit of the window the noises of the forest intruded. He heard clearly the bark of a fox and the distant scream of some luckless animal captured by an owl or other predator.

It was not long before the first visitor came to the room. A servant stamped up the stairs, came in, and quickly replenished the fire with wood from a pile near where Talon hid. Then he was gone and there was silence in the room but for the crackle of the fire and the low-pitched moan of the wind in the stone walls outside, seeking to come in through the rough wooden shutters of the narrow window. The noise from below drifted up the stairs.

Not very long after the servant had disappeared there was a light step on the stairs and he saw Petrona coming into the room. Talon was just about to show himself to her when a servant girl walked in behind her. He withdrew; he could not risk being seen by a servant who would surely talk, and then Petrona would be compromised.

They paused briefly to stand near the welcoming fire, but Petrona did not stay. She took the passage to her room followed by her servant. Their conversation faded as they went along the short distance to her apartments. The door opened and shut, once again he was alone with the silence.

It was not long before the servant girl came back, having finished attending to Petrona. Talon listened to her steps receding down the stairs. No sound came from Petrona's bed chamber. Once again he was about to move out of his cover to go to her room and wake her when he heard steps on the stairwell below. He drew back quietly into his cover.

There were heavy steps as more than one man came up. He listened and tried to watch the doorway but it was difficult, so he waited. Sir Guillabert, followed by the bishop, walked into the room still talking and then there were two more sets of steps. He reasoned that they were Marcel and the priest's. He decided that Roger had probably passed out below, dead drunk.

The men were well into their cups and wanted more for the evening. Guillabert shouted for more wine while the chairs were shuffled about. It was cool in the evenings now so the fire was welcome.

Talon heard them settling into their respective chairs; someone came and sat down with a thump and a creak of the wooden chair just in front of his hiding place. Then he heard the hurried steps of a servant bringing sweetmeats and more wine. There was idle talk while the guests were served, then when the servant had retired the men got down to the main subject.

Sir Guillabert opened the conversation. "My Lord Bishop, we have already decided the ownership of the mills, but I need to know what your intent is with regard to the de Gilles fort and the remaining properties once the decision is handed down from the court."

"My dear Sir Guillabert, I would have thought that it was obvious. You shall have the fort but we shall share the profits from the land. The Church has no need for a castle, but the revenues from the land, the ferry, the water rights, and the mills, is considerable.

We can both do very well from these sources, I am sure," the bishop replied throatily.

The voice came from only a couple of feet away from the crouching Talon. He could even smell the heavy perfume the man was doused with.

"I get the village?" Guillabert asked.

"I had thought that we should discuss this," the bishop said comfortably. "The revenue from the woods and the fields on the land Sir Hughes occupies is considerable. I think we need to divide this into equal portions. There will be the need of a priest loyal to me in the village. You do, after all, have this castle."

There was a silence for a few minutes while Sir Guillabert digested this.

"Who is to get the mills, Father?" Marcel asked.

His father grunted. "Marcel makes a good point, m'lord Bishop. We could have one each; they bring good revenue. Let's not forget the river rights, either. I want part of that; I've earned it, by God."

"I shall thank you not to blaspheme so much in my presence, Sir Guillabert. It is unseemly before God's servants. But I do not see a complication there, one each." There was a short pause. "Did I hear right earlier? That you have taken a maiden and Sir Hughes' young son prisoner?"

"Young Marcel here 'found' them wandering in the woods by the riverside. He felt it his duty to protect them, my Lord. You never know these days what dangers reside in the woods. Why, only the other day some of my men were attacked and cruelly slain by vagabonds and rogues."

The bishop chuckled. "I hope you do not have Sir Hughes banging on these gates demanding them back before I leave."

"He doesn't know where they are and certainly not that I took them, Sire," Marcel said thickly. He sounded heavily into his cups.

"The girl is worth nothing and will do for a bed companion for one of my sons, but we will use the boy to keep Sir Hughes from making any rash decisions before the court is concluded," Guillabert said with satisfaction. "Well done, Marcel; you did very well."

"What is this I hear about there being some moneys left by your uncle before he died?" the bishop asked silkily, changing the subject.

There was a pause, "I have heard a rumor, but nothing more," Guillabert said carefully. "I expect it was only a rumor. Should he have had any I am sure it would have been discovered by now. I ransacked the castle and the fort before that God-cursed de Gilles came back from the Holy Land."

"Your uncle was a wealthy man, Sir Guillabert. I wonder indeed if he might have had coin hidden somewhere when he died."

"I was not there to hear him say so," Guillabert said. "It was a frightening time for all. You will recall that my own wife died during the time before this last one."

"Yes, I recall the time, and she died alone," the bishop said dryly. "You realize that although the decision of the court is a foregone conclusion, you might still have to force Sir Hughes out of the castle."

"That will be arranged. He will not make it back to the castle after the court hearings. My people will deal with him and that whelp of his long before they get home."

The bishop gave short a bark of laughter. "I hear that whelp of Sir Hughes is making life difficult for Marcel here," he said unsympathetically.

"That will not continue for very long hereafter, my Lord Bishop," Marcel snarled truculently, "One way or the other, I shall finish that heretic."

"Oh, heretic, you say? What is this I hear?" the bishop demanded.

"You might not know this, my Lord, but he lived for many years among the Saracen and as such is a heathen," Marcel blurted out.

"My Lord, I believe this to be true." This came from the priest who had remained silent up to now. "I had occasion to talk to a priest who traveled the same road from the coast. I also had cause to meet him when I went to the de Gilles fort to remonstrate with Sir Hughes about the lawful will of your uncle Sir Guillabert. He is impenitent and without doubt a dangerous heretic in his heart."

"How interesting! Then we should remove the boy from the game using all the power of the Church to do so," mused the bishop. "That means prison and a trial for heresy. There is only one route out of that prison and it is to the stake. This removes any subsequent claims to the land. Finally, there is the young brother whom we have here, in any case."

"Indeed, my Lord Bishop."

"Then you should see to it that he does not inherit, either," came the chilling comment.

There was a silence for a couple of long seconds and then the sound of a hand slapping a thigh. "You are not a man I would cross lightly, my Lord Bishop." Sir Guillabert laughed a nasty laugh that sent chills down Talon's back. Everybody else laughed.

In his hiding place Talon felt his anger rising. These men had decided upon the complete destruction of his family and the bishop was abetting them.

The conversation became desultory after that. The bishop decided to retire and was seen off by the unctuous Guillabert and his son. The priest went back down the stairs after bidding all good night. Father and son stayed and drank more wine while they discussed the visit and its implications. Marcel was slurring his words while he talked about the future. It was clear that he wanted the fortress for himself and was urging his father to grant it to him. But Guillabert chided him for neglecting his brother, chuckling at the silence with which this was greeted.

Talon wondered if it would not be a good idea to kill them both right there and then, but the risk of one or the other shouting for help was too great. He needed to get out of the place and find Aicelina and his brother, then take the information home.

Eventually, both men left for their respective bed chambers. The room darkened as the candles went out one by one, leaving only the glow of the embers in the fireplace to light the room.

He could hear snoring from the chambers where Guillabert slept and once again he thought about taking the man's life. It would be so easy. He thought about the bishop and made up his mind: He would kill the bishop; that man was the pivot of the whole plan. If he could he would take out Guillabert as well, as the man still posed a threat. His anger threatened to overcome him, but he realized that if he was to achieve his purpose he must stay icy calm. He took a deep quiet breath, stood up, and made his way carefully toward the entrance that led to the bishop's rooms. The noise from below had died to a murmur as the remaining men drank themselves senseless with what was left of the wine and beer. There would be a lot of thick heads in the morning.

He was close to the doorway to the bishop's rooms when there was a noise on the stairway below. Talon looked around frantically for a hiding place in the short corridor, but there was nowhere to hide. Hastily he retreated to his previous place of concealment and hid there waiting.

Two men came up the stairs, one of them the priest, who asked for more light. He had work to do he told the other and this was as good a room as any. It was clear that he was talking to a servant who brought more candles and left him alone. Talon watched the priest while he settled into his chair and began to work on some papers. The light of the candles flickered and danced in the draft that came up the stairs and window but the priest concentrated on his work, oblivious of everything.

Talon eased himself out of the hiding place and moved silently across the room. He moved so lightly the priest could not have seen even a flicker from the candle flame. Talon came to the opening which led to Petrona's apartment and was just crossing this to get to the stairway when the priest suddenly stood up and stretched. He turned as he did so and faced directly toward where Talon had been.

Talon slipped silently into the room where Petrona slept. He could hear her breathing quietly in the darkness, very close to him as he stood inside the doorway. To his dismay he heard the priest coming along the short corridor toward the door, it could only have been the priest. After a very hurried fumble he located the latch wedge and slipped it into place. Then, to his astonishment, there was a light knock on the door. Petrona slept on. There was a furtive attempt to open the latch, but as it held this soon ceased. Then there was another knock, this time more urgent.

Petrona stirred and sat up in the bed. It was impossible for her not to see Talon within a second. He turned and grasped her by the shoulders with one hand and put his other over her mouth and whispered urgently for her to stop and listen.

"It is me, Talon. Listen, Petrona, the priest is outside and wants entrance to this chamber. Did you agree to that?" She calmed and then shook her head vehemently.

"You must call back and threaten to wake the house if he persists."

He released her and took his hand off her mouth. His heart was beating wildly. She could denounce him then and there and he would be dead, or she could help him. He waited tensely.

There was another knock on the door and a whispered request, barely audible through the thick wood of the door, and again there was an attempt to open it.

"Go away, whoever you are, or I shall call the servants," Petrona called out in a loud tone.

Talon let out his breath. The sound of someone leaving could just be heard outside. Talon listened intently and thought he could hear the priest go down the stairs. He could hardly believe it had happened. The man had actually thought he could bed the girl. He wondered what the brothers at the abbey would have thought of that. He would have laughed if it had not been such a tense situation.

He did not have time to reflect long, however.

"Is that really you, Talon? What are you doing here, in God's name! In my bed chamber, too! Who was that outside my room just now?"

He gave a vague answer. "I got into the castle to find my brother, Petrona, and then I decided I wanted to see you again. The man outside was the priest."

"The priest?" She gave a giggle. "I knew he wanted to bed me. He hinted all night while father and the bishop were talking to each other. The disgusting toad!"

There was a silence, then a hand came out and grasped his shirt to pull him down into the bed with her. He put out a hand to stop himself from falling over her and it landed on her breast. She gave a subdued gasp. He discovered that she was quite naked. He pulled back but she held onto his tunic firmly.

"You have found me now, Talon. What do you intend to do?" she purred.

"Can you tell me where they have taken my brother and his nurse?" he whispered back urgently.

"I cannot believe Marcel would do what he did, Talon. I am sorry for your brother. Do you really think you can rescue him?"

"If you can tell me where he is locked up I am sure of it."

"They are held in the strong-room near to the kitchens. They are under guard."

"How many guards are there?"

"Probably one or two of my father's men." She gave him clear instructions on how to get into the kitchens and then the strong-room where the prisoners were held.

"I thank you, Petrona, for your kindness, and now I must leave." He was about to pull away but her hand gripped his shirt harder.

There was a silence for a couple of seconds and then she whispered. "If you leave me now Talon, I shall be hurt. Are you a gentleman or not? I would know."

He moved back from her, still sitting on the bed. "What would you have me do, Petrona?"

There was a tense silence. He waited in the darkness. There was a rustle of the linen bed sheets and the bed creaked. He sensed that she had settled back into the bed.

Talon said nothing. Petrona, thinking he wavered, raised her voice. "I am in earnest Talon," she warned.

"Petrona, I need desperately to release my brother. You may not know it but your father and brothers mean him harm."

"They only want to keep him 'til the trial is over, they told me so."

"Petrona!" He put more urgency into his voice. "I have to get him out of here or he might not live. I know what your brothers have told you, but it's a lie."

Again there was silence, but this time he could sense her uncertainty. Finally, she said, "If you must go, then go!" Her voice had become sharp and he even wondered if she would betray him.

He knew Petrona wanted him to tarry and he even suspected that she had been inviting him into her bed but he thought he had managed to persuade her to let him leave.

He decided that at least she was entitled to a kiss of thanks and leaned over her and aimed a kiss at her lips. He connected but then she wrapped her arms around him and returned the kiss forcefully. He finally managed to extricate himself and sat up, holding her hands in his.

"Goodnight, Petrona, and God bless you for helping me."

"Go, Talon, for I am close to keeping you with me," she whispered and sitting up, she kissed him again. Then let him go and lay back in the pillow. "Goodnight, Talon," she whispered.

Talon eased himself out of Petrona's bedchamber. He looked very carefully for evidence of the priest, but that worthy had gone to bed it seemed, his ardor thwarted for the evening.

His pulse still pounding from his encounter, Talon went cautiously down the stairs, listening for any signs of activity below. He need not have worried; most of the people in the hallway were asleep except for a few too drunk to notice him slipping by.

The servants had departed for their beds, leaving the scullery servants to sleep where they could. He stepped carefully along the filthy flagstones of the corridor that led to the kitchens, strewn with bits of vegetables, bone and flesh, already stinking of rot. He nearly trod on the tail of a cat half hidden in a corner eating some piece of meat. It hissed at him and fled into the darkness. Once there he was forced to take care, as it was only dimly lit by a dying candle and the flag stones were slippery with blood and filth from the guts of the slaughtered birds and small animals. He could hear rats already out squeaking and rustling among the filth.

He traversed the length of the kitchen. Peering around the corner of a doorway that led into the dark recesses of the pantry, he spied a guard asleep against a doorway. There was no sign of the other. Talon knew he would have to either kill the man to get to the door or bluff his way. Deciding upon the latter course he walked boldly up to the man and kicked him in the thigh.

"Wake up, you idiot," he hissed. "The master will have your head if he finds you like this."

The man stirred slowly awake, mumbling.

"I have come for the boy. The bishop wants to see him and the girl is to be taken to Sir Guillabert. I shall do that, too." Talon spoke quietly, not wanting to wake anyone else.

The guard looked up at him and then sat up. He peered at the uniform Talon was wearing; as it was that of the bishop, he didn't seem to want to dispute it.

"All right, all right, hold your piss, I'll get the key," he grumbled, clearly upset at being awakened. He fumbled around on a nearby bench and produced the heavy key which he gave to Talon. "Sir Guillabert wants a piece of leg, eh?" he leered.

Talon grinned and shrugged, spreading his hands. "I don't care what they want, they are the masters and I just do their bidding then I can go to bed."

The guard now sat on a three-legged stool and rubbed his face with a pair of dirty hands as though to clear the cobwebs. "Here, take it, and open the door yourself," he growled, looking around for a drink.

Talon was happy to oblige. He took the key and ran it into the door lock then pushed the stout wooden door inward. He could barely see inside, but there was a scuffle as though someone was trying to hide and then silence. Talon pretended to be annoyed.

"Hey, you in there, come out where I can see you. I have to take you to see the bishop and no nonsense."

First Aicelina came slowly toward him a defensive look on her face that became incredulous, followed by a suppressed gasp of surprise when she recognized Talon despite his crude disguise, standing there looking belligerent.

He quickly put a finger for the briefest moment to his lips and then spoke again. "Get out of there, you, or I'll come in and get you."

Aicelina turned and whispered something into the darkness. Guillaume came out of the dark hesitantly, his eyes wide, staring at his brother in the doorway. Aicelina whispered again, put her finger to his lips and took his hand. He said nothing but continued to stare at Talon.

"Come along, come along. I haven't got all night," Talon said roughly and he made a threatening gesture toward them. Guillaume was scared enough to actually shrink from him.

The two came out of the darkened space and into the candle-light. The guard looked blearily at Aicelina and his eyes widened. Even in her dirtied dress and with her hair disheveled she still looked very attractive. The guard muttered a curse and stood up as though to move over to her.

He never made it; Talon quickly picked up the stool the guard had been sitting on and brought it down on the back of his head with a sharp crack.

The man fell forward without a sound. Hurriedly, Talon reached down and grabbed the guard's feet and dragged him into the pantry room. After locking the door behind him he looked up; Aicelina, still holding onto Guillaume by the hand, was peering out into gloom of the larger kitchen to see if anyone was coming. Talon admired her composure; despite the ordeal she had been subjected to she seemed to be able to keep her wits about her and remain alert.

He joined them and then he moved forward, beckoning her behind him. They scurried across the filthy floor and made it to the entrance to the short corridor that led to both the hall and the outside doors.

No one moved but there were loud snores coming from the hall as they moved by the entrance. They crept past the door that led to the stairway and Talon glanced up into the dim space. No one moved upstairs. They had almost made it to the doorway when he heard footsteps outside the wooden door, which was closed and latched. Someone was coming to the door from the other side. Talon pushed Aicelina back against the wall into the shadows and waited. He prayed that it would be only one man. The door was unlatched and pushed open; Talon could only make out a single guard in the semi-darkness, standing on the top of the outside stairs, carrying a spear and a flaming torch above his head. He was about to enter when he saw Talon standing boldly in the entrance.

Talon was still dressed in the livery of the bishop. The man peered at him and seemed to recognize the uniform.

"You are up late, man," he said.

"Bishop's business; he never seems to sleep. God's blood, but I am tired," Talon said, moving closer to the man who stood in his path. "What are you doing here?"

"I am going to relieve the guard for the prisoners..."

He got no further. Talon seized his shoulder with one iron hand and with his right stabbed the man up under his rib cage. The man gasped and dropped the torch. Before he could cry out, Talon had his hand over his mouth and held him. There was a weak struggle, but the man was mortally wounded and he soon sagged in Talon's arms to the ground. Talon glanced around to see if anyone had witnessed the killing.

The torch was still on the ground at the bottom of the short flight of stone stairs, flaring; he could see Aicelina in its flickering light as she moved into the doorway. She had her hand over her mouth but still clutched Guillaume tightly. The boy was white-faced and shocked at what he had witnessed but still held his tongue.

Talon hurried down the stairs, stamped out the flames, and then returned to drag the man down the stairs into the deeper darkness of the wall. Aicelina followed with Guillaume. Talon then led the way toward the place where he had come down from the battlements. The yard was silent but he was concerned that there might be some of the hunting hounds loose in the yard. The ones he had seen the last time he came were fearsome animals and he knew he would have a bad time of it if they attacked.

They made their way across the yard, keeping to the darkest shadows, and finally to the base of the stone stairs that led up to the battlements. Talon had the guard's spear and his knife out and led the way. When the got to the stairs, he picked up his bundle of clothes from the dark recess where he had left it and gave it to Aicelina. Then he motioned her to go up the stairs as quickly as she could. She took Guillaume's hand and went lightly up the steep stairs with Talon hard on her heels.

They made it to the top without incident; Talon peered along the ramparts in the darkness. There didn't appear to be any movement by the guards. He suspected that they were probably asleep or even drunk. The discipline in the castle seemed to be very lax.

He found the rope and tugged. There was an answering tug back. He pulled one end up and tied it round Guillaume's chest. "Hold onto this, little brother, and do not fear."

Guillaume looked up at Talon and whispered, "I am not afraid, Talon."

Talon grinned his approval in the dark and then lifted Guillaume over the edge of the wall and, taking hold of the rope, lowered him down the outside wall. He could see nothing below in the darkness but imagined that the Welshmen would get over their surprise quickly enough when they found Guillaume.

The rope went slack and then after a few seconds there was a tug. He pulled it up quickly and turned to Aicelina who had stood behind him saying nothing while he was engaged. He reached behind her and took the end of the rope and tied it level with her chest. "Can you hold on while I lower you?"

She came close to him. "I can hold. Come quickly after me, Talon," she whispered, her lips brushing his cheek. She tossed his clothes over the side. Then he helped her over the edge and carefully lowered her down. There still seemed to him to be some distance to go before she was on the ground but he heard something. He turned quickly and looked back down the stairs they had just come up. From his position against the wall he could only just make out the floor of the yard below.

It was a moonless night but despite the few clouds in the sky some stars were out and this gave enough illumination for him to see two dark shadows racing toward the base of the stairs. They were the huge deerhounds he had seen before. He broke into cold sweat. He would be no match for the pair if they managed to get onto the battlements with him.

He speeded up the lowering process and then just as the rope went slack he dropped it and grabbed the spear. He stepped quickly toward the top of the stairs and hurled the spear at the first huge dark shape that was coming at terrific speed toward him. There was a choking yelp and then the shape twisted away and fell over the side, landing with a loud thump.

The second deerhound bayed, a terrifying sound in the quiet of the castle. It hesitated, still baying, but that gave Talon just enough time to leap to the edge of the wall, grab the loose rope end and swing out from the top of the wall. He prayed as he went that the other end had been tied off. Just as he was about to lower himself the hound poked its huge head over the edge of the wall and they were face to face. The creature lunged at him, which brought its slavering jaws within inches of his face. the animal was growling and snapping ferociously; specks of saliva struck Talon's cheeks. Talon wasted no further time; he slid down the rope ignoring the burning on his hands and landed in a heap at the bottom of the shallow moat. Figures rushed out of the night to grab him and get him out of the odious trench and back onto his feet.

Above them there was pandemonium. They could see men carrying torches running along the battlements toward the still baying hound. There were shouts and all the clamor of a castle coming awake from an alarm.

"You seem to have stirred up a lot of trouble there, Talon, Bach. They sound just like the English after we have finished a raid on them. We have been worried sick that they had caught you," Gareth exclaimed in a whisper as they ran for the edge of the woods. There was a snapping sound from the walls and a couple of barbs from crossbows thumped into the ground nearby. They ran harder still.

Others from the group came up to them as they came into cover, wanting to know what had happened. He heard the twang of a bowstring and an arrow sped toward the people on the battlements. There was a shout of alarm seconds after it had flown.

"That should keep their heads down!" Drudwas laughed with satisfaction.

"I had no choice about the delay; I could not find Guillaume and Aicelina," Talon said.

"If you don't mind me saying, m'lord, but you smell a bit different."

Talon cursed Gareth's sharp nose and said quickly, "I had to wear a pomade, Gareth; the bishop's people all stink of incense and other smells." He decided that he should dive into the pool by the fort before he went into the grounds in case someone else got a whiff of him. To change the subject, he said, "There is a dead man at the base of the walls, Gareth. We need to..."

"We heard the body fall, Talon. We have taken it deep into the woods. No one will find it."

Talon nodded in the dark. "It doesn't matter now; I had to kill another inside. I have learned much this night and we need to tell my father and Sir Philip. I shall tell you as we go. We have to leave, Gareth; they will guess soon enough what has happened and then turn the other hounds loose on us. We must to speed away!"

They melted deep into the darkness of the woods, still unseen by the men on the battlements. Talon knew that they would find the dead guard soon enough, and the missing prisoners, and then the hunt would be on.

The Welshmen led the way unerringly through the dense woods. Guillaume was perched on Drudwas' back, clinging to his neck with all his might. The strong Welshman didn't seem to notice the boy's weight. Talon came in the middle, helping Aicelina as they ran. Although she was in a skirt she had tucked it up around her waist and he got a tantalizing glimpse of her white legs as she ran alongside. Gareth and Ap-Maddock took the rear. Soon enough, although they were already deep into the woods, they heard the distant baying of several hounds loose behind them. The whole group paused for an instant of alarm to listen to the chilling sound and then ran on with greater urgency. Talon knew that these great animals would corner them quickly enough if they caught the scent, which he had no doubt that they would.

"They will catch up with us very soon, Gareth," he gasped as they ran.

"There are streams ahead, Talon; we are heading for them. It will not be long now and then we shall to go downstream and throw them off the scent."

"There will be men with them, I would not be surprised," Drudwas said from under his load.

"Go you with Talon and Drudwas, Devonalt, while me and Ap-Maddock will lead them a merry chase through the woods," Gareth ordered him.

Talon nodded in the darkness. It made sense but it was dangerous. He had no doubt that Gareth and Ap-Maddock were capable of leading the hounds away from their proper quarry. He just hoped that they did not become victims themselves.

Almost as though he had a map in his mind and could see clearly in the dark, Devonalt brought them to a wide and shallow stream. In the quiet of the night the only sound was the rippling sound of the water over the stones and the distant baying of the hounds echoing eerily in the forest as they followed their trail.

Talon turned at the water's edge in the darkness and gripped Gareth by the hand. "Take care, my friend. God speed, and do not get caught."

"I have led many an English hunting party around in circles back on the Welsh borders, Talon. We will be safe. Go quickly downstream as far as possible before you leave. Drudwas and Devonalt know the way."

Talon gripped Ap-Maddock by the hand in the darkness. They shook in silence and then Talon and his party plunged into the shallow cold waters and waded downstream. Gareth and Ap-Maddock disappeared into the dark almost immediately.

Their party, led by Devonalt, waded carefully along the middle of the stream; it was uneven and they often barked their shins against rocks that protruded from the bed or fell into a deeper pool. They stopped to listen after wading downstream for about a hundred yards.

The sound of baying grew louder as the hounds with their scent now firmly in their noses rushed up to the edge of the water. Everyone held their breath as they heard the baying and then the shouts of the huntsmen as they ran up to the milling hounds.

Soon enough one of the hounds caught a scent and it began to bay, a chilling sound that filled the night, echoing into the depths of the woods. The others seemed to catch it and they, too, began to bay again. There were more distant shouts and the whole group moved away, going upstream. The baying soon became too distant to hear and the forest quieted again.

The group listened for a few more minutes, then continued cautiously downstream. On occasion one or the other of them would slip and there would be a splash. The whole group would freeze for a minute or two as they listened to any sound that might indicate danger. After what seemed to be an hour, Devonalt called a halt and they listened again to the forest. It was pitch-black all around but apart from the odd rustle in the undergrowth there was no sound to alarm them. An owl hooted in the distance and the faint sound of a fox yapping followed, but otherwise the forest was silent.

He turned to Talon and whispered, "We can leave the water now, m'lord. We should hasten to the fort as there are still places they could catch us if they decided we slipped them at the stream."

They all struggled out of the water and stood dripping on the bank. Talon took hold of Aicelina's hand. It was wet and very cold. "Will you be all right?"

She took his wet sleeve in her grip; she was shaking with the cold. "I will be better for a warm blanket and a hot soup. I shall be all right, Talon, but I am very cold."

She was soaked from the shoulders down and shivering violently. He took his damp over-smock off and placed it over her shoulders but there was otherwise nothing he could do for her except to say, "We will warm up as we move through the forest. It won't be long now before we are at the fort." He had to make a conscious effort not to let his teeth betray him, as he was numb with cold himself.

"God willing we will be protected for the rest of the journey," she responded her through her chattering teeth.

He admired her composure. She had not behaved as though frightened but he was sure she had to be despite her seeming calm. Talon turned and gave his brother a reassuring pat on the back, but the boy was too tired to do more than mumble something and continue to cling to Drudwas' broad back.

The party continued on its way guided unerringly by Devonalt, who had an uncanny sense of direction in the depths of the black forest. It was almost dawn by the time they arrived on the outskirts of the village, which was still asleep.

Still being cautious, they kept to the edge of the forest as they approached the fort. It was very quiet and still dark, that false kind of dawn that indicated light, but is still a short time from the sunrise. Talon could see the dark shapes of men walking slowly along the top ramparts, awake and alert at even this early hour. He nodded his approval. His father had learned his war craft in a hard country and was using it well here. But his instinct was nagging him, he still felt somewhat unsafe. Then Drudwas raised his hand for silence. He pointed toward the edge of the forest to the south of the fort several hundred yards away.

He turned to whisper to Talon. "I thought I heard the sound of a horse, m'lord. Why would there be a horse over there?"

Talon wondered at the man's ability to hear what no one else could, but he was not going to contradict Drudwas. What horses would be loose during the night? The others crouched while Talon and Drudwas stood and listened and watched.

"We have to move closer, Drudwas," Talon said. "I cannot hear from here." He believed implicitly in what Drudwas might have heard. He looked at Devonalt. "Wait here with Aicelina and my brother while we go and find out what is going on."

The man nodded and the two men moved slowly and carefully along the edge of the woods toward where Drudwas thought he had heard the horse. They had only moved fifty yards when there came the sound of another faint jingle. Both froze as they heard it and looked at one another, then without speaking melted into the undergrowth on the edge of the woods. There was no doubt about it: there was a horse, perhaps two, in the forest ahead. The enemy was waiting for them to come to the fort in the hopes of intercepting them before they could get to its safety. He wondered which one of the Guillabert family had thought of this.

Talon whispered to Drudwas, "Can you get close enough to find out how many of them there are?"

Drudwas grinned in the darkness. Talon could see his remaining teeth gleam. "I can stroke their horses' necks while they talk and they will not see me, Bach."

"Make sure you come back alive, my brother."

Drudwas disappeared noiselessly and then Talon waited. The dawn was about to break and still they could not move until they knew who was there to intercept them. He fretted as the light grew, wishing that he had taken a chance on getting to the gate before the enemy knew they were there. But he also knew that sharp eyes were watching the green swath before the fort and they would have been run down by the horsemen before they got there and the men on the walls were able to get the gates open.

He heard the faintest rustle and Drudwas was by his side. "There are four horsemen and five others who look like archers, but they have the crossbow."

The odds were not good. The two moved slowly and silently back to join the group. There they had a whispered council of war.

"We cannot just flee for the walls. They will run us down before we can get anywhere near," Talon said.

"We are three archers; could we not shoot them down before they come for us?" Devonalt asked.

"Too dangerous," Drudwas stated. "Remember there are four horsemen and five archers, and all are mercenaries; they will not be intimidated by us three."

"You're right, Drudwas, but can we even the odds with your long range before we make a run for it?" Talon asked.

"We are better in the woods than them, I am sure... you mean we try to kill some before we try to make a run for it?" Devonalt asked, realization dawning.

"Can you and I get close enough to kill some before the others run for safety?"

Devonalt nodded but Drudwas interjected, "I should go with Devonalt, m'lord. We two know each other and can run rings around them while you take the lady and your brother to the walls."

Talon thought about this. "Very well, both of you go to a position where you can kill without being threatened by the crossbows. Remember, they are only accurate up to forty paces while you can kill at one hundred and more. When you are in position, make the call of a nightjar. When you do, I shall fire an arrow at the fort to alert them. If they are awake, as I think they are, they will sound the alarm and then we will start to run for the gates. Do you kill as many as you can and then get out of there as they will hunt for you. We can then cover you from the walls."

The two Welshmen gave tense nods and disappeared into the darkness of the woods, heading toward the enemy positions.

Talon turned to Aicelina, who had been listening, and they moved very carefully toward the edge of the forest. It would all go very badly if they were seen now.

Minutes later they heard a distant bird call. Talon immediately stood up and shot an arrow high into the air toward the gates of the fort. He knew it was a long way for his bow, but his aim was good. The arrow landed with a hard thump on the top of the gates. There was a sharp exclamation on the walls and then a shout. Men peered down at the arrow and there were more shouts.

Talon seized Aicelina by the wrist, pulled Guillaume onto his back and they ran. The grass was wet from the dew which made it slippery but their strides were long and they ran for their lives.

Talon began to yell as they neared the gates. "Open the gates! We are Talon and Aicelina. Open the gates!"

They were about eighty yards off by then and the men on the wall were pointing toward them and shouting. Others turned and ran to open the gates but then other men pointed at the south end where some men were coming out of the woods; these men were about a hundred and fifty yards off when they emerged from the cover of the woods. Talon glanced off to where the men on the battlements were pointing, there were only two horsemen now but they were galloping hard and were followed by others on foot, crossbow men who ran very fast in spite of their cumbersome weapons.

Talon saw Belth on the walls and then heard his father's roar from within the fort and the gates began to open. Aicelina was running hard now just in front of him while he was beginning to feel the weight of his brother.

Panting now, Talon dropped his brother to his feet. "Run for your life, brother."

Guillaume squeaked something but then scampered after Aicelina, who paused to grab his hand and run as fast as she could toward the open gates, her skirts flying. Talon glimpsed her as she glanced back at him, but then the urgency of his own situation took all his attention.

He hurriedly notched an arrow and turned to face the oncoming horsemen. The nearest was only forty yards away by now and looked enormous on his huge horse. He was tucked deep into the saddle and well protected by his shield. He had a fearsome-looking lance aimed directly at Talon. The ground seemed to shake as the horseman came toward him.

Talon aimed deliberately at the oncoming horse. He loosed his arrow at twenty yards and it buried itself deep into the chest of the galloping animal. At the same time another arrow buried itself deep into the rider's right side. Belth had shot his arrow from the battlements. The horse nosed over in a somersault, tossing the its dead rider almost at Talon's feet.

Talon dodged the dead man's shield that flew past him to bounce once and then slam into the wall of the fort with a metallic clang. He looked around desperately for the other rider and saw that that man was also down, with two arrows in his back. The Welshmen in the woods had taken care of him. His horse was standing loose not far away. Talon could see the crossbow men shooting at the woods, but they were also trying to make their escape—they were now caught in a crossfire from the woods and the fort.

He turned to look up at the fort. The men on the walls were shouting and cheering and the gates were open. His father, mounted on his horse, followed by Philip and Max, rode out brandishing their swords. They galloped past with yells of greeting to Talon and then set about chasing the luckless crossbow men around the field, slashing at their running figures with their swords until none were left standing.

Talon didn't watch the end. He made his way tiredly through the gates to where his mother was standing, clutching Guillaume, holding him tight to her with one arm while she held onto a very ragged Aicelina, who was crying with relief. Even Guillaume had forgotten himself and was whimpering into his mother's skirts.

They looked up as Talon came in and he found himself in the middle of a collective embrace. Everyone was talking at once and there were more tears from his mother. This time a shaking Aicelina was also weeping.

Eventually they parted and Marguerite looked at Talon with tear-filled eyes. "I thank the Lord God for his kindness, he has been kind and has delivered you and your brother and Aicelina back to me. Now, Aicelina, you must get out of those soaking clothes and do the same for Guillaume or you will all die of cold, and then all will have been for nothing," she scolded them. "Talon, you look and smell like a badger, do you want a bath? You will take this brother with you and make sure he is bathed, too. Then I want to hear all about this adventure. Aicelina tells me that you rescued her from the castle of my uncle? Dear Lord and his Saints be my witness but that perfidious man has gone beyond all redemption now," she gasped out, her hand on her heart.

Just as she finished Sir Hughes and Sir Philip with Max right behind them came trotting in through the gates. They were followed by Drudwas and Devonalt. The men were exultant and grinning with their victory.

Without getting off his horse, Sir Hughes called over to the group by the hall doors. "We took care of the vermin, I don't think any got away. Talon, are you all right?"

Talon nodded. "I am fine, Father, and right glad to see you again. Hello, Uncle and Max. Drudwas, Devonalt, and Belth, thank you for your help. It was a bit close out there."

There were chuckles at that from the Welshmen and the onlookers gathered around.

"I think you were in more trouble from that shield the man tossed at you, m'lord!" Belth laughed. "It fair shook the walls of the fort when it struck, it did!"

Talon grinned at the memory and clapped him on the back. "Thank you, my friend," he said.

"Your Welshmen continue to make a good account of themselves, Talon. I hope you can pay them," Philip laughed.

"I am more concerned about Gareth and Ap-Maddock right now, Uncle. They led the hunting hounds away from us into the forest."

"Don't you be worrying about them, m'lord," Devonalt said. "Gareth is a clever man in the woods; they will be safe enough, God willing."

Indeed, almost as he completed the statement there was a shout from the ramparts over the gate. "The archers are coming, m'lord."

Chapter 11

A Swineherd

Talon held a family conference after an exhausted sleep and waking up when the sun was almost down in the west. The story of how Aicelina and Guillaume had been captured came out during the meeting. The two had been walking only a mile from the fort on the other side of the village. They were looking for mushrooms, hedgerow asparagus, and other plants, something they had done often before without any fear.

Horsemen had suddenly appeared on the wide path that led back to the village which was a good mile away. Sensing that they meant harm, Aicelina had seized Guillaume by the hand and tried to run toward the village and safety, but after a short chase they had been stopped as one of the horsemen rode in front of them, barring their way. Marcel had then revealed himself; they were all now standing in a small clearing in the wood next to the track.

He had stared down at them from his horse with a sneer on his face.

"Well look what we have found here, a maid and her babe," he had said with satisfaction.

Aicelina had been frightened, but had stood her ground with Guillaume at her side and faced him. She had demanded to know what he wanted and he had pointed to Guillaume. She had told him that he had no right to take the boy but Marcel had dismounted, thrown his reins to another rider and walked right up to her.

"It is not your place to tell me what I can or cannot do." he had snarled and then struck her hard on the side of her face with his gloved fist, knocking her down.

Aicelina confessed that there was little she remembered after that until they were dismounting in Guillabert's castle courtyard. She then went on to tell the assembled family and friends how Talon had rescued them and then the long night in the woods. Guillaume, who was there with them, piped up on occasion to correct a detail in the story that he felt was important.

There was a silence when she finished her tale. The assembled family and retainers were appalled at what they heard and even more so at the information that Talon imparted after Aicelina had finished.

Sir Hughes and Philip were raging with anger and demanded that he repeat several times what the bishop had said. Talon had not mentioned the threat against Guillaume. He was going to take care of that in his own time.

"Unfortunately, we have no proof other than your word, Talon," his father said kindly, patting him on the knee to take the sting out of the comment. "We will need more than that for the court, I'm afraid. But where Guillabert is concerned he is now my sworn enemy and God help him if he comes near here again. I am sorry, my dear," he said turning to his wife, "but your cousin and his sons have gone too far this time for me to forgive them."

Marguerite nodded. "I am forced to agree with you. Reluctant as I am to have a blood feud within the family, they leave us no option, God save us." Her face was pale and she sounded very sad as she said this.

Talon stood up and came over to her. "Mother, they have not treated you as family since you came back from *Outré Mere*. You owe them nothing, and now Guillabert has contemplated the murder of our family. That man has an evil heart and so does the bishop." He put his arm around her to comfort her and she leaned against him as though seeking support.

There was a lively discussion between the members of the family after this, even Gareth and Max were involved as they all debated the question about what to do about the grievous affront to them. It was clear to everyone that to rush off and lay siege to Guillabert's castle would be futile as they could barely muster enough men to man their own fort, let alone attack Guillabert in his lair.

Talon swore to himself that he would take care of the matter in his own way when the time came, but he did not discuss that with anyone.

Sir Hughes made certain that from then on no one from the family strayed far and that if they needed to go even just to the village, they must have an escort.

Life resumed at the fort and there was time for Talon to take his ease and enjoy the remains of the summer. Most of the Welshmen were out in the forest scouting for intruders; Sir Hughes did not want a repeat of the incident with Marcel. So far, after a week, they reported that there seemed to be no one in the woods who should not have been there.

Talon accompanied them when they went once to the edge of the forest and watched the activity at Guillabert's castle, but all seemed quiet there, too, although it was far better guarded than before. Sir Hughes and Sir Philip reasoned that Guillabert was nursing his wounds and most probably he had been cautioned by the bishop to take no further action for the time being.

They all sobered at the thought of the court case to come. The bishop was now declared to be on Guillabert's side and as they did not have any support from any other quarter, the situation looked bleak. But Sir Philip came up with an idea that seemed to have some merit. He told them that he had to go to Carcassonne and pay his respects to the Captain of the Order.

"Perhaps I will be able to get an audience with the Count and present our side to him?" he suggested hopefully.

After a private discussion aside with his brother, Sir Hughes addressed Talon. "I need you to go to Carcassonne for me. Philip is going to the Temple house there, and I think it would be a useful thing for you to be seen at the court. Philip will be paying his respects to the Count and I want to have you presented at the court on my behalf. I dare not leave our home under present circumstances but if you go with Philip in my place and explain the situation I am sure he will understand. I and Philip think that it is time to ask for some help if it is possible from the Count himself."

Philip nodded, smiling. "We shall leave in a day or so, Talon. Make sure you pack your best clothes. I have some business with the Temple and then we have to attend the court for a short while and pay our respects to the Count. Perhaps he will hear our case and provide some support." He smiled at Talon's surprised look. "We will go to pay homage to the Count of Carcassonne, my boy. Your father is expected to do this once a year at the very least. We will leave in a couple of days."

"Will it not be dangerous to leave with the situation as it is, Father?"

"You have a good point, Talon, but I shall have the Welshmen as my scouts to warn me if there is any treachery afoot. I do not think that Guillabert will make his move until after the court case. We will be safe enough if we are careful and no one wanders off too far."

"You will enjoy Carcassonne, Talon," said his mother. "It is a huge city, larger even than Paris. At least I hear it is. Beware of the intrigues of the court, my boy, particularly the maidens. They are as wolves and will snap a young man up within a minute." She pretended to look severe.

"Yes, Mother I shall be careful," Talon said dutifully and with a playful grin.

Sir Hughes chuckled. "Your mother is not interested in the lively world of the Carcassonne court. My dear, I swear that your life in the Kingdom of Jerusalem has turned you into a prude. He is going to the court of love." Hughes leaned toward her on the bench and tried to kiss her but got a gentle slap for his pains.

Marguerite bustled out cheerfully, calling for Aicelina. The men were left alone to discuss the journey and what might be said to the Count of Carcassonne should an audience be granted.

Talon later made his way out of the hall, having decided to bathe at the stream where he had been fishing with his brother. It was a warm August day and the thought of taking a dip in the cool waters was very appealing. He could not find Guillaume whom he assumed to have hidden, knowing that his brother wanted to throw him into a bath. Neither had he seen Aicelina, so he figured it was a good time to take advantage of their absence.

The pool he had in mind was deep, so that he could plunge into it and later perhaps tickle a trout out of it. Few came this far into the wooded hills so he was fairly sure of his privacy.

He told his men that he was going for a walk in the woods and not to worry about him, then walked out of the gates unobtrusively. His men by now knew that he could more than care for himself in the forest so they let him go unescorted without demure. Once clear of the village he headed up the slope to where he and Guillaume had spent happy days fishing through the midsummer weeks. It was now August and the forest hummed with insects and was sleepy with the summer heat.

He heard his name called behind him and looked back. Aicelina was hastening after him up the slope. He waved and then waited until she caught up with him slightly breathless and flushed from the climb.

"That takes care of my bath." He sighed but he was glad to see her nonetheless.

"Talon, are you going for a walk in the wood? I would accompany you." She seemed to blush. "It is not safe for me to be on my own in the forest now," she added by way of explanation.

He smiled awkwardly. "Of course you are welcome to walk with me. I shall be glad of the company. But how did you leave without mother or someone knowing?"

"I talked to Gareth and he told me to hurry and I would catch up with you, which would be safer for me." She smiled disarmingly.

He smiled at that.

Despite the fact that he wanted a bath he had no objection to her company, welcoming the unexpected interruption.

They walked on in silence. It was some way to the stream, nearly a mile in all, so they went slowly, enjoying the warm day. Despite this Talon was vigilant and trod carefully, keeping off the main paths; he did not want to be surprised by Marcel's mercenaries.

They disturbed a fox that had been sunning itself in a glade as they walked by. The sleek, red-coated animal got up lazily and ambled off into denser cover. They did not pause but moved quietly along the faint animal track until they were following the banks of the stream. Aicelina stayed close but said nothing, seeming to be content with just keeping near. He still intended go to the pool by the river as it was a quiet place where they could sit and enjoy the late summer warmth.

The woods were thin here, allowing the sun to break through, leaving a dappled pattern on the forest floor, and the light was warm on his face as he walked. He put out his hand to steady her at one point. She gave hers to him and he enjoyed the feel of her cool fingers as they slipped into his palm. Then it seemed natural for them to stay hand in hand.

They heard a splash as they came to the crest of the bank where the pool was. Both of them froze, startled, then crouched instinctively. Talon drew his sword and eased forward until he had a good view of pool and the surrounding banks. An otter was playing with its mate in the cool, deep water.

He smiled and indicated the playing pair to Aicelina, who eased forward to lie next to him and she too watched them cavorting and laughed silently. He liked her good teeth and her smile tugged at him.

The animals must have sensed that they were being watched because they slipped out of the water and with a backward glance in their direction wandered off into the undergrowth on the other side of the pool.

Aicelina stood up, as did Talon, but she walked to the pool and before his disbelieving eyes began to take off her long dress. The sun sparkled through the tree branches around the pool in warm patches. She was standing in one so he had a clear view as the sun lit her face and arms. Then her dress was over her head, followed by her shift and then she stood naked in front of him. The sunlight was full on her, illuminating her full round breasts with the dark nipples sharply defined against her white skin. His eyes strayed without a will of their own down her ribcage to her smoothly formed belly to the dark patch between her thighs. The long thighs tapered to two slim knees. He suddenly wanted to touch her and stroke those legs. She was well formed and slender. He had liked her slim ankles before and now his admiring eyes could do the same for the rest of her. Her long hair, which came down to her waist, was unbound and spread over her back.

Aicelina broke into his lustful thoughts. She looked at him and said as though she had divined his intent from the first, "Talon, did you not come to bathe, too?"

Then she was in the water, while he still stood on the bank admiring her form from behind. He felt a stirring in his groin that would not be stilled. She was humming to herself a troubadour song, and to his surprise he remembered the song from the time they had spent at the fair.

Talon was quite unsure of what to do. He stood on the bank and stared at her like a gaping yokel as she stood in the water up to her waist. All the while he was admiring the symmetry of her breasts and her taut stomach.

Aicelina turned toward him her hands covering her breasts self consciously said. "Talon, come into the water, I shall not bite." Her lips were curled into a little hesitant smile of encouragement.

Talon moved to the bank and began to undress. Aicelina regarded him frankly and without embarrassment; it was somewhat disconcerting. He eased himself into the cool water and sank gratefully into it.

She was only a few feet away and smiled at him. "You smelt like a rabbit when you came back from the castle. I approve of you bathing; few men seem to hereabouts, and your little brother is a badger about it."

Despite a twinge of guilt Talon could not help it, he laughed. She did, too. It broke the tension.

"I shall wash your back if you wish?" she offered, moving toward him, no longer covering herself and he could admire her more closely.

"How beautiful is the female form," he said.

She smiled at that but didn't answer, by then she was looking at his scars with wide eyes. "Did the lion do this to you?"

He nodded, then she was close and pushing him gently around so that she could wash his back.

The sensation of her hands on him was delicious, she had brought some kind of soap with her that she had taken out of one of her pockets before going into the water and this she now moved over his skin. He could not help it—the effect upon him was spectacular and he was becoming acutely embarrassed. He suffered the gentle torture for as long as possible while she washed him with hands that seemed to explore. Then he turned in the water and she allowed his hands to stroke her. They explored each other; she traced his scars but he simply enjoyed the slippery feel of her skin as his curious fingers traced her contours. Finally, he could bear it no longer.

"Aicelina, I cannot endure this for much longer," he croaked.

By way of response she slipped her hands down to his groin and played gently with his manhood.

Talon put his arms around her back and held her close. He could feel the warmth of her but he also felt himself growing hard against her stomach. She smiled again, but this time it was an invitation that was unmistakable. She leaned back as though to see into his eyes. She looked a question, but then he saw a kind of decision in her expression and she nodded. He bent toward her and kissed her right breast. Aicelina gave a low moan. Then he kissed her on the mouth, enjoying the soft, pliant feel of her unresisting lips.

Talon scooped her up in his arms and carried her to the bank. He laid her down on the tumbled clothes he had only just shed and lay down alongside her. The sun patch they lay within warmed their wet skin.

He leaned over her and tentatively kissed her again on her slightly parted lips. She reached for him, placed both hands on either side of his head and gripped his hair lightly.

They kissed long and deeply, holding one another in a light embrace. He drew away to then lean forward and kiss her in the hollow of her neck. She sighed and her hands moved to his back to tighten and encourage more. He began to caress her fair skin with gentle and wondering fingers, enjoying her curves and her responses to his movements. She lay quietly with her eyes half shut, seeming to be willing to abandon herself to his caresses. Her nipples became taut and she gasped when he kissed them, her eyes flying open.

Then she laughed softly into his amused eyes. It was not long before her passion grew and she pushed his willing hand downward toward the light bush at the junction of her long legs. Talon brought her to a point of trembling ecstasy, her body undulating under the gentle ministrations of his fingers. He was enjoying the giving of pleasure to this girl who gave herself to him freely without condition.

She gasped again and cried out, pulling him up over her. "Talon, please. I want you. Oh, yes," she cried as they came together. They lay quietly locked in this embrace for a long moment, savoring the union and then she began to move her hips as did he. They moved together slowly, he looked into her eyes, seeing them gradually widen as she began to feel the surge within her. Suddenly, she arched her back, clasping his arms, her lips slightly parted as she began to abandon herself to the sensations growing surely within her. They moved into one another more urgently toward a climax that left Aicelina crying out as she clutched at him in the throes of her passion.

They lay together for long moments when it was over, both reluctant to move. Talon finally rolled over onto his back and she shifted her head into the crook of his left arm, laying her head on his shoulder. A shaft of sunlight broke through the dark clouds gathering over head and warmed them as they lay together. Talon was sleepily enjoying the fresh scent of her hair when she murmured something.

Talon half turned, "What did you say?"

"I said that you are a very gentle lover. For a man who is such a fighter, you are truly a gentle knight."

Then she said something that almost made him sit up.

"I know there is not love between us, but I wanted to give of myself. Your mother told me of the Persian Princess and since then I can see that you wear your love of another on your sleeve."

"I-I am sorry, Aicelina," he stammered.

"Do not be sorry. I enjoyed the loving; and you are a very good lover. Women of Languedoc have the right to their own bodies. We can share with whom we wish... within reason," she added as an afterthought. She lifted her head suddenly. "You do not think ill of me for doing so?"

He grinned at her. "I am still bemused at the wondrous gift you have given me. How can I think ill of you?"

She nodded solemnly then, glancing up at the darkening sky, said briskly, "I could wish for more but it grows late and will rain very soon. We should go back to the fort or they will worry."

Talon realized reluctantly that she was right. They dressed hurriedly.

The light was rapidly leaving the forest; the ominous darkness preceding a storm was making the glade dark and cold. Almost as he thought about the possibility there was a crack of thunder and it began to rain.

Talon looked around for some cover and could only see a large overhang off to the side of the glade about fifty feet away through the trees where they might be able to shelter from the fury of the storm. He pointed to it and gestured that they should try to get under there.

She gathered up her long skirts in her left hand and seized Talon's with her other. They ran laughing in the rain toward the overhang, splashing though filling puddles of water along the way.

They came with a rush up against the rock wall of the overhang but it provided poor shelter from the lashing rain. He looked at her; by now their clothes were almost soaked. She brushed her hair back from her face and laughed up at him. He grinned back with a rush of affection for her—not much seemed to disturb her.

Talon released Aicelina and stood back from the rock, once again in the rain, looking around it to see if there was some better place for them. There was by now a wind blowing that lashed the tops of the trees and bushes all around. As he stood there Talon caught a glimpse of a darkness that showed momentarily in the wall of the cliff as the shrubs and small trees were waving to and fro to his right.

He splashed over toward it, leaving Aicelina cowering under the inadequate shelter of the overhang. She must have decided that she would rather be with him as she abandoned it and skipped over to his side as he investigated the opening—for that is what it was, an entrance to some kind of low cave. He pushed through the bushes at the entrance and, taking her hand, led the way at a crouch into the dry darkness that greeted them. Abruptly the noise of the storm became muted and they crouched in the low entrance watching the pouring rain and the wind lash the forest outside.

There was a dry, musty smell coming from behind them as though this overhang might have once been the lair of an animal. Curious, Talon turned and stared into the darkness behind him; he could see very little but what the lightning illuminated made him start. He squinted at an object lying just in front of him and moved toward it. He gingerly lifted the small bundle up to inspect it more closely. It was an old leather shoe, badly chewed by some animal, but inside it were some bones.

Aicelina gasped and made a hurried sign of he cross over her breast when she saw it and then pointed deeper into the low depths of the cave. There were more bones scattered about with some shreds of coarse cloth still clinging to them. His eyes had now become used to the darkness and he could see farther. He felt a trickle of superstitious fear and the hairs on his forearms tingled.

Stooping low, Talon stepped carefully over the scattered bones and saw in the back of the cave a skull lying near a small pile of rags. There were still a few strands of hair attached to it, the empty eye sockets stared back at him, and the lower jaw was nearby in two pieces. It was clear some animals had chewed on the dead person's carcass after he or she had died.

Talon felt the hair on his neck prickle and also made the sign of the cross, then turned to see if Aicelina was all right. She had retreated to the entrance and was watching him with fearful eyes. The natural superstition of being near a dead person was frightening even this courageous girl.

"I don't like it here. We should go now," she pleaded in a whisper.

He nodded. "This must have been a vagabond or some wanderer who died here."

But his curiosity was still strong. He squatted next to the skull, looking down at it, wondering how lonely a death this had to be. With no one to shrive the poor soul or act as a companion and stay in attendance while death crept up to lay his icy hand upon him, it must have been a lonely death, indeed. He glanced down to the pitiful pile of rags nearby and his attention was caught by a badly chewed leather bag lying among them. Rats had gnawed at the leather, creating a hole from which something had spilled out.

He put his hand out to touch it and realized it was something metallic. The small pile chinked as his hand disturbed it. He gathered up the frayed but heavy bag careful not to allow anything else to drop out and took it toward the opening to see more clearly what he had discovered. Aicelina leaned over his shoulder as he again squatted and poured some of the contents out onto the floor at the entrance to the cave. The storm had abated somewhat and there was some light left from the day. Coins and rings of indeterminate origin, blackened with time, fell in an untidy pile in front of them. One rolled to Aicelina's feet.

She picked it up and gasped. "Talon! It is money or some such thing. I have never seen so much. What's it doing here?"

"I don't know, Aicelina, but we must get back to the fort before it's totally dark. I'll take this with me."

He went back into the cave and hurriedly gathered up the remaining coins scattered about and placed them back in the leather bag. He muttered a quick prayer to the ghost of the dead person and then left. He glanced out of the cave and led the way out onto the small grass swathe surrounded by trees. They walked quickly toward the stream and pool. Glancing back, Talon could see no evidence of the cave from where they stood. The undergrowth hid its secret from prying eyes once again.

As they walked away from the stream Talon spotted in the gloom several different types of mushrooms half hidden among some grass close to an old rotten log.

He pointed at them. "Are those edible, Aicelina?"

"No," she exclaimed, pointing to some. "Those are very poisonous; just one will kill an ox. Some folk dry those others over there and put them in a soup—this makes them dream. Too much and a person has bad dreams, while a small amount will make them very happy and they become fools. Look over there! A septus; do you see it? The very big brown one; we will take for the pot. They are delicious with eggs."

She plucked the huge mushroom and placed it in the pocket of her sodden skirts. Not wanting to let their time run out so fast, he drew her toward him. He held her for a few long moments within the circle of his arms, her head on his breast, then it was time to go. She kissed him and put her hand on his arm and they walked back to the fort, which was in a state of alarm as people had missed them and were very concerned.

Marguerite scolded them both and told Aicelina to go get dry clothes before she turned to Talon and said in an agitated voice. "Where have you two been? We are all at odds because it is dusk and you came back so late! You of all people should know that it's dangerous to be out late in the forest. You had me so worried for you and Aicelina."

Talon wanted more than anything to distract this line of questioning, so he said quickly, "We were out looking for mushrooms and were caught in the storm, but look. I have something to show you."

He went into the darkened hall, took hold of a candle as he went and walked to one of the tables, where he let the bag drop onto the surface. It chinked noisily as it landed and a small coin rolled out of the hole in its side.

Marguerite put her hand to her mouth. "Whatever have you found?"

"Could this be the silver that your father was supposed to have lost, Auntie?" Aicelina asked, she had not left despite the scolding. However she did now have a blanket over her shoulders.

Talon lifted the bag and poured the remaining contents out. A stream of blackened metallic objects chinked and clattered onto the table. He pushed them together to form a good sized pyramid.

Marguerite called sharply to one of the housemaids to bring Sir Hughes and his brother. "Anna, come here," she called to another, older-looking maid who came walking shakily from the other end of the hall. The old maid, bent with age, stared at the pile of coins and rings on the table.

She gasped. "Oh, my dear Lord God save us! Where did you find those?" she asked.

"In the forest," Aicelina responded. "In a small cave, with a dead person's bones nearby; we were looking for mushrooms when the storm came," she added with a glance at Talon from under her eyebrows, who looked away, having trouble with a smile.

Anna made the sign of the cross over her breast. "Then it's true," she whispered. "May God have mercy on his soul."

"What in the Saint's good name are you talking about, Anna?" Marguerite asked sharply.

"My lady," the old woman quavered, "did you not know that your father had a store of silver hidden somewhere before he died?"

Marguerite shrugged. "It was but a rumor. No one believed it and none has ever been found... until perhaps now," she added uncertainly.

By this time Sir Hughes and Sir Philip, accompanied by Max and Gareth, had come into the hall to see what the excitement was about. They still wore their cloaks, damp from the rain, their boots muddy. Guillaume had also rushed in and was trying to get his hands on the pieces lying on the table.

His mother slapped his probing hand gently to dissuade him. "Not now, Guillau'; leave them alone."

They all stared down at the pile on the table in awe. The light from the candle gleamed off the edges of the coins, many crudely stamped with heads and words.

"Is this silver?" Sir Hughes asked, picking a piece up and rubbing it between thumb and forefinger.

"It is, m'lord," Anna said with some confidence.

"Why do you say that, Anna?" Sir Hughes asked.

"Do you know who the person was that we found with these?" Talon asked.

"Frobert the swineherd, m'lord." She looked frightened.

"It's all right, my dear, tell us what you know," Marguerite said gently.

Anna sat down heavily on the bench nearby and composed herself. They all gathered around to listen; behind them were many others who had heard the disturbance and were eager to know more.

Anna looked at Marguerite. "M'lady, your father was a good man and careful with his money. There never was a lot to be had, but the mills were a good provider. He ran the river and the ferry well and made sure that no one cheated him. In time it became known that he had stored some silver away for the hard times. He would always help the villagers when the harvest was poor. May our saintly mother Mary bless him and take him to her bosom, for he deserved it."

She paused for breath, crossed herself and then continued. "But all his silver could not protect him from the plague when it came. I remember it well; the summer was cold, there was much rain, which is not at all usual here, and there were many rats. Far more than normal, they seemed to be everywhere and the men and dogs could not kill them all. They seemed to herald the plague.

"God have mercy and forgive me, m'Lady, but when it came we were so afraid we all fled. Your father stayed, already abed with the fever. He told me to leave as he knew full well what he had. His mind was clear but his body was wracked with agony. Frobert said he would care for him as he did not fear the death. I still do not know why Frobert should stay as there was no particular bond that I know of between My Lord and the Swineherd.

"We did not come back until months had passed, as the plague lingers on, and we knew not what had become of your father."

She fell silent, then continued slowly.

"When we came back there were few left; the plague had followed many into town and field where they died like animals. There was your poor dead father still in his bed, just his bones. We gave him a decent burial, although only I and one of the field hands would pick up his remains and place them in the grave where he lies today.

"Of Frobert there was no sign at all, so I believed that he had fled, too, and perhaps would come home one day, but after a while I thought he might have died somewhere. Indeed, he did, but he must have found the silver and took it with him. He was punished for his sins. May God have mercy on his poor soul. The plague followed him even to where you found him. He would often, in safer times, take the swine into the forest to feed them. He knew the forest right well."

Talon looked at Aicelina, who stared back with frightened eyes.

"You mean he died of the plague, Anna?" he asked slowly.

"I cannot think of what else would have slain him. In those days men stayed clear of other men; they did not dare to even rob them there was such fear in the land."

Talon looked down at his hands and then again at Aicelina. "Could the plague still be on the bones?" he asked.

"That I know not, m'lord. It has been several years since it left us."

Talon turned to his mother. "I want to have a bath immediately, and then Aicelina's and my clothes should be burned. I have touched the bones and this bag belonged to the swineherd. I was taught that if there is disease around, then to contain it one must clean oneself and burn the clothes."

He noticed that everyone had drawn back from him and mentally shrugged. So be it; he was now in the hands of God.

His mother, not lacking in courage, chased everyone out of the hall except Talon and Aicelina and bade the servants to go and get hot water prepared.

Later, a well-scrubbed Talon in new clean clothes watched as the old ones were burnt along with Aicelina's dress. They stood together, somehow brought even closer by the situation they found themselves in.

The silver was cleaned by the reluctant servants who were afraid that something from the dead swineherd might linger on the silver as a curse; yet it was examined with awe by Sir Hughes and his family. Talon realized his father was now reasonably wealthy. He didn't know it, but he already was even before Talon found the silver. Talon had never revealed how much gold he personally possessed. He had intended to disclose his secret when the time was right, but the opportunity had not as yet presented itself.

This was the gold he had had on him when he was captured by the Templars back in Palestine at the castle of Montfort. This had been the gold that he and Rav'an had brought with them as they came to seek the Agha Khan. He was aware that their combined monies made them rich and resolved to tell his father as soon as possible. The opportunity came sooner than he had thought.

Sir Hughes, ever the generous man, wanted to give some of the silver to Talon who flatly refused it, saying he had gold of his own from the Holy Land and would share that with his father when the time came to rebuild the castle out of stone. His father had been puzzled by the statement, but Philip confirmed it when his brother discussed it with him later on.

"Your son has gold that he brought back from his adventures in the infidel countries, Hughes. He has no need for any of the silver. Keep it and build a castle to protect your family. This fort is not a fit place for one such as you. Talon will for sure share his wealth to make a castle of stone for you and the family. Our family deserves better than this miserable fortress."

For Talon the relationship with Aicelina was now permanently changed, but she was as cool as ever the following days. They did sit and talk more often, which he enjoyed, but she made no effort to invite him to her bed during this time. He wanted to know more about her faith and she began to open up to him slowly.

"The people of our faith are Christians," she insisted, "but we were not of the Church of Rome, and in fact disapprove of its path. I am angered at the corruption of the bishop of Albi," she exclaimed, and Talon could not disagree with her. "To my people, our faith in God is of the light. The evil ways of men that the church often seems to sanction is contrary to our beliefs."

"But where are your churches and places of worship?"

"We worship in the fields and woods and our houses. There are no bishops, but there are Bons Homes who are elected to be leaders in conferences."

"What of the women? Are they bonded to the men, too, as in other societies?"

She looked uncomfortable at that. "Women in all societies are bonded to their husbands, it is true, and this is the God-given way. And it is true, women are considered unclean to the men of our faith and the Bons Homes are not supposed to consort with them."

He looked bewildered so she shrugged and told him that it was complicated and that they would have to talk some more about it one day. They were interrupted as usual by Guillaume who'd been on the lookout for Talon and wanted to play at archery. Talon left with a backward smile at Aicelina, who waved him off and turned back to her duties.

Talon thought about it as he practiced with Guillaume and helped him with his bow. He was interested in the fact that these people did not feel the necessity to be bound to the Church of Rome, even though the Church seemed to be involved in every facet of life. It appealed to him all the more, not least because he had been raised in part by the free-thinking Ismaili, who were also considered heretics by the other two Muslim sects.

Talon spent time with his archers, making sure that Gareth kept up the patrols in the forest and ensuring that no strangers came anywhere near the castle without his knowledge. They all agreed that they did not want to be surprised nor discomforted by another visit from Marcel and his roving band.

Gareth had appointed one man to be close to Aicelina and Guillaume at all times. They did not discuss these arrangements with either Sir Hughes or Marguerite as Talon did not want to worry his father nor mother unduly, but he was concerned enough about the threat he had heard to safeguard them.

However, the raids on the outlying farms had stopped, which gave them hope that Guillabert was staying low and waiting for the trial.

There had been a training program going on during the last few weeks. Talon had, with Sir Hughes' permission, gathered volunteers from among the villagers who wanted to become men-at-arms. The fort's few retainers who had been men-at-arms, with Max leading and giving shouted directions, as well as the Welsh-men all worked hard to bring them up to some standard where at least they could hold a pike and even shoot a bow in two cases. Feremundus was put to work making spearheads and blades and went at it willingly with the help of the boys and other men.

"It's not much of a defense if Sir Guillabert decides to come and visit," Talon told Gareth morosely.

His friend nodded equally soberly. Some of the recruits were dressed in the captured hauberks and helmets, a couple of which were oversized for their occupants, making them look all the more ridiculous. Talon and Gareth watched them stumble about in the muddy field in front of the fort with pitchforks and the odd pike as Max tried patiently to move them forward in straight lines or to form defensive positions.

"We are indeed very thin on the ground, Talon, Bach. But go you and see that prince or Count of yours, and tell him what you know and may be *he* can do something."

Chapter 12

Carcassonne

A few days later Talon, Max, and Sir Philip left with a tiny escort: Anwl and a groom. They made good progress and arrived within view of the city late in the evening of the third day. It was clear that this was the seat of power for Talon had plenty of time to observe the countryside as they rode. Most of the roads were simple tracks except when they ran along a former Roman road. Then it became paved with great flat slabs but sometimes even here, because nothing was maintained, that became a problem as the great stones were rising at odd angles from the earth, often broken, making it difficult to ride past them.

They came down from the high hills above Mas Carbardes and from the slopes when Philip pointed to a distant blur on the low slopes many miles away.

"That is the city of Carcassonne, Talon."

They had yet to cross the wide, flat plain that the city dominated. As they rode, Talon found that more and more the distant city seemed to rise above them. It was situated on the northern slopes of the foothills that eventually led to the Pyrenees. These distant mountain peaks gleamed with a crest of snow in the sunlight.

Traffic increased as they drew near to the city. Several roads converged upon the wider road that led to the gates, where carts and wagons drawn by slow oxen moved too slowly for the mounted men who had to ride around them. Talon noted that other riders paid scant respect to the peasants, often shouting abuse as they rode by. The peasants, often too poor to be dressed in anything other than one overshirt and a leather cap or straw hat were, it seemed, unable to respond for risk of a beating from the riders, so they shrugged and hunched their shoulders stoically.

Philip and Max seemed oblivious of the peasants, but not Talon.

He noticed that once when a particularly unpleasant knight had gone by a group of carters and their wagons, the carters shared a joke at his expense, followed by sardonic laughter and accompanied by discreet obscenities with their hands. The particular group that he was observing suddenly noticed him watching them and hurriedly adopted the normal pose assumed by the peasantry, servile and downcast.

The carter's wife, though, stared back up at Talon with frightened eyes as though she knew they had stepped well out of bounds and been caught. As they rode by Talon grinned down at the cart driver, nodded and winked. The man after a brief moment of surprise grinned back a black-toothed smile of relief.

The small group paused on a hillside that gave them a view of the city. The evening sun was lighting the walls and battlements of the city in a golden glow. Talon was struck by the magnificent fortifications, among the best he had ever encountered. This was without doubt the largest city he had seen in Christendom thus far. It made Albi and the other fortified towns he knew look rustic by comparison. This matched anything that existed in the world he had been familiar with in the *Outré Mere*. Philip turned to Talon and pointed. "This is one of the great cities of the Languedoc lands, and that includes the kingdom of France and England, I would wager."

"Indeed, it would seem so, Uncle; the ruler of this city must be as rich and powerful as a king."

"Yes, he is a powerful man, but still he is not a king. He is a Count and Viscount of many areas of the Languedoc and indeed Albi, our nearest town and region. Henry of England would like to have this city and indeed Toulouse for his own to add to his already extensive holdings of Aquitaine, but he failed to take it not so long ago. Just the once our own king managed to outwit the fox himself and hold onto Toulouse. The politics are difficult in these parts." He scratched his side reflectively. "Well, we shall have to hurry or we will not be allowed in; the gates shut at Vespers. Come along."

There were the usual gibbets and iron cages along the slopes that led to the approaches to the city, most of them occupied by the skeletal remains of former criminals and traitors. The stench of the dead enveloped the riders who held cloths or their sleeves to their noses as they rode by. The horses would skitter with apprehension at the noisome stink. Talon could see heads in various states of decay along the gateway battlements. No one remarked on this, other than to hold their noses when the wind shifted in their direction.

The walls were at least fifty feet high and seemed to Talon, craning his neck, to be a hundred. They were well made of light-colored, well-fitted stone that gleamed in the evening sun. The towers with their pointed slate roofs, set at regular intervals along the walls, seemed to reach to the sky. Upon most of the towers were flags, but above the gates was the unmistakable banner of the Viscount of Carcassonne of the house of Tranceval and the Tranceval shield with three gold horizontal bars with rows of what appeared to Talon to be spearheads with three dots above them in between. He assumed these to be trees.

The walls had stout overhanging defenses of wood which Philip, who knew a thing or two about castles, told Talon were called hoardings. They had openings in the floor of the battlements for dropping stones or filth upon attackers' heads. Talon noted that there were slots for archers to fire directly down upon the luckless wretches sheltering at the base of the walls. His practiced eye told him that even he would find it difficult to scale these walls without a rope, although he wondered if Reza would be daunted by them. His Persian brother was like as spider on smooth surfaces. If he were to try for entry into this city he would probably have to use stealth and enter the gates in some disguise. He asked Philip why the walls sloped outward at their base, assuming it was simply to stabilize the walls.

"They drop big stones from the hoardings that strike the slope and then fly straight into the massed ranks of the enemy and can kill or maim many." Phillip told him.

They rode up to the angled gatehouse on the outside of the moat, which was actually a wide swathe of land dug out around the castle where grass was growing and men were exercising horses and practicing swordsmanship with one another at the base of the great walls.

Philip and his group waited in line for the traffic to ease before they could cross the narrow bridge constructed of stone with wooden floors that could be pulled up in the event of attack. As soon as the sentries saw the Templar uniforms they were admitted without even being questioned—once again Philip and Sergeant Max wore their own passport. Philip was a large man so he stood out among the crowd, looking imposing, and he was shown a lot of respect by the city guards as they rode by.

Max pointed out the murder holes in the arched roof above them as they rode under the gatehouse between two raised portcullises. "They can trap the assaulting troops between the two portcullis'. Then they open the roof above, see there?" He pointed up at the trap door above them. "That's where they roll rocks onto the luckless wretches or pour boiling water on their heads."

Talon thought about that for a minute and decided that this was a very modern, very defensible castle and city. He began to respect the engineering that had gone into the building of it. He reflected on the poor fort that his father lived in, and he decided that something had to be done about it. Between them they could afford to build a respectable stone keep that would have high outer walls and tall towers at least, nothing like this, but much more fitting for a man of Sir Hughes' stature.

They could have billeted in the Temple house which was very grand when compared with the one at Mass Dieu, but Philip wanted to stay at an Inn as that gave Talon more freedom of movement. Their lodgings were basic, but adequate, as far as Talon was concerned.

The next day Philip went off to pay his respects to the Master of the Temple House, taking Max with him. Max returned briefly to tell Talon to look around the city as they would be staying with the Master on Templar business, but he should be back by noon so that they could attend the court after their meal. The Master of the Temple House was going to take Philip with him and Talon was told to dress his best and to be present. He was left to look around with Anwl.

Talon enjoyed walking about the narrow streets, seeing how life in a town of this size carried on its daily life. The town seemed to be full of people moving in all directions; the crowds pushed and shoved cheerfully in the narrow, smelly lanes. The top floors of the houses leaned out over the streets so as to almost touch so that the light was somewhat limited. In a way that was good as some of the objects and piles lying in the center of the street and piled against the walls did not bear investigation, giving off such a stench that they made one's head ache.

It was a relief to come out into the wider space of the market square. There they saw a church with the foundations of a cathedral being constructed nearby. The construction site was swarming with laborers and masons working like ants, doing all the complicated things that were needed for the building of such places.

Talon led the way into the church to light a candle to Jean de Loche, his friend the priest in Persia, who had died there. He also prayed for his other friends and begged that God would allow him to return and find them. He had had no news of the two young people who meant so much to him since he left them. Their escape from Alamut, the sinister castle in the mountains of northern Persia, and their final meeting with the Agha Khan, had brought the three of them very close. Rav'an and Talon had even become lovers. Despite everything that he had encountered here in France these two were never far from his mind. But he was almost at the point where he mourned Rav'an because he could not imagine that she would be allowed to live if she carried his child.

Anwl was as agog as Talon at the sights and sounds all about them. He confided to Talon that Wales had no towns that were in any way comparable to this magnificent city, but he had heard that the English did. It was a city called London, where the English king lived. Perhaps another called Chester, but he wasn't sure. They were both appalled at the number of beggars who were to be seen everywhere on street corners or hobbling on crutches with one leg missing, dressed in foul-smelling rags. Most of these wretches seemed to be in dire straights; particularly the one or two lepers who were given a wide birth.

"We have no people like this in my country," Anwl exclaimed in disgust. "Will the Lord of this place not protect his own?"

"I don't know why it is so here, but where I lived in Persia there were also many beggars. I saw them in this huge city called Hamadan and again in Isfahan. These cities were much larger than this place, but still, the presence of beggars seems to be a part of city life." Talon reached for a copper to toss to a starving woman who clutched an equally thin and wasted child. "It would seem that they are to be found in every city. It is a curse."

"We do not have these kind of people in my land," Anwl stated firmly. "If a man is very poor there is always the tribe to protect him and give him work so he can hold his head up among other men."

There were an abundance of vendors and assorted stalls selling anything from flyblown meat off newly slaughtered goats, to rough, homespun woolen bolts, to fine cloth from abroad, and copper utensils. Men and women were shouting their wares to the world at large and calling to anyone who even glanced at them, trying to entice them to examine their produce. More than once a pretty maid would call out to the two men and sway her bosom at them in an unmistakable gesture that would draw envious looks from the men and appraisal from the other women. Anwl nudged Talon once and gave a gap-toothed grin as a girl who sold flowers sidled up to Talon and, as she placed a rose in his hand, kissed him on the cheek.

"What is a handsome young man doing on his own, in streets full of young maidens, and not one of them on your arm?" she cried amid the laughter all around.

Talon could only grin, his face red with embarrassment, and take her coarse, work-scarred hand and bow in a clumsy show of gallantry. This earned approving cheers and more lewd comments as to what he should do with the other hand. He tossed her a copper then they moved on.

He noticed that there were monks and priests aplenty here in this town. The abbot had explained to Talon that the priests who stayed in the cities were often men of education who served a bishop or a more powerful man like the Count, providing him with the means to correspond and stay abreast of events farther abroad.

"You should remember that monks take vows, but that's not always true for the men who look like priests. They are as often as not advocates, men of ambition and education who serve powerful men in the hope of advancement to some lucrative position with a bishopric as title," he had told Talon with a wry smile.

The city boasted large houses that he had not seen in Albi; only that of the Bishop of Albi's came close to the size of some of the new merchant houses here. He could see that there was real wealth in this city as the new men of means, the merchants, established themselves under the protection of the Count.

Before too long they heard the bells toll for the half hour before noon and rushed back to their inn. Hurriedly, Talon changed into his best clothes and prepared himself for the visit to the Palace of Count Roger de Tranceval, the Count of Carcassonne.

There were hurried introductions as Talon met the Master of the Temple, Sir Gualhart, then they were off at a brisk walk to the palace. The Knights wore their ceremonial garb, which consisted of white tunics known as surcoats with the red cross sewn onto the left breast over a full mail suit. They both also wore a white woolen cloak with red edging and again a red cross sewn onto the top left corner. The only difference it seemed to Talon was that the Master wore the same badge of office on his cloak as had the Master of Mas-Dieu. The two men wore pointed helmets that left the face clear, and had a distinctive eastern look with a cotton cloth wrapped around the helmet's base not unlike a turban. Templar dress had changed much since the beginnings, Philip informed Talon. They were among the few allowed to carry a sword into the council chamber of the Count.

Talon wore his green tunic with a new doublet his mother had cleaned up. It was well brushed and darned, but he was self-conscious in his tight-fitting hose. He wore neither cloak nor sword but carried a dagger hanging off his belt. His old calf-length boots were scruffy to say the least although he and Anwl had tried to bone them to some kind of a sheen with some goose fat and a goose thigh Anwl had obtained from the kitchens.

After a perfunctory examination they were admitted by the guards at the gate of the huge building. It was a fortification within the city walls themselves; and once again it was the Templar uniforms that were their passports.

Talon was struck by the beauty of the stone work. Craftsmen who knew and understood stone had done magnificent work on the arches and pillars that lined the passages within the confines of the palace. Everywhere he looked there were chiseled decorations on the pillars and over the doorways. There was wealth here; it was quite unlike the castles of the Holy Land which were massive, stark, defensive fortresses. Talon realized that this was a palace that was designed for living. Thus, while it had formidable defenses; within it people enjoyed the luxuries of life.

They continued through several more arched doorways, each with its liveried guards standing in full chain mail and helmets, pikes at the guard. Soon they came to a slightly smaller door that was made of thick, well carved oak, with two men standing in front of it wearing swords. They were not ordinary guards; instead, they were knights wearing the Count's livery—the same colors and forms that he had seen on the banner above the walls. After asking their business the one on the right opened the door and spoke quietly to someone within.

"This is the council chamber for the Count," the Master said in an aside to Philip.

The door was opened and they were announced loudly to a gathering inside the candlelit room. It was smoky and stuffy inside, and there were many people standing around on either side of the aisle they now walked down. In the dim light he noticed crowded aisles to the sides and that there were many pillars supporting a high, wood-beamed roof from which hung in great profusion banners and flags of different colors and insignia.

The Master of the Temple strode forward with Philip just one step behind, while Talon walked two paces behind them. They had to skirt the huge fireplace where smoldering logs burned.

At the far end of the hall sat a heavyset man on an ornately carved wooden chair raised on a dais. Standing in attendance were several knights, also a richly dressed man in clerical dress comprised of an over-cloak of fine dyed red wool with Church insignia. There were several other men in rich court clothing standing nearby. They all looked very important to the bemused Talon.

On either side of the aisle were men and women in the height of fashion. Many were dressed for riding—presumably the hunt in the morning had just finished—while others wore clothes befitting an elegant party. Talon became acutely aware of how shabby his clothing was by comparison, but he did not have much time to worry about it—they were fast approaching the man seated on the throne.

There had been a low murmur of voices as they entered which hushed as they came up to the throne.

The Count was an imposing, solid-looking figure; to Talon he seemed more suited to riding a horse than sitting at a table strewn with papers. His thick forearms, presently encased in tight-fitting silk sleeves, were lying at rest on the arms of the chair. But his strong hands were holding a parchment, not a sword. Talon thought he would be able to twirl a heavy sword should he have to.

The three men halted. Talon took his cue from his uncle and went on one knee and bowed his head, then they waited.

Roger de Tranceval, Viscount of Carcassonne, Razés, Albi, Nimes, Bézier and Agde, a man of enormous power second only to the Viscount of Toulouse in this whole region, observed the three men standing in front of him in silence for a moment or two; and then he said in a deep voice, "Master Gualhart, I greet you. Who is this you have brought with you today?"

The Master of the Temple straightened. "Greetings, Sire. I have brought one of my brethren of the Temple, Sir Philip de Gilles, who has of June this year arrived back from the Holy Land. With him is his nephew, Talon, who distinguished himself against some pirates who would have taken their ship. He thwarted the attempt with great courage and aforethought."

Talon heard a murmur on interest from those nearby who had heard the exchange.

The three of them were now standing in front of the seated Count.

"Greetings, Sir Philip, and welcome to my court. I look forward to hearing of the Holy land," said the Count, then glanced at Talon. "Stand forward, Talon, nephew of Sir Philip, so we can see you." Talon stepped forward in front of the Master and Sir Philip and bowed low.

"Why, he is a very young man, almost a boy," the Count exclaimed.

"Sire, this 'boy' killed many of the pirates and saved me, my sergeant, and many pilgrims from certain death or enslavement by his quick thinking," Philip stated. "He is well able to take care of himself and others with him."

The Count looked interested. "You shall have to recount the tale to me later today, Sir Philip. Is he yet a knight?"

"No, Sire, he is not. Although it is within the purveyance of the Master of the Temple to knight him, we have brought him to you for that honor. I stand before you to testify that Talon De Gilles, son of Hughes de Gilles, has distinguished himself in battle satisfactorily and shown leadership in combat. I am here to petition you, my Lord, to knight him and to accept his fealty to you as his father owes it to you today."

It was a long speech for Philip and left a stunned Talon rooted to the ground, staring up at the Count, who regarded his surprise with amused eyes.

The Count smiled but then turned to the Master of Templars. "Do you concur with Sir Philip, Master Gualhart?"

"I do, my Lord," the Templar Master rumbled.

The Count stood up, "Bring me my sword." he ordered. When it was in his hand, he said, "Kneel, Talon de Gilles."

Talon crashed to his knees.

"Do you, Talon de Gilles, swear fealty to me on your father's honor and that of your high-ranking sponsors, Master of the Templars Sir Gualhart and Sir Philip de Gilles? Do you swear to be my vassal and to protect my lands from all my enemies even to the loss of your own life?"

"My Lord, I do," Talon croaked as he gazed up at the Count's stern visage.

The Count placed his hand on Talon's shoulder and held the pommel of his sword in front of his face. "Give the kiss of fealty to my sword."

Talon leaned forward and kissed the hilt of the sword. As he pulled away he received a buffet along the side of his head that made his ears ring.

"Let this be the last blow you receive unanswered, Sir Talon.

"Then rise, Sir Talon de Gilles, Knight of Carcassonne and liege knight to my name."

Talon stood shakily to his feet and looked straight into the gray eyes of the man who stood before him. He saw a smile on the scarred face as that man assessed him from up close.

"Yes," he mused, "you might be young, but I sense that you are indeed a fighter, Sir Talon. You have that look," the Count murmured below the sudden noise of the crowded floor as he embraced him.

"I am honored, Sire, deeply honored," Talon said. He took a step back to join the other two men.

"I expect to be given a detailed report of how you left events in the Holy Land at supper tonight," the Count said to Sir Philip. "Again I bid you welcome and invite you to the festivities this evening." He turned to one of the men standing near his shoulder. "My son, take the young Sir Talon and entertain him this afternoon. Show him our palace and introduce him to your friends."

Talon bowed again to the Count. He turned to his uncle, who was beaming hugely at him. He grinned and reached out to grip his uncle's arm. "You are full of surprises, Uncle. Thank you, and also you, sir. I am deeply in your debt." He addressed the Master of the Temple with a deep bow who gave a short bow in response and smiled.

"Your uncle thinks very highly of you, lad," he said quietly. "We hope one day to have you as a Templar."

Talon turned, aware that someone was just behind him. He saw that the son of the Count was the young man he had locked eyes with at the fair in Albi. The recognition was mutual.

Chapter 13

Recognition

"We meet again, *Sir* Talon," the young man drawled, but he smiled as he said it.

"Indeed, Sire. Well met," Talon said. He bowed respectfully.

"You may call me Roger, Talon. I like it that way. Come, we should leave the Templars to talk to father; it will be about money, I am sure."

Talon bowed respectfully to the Count, but he was deep in conversation with the Master of the Temple with Philip with several of his advisers in attendance. He did not notice them leaving.

Roger walked Talon down the aisle between the company of lords and knights who called to him, asking him to tarry and introduce the new knight, but he waved everyone off with a smile.

"I want to hear all about the battle where you distinguished yourself so well and also to introduce you to my circle of friends," he said as they left the noise of the hall behind.

They went by way of numerous corridors and passages, manned by men-at-arms with liveried servants hurrying hither and thither while they strolled along.

Roger questioned Talon closely on the action with the pirates. The young man at his side applauded his plan to use pitch; Roger was delighted with the story.

They came to a medium-sized garden with large, well-tended hedges and lawns. There was a small fountain in the middle that Roger pointed to with pride. "We took the idea from the Moors in Spain. They seem to know how to make good gardens and they know how to make this kind of 'fountain,'" he said proudly.

Talon looked at the fountain and stopped still, memories threatening to flood him with desolation... but he had no time to reflect. A group of other young people came running out of the doorway they had just exited and rushed toward them.

"Roger!" one of the two young men called out. "We saw you leave and then we lost you. Introduce us, m'Lord." They ran breathlessly up to the two standing on the path.

"Why, this is Sir Talon de Gilles, one and all, newly knighted by my father," Roger exclaimed. "Sir Talon, this is Lord Andreu de Béziers, whose father's lands are within the Duchy. He is one of my cousins. Then there is Lady Elena, his sister." Roger was exaggerating their titles, an impish smile on his lips. Talon decided that he liked the young Count.

Talon bowed to both the newcomers, aware that the girl was watching him curiously with wide, gray eyes.

Roger went on to introduce the other three as Lord Donate de Baucaire, Lady Galiana de Castres, who was visiting the Count with her father—a baron who held Nimes for the Viscount—and Lady Sybille de Foix, also on a protracted visit with her parents.

They were all of an age with the young Count, which was the same as Talon. All were well dressed in the height of fashion, eager and full of interest in the newcomer in their midst. He was forced again to describe the battle with the pirates to which they listened with excitement. They were unabashedly glad that the pirates had perished the way they had, exclaiming on his strategy, and asking more about the Welsh archers he mentioned in his report.

"You've lived all your life in the Holy Land, Talon? Tell us more of that land. We know almost nothing of it and who's doing what at any time," Elena asked.

Talon hesitated. "It's true I lived there all my life, my Lady. But I can't tell you much of what happened in the Holy Land for the last five years... as I was not there," he finally said, reluctantly.

There was a stir among them. "Then if you were not in the Holy Land, where were you?" Roger asked, obviously intrigued.

"I was captured by the Ismaili, who are known also as the Saracen, and taken to Persia."

There was an audible gasp.

"How then did you escape and come to be here now?" Donate asked skeptically. "We hear of terrible things they do to their prisoners and none seem to come back when taken. We hear that they eat babies and rape and pillage wherever they strike."

Talon laughed at this. "I think that they do as we do when they've taken a stronghold, they take booty and the spoils of war. It's a very long story; are you sure you want to hear it?" he asked. He was reluctant to tell his tale but it seemed too late now.

"Sir Talon," Roger said as pompously as he could, "you whet our appetites and then would deny us the sustenance? Shame on you, sir! We want to know all." He laughed. The others agreed loudly. They all looked for a place to sit and Roger sent Andreu off to find a servant to bring them wine and sweetmeats.

"We cannot have a story without wine," he said to approving grins from the others. While the others chattered, Talon had time to observe the fine clothes these young nobles wore and to compare it to those of his family in Albi. The young maidens wore the *bliaut,* long dresses of many shades and colors. Elena had bands of elaborate embroidery at the high neck and the very wide sleeves that almost trailed on the ground when she let her arms down. The ladies' dresses were made of fine imported fabrics instead of plain cloth; Elena's was of creamy satin, sewn with pearls down the front which set off her slim figure and light features very well. He could see that the *bliaut*, worn over a chemise and laced tight, showed off every curve of the young noblewomen. Elena wore a *gironee* or separate skirt, and her companions wore full-length *bliauts*, which fell to the floor in many folds, and again of expensive material, silk or satin. They all wore a belt, the *ceinture*, but again these were woven with silver or gold thread. Peeping out beneath the dresses were silk *sollars*—slippers—with pointed toes but nowhere near as long as those of the men folk.

Although the maidens all wore a *guimple* or head veil of fine almost translucent material, it was much more casual than the average person he had seen in the town, and revealed their hair. Being noble maidens almost all had a band of silver or gold holding the *guimple* in place on their hair—which was in Elena's case tressed—and fell down to their waists. Again Talon was struck by the elegance of their dress, but there was little in the way of jewelry on their persons except Elena who wore a broach.

The young nobles were no less elegantly dressed in tight hose that was of expensive silk or very high-grade English wool, with an over tunic of fine material with fur at the sleeves that were distinctly tighter than those of the maidens. They all wore a cloak of brightly colored wool with ermine edging held in place by silver chains, or richly decorated leather with gold clasps. Their hair was cut more or less like his, straight across the front and long at the back. They sported richly decorated belts from which hung small purses and the inevitable dagger in a jeweled or silver scabbard.

Andreu hurried back with a servant and several glazed jugs of wine which were poured into leather mugs for the people seated all around Talon.

Talon told the story as simply as he could, the capture, the awful journey to Persia, the horror of the frequent executions, the training for the boys, and then the fight with the lion.

They exclaimed at this last, excited by his tale, but one of the girls reached to point at the long scar on his jaw. "Was that one of the scars put there by the lion?" she asked. She seemed excited by the idea of the fight with such a dangerous animal. "How big is this animal? Is it as large as a horse? Does it look like the heraldic paintings of it?" she demanded to know.

"There are lions in Palestine and in the mountains of Persia and they are about as big as a pony, but with shorter, stronger legs and huge claws on their paws. They are very fierce and they eat goats and kill men if they are not wary," Talon said, smiling.

"For a boy the age you were when you met the lion that is huge! Were you not a little frightened of the beast, Talon?" Roger asked.

"Roger, I was so scared I nearly drowned with terror. The animal landed on me after it had killed itself on my spear and carried me under the water."

The others laughed merrily at this description.

"I doff my hat to you, Talon. You do not embellish but tell it as it was. For that you have my respect," Roger stated, still laughing.

"We have bears and wolves in our forests and wild boar, but no lions," Donate said.

"There are still dragons in the depths of the high mountains far, far to the east, are there not?" Lady Galiana asked innocently.

The others laughed at her but although they mocked her, Talon sensed that they were not sure of themselves.

"There are no dragons left in Langue d'Oc, Galiana," Andreu said scornfully.

"How do you know, brother?" Elena asked, taking Galiana's side with an impish grin.

Lady Galiana asked Talon directly, "Well, I shall ask Sir Talon. Do they have dragons in Persia, Sir Talon?"

He smiled. "I was told that in the past there were many dragons and demons in the lands of Persia, but a great hero called Rostam slew most of them so I can't tell if there are any still there today, my lady."

They plied him with questions about his story and how he had managed to escape. He was deliberately vague about how he had been treated by the Templars. The knights were not to be accused in this company, he surmised.

It was well into the evening and the bells of the city were ringing evening Mass when he had finished. He had glossed over much but the main story was there. There was a long silence when he stopped.

Roger and the other young men were looking at him with new respect; everyone seemed to be reassessing him. Each was thinking his own thoughts.

Finally Roger said, "You have led a life that none of us could have imagined. I am glad to know you. It is now our turn to entertain you, and so we shall." He looked around. "This evening there is to be a feast in honor of a dignitary from England. My father will have him seated at the high table with your uncle, Talon. He will want to hear all about life in the *Outré Mere*; news is hard to come by. We will be seated along the side of the high table and we shall have troubadours and jugglers, dancers and singers."

"With perhaps even contortionists and acrobats," Donate added.

"You only like to watch them because they are mostly girls and often naked, Donateie," one the girls teased. Donate had the grace to blush while the others teased him.

Talk came round to the news that there would be a famous troubadour at the feast that night.

"He shall sing the ballads of Aquitaine and of the arts of love," Lady Galiana told them, "Perhaps even of Tristan and Isolde."

The young men smirked with derision. "You ladies are always mooning over the latest songs from these people. What of the art of war?" Lord Andreu asked.

"Our Queen Eleanor said that a knight was not meant to be merely a man of war, but able to woo a lady with fine knowledge of the art of love as well," Lady Sybille said defensively.

"I am sure that Talon is well familiar with the art of love as well as war," Elena said archly, her eyes directly on him.

Talon gazed back at her solemnly. He paused as though thinking carefully, but he had already decided to enjoy himself and to enter into the spirit of the exchange. "That depends, M'Lady. I am no troubadour, so I would be a willing student of one who knew all there was to the art of love." he said innocently, looking directly at her.

The others laughed outright at this and it was Elena's turn to be teased. She tossed her head and laughed with them, her eyes still on Talon, a slight blush on her cheeks. He smiled at her with his eyes and her blush deepened.

"It is clear that Talon is not to be tested in that arena," Roger said, his eyes assessing the situation.

Talon was struck by the gay innocence of the young people around him. He felt sure that the young men at least were probably good with weaponry, it being a prerequisite for young lords of the time. All the same he felt a lot older than the group he was with and somehow detached. He noticed that Roger had disappeared but that the others were still walking slowly in the direction of the feast hall. Elena had him firmly anchored by her side, her arm linked in his.

He again felt acutely conscious of his distinct lack of finery and hung back; but Elena pushed him on, seemingly quite unconscious of his deficiency and determined to have him with her.

The bells tolled again and it was Vespers; time for the feast to commence. Elena told him that the young people were expected to be present in the hall before the Count came to the table, so they walked quickly along the passages together with other hurrying people heading toward the Great hall where the feasting would take place.

Roger had warned Talon that there would be much pomp and ceremony. The arrival of an ambassador from Henry of England was an unusual event and meant that something was afoot. Talon was discovering that he was woefully unaware of the events generated by the two kings of England and France as well as the alliances that were being sought with men like the Count of Toulouse, Carcassonne, and Burgundy to the east.

Sybille, who like others of her noble class, could recite from memory the names and titles of most of the gentry in the Languedoc, Aquitaine, and beyond, briefly explained the convoluted state of affairs in the land as it was then.

"The Count, a very powerful noble in his own right, still owes fealty to the king of France, as does King Henry II, himself." She arched her eyebrows at him.

To Talon it was as confusing as the interaction of the Sultans and princes in Persia. He was further puzzled to learn that the king of France probably had much less land belonging to him than most of his powerful nobles, but because he was the descendant of the great Charlemagne he held the title nonetheless. "Why then does Henry of England have to pay him tribute, when he is king of far greater lands than those of the king of France?"

There were snickers at that and he felt embarrassed, but Elena spoke up.

"Do not be surprised at our contempt for our own king, Talon. King Louis the Pious has lost all respect from his subjects, not least because of the way he discarded Eleanor, but also because he plays the monk and not the king. Henry Deux may be his vassal, but Philip dare not demand anything in the way of 'tribute' as you call it. He is a weak king."

"Do they war with each other?"

"Constantly," Donate said, unexpectedly. "They mainly war over parts of Normandy in the north, an area known as the Vexin, which they squabble over interminably. Ever since he took Eleanor as his wife, Henry has been in possession of Aquitaine and Normandy as well as England and is now the most powerful king of all the three great Christian kingdoms. He would like to have the Languedoc on his side, too. Why should he want to continue to be the vassal of a man like Louis?"

"Do not forget that Louis, despite his divorce from the queen, still covets the Aquitaine."

"Why then does this Henry not just conquer what's left and have it all?" Talon asked.

"Because it would be too much even for him. Even a king as powerful as Henry knows the value of balancing one enemy against another. My father taught me that and Henry has to balance a lot of enemies against one another to know any peace at all.

"He has his hands full with the barons of Normandy and Aquitaine, truth be known, who are a quarrelsome group and don't want an 'English' King. It would be easy to take the Isle de France and depose Louis, but Henry would find the other nobles of the Frankish kind to the north of here and even the lords down here in Languedoc in fierce opposition to him and he could not contain them for very long," Roger explained.

"Let us not forget his son Richard, who is rumored to be against his own father," Andreu put in. He had been listening quietly to the discussion up to now. "Mark my words, *mon amis*, we shall hear from Richard in due time."

"There is a rumor that Richard is not Henry's son at all but that of his queen and a nobleman from Aquitaine, Geoffrey of Rancon," Elena whispered to Talon.

Talon was surprised to find Elena at his side; she had disappeared earlier. Now she placed her hand on his arm. "Will you be my Gentle Knight for the evening, Sir Talon?"

Roger, who had left briefly to talk to someone, rejoined them and overhearing, laughed. "Beware, Talon. An invitation of that sort can be interpreted many ways here in Occitania."

The others laughed gaily at this and fell to joking. The maidens gave as good as they got from the youthful noblemen. The party arrived in time to be loudly introduced to the crowded hall. It was a huge hall, ablaze with candlelight, with many pillars supporting a roof that soared into the smoke-darkened rafters high above.

Talon noticed enormous tapestries along the walls, depicting hunting scenes and battles fought against other armies of men or even dragons. Here, too, there were many banners with a confusing array of coats of arms, which he learned were just beginning to come into fashion. He noticed shields hanging from the pillars with many different designs upon them and assumed them to be booty taken in battle.

He was again surprised to feel and see green rushes beneath his feet and wondered at this habit of putting down a grass in a hall. The air was thick with talk and the sound of horns and bells as more guests arrived to be greeted by their friends in the huge hall.

As many as two hundred people of knightly and noble ranks, men and their ladies, were standing around in groups, gossiping, or seated at the long tables already drinking the Count's wine and mead.

It was clear that Roger was popular as there were calls from all sides to tarry and share a goblet of wine. This he did and often as not introduced Talon and his friends from the other counties. Talon noticed that there were few glass beakers to be seen here, for all the riches displayed. There was much silver in the form of dishes and goblets, but somewhat to his surprise he saw little gold. Unlike the women of wealth in the eastern countries he had visited, the women here did not wear their husband's fortunes on their arms and necks.

He was left alone briefly so he looked around at the company of barons and knights with their ladies talking loudly to one another, some, including the ladies, well into their cups, leaning across the laden tables that were heaped with huge dishes of food. Elena came back from talking to some friends and took his arm again.

"Come along, Sir Talon. We are seated with Roger over there." Elena pointed to where some servants were preparing a table that was off to one side of the high table.

"From there we can watch the high table and still see the entertainment. I am looking forward to the singing tonight."

"I heard one of the troubadours, as you call them, in Albi and liked his songs," Talon said. "He was bold and played to the girls. He was certainly entertaining; everyone enjoyed his songs."

"Many of them owe their patronage to Queen Eleanor, who encouraged them to come to the halls of lords and sing of love. It is now customary to have a troubadour sing at a banquet and my Lord Viscount of Carcassonne always has a good feast."

They were interrupted by a trumpet blaring near the high table and all in the hall stood for the arrival of the Count of Carcassonne. The Count made a grand entrance from behind the leather curtains that led to his private quarters; he was richly dressed and bejeweled. With him was another thick set man dressed somewhat differently to that of the assembly, but equally richly clad with ermine on his collar and a warm cloak of rich blue wool and a red tunic embroidered with three gold lions.

Talon observed that the Count had his lady in attendance. She was a striking woman who had once been very beautiful and still carried herself with grace and dignity although her youth was behind her. Her gaze sought her son in the crowd next to Talon. She smiled at Roger, who gave low bow, smiling up at her, obviously pleased to see her.

Her gaze moved away from him as she looked over his company, then they rested on Talon for a long moment as though assessing him. He looked back with interest and then politely bowed toward her. There was a flicker of a smile and then she and her husband were moving forward to the grand table.

They were seated by obsequious servants along with their guest and another man in rich red robes that Talon assumed were the clothes of the Church—a small red cap on his tonsure gave him away. Talon noticed his uncle and the Master of the Templars seated nearby. They would be kept busy with questions about the news from Palestine, no doubt. His uncle had told him that the Templars had one of the best information services available to the western kingdoms.

The Count lifted his arms almost as a blessing and the entire assembly bowed their heads while the man in red clothing said grace. Talon, who was unfamiliar with this procedure, lifted his head to observe the crowd and listened to the sonorous voice as it intoned the prayer for the day. He glanced toward the high table and was surprised to see the Countess observing him. Their eyes locked for an instant and he wondered what was in her look, but then he felt compelled to look down and thereafter kept his eyes down until the prayer was over.

The assembly seated itself with a lot of bustle and noise as the feast got under way. The toasting began almost immediately and the Count was busy responding or calling to his people among the crowded tables below his own. A group of minstrels were playing on the other side of the hall, their music all but drowned out by the noise on the hall floor. Talon, who had found his interest piqued, observed that the Countess ate sparingly and spoke barely at all.

Elena leaned near to him and whispered, "Our Countess has noticed you, Sir Talon. Roger must have told her about you. I fear that you will have to spend the evening telling her of your adventures, and I shall not have you as much to myself."

"Would you not be allowed to come, too, should she request my presence? Surely Roger would ask for you?"

"We shall ask Roger directly. Roger, your mother had spied Talon; I am sure she will demand his presence later. Perhaps you have talked of him?"

Roger laughed. "How could I not. Elena? I am sure we will all be present tonight at my mother's chambers to listen to Talon recount his adventures in the Saracen lands."

Elena beamed and then resumed their conversation regarding the troubadours.

"Our Queen Eleanor of Aquitaine cultivated them in her court when she ruled in her land, taking after her father and Grandfather William, both of whom loved the arts. She is now instead in that cold and misty place, England. I wonder that she wed King Henry although they say he is a vigorous man and certainly commands respect."

"I know nothing of either the king of France or of this Henry of whom you speak, Elena. Have you met them?"

"Oh no, of course not! I was too young to have been at Queen Eleanor's court when she ruled Aquitaine; and of course no one has seen the king of France, mainly because he spends most of his time wearing out his knees praying to Our Lord for absolution."

"Why, has he committed so many crimes that he needs to beg for absolution?" Talon asked.

Those nearest him who overheard, laughed at the comment, but now Talon did not feel stupid as they made it plain they wanted to help him understand their world.

Galiana leaned close to them as they talked; she had been listening. "Our great king Louis is a deeply pious man, Talon. It is said that he abhors the flesh so much that he prayed for an immaculate conception by his queen but was sorely disappointed."

"Who is his queen?" Talon asked.

"He has no queen at present, but once it was Queen Eleanor who is now Queen of England and who now has three surviving sons to date by the lusty Henry," said Elena with a wink.

"So does the King of France have no heir?" Talon asked, intrigued.

"If he begets an heir it will be a miracle in itself, but I have no doubt that someone will oblige and help him somehow," Roger said, joining in the conversation with a grin. The others tittered.

"So the king has only one wife?" Talon asked innocently.

They all laughed again. "He has only one wife who is the Queen, Talon. He divorced Eleanor on some trumped-up charge which suited everyone although it was bitterly unfair to that lady. She is worshipped in her own lands and Louis is considered a man of no honor because of it," Sybille interjected.

"Why do you ask if he had only one wife, Talon? Is it so different in the Saracen world?" Roger asked curiously.

"I recall that the Sultans could have as many wives as they wished, and many men of the Arabic lands have more than one. It is allowed that a man may have more than one wife, but must be able to keep them well."

There were amused gasps from the girls and raised eyebrows from the youths. They were all seated facing the center of the hall which was a wide cleared space in which the servants ran about carrying trays of food, some of which was finding its way to their table.

"These Sultans must be men of great status and vigor," Sybille remarked with a smirk to Donate, who laughed. The others laughed, too, but they were intrigued nonetheless.

"It is the custom; one of the most important things for the Sultan to do is to have many heirs."

"But if he breeds many heirs, who then assumes the throne when he dies or is killed?" Roger asked.

"There you have it, My Lord. By law it should always be the first born, but they often fight for the right of heritage and then the winner, usually the strongest, sets about killing his siblings to ensure that they cannot cheat him of his right in battle or by stealth later."

After this the questions came fast and he was hard put to answer them all. But then the food arrived in trays delivered by the harassed, sweating servants, all in the Count's livery. He had time to study Elena, and found himself approving of her. She was an attractive girl who had a graceful neck, her fair hair combed high onto her head leaving her high forehead and slim long neck exposed. His glance took in her well-formed body that the expensive clothes did nothing to hide. She had a thin chain around her neck with a silver cross attached but he had noticed that the people all seemed quite pious; many women wore a cross of similar type so he did not remark it very much. She must have noticed his scrutiny as she turned and gave him a frank look and then smiled at him. He smiled back.

He also noticed that there was a good deal more formality at the high table. The Count leaned toward his guest and often offered him a morsel, pointing to a new plate of oysters or pheasants tongue, boasting lightly that his cooks were among the best in Christendom. They seemed to be involved in an earnest and very serious discussion that included the clergyman and the two Templars. He wondered what they might be discussing.

Talon concentrated on his food and found that something was missing. There were few vegetables to go with the meats. It was true, here was some baked roots and some fresh cabbage, but few people seemed interested in them. For the most part they ate meat or pastry and the variety was staggering, from seafood to hunted venison or boar.

He wondered if he would ever see a fig or an orange again, as he had not up until now. He longed for a pistachio nut to crack and chew. There were plenty of apples and he enjoyed the cooked plums and cherries that were plentiful with the meat. Elena pressed a pear onto him, eating another with obvious relish and letting the juice drip down her chin until he was forced to wipe it with a corner of the linen over-cloth provided for the purpose, both laughing as he did so.

Talon had to ask what some of the food was, for it was quite new to him. Elena pointed to platters of oysters that had come fresh from the sea. There were boiled mussels, which he had never seen before. There were numerous game birds that positively stank to the point where he almost had to be rude and hold his nose. He asked why they were so rank. His amused companions told him that the game birds were hung for days after being killed to make the flesh tender. Talon had to agree after taking a tentative bite; the flesh was tender but it was difficult to get past the smell all the same.

The pies arrived, some filled with starling carcasses that had been roasted before being placed in the huge dish with a crust baked over them. There were huge fish on long silver trays that they called *brochets* that were pulled out of the river along with trout. He sampled the trout that had been baked with toasted almonds, knowing how that tasted and again finding it delicious, and then tried some other choice bite that Elena had placed on his plate.

Being noble they ate off silver plates but he noticed that most of the gentry seated on the lower tables were eating off pottery plates while farther down the hall among the lesser knights they ate off trenchers of thick bread that were replaced after each course.

Here too people ate with their hands and used their knives to cut the food up before they took it to their mouths, or even cut it off the larger part when it was between their teeth. Before long his young companions all had juice and gravy on their chins as they happily indulged themselves. Servants came along behind them and gave them clean towels from time to time, but Talon noted that the young men and even the girls were not above wiping their mouths with the sleeves of their tunics or dresses.

Wine flowed freely, as did mead that he was careful not to drink, knowing full well what the mixture would do to him. Others seemed less inhibited and before long there were quite a few men staggering drunk in the hall.

Talon had been so engrossed with the food and conversation with his newfound friends that he failed to notice that there were was something brewing in the lower hall.

Two men, richly dressed but obviously drunk, had engaged in a quarrel that came to knives drawn. They staggered out onto the center of the hall in between the tables and slashed at one another with deadly intent. Even the minstrels stopped playing to watch, agog. There were shouts of encouragement and ribald comments as the two tried to stick one another with their long daggers.

The Count was not amused. He reared up at the high table with a roar of anger and shouted down the hall with a voice that dominated the raucous shouts of the crowded hall and even intruded upon the two antagonists' dulled senses.

In the silence that ensued the Count yelled, "Stop this brawl at once. You dare to fight in my hall after taking salt at my feast, in front of my guests? Guards, arrest these men at once. Throw them in the cells where they can sleep off the wine and in the morning they shall entertain us all at the lists. We shall see how well they do when sober."

His guards came running with pikes and swords drawn to seize the two men and hustle them out of the hall to the jeers and laughter of the rest of the crowd. The Count sat down, clearly out of sorts with the event. The remainder of the guests settled down to eat more of the good food he had provided and before very long the hubbub of conversation and activity had resumed as though the incident had never happened.

Roger glanced at Talon. "You are witness to the hot blood of the Languedoc. Men often carry a feud to the death in this land. I would that the knights and retainers were better mannered. Those two have had a grudge for years. I expect one to die tomorrow at the lists; they hate one another."

"I was surprised, my Lord, but your father is obviously respected and rules with a strong hand, so it would seem this does not happen often."

"That's true, but every year at this time when men come to pay their yearly homage some old grudges resurface and have to be cleared at the lists," Roger replied.

"The sport of jousting is forbidden by the Church, but all the same, men will fight, so it is better that they fight in a place where all can see it a fair fight," Donate told Talon.

The incident was forgotten as the night's entertainment began. The first was as Donate had hoped: the jugglers and acrobats. A group of five people, naked except for loin cloths, came running into the hall. To Talon's surprise one of them was a young girl of about sixteen who was as slim and as lithe as the youths she worked with. While she, too, wore a brief loin cloth wound tightly around her waist and between her legs, her small breasts were uncovered. The whole troop was glistening from oil they had rubbed onto their skins. They danced and weaved their way to the front of the high table and then began to juggle colored balls.

They tossed them high into the air, catching and moving them effortlessly about from one to the other, shouting out as they caught the balls and passed them along. Then they moved on to juggling wooden clubs like batons. Talon glanced surreptitiously at his companions: His youthful friends were all watching the girl avidly while the girls were simply watching the jugglers' skills. Elena caught his eye and smiled secretly at him. He smiled back.

The group had now gone on to juggling with knives and turning somersaults on the floor. They would jump onto a cupped pair of hands with shouts and calls of encouragement and leap high into the air, turning back flips or somersaults with bewildering speed. The crowd loved it and shouted for more. Their display was skilled, and impressive enough for people to throw coins their way after they had finished and stood panting and bowing to the approving assembly. A servant brought a small bag of coins from the Count for the leader of the group and then they were gone.

The small group with Talon was exclaiming on their skill while the girls teased Donate on his lust for the maiden. He blushingly fended them off, but it was clear that he had enjoyed watching her.

Then it was time for the minstrels to play and sing songs of the Languedoc and Aquitaine. Drunken conversations were hushed by people wanting to hear, and the first came into the hall and commenced one of his songs. He was a slim, olive-skinned man with a dark mustache and flashing teeth whose skill within a few strums of the stringed instrument he carried soon had the attention of the whole hall.

His first song, to warm up the crowd, was a very popular song that everyone knew and which many joined in singing:

If he sings, let it sing
He does not sing for me
But for my sweetheart
So far away from me

At the end of the meadow
There's a poplar with a hole
The cuckoo sings there
It may have made its nest

If he sings, let it sing
He does not sing for me
But for my sweetheart
So far away from me

Those mountains
Are so high
They prevent me from seeing
Where is my love

If he sings, let it sing
He does not sing for me
But for my sweetheart
So far away from me

Those mountains
Some day will lower

And my love
Will come back
If he sings, let it sing
He does not sing for me
But for my sweetheart
So far away from me

He sang songs in a rich baritone that Talon had never heard before and because of the dialect could not fully understand. The crowd in the hall knew it well and they often joined in singing or simply shouting the words as he played. Elena and Sybille sang gaily along.

The minstrel could not fail to notice the group of young nobles at Roger's table so he came over at one time and placed his foot on a bench nearby and regarded them with a smile. "My fair young lords and ladies, it is clear to me that you have the advantage of youth with you. Here is a song for you to ponder."

They all clapped and waited while he pretended to compose himself. He strummed a couple of notes and began.

Oh Youth. Go with reckless faith,
And trust the flattering voice,
Which whispers, "Take thy fill till death.
Indulge thyself and then rejoice.

Or surely by end of every setting day
Some passed delight you'll mourn
As flowers shall die along our way
Till you too die lost and forlorn

So take the world's garish feast
Drink of her first charming bowl
Infused with all that fires the lonely breast
And cheat the morbid darkling soul

And yet as loud the revel swells
The love fever'd pulse beats higher,
Did you taste the nectar from the well?
A man would fain slake his fire.

A lady's love is not always given
But to those who would dare to take
That which is oft in jest forbidden
Passione'd love is surely theirs to make.

The Minstrel finished with a flourish of notes and bowed toward their table, receiving the applause and laughter with a wide smile. Roger threw him a few coins which he deftly caught and pocketed with a murmured thanks and a deep, sardonic bow.

He bowed again toward the high table then walked to the middle of the room where he continued to entertain the noisy crowd, which asked him for more old favorites. While the huge candles sputtered hot wax and threw long shadows about the walls and servants replaced them with fresh ones, the crowd hushed and listened raptly. He sang of Charlemagne and Roland, of Arthur and Guinevere, and of the forbidden love between her and Lancelot.

He did indeed sing the Ballad of Tristan and Isolde, much to the delight of the ladies who explained the song to Talon as being an ancient song from Brittany and Cornwall about love gained and lost. Many the tear was shed for Isolde by the time the Minstrel was done.

The troubadour took on a more reflective mood and sang about Thierry d'Argonne, one of the great warriors of Charlemagne and his battle with Pinabel, Ganelon's kinsman and champion, in fierce single combat. Ganelon had been accused of causing the death of Roland and many thousands of other men through treachery. So the question of his guilt had to be decided in single combat between two champions. Pinabel struck Thierry on the helm, but according to the poem, God protected him from death.

Thierry returned the blow, which split Pinabel's head. This victory resulted in Ganelon's conviction of guilt, and his immediate execution. The menfolk who knew the legend were full of praise for the song and threw coins at the man who again collected them, bowed elaborately, and left.

It was not long after the minstrel had departed that Lady Roseanne rose and amid the bows and polite words left with the same grace with which she had entered the hall. Before she left she whispered into the ear of one of her ladies, who nodded and looked at Roger and his friends.

Soon after the lady in waiting came through the hall to ask Roger if he would attend his mother in her chambers and that he should not forget to bring his friends.

Chapter 14

Tournament

The Count prepared to leave the hall not very long after his lady had retired. When he stood up there were renewed toasts and vows of loyalty, which he returned, or made some joke. He left with the English ambassador alongside, no doubt making for his private chambers. His departure seemed to be a signal for the drinking to begin in earnest. The young Count turned to his companions and indicated that they should also leave as they were to go to his mother's chambers. Talon followed the group of young courtiers as they left the great hall.

They made their way along darkening corridors with arched columns and flagstone floors that echoed to their footsteps, a sharp contrast to the noise and light of the Great Hall. Then they climbed stone stairs toward the Count's private quarters. The young Count was recognized by the men-at-arms at the doorways they passed through; they saluted him smartly as he went by. He called out their names in greeting which was received with a grin of appreciation from the guards.

The group came to a wooden door with two sentries placed either side who brought their pikes up as he approached. One rapped on the door to attract the attention of those within. It was opened by one of the queen's ladies, who motioned them inside with a respectful curtsey and welcoming smile to Roger. The girls went in first and headed straight for the Lady Roseanna, who greeted them each in turn with some words and a kiss on both cheeks.

The room was brightly lit with candles; obviously the Count lacked neither money nor resources to maintain a grand lifestyle, Talon thought, thinking of the dank, dark fort his parents lived in.

He was hanging back while the others greeted Roger's mother, who admonished her son, "Roger, I trust that you are making sure that your cousins are well entertained this evening?"

"Indeed, Mother, we have been well entertained by Sir Talon here, who has lived a life unlike anything I could have imagined. Talon, come and greet my mother."

Talon walked toward the regal lady who watched him as he came with a slight curl to her full lips. He wondered what she found so amusing, but maintained a polite smile on his own face as he came up and bowed deeply to her. He kissed the delicate hand that was presented to him and received a gentle squeeze as he did so.

"I am told by my son that you have had many adventures in a land that none of us know anything about, Sir Talon. Will you not indulge me and tell some of the same tales again and more this early evening?"

"My Lady, if you so wish, then I am at your service," Talon said looking again into the bright hazel eyes.

She smiled at him. "Do not be discomforted, Sir Talon. I surmise that you are a reluctant narrator, but have pity upon us, for we do not know of the lands you have traveled and would learn from you."

He smiled back, disarmed. "My Lady, it would be difficult for anyone to refuse your request. In my own poor way I shall attempt to paint a picture of where I've been and what I've seen."

There were more than ten people in the room, which was warmed by a fire in a recess in the thick, stone wall. Leather and wood-frame chairs were placed nearby for her ladyship and guests. The group of new friends either sat or stood around in a close circle as the ladies-in-waiting made Lady Roseanna comfortable. She motioned Talon to sit opposite her on the other side of the fireplace. Roger sat on a cushion near his mother and leaned against her knee. Her hand strayed to play with his hair from time to time. There was obviously a strong bond between them. Mulled wine was ordered and Talon was presented with a silver beaker of very good local wine to drink while he talked.

He was pleasantly surprised by the curiosity of Roger's mother, who appeared to be interested in all things about the Holy Land. He had to recount yet again the story of his battle with the pirates, which brought applause and much praise from the ladies-in-waiting.

Elena wanted to hear about the lion all over again and he told that story once more. He left out his sadness at the loss of Jean de Loche, his mentor from those days, and concentrated on the stories which appeared to fascinate his audience. He watched Lady Rosanna as he told the story and she in turn appeared to listen closely to every word. Her eyes rested on him often during the telling of the tales.

The candles were low and the flickering shadows deeper when he finished. There was a brief silence and then a babble of conversation began as though people had been holding their breath. Talon turned away from them and gazed into the glowing embers of the fire, alone with his memories for a few moments.

He was interrupted in his reverie by Lady Roseanne, who asked where Talon was staying. Talon replied that he was staying at an inn near the Templar stronghold on the other side of the town.

Lady Rosanna stood up and the audience was over. Hurriedly standing, too, Talon bowed over her extended hand once more.

"You have provided me with much to think on this night, Sir Talon. I wish to hear more of the people of those faraway lands. To listen to you they are not the savages we perhaps think they are, and yet they are our enemies in God's eyes. We shall talk some more tomorrow in the gardens. Roger, you will bring him with you tomorrow?"

"Willingly, Mother," Roger said. "We should bid you good-night, and take our leave until tomorrow." He kissed her on both cheeks and then led the procession out of the door into the cooler and much darker corridor outside.

Talon found that a small, cool hand had been inserted onto his arm and, looking down, he saw Elena close by. She squeezed his arm and walked with him among the happy group as it headed this time toward the entrance of the palace. As they walked in the darkened spaces, Elena reached up and gave Talon a swift kiss on the lips, but said nothing. In the darkness of the corridors they walked along, it was not hard to stop for an instant and kiss her in return as was expected. She returned the kiss with passion to the point where they were left alone for a few paces while the others continued talking and teasing each other, seemingly oblivious of them. Elena reached out and took his hand, then placed it on her breast.

Talon felt a jolt in his groin as she did so; it was clear that she was excited and wanted him to go further, but just then the young Count called back to them to stop playing in the dark and catch up. Elena sighed with exasperation.

"Roger has his instructions, Talon. I shall wish you a goodnight from here and God speed to your bed. I shall go to mine but I fear that after all the adventures you have told us, I will not sleep very much this night!" she whispered and gave him a peck on the cheek.

Roger was going to see that Talon went home this night and Elena was to behave. This drew much teasing and laughter from the others in the group, who were also behaving toward one another very amorously.

Talon fell into bed that night with much to remember and the feeling that it would be nice to stay a while longer in Carcassonne.

Indeed, it seemed that Philip was in no hurry to leave either, as over breakfast he told Talon that he had an audience with the Count that morning and Talon was to attend.

"There will be jousting this afternoon, Talon, which the Count wishes us to attend with him."

Talon realized that he needed to do something about his wardrobe. He excused himself and with Anwl in tow hurried off to the town center to look for some new clothes. While he was at it he decided to buy some for Anwl, whose clothes were positively ragged.

Talon returned to the Templar stronghold feeling very pleased with himself. He had on new bright green hose, a new linen undershirt, a well-stitched tunic that came down to the middle of his thighs and a well-made doublet with a snug fit. He had a new cloak that was embroidered around all its borders and hung off his shoulders with a fine silk rope entwined with silver thread. He was not at all sure that the hose that now clung to his legs was what he really wanted, including the long pointed slippers he now wore, but the tailor had insisted that it was all the style. Looking about at other young men of the same age and class Talon was hard put to disagree.

Anwl was very pleased with his new clothes and spent a lot of time looking at himself in anything that would reflect his image, from bright copper pots to puddles of water. "My Prince in Cwmry will think I am a nobleman when I come back in all this finery, M'ilord," he stated firmly.

"We need to buy some of the same for Gareth and the others, Anwl. or they will be mightily envious of you."

Talon knew that he was still not dressed in the height of fashion. Also having insisted that he be provided with a trough and hot water he divested himself of the new clothes and to Anwl's horror and the Inn maid servant's frank amusement as she brought the pails of hot water he proceeded to take a bath. Now at least he would feel cleaner.

He was luxuriating in the trough of tepid water when his uncle banged on the door, demanding to know what was taking him so long to get ready. Talon clambered out, dried himself with one of the coarse linen sheets, and donned his new clothes. Max accompanied them this time as they walked hurriedly to the Count's palace. They were again admitted easily because of the Templar uniforms.

They were taken to a different place this time, up some stairs to a chamber which seemed to serve as the Count's office as it was full of parchments in buckets and in racks on the walls. There were several clerks writing in a corner, but the room was dominated by the Count himself, who sat at ease in an oak settle by the window. He had been talking to the Englishman and both turned and watched Philip and Talon come in. Max stayed outside.

Both Philip and Talon bowed low and stood waiting for the Count to speak.

"Ah, Sir Philip de Gilles, and our newest knight, Sir Talon de Gilles, welcome! I wish to introduce you to my honored guest, Sir Guy, Count of Northumberland, emissary to His Royal Highness, Henry, King of England, and Prince Richard, his son."

Philip and Talon both bowed respectfully toward Sir Guy, who nodded pleasantly and walked over to them. He held out his hand in a gesture of friendliness. Talon was impressed with the strength in the man's grip.

"I have heard last night from Sir Philip here that you are just back from the Holy Land, and would hear more of it from your own lips. I understand from the Countess, who told us this morning about you, Sir Talon, that you were even a prisoner of the Saracen and lived to tell the tale."

"Talon has indeed come back from the far eastern countries, from Persia, where he was taken as a captive. But later they let him free and he found his way back to us in Palestine." Philip confirmed.

"Tell us more of the Kingdom of Jerusalem, Sir Philip," the Count demanded. "I did not get the opportunity to talk to you very much yesterday as we were involved in other matters."

"I can tell you more of that than I can of the countries beyond, Sire; Talon can feed your curiosity regarding that."

"Well, what of the Kingdom? Is it going to survive?"

They were seated in carved fruitwood chairs, provided with wine, and the conversation centered on the Holy Land. Sir Guy listened attentively, only occasionally asking discerning questions.

The Count was obviously intrigued at the number of questions and finally asked, "Sir Guy, you are clearly keen to know all there is about the Holy Land. Is my Lord King Henry contemplating a crusade to those parts?"

"My Lord you might well ask why I am so eager to hear of the Holy Land; but it is not for my Liege Henry, but for his son, Prince Richard. Although young, he is very curious about the *Outré Mere* and demands to hear all that I can tell him on the subject. I have to bring him information on the disposition of the forces in the Holy Land and how they are doing against the Saracen. I am much in your debt for letting me talk to Sir Philip and his nephew. Besides, My Lord Richard is in Aquitaine at this time."

The Count was obviously surprised but he also looked interested. "If Lord Richard is so near, why then did he not come to see me himself?" he asked, somewhat archly.

Sir Guy laughed. "You know only too well, my Lord. He cannot afford to have spies report back to his father that he visited you even for the most innocent reasons."

The Count laughed. "Right you are, Sir Guy. But it interests me that the two cannot seem to get along for even the shortest time."

"The one is a lion, sir. The other is truly the lion's cub and would have a country to rule, young as he is. Henry holds the reins very tightly over his impatient sons."

"Queen Eleanor, is she, too, back in Aquitaine?"

"No, she remains in England. Prince Richard came to these parts on her behalf. His father only just allowed it. He distrusts his vassals and, I fear, Richard as well."

"What of John, the other son? Is he in his father's favor while Richard is out of it?" demanded the Count.

"Prince John is better thought of as the bungler. He tries to rebel and only makes a fool of himself. The king does not trust him, either, but knows which one to watch the most. It is not John."

"I am sure that Sir Philip de Gilles of the Templars and Sir Talon here will be happy to provide you with all the information they can on the subject of the Holy Land, Sir Guy. Will you not stay a while longer so that we can indulge this curiosity?"

Sir Guy bowed. "Thank you my Lord, as ever, you place me deep in your debt."

"I hope to place Prince Richard in my debt in time, Sir Guy. As we both know, the yoke of France is irksome to one such as I."

Talon had been listening to the discussion with interest. He was witnessing the interchange between powerful men; it surprised him that their loyalties were out in the open. It was clear to him that Sir Guy's loyalty lay with Prince Richard and not fully with the father. He was impressed that the Count should trust Sir Guy with the understanding that he chafed as a vassal to the King of France. This could be construed as treason, but had he not sworn to protect the Count with his life? This meant that his first loyalty was to the Count before even the King of France.

Sir Guy smiled. "Then it is settled, I shall stay longer. My Lord, I understand there is to be a joust today. I would see the knights of your table demonstrate their prowess."

Much later, the Count stood up stiffly. "Sir Guy, I have to attend my councilors for a while; shall we continue this discussion later today? Perhaps after the tournament?" The English lord stood as did Philip and Talon. He turned to Talon. "Did you learn anything of the way the Saracen make war that you can show us here in Christendom, young knight?"

Talon was very much aware that he was being watched carefully by all the men in the room, even the clerks seemed to be listening.

Philip spoke up. "Sire, I have seen Talon perform feats with a bow that I doubt few others can match. He tells me that he learned it in Persia. Talon, will you not demonstrate to my Lord the Count this skill? My Lord, it is wondrous what he can do with a bow while on a horse's back."

The Count and Sir Guy looked interested. "Then you shall perform for us all after the jousting is done, Sir Talon."

Talon bowed acceptance and they were ushered out by a servant. As they departed, Talon heard the Count say, "The tourney will be in your honor, Sir Guy; there will be a mêlée for the young knights, led by my son, followed by another led by my captains, against the knights of My Lord of Toulouse, and then some single combat bouts."

As they walked down the cool corridors, again accompanied by Max, Talon turned to his uncle. "Now you've placed me in a pretty pickle."

"Indeed not, Talon, it is good to be able to show off one's martial skills. The jousting will be entertaining, but your skill with a bow is remarkable. You shall do well, I am sure." Philip patted him on the shoulder.

"I agree with Sir Philip, Talon," Max said. "It does a knight no harm at all to be known for his skill at arms and you are very impressive on horseback."

Talon said nothing. He knew he could perform well on Jabbar but he would have preferred to be less conspicuous. It was not in his nature to advertise his skills to others except in situations that demanded it.

They walked down the stairs and were about to leave when a servant wearing the livery of the Count, who had been hovering at the main entrance, came up to them. He bowed respectfully. "Sirs, my Lord Roger would see Sir Talon de Gilles. Which of you is he?"

Philip clapped Talon on the shoulder. "I think you are in demand, Talon. Go with this man. I will be returning to the Temple. I shall come later in the day after prayers to watch you show these people what real horsemanship is all about."

He and Max walked off, leaving him with the servant. Talon followed the servant to the chambers of the young Count Roger and was greeted by his friends from the evening before. All gave a kiss of greeting but he sensed that Elena gave him more than a mere greeting. He looked into her eyes after they had exchanged greetings and saw a promise there that heated his blood.

"We were wondering what could keep you with my father for so long, Talon," said the young Count.

"He was interested, as is everyone, in what goes on in the Holy Land, my Lord."

"Was the ambassador Sir Guy with him?" Andreu asked.

"He was. He is with Lord Richard, who is in Aquitaine at this time."

There were gasps of surprise. "The young Prince Richard has gained a reputation for valor that is second to few other men. So close. We so wish that he would come to Carcassonne," Galiana said wistfully.

"That is precisely what your father said, my Lord Roger." Talon looked over at Roger significantly. The young Count smiled back.

"My father would indeed like to meet Prince Richard in person, but it would be dangerous for both, I fear. One must have a care as to whom one meets and when."

"I hear that there is to be a picnic on the lawns of the garden for your mother, Roger, and we should not be late." Galiana said. She led the way out of the Count's chambers.

As they strode out, Roger walked alongside Talon. "I am to be in the tourney this afternoon. I am to lead the young knights in a mêlée before the main event. Would you care to be one of my knights?"

"I am honored, but I also have to collect my horse and bow. My uncle, God Bless him, has told the Count of a skill I have with the bow and now I have to demonstrate it to all and sundry."

"You could do both. How do you feel about that?"

Talon hesitated for a second. He remembered the messy mock battle fought on the grass at Albi and wondered, but then he reluctantly decided that he needed to know how to fight like this. Besides, his uncle would be upset if he refused. He nodded. "I will fight alongside you, sir."

"That is excellent, Talon," Roger said. He passed the word to the others, who were equally excited at the prospect of seeing Talon perform in the mêlée alongside the young Count as well as to demonstrate his skill with the bow. Andreu and Donate laughed back at them and warned them both that they were on the other side and not to expect any quarter.

He had no time to worry about how well he would do when the time came, for they dragged him down to the gardens of the palace where he was once again presented to the Countess. He admired her beauty and the way she looked at him, but once again he was unable to decipher her expression. They passed a very pleasant lunch on the lawn. The cooks who worked for the Count were very well trained. Talon found that he was eating fare that was simple but presented in such a way that a person made a new discovery each time he took another plate from the hovering servants.

There were many different pâtés from very fine to coarse but each tasted delicious The pâtés and the other pies and sweetmeats were set among olives that had been marinated in olive oil and dusted with dried herbs of all kinds, including lavender. There were cheeses of such variety that he had no idea which to chose; but Elena helped him, laughing at his bemused expression. Then of course there were the wines that he enjoyed, but he had half an eye on the time and did not want to drink too much before the tournament. His companions did not seem to care and ate and drank with gusto.

The Countess again asked him to sit near and to tell her more of his adventures in the far land of Persia, which he did. He was beginning to enjoy her attention and that of the others in this group, who seemed eager to hear more of the great lands to the east of the Holy Land. But he also noticed that Elena was not so pleased with the arrangement—she fidgeted and looked at the sun often.

The countess at one time leaned over to him to present him with a small tidbit. Her fingers brushed his lips as he took the sample. She leaned back and smiled at him. "You remind me of a wild animal that is caged, Sir Talon. I was not sure that I would keep my fingers."

"My Lady," he protested, "not even a caged lion could bite the fingers of one so lovely."

The assembly clapped at his response, but Talon finally realized that the countess understood him all too clearly.

She smiled back and said gently. "You have left something behind in those strange lands, Sir Talon. Only a woman could know."

He felt himself become hot and stammered a feeble reply that seemed only to confirm her assessment.

"So I was right, it is a woman," she murmured in a very low voice.

"A princess, my lady," he all but whispered, his face ashen. How could she have divined this? he wondered.

"May God bring you together one day. I shall pray for you," she said quietly. Her eyes lingered on his for a moment.

It seemed to Talon that they were within a space only they were aware of for a couple of long moments and then they were back into the conversation all around. He was relieved to note that no one else seemed to have heard the interchange. The boys were wagering on their particular side's chances of winning the mêlée.

Talon had to excuse himself and run all the way to his lodgings to find Anwl and to prepare himself for the jousting. He was eager to see what the knights of this great Count could do in a mêlée. He was nervous about his capabilities on the field during the mock battle alongside the prince, but he was reasonably confident that he could handle himself.

He had Jabbar, who responded immediately to every command, either through his back or leg and hand; they were as one together, which would enable him to concentrate upon the fighting without having to worry about controlling his animal. He rode Jabbar toward the great fields outside the city with Anwl and the groom in attendance and reported to the master of ceremonies, who had already been warned by one of the Count's men that he would be along and asked him what he needed in the field. He was told when to arrive for the mêlée which was to be approximately mid-afternoon, so he had time to watch some of the individual jousts before he, too, had to put on the chain mail that he had brought from home. Philip had told him to do this even though he had not been sure he would need it. The fine chain links were lighter but of better steel than the heavy hauberk and leggings of the local knights.

Talon gave instructions and then dismounted and tossed the reins to the groom who would care for the horses while Anwl would watch the equipment until needed. Max came over and elected to stay with Anwl.

Talon had been instructed by the Countess to come to her stand where she and of course the Count would be watching the jousting. He was allowed in by the sentries and went toward the waving group of young friends who stood off to the side of the thrones where the Count and his lady would be seated.

Talon was impressed with the pomp and ceremony; it reminded him of the days he had attended the polo matches in Isfahan. There was an enormous crowd; it seemed as though fully half the city's residents had come out of the city onto its fields. Obviously, although frowned upon by the Church, the sport was very popular here in Languedoc.

There was much blowing of trumpets, flags were flying lazily from high standards in the light breeze, and knights strutted about in their chain mail, either on horseback or on foot. All seemed determined to be seen and noticed by those in the Count's stand. Talon mentioned to Roger that he was utterly confused by all the emblems and designs on their surcoats.

Roger smiled. "You, too, will need your own coat of arms, Talon. You're a knight now."

"Is every knight meant to have a coat of arms, My Lord?"

"It's quite new, but the answer is yes. It has recently become the fashion. Each knight should have an emblem of his own to distinguish him from all others, especially on the battlefield. He can be clearly seen in the confusion of battle and thus his men can rally to him." Roger instructed Talon briefly on the growing art of heraldry, naming men who bore an emblem on their surcoat, the coat of cloth that was worn over the chain mail hauberk. "You will see the emblem also on men's shields when they go into the jousting field in front of us, Talon."

A trumpet sounded and all stood up as the Count and his lady were led to their thrones and seated. Talon noticed Sir Guy in attendance as the honored guest who was placed to the Count's right hand. The countess looked around, spotted her son and his friends and smiled at them. Her gaze rested on Talon briefly; she smiled, and then she turned to look forward. Talon felt his arm squeezed and looked down at Elena, who was holding onto him with a tiny frown on her face. Was it jealously, he wondered?

There was another blast of trumpets and a man in very ornate clothes walked forward of the stands and turned to the Count. Bowing low he addressed the Count and his assembly. "My Lord, My lady, honored guests, and friends. We are to be honored today with a great show of courage and of skill with weapons and by the knights of my Lord the Count of Carcassonne and those of my Lord of Toulouse."

There was applause from the crowded stands. This was to be a very big mêlée involving almost sixty knights. The crowd sensed that there would be bloodshed on the field today.

"There will first be individual bouts of knight against knight with lance and sword, followed by a mêlée of younger knights, led by the Count Roger of Carcassonne, and those of Toulouse, led by Lord Andreu and then the senior knights as the finale," the man shouted.

The crowd cheered and clapped at the news. Roger and Andreu, looking tense, nevertheless laughed and clapped with them.

Roger turned to Talon. "Donate will be with Andreu. Remember, Talon, this is a joust, do not use your sword to kill, just to unseat and subdue your opponent. If you see any foul play, call to me and we will deal with it together. Andreu and Donate will be watching, too."

Andreu nodded. "We are friends on this field and do not want injury, although there will be some. Donate and I will watch for you, Roger."

Talon nodded. "I shall be careful, my Lord. I shall be watching your back, have no fear."

The young Count looked at him hard. "I shall fear not, my friend. I am sure I can depend upon you."

There was a sudden blare of trumpets and the first single combat joust began.

Both knights were riding horses that were of much finer breeding than those he had seen at Albi and clearly knew what they were about. The men, who were clad in mail from head to foot and wearing heavy, flat-topped steel helmets with nose guards, rode sedately up to the stands to greet the Count and his guest while their grooms shouted their pedigree to the crowds.

Roger whispered to Talon that these were the men who had had the brawl in the Count's hall the last night. "Here is their chance to settle the dispute for all time."

The Count waved the two men off whereupon they cantered to either end of the field. At the call of the trumpet they began to gallop toward one another; the huge horses' hooves tossed up clods of earth as they galloped. They came together with a crash that shook the ground as lance splintered on shield. One rider was rocked back in his deep saddle, almost coming off.

The crowd roared its approval and urged the riders to do it again. New lances were presented and they rode back to their ends of the field. Once again they charged each other and again crashed into one another head on. This time the other knight was struck directly in the center of his shield with enough force to topple him right out of the saddle. He tumbled to the ground and lay there while his horse galloped away. The mounted knight, not wanting to lose the opportunity, hastily dismounted and ran toward the other to force the surrender, but was too late.

His opponent had scrambled to his feet and was now waiting for him. They set to with swords and shields. It was clear that this was a grudge fight and soon some blood from superficial wounds began to show against their chain mail; both men were bleeding from the nose and other cuts to the face.

Talon was interested to note that the fighting men knew how to use the whole of the sword from the point of the blade to the pommel and the hilt. If a blow could not distract an opponent, a thrust or a shove with the hilt of the sword at the face would, and often the edge of the shield was used as a weapon, too. Both men went at it savagely for about ten minutes with a wildly cheering crowd before one slipped to one knee and was then taken down hard by his opponent with another blow.

He lay stunned for a few seconds, his shield discarded. His opponent seized his chance and stood high over his victim and with a shout raised his sword high overhead and brought it down hard onto the exposed neck of the man on the ground. There was a sickening crunch heard clearly across the field, as the sword cut through the untempered chain links and partially severed the man's neck. The dying man convulsed briefly and then lay still in a gathering pool of blood.

The victorious knight stood up and received the cheers of the crowd, which liked the sight of blood. He staggered sweating over to the Count's enclosure, received applause from many there, and a few words from the Count. It was clear that the Count was not very pleased with the outcome, but the deed was done and in public so there was little to say. He offered a few words of admonishment and the man hobbled off, looking chastened but also relieved.

Men came and carried the dead man off the field and threw straw over the blood-soaked grass.

Talon watched with interest as more than a dozen bouts, of a less grudging nature this time, were fought in a similar manner, and then it was time for the young Count to lead the mêlée. They took their leave from the ladies and hastened off to arm themselves. Elena swiftly tucked a kerchief into the collar of Talon's mail shirt which he self-consciously fingered in some surprise.

"Do you honor me in battle, Sir Knight?" she asked him archly.

He grinned, embarrassed. "I will surely try, My Lady." There was some laughter at the exchange but he noticed that Elena was watching Countess Roseanna, who laughed, too.

Talon's chain mail evoked some interest as it was clearly of a much better make than that of the knights he was now grouped with. His was of fine-tempered steel and theirs was of iron that could not resist the thrust of a good steel blade.

Most of the young men gathered around the Count waiting for the mêlée to begin were of much the same age and were looking forward to the bout. Everyone was armed with a sword and lance. Their hauberks of chain mail covered them from head to waist while chain trews reached to their feet. They all sported a steel helmet with a nose guard. They were familiar with the rules and were full of bravado as to what they were going to do to the other side.

The trumpets sounded and they mounted up. The Count had loaned Talon a huge Destriere as he pointed out reasonably that Jabbar would not survive the overwhelming weight of the combined charge they were about to face. The horse was in fierce mettle and although larger than Jabbar, managed to prance, his neck arched and his eyes rolling. He shook his head, making the harness jingle, indicating that he wanted to run, and then he tried to buck. Talon, feeling that he was riding an animal of enormous energy, held him firmly with his left hand and guided him with his legs to see how responsive he might be and was pleasantly surprised to find that the animal moved well under his guidance. He was careful to keep his spurs off the sides of the animal for the time being. The horse felt ready to explode underneath him if he were not careful.

They walked their horses onto the field and faced the other team of twenty young men who were glowering at them from ten yards away. Talon had time to observe the others and take stock of them while the herald was announcing the bout. This was to be a simulated battle, commencing when the trumpets were blown, where men would be knocked off their horses and remain on the ground unconscious, or would have to get to their feet and continue until forced to surrender. The winners, after the trumpets had blown again, would be the ones with most men on their horses or standing on their feet.

The herald finished his long-winded speech and the young men saluted the Count in the stands with their lances and shouted their names. They wheeled their horses and cantered to their respective ends of the lists.

Roger turned to Talon. "Talon, stay on my shield side; we'll fight together." He sounded tense.

Talon nodded. "Yes, my Lord."

There was another blast from the trumpets and they were off. Head and body tucked in behind the shield and the lance straight out as steady as he could hold it, Talon had no trouble putting his horse into a gallop to follow the Count who was racing across the field; the Destriere wanted to run.

There was no order to the attack. It was just a wild charge across the green field to collide with the opponents. Talon raced his horse alongside Roger's so that as a pair they hit the other young knights charging the other way. Talon focused on a man coming directly at them slightly onto his side, pointing his blunted wooden lance at the center of the man's shield. Another tried for Roger, who deflected that lance just as Talon's struck the edge of his opponent's shield. It splintered but must have slammed the shield back onto the man's nose piece, for the young man toppled off his horse, unconscious and well out of the fight. Roger was shouting for his men to rally, waving his sword in the air and seeking combat from his foes. Talon kneed his horse alongside and received a grin from the Count.

"That was a good hit! Have you done this before?" he yelled and then he was too busy to listen for a response. The din of mock battle was everywhere as the young men shouted and yelled taunts and challenges at one another, following this up with reckless displays of courage and fierce attempts to unhorse their opponents.

Talon swung round just in time to deflect a blow from the sword wielded by a youth who had ridden in at a sharp angle. It was Donate.

"Hey, Talon, now you must fight for your life," he shouted, grinning through the flat nose piece of his helmet.

Talon grinned back, danced the Destriere out of the way with a touch of his leg and then spurred the horse hard into Donate's, knocking it off balance just long enough for Talon to aim a careful blow to Donate's shield shoulder where it was exposed. It proved effective as with a curse Donate had to pull his horse up; his shoulder was suddenly numb. He slumped in pain over the pommel of his saddle. With another kick to the side of his own mount Talon brought his horse in hard just behind Donate's which allowed him to strike Donate between the shoulder blades with the pommel of his sword. Donate's eyes crossed and he slipped sideways off the saddle and tumbled to the ground.

Talon looked around for Roger and saw that the young Count was surrounded by three opponents. He was fending them off vigorously, but they were about to overcome him by sheer weight of numbers. Talon danced his very hot and eager Destriere forward and with two bounds he crashed into the rump of one of the men surrounding the Count. Talon reached forward and delivered a sharp blow to that man's sword arm just below the shoulder. It would have cut off an arm not covered with chain. As it was, it bruised the man's arm so badly he dropped his sword and turned with a yell of pain and surprise. Talon had ridden alongside, transferred his sword to his shield hand, then seized the youth by his belt and tipped him off his horse to fall with a yell to the ground.

Then Talon was alongside the Count, who swung his head to greet him. He grinned from behind his nose guard, sweat pouring off his face. "That was timely, Talon. I thought you had abandoned me!" he shouted hoarsely.

"I had a little business to settle with Donate, my Lord."

"You unseated him? Then let's deal with the others. I believe we're winning."

They set to and by dint of excellent control of their horses both managed to outmaneuver their opponents and unseat them. They paused after this to take stock of the situation. The noise of steel clashing with steel and shield still rang out. The youths were becoming hoarse and tired now, but their enthusiasm was barely diminished. They still swung their swords at each other with wild abandon, and in some cases they drew blood, but it was unintentional.

Roger pointed to a small group of men who were doing well against his own men.

"Come, Talon. There is Andreu, let's go and take care of him, for then we really shall win."

They galloped the few yards as a tight pair and crashed into the group that failed to react in time. Talon and then Roger managed to unseat their opponents in quick succession, which left Andreu and one other well on guard and equally determined to finish the bout their way.

Andreu went for Roger with an exuberant shout while the other, a very stocky young man, made for Talon, trying to shove him aside with his horse. But Talon's Destriere had other ideas. It was pulling excitedly at the reins, trying to have its head, although still manageable, when suddenly it reared, striking out with its hooves at the other horse. The rider pulled up in alarm in the face of the flailing hooves. Talon rode the horse up easily and then realized that he had another tool in his armory. He spurred his animal hard just as it came down onto all four feet.

It squealed with rage as the sharp points dug into his flanks and jumped straight at the other man and horse. Talon's Destriere struck the other on its side with its chest just where the rider's leg was. The rider screamed with pain, but the force continued and both horse and rider went down under the Destriere's hooves. Talon quickly hauled his horse away to avoid hitting the downed rider, who was sprawled out, clutching his leg. Talon hoped that he had not broken it.

Then it was over. Roger had unseated Andreu, who was ruefully holding his arm but standing. Most of the Count's riders were still mounted. The trumpets sounded and they looked around.

To Talon it did look like a battlefield. There were young men limping off the field or simply lying where they had landed, holding an arm or a leg. Riderless horses were either galloping about the field or calmly grazing. Broken lances discarded shields and swords were laying all about. Roger's team cheered hoarsely, adding their shouts to the cheering crowd of supporters who were screaming applause.

He took off his helmet and swept it in a happy flourish toward his parents, who were standing with the others, applauding. Roger wiped the sweat from his eyes and then searched the remaining men, complimenting them one by one. Then his eyes fell on Talon.

"Sir Talon, you are a true knight. Well, you are knighted. You proved your worth today."

"Thank you, Sire," Talon said. He was pleased he had escaped unscathed from any injury; some of the young men would need a physician tonight or most likely one of the dreaded Leeches, as they were known. He turned his horse to look for Donate and then rode over to his new friend. He dismounted quickly and walked the last few yards to kneel in front of where Donate was standing, watching him.

"I hope you are not injured, my Lord?" Talon asked concerned.

Donate laughed ruefully and shook himself. "Stand up, Sir Talon. Apart from a very sore back I am fine. You proved to us that you are a real warrior today. I am truly impressed with your horsemanship. Here is my hand for the new friendship we have, Sir Talon." He grinned as they shook and then he clapped Talon on the back. "That was right thirsty work. I am ready for some wine. Let us join Roger and the ladies and watch the next fight."

Talon smiled, happy that Donate had been so sporting and gripped his arm. "I am in full agreement, my Lord."

"Nay, Talon, we are friends and friends will have names. I am Donate to you this day."

They led the still dancing Destriere back to the horse lines and Talon turned him over to a hovering groom. When they returned to the stands they were greeted as heroes. Talon, because he was the stranger among them and had done well, was rewarded with much praise.

Elena flung her arms around his neck as he came up and kissed him full on the mouth. "You are truly a warrior, Talon, cunning and masterful on the horse!"

Even the Count laughed and waved to them from his seat and Philip, who was nearby, grinned his appreciation.

Roger was still very excited as were his companions who did not seem to be put out unduly from their loss. They exchanged banter throughout the next mêlée, which Talon was unable to pay much attention to; Elena was demanding much of his concentration.

Soon enough the clash of arms out on the field subsided and the herald was once again standing in front of the Count. But this time he was announcing that Talon was about to put on his demonstration. Talon rushed off to the tents where Max and the Anwl were standing, holding an impatient Jabbar with the bow and quiver waiting for him. Talon mounted and took the bow and quiver, placed the quiver in its place under his left thigh and, giving an impatient Jabbar a pat on the neck, cantered onto the cleared field. He danced Jabbar slowly up to the stands and then swept an elaborate bow from the saddle toward the Count and his Lady. He noticed his newfound friends were gathered behind the chairs of the Count and his guests and were waving enthusiastically at him, to which he replied with a touch of his fingers to his cap which he now wore instead of the helmet.

Behind him men had finished positioning a long, thin pole, about twenty feet high, to which were tied two pigeons that fluttered frantically at the end of a string tied to their feet. Talon set Jabbar into a light canter in a circle around the pole about twenty yards out from the center and lifted his bow. Taking his time he circled twice and then notched an arrow into the string and aimed. The pigeons had settled on top of the pole and seemed to be resting. Talon loosed an arrow at the pole just below the pigeons' feet. The arrow struck the thin pole just below the birds and the crowd hummed, to them it was a near miss.

There was an appreciative murmur from the crowd at this display, but although it would have been a good shot at any time Talon had simply wanted to make the birds fly.

As soon as they took off he knocked another arrow in the string and standing in the stirrups in one fluid motion aimed and loosed the arrow at the flying birds.

The arrow struck one bird true, piercing it through the breast. There was a small cloud of feathers and the bird collapsed on the end of the string and hung limply against the post. The crowd roared its approval and pointed with obvious amazement at his skill.

With Jabbar still cantering in a circle around the pole Talon loosed another arrow at the remaining bird and again his arrow flew true to bring that bird down as well.

Talon cantered slowly toward the stands where his friends stood clapping and cheering; he bowed once again to the Count and his lady.

The Count indicated that he should come closer. "You are a skilled horseman, Sir Talon de Gilles, and we have seen you in a mêlée where you acquitted yourself well. What can we do to reward you for such displays of arms?"

"My Lord, I would see justice for my father in the court of Albi this coming month. That is all I ask, Sire."

The Count turned to Philip, who was standing nearby in his Templar uniform. They conversed in undertones as the Count asked questions. Then he nodded and turned back toward Talon. "I shall see to it, Sir Talon de Gilles. You may inform your father, Sir Hughes, that I will see to it that justice is served."

Talon swept off his cap and bowed deeply from the saddle. "Thank you, Sire. I am very grateful."

He cantered Jabbar off the field, amused that others were now riding their horses onto the field with bows and trying to emulate the feat he had just performed. Arrows were now flying into the crowd from badly aimed weapons, eliciting shouts of surprised anger as people dodged them, or in a couple of cases striking an unwary target.

Max and Anwl greeted him warmly at the tents as he rode up. "That is quite a thing to see. I have not even seen the Saracen perform this feat before. Did you learn it in Persia?" Max asked as he took the reins and patted Jabbar on the neck.

"I did. We were encouraged to do this sport when we were boys. My friend Reza was even better than I at this game."

"Well, Talon Bach," Anwl commented dryly, "you might need to provide some instruction on how it's done; the men out there are about to do much mischief with their bows. I have not seen one come even close and their arrows are flying in all directions. Watch out, my Lord!" he yelled as an arrow flew by, much too closely, and thudded into the ground close by.

A trumpet sounded the end of the events and people began to leave.

Before they left, however, Anwl said something that made Talon pause. "There is a man who has been hanging about our lines this afternoon, m'lord. I saw him this morning when we were in the town as well. It seems like he is watching our every move."

"Where is he now?"

"As soon as you rode up he disappeared. Almost as though he didn't want to be seen."

"Did you see him Max?" Talon asked.

"No, I was too busy watching the show you were giving."

"If you see him again tell me quickly and as quietly as possible, Anwl. I would like to know what he wants."

"Certainly, m'lord," Anwl said, "I shall."

Chapter 15

Mission

The following day Talon was woken by Phillip again banging on the door. "Wake up Talon! We are summoned to the Count's palace," he bellowed.

Hurriedly climbing into his clothes and dashing water over his face, Talon joined Phillip at the entrance to the tavern where he stood waiting impatiently, his cloak billowing in the light breeze.

"Don't we even eat breakfast Uncle?" Talon asked plaintively. He had come to bed late and his mouth tasted dry and wooly.

"The Count waits for no man, my boy. We had best leave breakfast till later." Phillip advised.

"What have we been summoned for Uncle?" Talon asked hurrying alongside, buckling his belt a little tighter and adjusting his sword.

"The Good Lord knows: I have no idea what it could be for, Talon. I had hoped that we might be on the road back to your father today. We'll see." Phillip said as they gained entrance to the palace and walked at a brisk pace along the cobbled road of the inner keep. They were met by a page who guided them to the chambers on the upper floors they had visited the previous day.

As they entered Talon noticed that Lord Guy was again with the Count, and that the hard faced individual was standing in the corridor glowering at them as they entered.

Neither Phillip nor Talon paid him more than a cursory glance before the door was shut and their attention was focused upon the Count and his guest who were standing by the window.

The Count turned and greeted them.

"Good morning Sir Knights. Ah, Phillip, I want to talk to you more about the *Outre-Mere* but at this moment I have something else to discuss. Will you take water or wine?"

Sir Guy walked forward and greeted both. "I am pleased to see you again, Sir Phillip, and you, Sir Talon. Your demonstration of horsemanship with the bow yesterday was remarkable indeed."

The Count called over to one of the men in the corner who was furiously scribbling, the sound of the scratching quill came clearly to their ears in the quiet room.

"Have you not finished yet, Michal? My Lord Guy is impatient to leave."

"Almost ready my Lord! Almost done," squeaked the man and continued to scribble. Another monkish figure hovered over him whispering words that he wrote down.

The Count turned back to Phillip and Talon. His gaze fell upon Talon and he contemplated him a moment before speaking.

"Sir Talon, you demonstrated excellent horsemanship and good weapons skills yesterday, apart from your skill with the bow which will be talked about around here for a long time. I could not fail to notice how well you protected my son in the mêlée. That was the mark of a faithful and trustworthy knight."

Talon blushed with embarrassment. "I was only doing what I thought was the right thing by my Lord Roger, Sire."

"Quite so! It is with that in mind that I am now commanding you to accompany my Lord Guy to Aquitaine as a messenger to bring back certain information that I am desirous to receive."

Phillip half rose in his chair real surprise on his bearded face. "My Lord! Talon is young and what you are asking of him is a high responsibility. With deep respect Sire, why could not one of your other more experienced knights act as the messenger?"

The Count glanced at him sharply and said. "Sir Phillip, you have a right to ask and I am well aware that you were expecting to leave very soon for Albi where there is pressing business. Indeed I would not ask this of Talon but that he is quite unknown in the regions to the west of here and therefore will pass unnoticed. I can assure you there is little danger for him, whereas another of my knights might well be recognized and betrayed. Do you get my meaning?"

Phillip subsided reluctantly.

The Count continued. "Also I have heard reports of Talon from both yourself and also my son, beyond what I myself have seen, that tell me he is exceptional for his age and well able to take care of himself. Am I mistaken in this?" he demanded almost aggressively.

Phillip glanced at Talon and nodded. "I will not protest further my Lord. I would leave it up to Talon to respond."

Talon was excited at the prospect of an adventure on behalf of the Count. He glanced at Philip who nodded, but looked unhappy.

"My Lord, I am yours to command," he stated simply.

There was nothing else he could say. His heart was beating a little faster at the thought of a mission for his Count so soon after having been knighted.

The Count gave him a warm smile. "Well said, Sir Talon. This will be an interesting diversion for you and in the best of company." He indicated Lord Guy, "There is every chance that you will meet and talk with Prince Richard of England. He will be very interested in hearing about the *Outré Mere*."

At that moment the scribe finished writing, he sprinkled sand on the parchment and then, blowing and shaking it to remove the last of the fine sand, he took it over to the Count for him to read.

The Count looked the document over carefully. It seemed to Talon that this was not the first draft but this time the Count nodded his approval and called for the sealing wax. This was presented by the other scribe and a huge blob of red wax was dripped onto the now rolled parchment, held with a blue ribbon, then the Count stabbed at it with his ring bearing the crest of his family. Talon did not see the contents of the parchment; neither did Lord Guy.

The Count handed the document to Lord Guy and said. "I wish you God speed, my Lord. If you will wait in the courtyard I shall send Sir Talon to attend you forthwith."

Count Raymond bade good bye to Lord Guy then he told everyone except Phillip and Talon to leave the room. The monks bustled out clutching rolls of parchment, papers and pens and ink.

When the door was firmly closed the sound of parting steps had receded the Count turned back to the men in the room.

"Good, now listen carefully as this information is for the ears of only those within this chamber.

"I am sending a written message with My Lord Guy to Richard. Prince Richard is in Aquitaine and is seeking my aid. His father is making noises about moving down from Normandy to crush what he sees as a rebellion by the Prince. I intend to offer help in the form of men and treasure to show good will for the future.

"None of this must ever reach the ears of either his father, Henry, or King Louis—do I make myself clear?" he demanded, his voice low but hard.

Both men nodded their agreement.

He turned his stern gaze upon Phillip and said. "Sir Phillip, the only reason I have included you is that you are somewhat of a guardian for this young man, and you are a relative. I am also aware that your allegiance is to the Church of Rome, so you are here on my trust. Do I have your word that none of this will go further than this chamber?"

Phillip stood up and faced the Count and placed his hand on his heart. "You have my word as a Templar Sire. Nothing shall go beyond this chamber."

The Count nodded and continued. "Talon, you are to remember the numbers I give to you now, as none of this is written down in the parchment I have given Lord Guy. The information will be delivered by word of mouth by you only. I trust Lord Sir Guy implicitly, but I do not know if there is a spy among his retinue. The damned scum are everywhere; both those of King Henry, but also those of Louis. I have to be very careful. I would therefore rather not compromise him or the Prince with damning information in writing. However, everyone will know that Lord Guy came to visit me, so he must go home with something to show for his troubles; that will throw the spies off the scent."

He then proceeded to list the men, horses and supplies he could provide and where they would be available. When done he told Talon to repeat verbatim what he had said and was pleased when Talon made no mistakes.

"Go with God and may he protect you and Sir Guy and bring me the news I wish to hear in haste," he said by way of dismissal.

Talon had arranged to meet Sir Guy at the north gates within the hour. He had Anwl snatch some food from the Inn kitchens then bade a hurried good bye to Phillip who was decidedly unhappy at this unexpected turn of events, as was Max. Anwl on the other hand was excited and made haste to get their baggage ready so that they could ride immediately.

Talon told him, "I am assured by the Count himself that this is a routine visit and we are to meet the great Richard of England, Anwl."

"I have never seen an English Prince, Milord. Not like our Princes in Wales, I think me," responded Anwl happily.

Anwl, although not as good a rider as Talon, was competent enough on a horse so it was not long before the two of them trotted their mounts toward the gate and were greeted by Lord Guy, who was impatient to leave. Alongside him on a charger was the man who had been lurking around the corridors while the Lord spoke to Count Raymond. The man glowered at Talon but said nothing and Lord Guy did not bother to introduce them. Talon noted the huge sword the knight carried on a belt over his shoulder. It was two handed and looked very businesslike.

They were seen off from the gates of the city by a curious crowd who had not seen English knights or men at arms before. The brightly colored pennants on the tips of the lances snapped in the breeze and the horses, sensing an adventure, were stepping high, arching their necks and chomping on their bits. Men sat their mounts stiff and proudly as they were sent off with a cheer from the friendly people of Carcassonne.

"We will head along the main road towards Toulouse but then take the southern route around the city, as I do not wish to stay there overnight. Too full of people loyal to the King of France, I fear." Lord Guy told Talon.

"Where are we going, my Lord?" asked Talon who had no idea as to where Toulouse might be let alone any other place in the country.

"We will travel northwest till we are in Aquitaine and once within the borders we will find the road to Auch where I hope that the Prince will still be hunting," said Sir Guy.

Talon looked back at the men who accompanied them. Sir Guy had only six in all, but tough looking men who were undoubtedly English from their light beards and huge mustaches. They were all well mounted and armed. Their faces and eyes half hidden by the flat topped iron helmets and long nose guards gave the men a forbidding aspect.

The one man who Talon was concerned about was he who stayed close to Sir Guy. He disdained to wear a helmet but wore a good hauberk of chain with a chain hood which was pushed back over his shoulders leaving his shaved head clear. It showed off the scars on his face and only half an ear on the left side of his skull. He sported a wide yellow mustache and his hard blue eyes never seemed to miss anything.

In an undertone Talon mentioned the man to Anwl and pointed him out saying, "I am not sure of this man and I do not trust him very much, although apparently Sir Guy does. I suspect that he speaks French so be careful what you say in front of him, Anwl."

"I shall, m'lord." said Anwl. "But he is not likely to understand my French in any case." He gave his gap-toothed grin to Talon who, knowing exactly what Anwl meant, laughed quietly. He was excited at the prospect of this unexpected journey into Aquitaine. He wished only that he could have had time to say good bye to his new friends.

They rode for the rest of the day following an old Roman road that led over rolling forested hills. Their route took them over some well made stone bridges and across wide fords. The forests were full of game, and it was not hard to pick out deer watching them from the shadows or even crossing their path. Lord Guy did not tarry to hunt, although many were the times Talon could have brought down a small deer for supper without getting off Jabbar. However, Lord Guy seemed impatient to get to his destination without delay.

Some times when the hills were less densely populated with tall stands of trees they were afforded spectacular views of the distant snow clad mountains to the south. The road that they followed towards Toulouse was well used and not in good condition. They frequently passed slower parties of merchants and the occasional group of monks or pilgrims going in either direction. Often the people going their way would call out to ask if they could accompany the armed group for protection against robbers on the road. But Lord Guy would not tarry for them so they were left behind to fend for themselves.

They did not encounter any delays, so they made good time and by evening they were near a small fortified village where they were permitted entrance and stayed the night at the only inn of which the village could boast.

That night, over local beer and wine and a haunch of roasted mutton, Lord Guy became an entertaining host who asked many questions about the *Outré Mere* and in turn told Talon about his native country, England. His own estates were extensive and located in the great valley of Thames, as he called the river not very far from Oxford, a city of learning, he explained. He laughed at Talon's attempt to pronounce the name of the river.

As all this was very new to Talon he listened with interest and asked many questions of his own that Lord Guy was happy to answer.

Talon wanted to know about this legendary Prince of England and Lord Guy told him what he could.

"He is known for his fighting skills and his great strength, Talon. You have already seen the mêlée and have indeed taken part in one; however when the Prince joins the one side, the other is immediately at a disadvantage and is bound to lose. He is a big man and when he strikes, even without intent to maim, a man falls, it's as simple as that!"

"Does he have brothers or sisters, my Lord?'

"He has two brothers, neither of whom is close to him in physique nor ability. However King Harry, who lacks nothing in cunning, sets the brothers against one another, so that he can rule and they cannot unite against him. He is jealous of his kingdom and will not share it." He lowered his voice when he said that and winked.

"But the one both the King and the Prince need to watch and to be very careful of is John, the king's other son. That man has brains and could make a good administrator one day. If the two could only work together, they would make a pair hard to defeat in any Christian land."

Talon went to bed that night somewhat confused as he tried to understand the makeup of the English Royal family.

The next day they left early and rode hard but with more care as they were now within the environs of Toulouse and Sir Guy did not want to draw unwanted attention to his little band before they could make a diversion around the south of the city. As he pointed out there would be awkward questions to answer as to why a party of English were in the area and had not visited the city to offer their respects to the Count of Toulouse or even request permission to cross his land. Two of the men were well forward of the main group watching for any large party that might be on the road going the opposite way.

But while traffic did increase, as Toulouse was a large trading city, no parties of high rank came the opposite way. They were not accosted and the day passed uneventfully.

While there was not a great increase in tension, the men were more watchful of their front and the undergrowth on the side of the road; and consequently so too was Talon and Anwl. Sir Guy turned in the saddle and said to Talon.

"I am expecting to be met by a party led by one of Richard's most trusted knights at the border. I will be more comfortable once we've crossed that line."

To Talon, who felt that he was within the bounds of his own country, the statement seemed odd, but he had had the rudiments of an understanding given him by his young friends the previous night and understood that the land of Aquitaine was firmly in the hands of an English King; hence it was, in effect, another country.

They crossed the border of Aquitaine into a region Lord Guy called Gascony without incident, although there was little to indicate that there was actually a border other than a tower at a crossroads, and even that was abandoned. However, the men now visibly relaxed and Sir Guy seemed to think the journey from here on to Auch was going to be straightforward.

"We are to be met close to here by Sir Nigel of Norfolk with an escort, so keep your eyes open, Talon, as they should be waiting for us near here."

Night was drawing in so Talon was also looking for a likely place to either camp or, if they came across an inn, to stay the night. However, as the evening drew on it looked as though they would be camping. In fact the dusk came down fast after the sun had set; so Sir Guy reluctantly agreed that they should make stop, near to water if possible, and not continue in the dark as a misplaced foot by a horse on the rough road might mean a bad accident. There was no sign of the people they were to meet.

The two forward scouts located a ford just a bit further along the road. Here they could get off the road into a meadow of tall grass that seemed to have been cut naturally into the surrounding forest. They could hobble the horses and sleep on the swathe of grass under the branches of a stand of large oaks and elm trees near the middle of the field.

As they rode into the field they all noticed a herd of five small deer on the far end of the long meadow. Lord Guy stopped his horse to watch the animals and so did everyone else.

"My Lord, it is a long shot but my man here could bring one down for supper." Talon whispered.

Lord Guy nodded slowly. Talon indicated to Anwl that he could try for the deer. Anwl had to dismount; as he did so the deer, having seen men on horses, had not been alarmed, but now one of the intruders was on his feet they sensed that something was wrong and began to head slowly for the shelter of the undergrowth.

In one swift motion Anwl stepped forward of the horses, notched an arrow and sent it on its way with a loud twang of his bow string.

The arrow sped in a low arc for nearly eighty yards and struck true. One of the small deer leapt into the air and fell to the ground. The rest disappeared like magic into the woods. It was an impressive shot of some distance and in poor light; there was a murmur of approval from the English men at arms.

Anwl was off running, his knife out to finish it off while the troop of men dismounted and prepared the camp.

Once a fire had been made they all ate fresh venison along with some stale bread and cheese provided by the soldiers. One of the English pointed with his chin at the long bow that Anwl carried and said something to Lord Guy.

He turned to Talon and said, "That was a difficult shot for anyone in this poor light. They say that looks like a long bow of the kind that the Welsh carry. Where did your man learn to use it?"

Talon thought quickly. "My man learned the use of it from Welshmen in the Kingdom of Jerusalem, my Lord, and has used it ever since to good effect."

Lord Guy translated for him and the men smiled and showed their appreciation for the meal with signs and smiles. Later Lord Guy and his bodyguard sat aside and talked quietly together while the English soldiers sat close to the fire.

It was odd to listen to the men talking in their native tongue. Although there were some half-hearted attempts to communicate, as neither Talon nor Anwl spoke English, it petered out and they went over to their hobbled horses and sat talking together in low tones. Night fell and the forest all about them began to come alive.

Talon and Anwl bedded down some way from the other men, near some dense bushes on the edge of the field. It was more from habit than anything else. Both knew the value of having cover

nearby. They could hear rustlings and the sound of small animals as they scurried about on the dried leaves of the forest. In the distance an owl hooted and a fox yapped. Talon enjoyed the feel of the forest again and he sensed that Anwl did as well. It was not long before the English camp settled down to sleep.

Talon slept lightly as was normal. He had noticed that although guards had been set at dusk no one relieved them and in consequence when he got up just before dawn to go into the bushes, he could make out no men standing where he assumed the guards might be. He shrugged but when he came back to his rough bed of leaves he heard a whisper from Anwl.

"M'lord, have you been hearing those noises?"

"Such as?" Talon responded in a whisper.

"I woke some time ago and thought I heard horses some ways off, the other side of the ford perhaps, but then that stopped and I went back to sleep. But then I heard a cry in the same direction. I am sure it was not an animal, m'lord. I think there are others nearby and for what reason I do not know. We should be on our guard."

Talon had been kneeling to hear Anwl better but now he lifted his head and both concentrated on listening to the sounds of the night.

Although Talon heard nothing to worry him he decided that Anwl was right; the Welsh lived by their woodcraft and the forest seemed to have gone very quiet, although he did not hear any other sounds that might betray human movement in the woods nearby.

The eastern sky was just beginning to be streaked with light; it was almost dawn and he thought it would be a good idea to wake the others just in case.

He got up and walked over to the dark group of prone bodies where Lord Guy and his men were sleeping. He was greeted with snores as he approached but he had not counted on the bodyguard of Lord Guy. The man was on his feet faster than Talon had expected with his sword in his hand.

"Who goes?" His voice was full of menace.

Talon stopped and even took a step back, his hand on his own sword.

"It is I, Talon. I wanted to wake you. We, myself and my man, have heard movement and noises that are not entirely those of animals and I came to tell you that we should be on our guard."

The big man moved the point of the huge sword away from the direction of Talon's midriff. He was silent, seeming to be digesting the information.

"From where did you hear the noises?" he asked in passable French.

"To the northwest along the road." Talon pointed.

"I shall wake them, it's almost dawn anyway."

Talon turned and walked away. He had done what he could, but now he wanted himself and Anwl to be up and mounted so they could leave in good time. Suddenly the woods about seemed to contain menace, and he felt very exposed in this field with little cover.

They had just finished tying down the blankets on the saddles and were watching the rest of the men and the English Lord doing the same when they all heard the sound of horses' hooves on the distant road.

Talon mounted up, as did Anwl, and Talon called a low warning to Lord Guy. Immediately the English mounted and as a body rode out onto the roadway, every man alert for trouble.

They were greeted by the sight of several well mounted knights in fine chain armor and bright cloaks walking their horses down the road towards them followed by many men at arms, some on horseback. The knights were still on the other side of the ford and about a hundred yards away, but could be clearly distinguished in the early morning light as men of substance. Behind the knights were men at arms and footmen with pikes with others carrying crossbows.

Sir Guy and the English all relaxed. "These are the men we were expecting." Sir Guy said to Talon.

But Anwl gave a low exclamation. "Talon, do you see what I see?"

Talon did see. The man in the front of the group coming ever closer seemed to be swaying in the saddle and looked ready to fall off. In fact his eyes seemed sightless to the point where he could have been dead. Another man rode very close to him almost as though he might be supporting him in the saddle.

Talon felt a whisper of dread slither down his back. How was a dead man riding towards them? But then he realized that Sir Guy had not noticed and was urging his horse forward with a shout of greeting.

"Sir Guy!" Talon called.

But Sir Guy did not hear him and continued towards the on-coming men.

"Nigel! We were expecting you last night! Where have you been?" he called as his horse splashed into the river.

At that moment the man who Talon considered Sir Guy's bodyguard seemed to sense danger because he bellowed something in the English tongue to Lord Guy.

It was clear to Talon that he had suspected a trap and was shouting a warning. Sir Guy glanced back once and then forward when he too realized that there was something dreadfully wrong. He tried to turn his horse, but by then it was too late as the advancing men were now very close. The man in front slid sideways in the saddle and fell to into the water. No one seemed to care; instead there was a shouted order.

"What is this?" Lord Guy shouted at the helmeted men bearing down on him.

But they did not reply, instead they spurred forward, dropping lances and couching shields as they came on with deadly intent at a gallop directly towards the small party of Sir Guy. Someone shouted.

"Do not kill him, I want him alive!"

Sir Guy was ridden into and beaten off his horse into the water before he could even draw his sword, then the armed men swept by. The horses splashed into the ford raising a huge spray that flew higher than themselves. The whole effect was made even more sinister by the way the dark knights hidden behind their shields and their faces covered and long lances pointed directly towards them seemed to be not of humankind. In that instant, time seemed to stand still.

Talon's gaze flicked to several footmen running over towards the dazed Lord Guy as he tried to sit up in the river, their spears pointing at him.

He immediately realized that there was treachery about, but he knew nothing of its significance other than that his survival depended upon being quick and agile and above all escaping. The bowmen had dispersed to the sides of the road and already their bolts were whispering through the air and some had already struck men and horses nearby with sickening thumps. Those men tumbled off their horses to be ridden over by the charging knights who crashed into the small party of English soldiers, the shock taking men and horses down.

By some miracle neither he nor Anwl were struck, perhaps because they were at the end of the file of men. His heart in his mouth Talon directed Jabbar to the right down the side of the road back towards the field they had only just vacated, shouting for Anwl to follow.

Looking back it seemed as though the group of men who they had just been with had been destroyed. There were only two men left on their horses, and one was the man who guarded Sir Guy. But the screams of dying men and horses were loud in the cold morning air.

This man, seeing that he had no chance if he stayed, slashed his way out of the mêlée shouting his war cry and driving through the men all around him. On his way out he cut off a man's arm, who fell with a shriek to the ground to join the others, and then the great sword hacked another almost in two as he sat in the saddle. That man died in welter of blood without a sound.

Then the man was through the surrounding men and pounding after Talon and Anwl. But he was followed by a hail of arrows, one of which struck his horse in the flank. The horse took the big man well into the field before it nosed into the ground and tossed him forward almost at the feet of Jabbar.

Talon had his bow out by now and loosed an arrow at the group of men just beginning to ride into the field behind the man now at his feet. They were forty paces off but his arrow did some damage as there was a shout of pain and a man fell off his horse. The loose horse galloped across the field but in the wrong direction or they might have captured it.

Lord Guy's bodyguard staggered to his feet looking dazed. Realizing what had happened, he recovered his huge sword then looked up at Talon, his eyes blazing.

"There is treachery here! You must survive and you must deliver the news to Prince Richard. Tell him of this and tell him I died well."

"Who are you that I might tell him?" Talon called down at him while he watched the enemy riding towards them, the archers stopping to wind up their bows before notching a bolt. They seemed to be coming towards them much too fast. He glanced up and saw a mounted man with a wide bearded face, his helmet off, who shouted something in a language he did not understand but the meaning was clear. The men on horseback were determined to kill them.

"I am Sir Bertrand! Tell the Prince that Lord Guy is taken by Cumberland. Now go! Go! I shall hold them as long as I can. Go! God protect you!"

He turned and strode towards the men coming towards him brandishing his sword and shouting something at his enemies.

Talon glanced at Anwl and nodded. They wheeled their mounts and galloped towards the far end of the field. As one last act of defiance Talon hauled his bow out and, turning full in the saddle, sent an arrow arcing into the ranks of the footmen and archers. He had the satisfaction of seeing another one of them fall to the ground. Seconds later the two rode into the bushes and urged their horses through the forest at a flat out gallop. The last Talon saw of Sir Bertrand was his whirling sword and a man on horseback falling to the ground. That man would give a good account of himself before he went to meet his maker.

But Talon noticed with a trickle of fear that some of the men on horseback had bypassed Sir Bertrand and were giving determined chase.

"Hurry, Anwl, we must ride for our lives! They're following us!" he called.

Jabbar needed no persuasion to run and being a very nimble animal dodged and weaved among the trees without needing guidance, but it was mere chance that a low hanging branch or animal hole in their path did not bring either horses or riders down as their horses fled through the dense woods.

The enemy followed hard on their heels, crashing through the woods in hot pursuit, yelling and hallooing like hunters after their quarry. The footmen with bows also gave determined chase, stopping from time to time and shooting at the fleeing pair as the bolts thumping into trees nearby attested.

After some frantic minutes of dodging and weaving among the trees the numbers of people chasing them seemed to thin out as their horses tired or they ran out of breath, but there were several very determined men still after them.

Talon glanced back at Anwl and called, "How many do you think are still there?"

"I think there is one horseman, maybe two, and some runners." Anwl called back, his head only a few inches off his sweating horse's neck. He was not as good a rider as Talon and was hanging on for dear life to his charging mount.

Talon estimated that the men giving chase might be far enough back for him and Anwl to turn the tables with their bows but it would be close. These were very determined men.

They galloped up a low bank into another dense thicket which slowed the horses, the saplings whipping and tearing at horse and rider. It was at this instant Talon decided to make a stand. He hauled on this bow and quiver then leapt off Jabbar calling to Anwl to do the same.

Both men tumbled into the bushes in untidy heaps, letting their horses run on. Talon was sure that Jabbar would not go far and would wait. Recovering his bow Talon pointed to the thicket and ran back the couple of yards towards it.

The two crouched, tried to catch their breath, checked their bows then pushed through to the edge of the thicket on the top of the bank. They were just in time to see a rider hurtle out of the thickets on the other side of the small clearing and gallop straight towards them. The horse was lathered with foam and sweat and it kicked up clods of the loamy soil as its rider spurred it ruthlessly onward, lashing at it with the flat of his sword.

Talon and Anwl loosed their arrows at the same time. They heard the audible double thump of the arrows striking the man in the chest and his choked cry before he tumbled off his mount to hit the ground and slide to within twenty yards in front of them. The terrified horse galloped up the low bank then right past them, almost knocking them over as they knelt concealed in the thicket. The sound of its pounding hooves died out as it disappeared into the forest. They hurriedly notched another arrow each and waited. The man in front of them lay sprawled in a lifeless heap half covered in leaves.

They did not have long to wait; two more men came running hard along the thin track left by the rider and almost fell over his body. Two arrows found their mark and the men fell with choking cries and died nearby.

It was time to leave. Talon guessed that others following would hesitate before continuing the chase once they saw their dead companions.

Running now, the two left the scene and hunted for their horses. As he had expected, Jabbar was grazing about a hundred paces away having found some nice green grass to occupy him, while the other mount was nervously eating just a little further on.

It took a few tense seconds to capture that animal and then they were mounted and again riding hard.

Talon thought he heard some shouting and guessed that the bodies had been discovered; but it was not long before the shouts faded to nothing and Talon felt it safe to slow their headlong rush. He stopped Jabbar on a small rise, both to rest the blowing horses and to listen for pursuit. But for the sound of small birds in the uppermost branches of the tall trees, the forest was silent.

"We have to find our way out of here and head north to a place called Auch. I remember Sir Guy talking about that town. He said that Prince Richard would be there hunting. The Prince is waiting for a message from Sir Guy, but I do not think it will be delivered now," he told Anwl.

Anwl, who was quite at home in the forest, indicated that north was in the direction he pointed and they could proceed. They dismounted to rest the horses, which were still blown from the mad dash out of danger, but all the while they walked they listened to the forest for any clue as to who might be following them still.

Anwl was aggrieved. "I thought you were told this was to be a gentle visit to a Prince, Talon? This is not gentle!"

Talon was anguished. "For the love of God, I do not understand what is happening, Anwl. But I fear our good Count anticipated this, or something like it, and now we are to deliver a message to a place I have never been, to a man I do not know, and have never even seen before."

"Do not fear, m'lord. If we can find the road again we might be ahead of these men and have a chance of making this Auch place before them. In which case you can bear witness against them. Would you recognize any of them again? In any case, we must find the town you speak of and try to find the Prince, should we not?" he asked anxiously.

Talon shook his head. "There was only the one with his helmet off, a man with red hair and a wide face. He I would recognize in the middle of a pitched battle, but none of the others... not one, God curse them! Sir Bertrand called a name. Cumb'land I think it was, but I am not very sure. What did Lord Guy do to deserve this? I don't think it was meant to end in this manner," he muttered,

"Come Anwl, You're right we must press on and try to get to the town before those murdering cutthroats."

They rode all the rest of the morning and well into the afternoon before the forest began to thin out indicating that there might be signs of human habitation and cultivation. They rode with extra care after this, staying away from any large tracks, keeping instead to the narrow trails that wove in and out of the stands of trees. Despite this, they ran into woodsmen who had been cutting trees and charcoal maker huts along the way. None of these filthy and ragged people tried to stop them however, other than to greet them respectfully with curious looks. They appeared to be pondering as to what two riders were doing in this remote area of the forest.

Anwl with unerring accuracy held them in a north westerly direction, saying that the road had followed this course before they left it. Late in the afternoon they passed what looked like a monastery perched on a hill, and Talon would have dearly liked to have taken shelter there. But, even with his fears and uncertainties, he knew their mission was to find the Prince and warn him of the treachery, despite the unknown dangers that might await them in the town.

Soon after they crested a hill and saw what appeared to be a sizable town in the distance. It was seated on a high wide hill and contained what seemed to be a church or cathedral and a massive castle with many tall towers, all clustered tightly together. The town had high walls built all round the one side they could see. There was a river flowing at the base of the hill providing further defense against a would be besieger. They could see boats sailing up and down the water.

It seemed to the two weary travelers that this must be the town they were seeking.

"I wonder if that is Auch," Talon asked himself.

"It is a great town, m'lord. It seems to be almost as large as Carcassonne. We have no choice but to ask," said Anwl. "There are carts down there, we could ask the farmers," he added pointing.

With great caution they approached the carts stopped on the side of the road where some peasants were seated eating and Talon asked them the name of the town.

He was told it was indeed Auch and that, yes, it was known the English Prince was in residence. The peasants were going to the market which was to open the next day.

"Have you seen any other travelers going along this road towards the town today?" asked Talon.

"No m'lord, but there was a large group of English going the other way last evening. Most of the travelers around here are the pilgrims."

Talon turned to Anwl. "It must have been the men we had the misfortune to encounter, Anwl. You were right; we are ahead of them and must get within the gates before nightfall and hide."

Thanking the peasants they galloped the last mile or so to the city gates, arriving in time to join a party of peddlers and other people with laden donkeys who were about to gain admittance. There were the usual heads on spikes above the gate and even a corpse hanging from the limb of a nearby tree to greet them.

The soldiers waved them in and the two trotted their horses along the cobbled streets towards the center looking for the entrance to the castle.

They passed the by now familiar mounds of filth at every corner, and the sides of the street they rode along were piled with dirt and other stinks that made Talon want to gag. There were a lot of people milling about near the center of the town at the entrance to the large twin towered church.

"They are pilgrims, I think, m'lord," Anwl told Talon when he asked. According to Anwl the men and women carried the staff and cup that was associated with those on a pilgrimage, some even wore elaborate badges on the front of their tunics indicating from where they had come. Talon wondered if this town contained a famous shrine. He'd heard about those.

He thought that he could ride up to the gates of the castle and demand entrance to see the Prince. But in this he was to be disappointed, as the guards were English and spoke only a smattering of

French. They were not interested in a young man impudently asking to see the Prince for whatever reason. Talon even tried to invoke Lord Guy's name but they were not interested in that either. They barred his entrance with long pikes and made it clear that if he tried to ride past they would use them.

Angry and frustrated, Talon turned away and he and Anwl set about finding a likely place where they could stable their mounts and hide themselves while they decided upon their next move.

Not far into the town they had passed a narrow street where they noticed a hostel, so they went back and turned in there. For a few coppers they were given stalls for the animals which they unsaddled and rubbed down, then fed.

But finding accommodation was hard and Talon had to pay a high price for a room they would share in a rundown inn. The landlord told him that all the rooms were taken because it was the season for pilgrims heading south and Santiago de Compostela.

"Where is this shrine?" asked Talon innocently.

The man smirked at his lack of knowledge. "Why, everyone knows it's on the other side of the Pyrenees mountains and a long way from here. These poor fools have a long, long way to go and many a trial ahead of them. They will worship at the cathedral here and then make their way in large numbers to the south, and we will have a little peace for a while. That is when the English will have left too. Those soldiers are animals, they drink and whore like there is no tomorrow!" He gave another gap toothed grin and told them where to find their room.

"I have to gain entrance to the castle and find the Prince urgently," said Talon to Anwl. While they were leaving after the altercation with the guards Talon's eyes had been busy. The fortifications were nowhere as good as those of Carcassonne nor quite as high; and he felt reasonably certain that he could gain entry, if he had to, by other means.

Later that afternoon they were seated at the table of a nearby tavern eating a stew of goat's meat and a huge loaf of bread washed down with a flask of sour wine. As dusk drew in, the tavern began to fill up. A girl in a dirty apron walked round the tables lighting thick candles, while the tavern keeper stayed near the kitchen and shouted orders to people bustling about within.

Most of the customers were French speaking, either peddlers or merchants, with the occasional farmer and better off pilgrim. There were some English soldiers in a corner drinking mead and playing dice, their spears stacked untidily in a corner. Apparently they felt secure here in this inn.

Anwl glowered at the English soldiers, muttering a curse in Welsh under his breath. Clearly he did not like them; but, apart from that, he concentrated on the conversation with Talon.

"I shall go into the castle tonight, Anwl. We just have to find a quiet place where I can climb the walls undisturbed." Talon whispered.

Anwl looked across at Talon, his eyes questioning, but he nodded. He knew enough about his young leader to know that if he said he could get into the palace, then he could.

Talon had purchased a small square of parchment from a street vendor and a quill and some ink. He busied himself with the note he was writing while Anwl kept watch for any unwelcome intrusions. The girl came and lit their candle and expressed interest in what Talon was doing; but he paid her no attention and Anwl waved her away. She left with an irritated swing of her hips.

Once the note was completed Talon blew on the wet ink to dry it then folded the scrap of parchment carefully into a small package which he put into the folds of his tunic. They were now dressed in common homespun clothes which a few coins had purchased and were therefore indistinguishable from anyone else in the room. They carried only knives on their persons having reluctantly left their bows and swords in the flea-ridden room they had rented earlier.

They finished their meal and pulling the hoods of their outer tunics over their heads to hide their faces they walked along the main road of the town. They joined the last crowd of the day as people made their way to their homes or traveled toward other drinking taverns.

There were several in the town, the one nearest the gates of the palace was full of off duty English soldiers who were well into their cups, some singing drinking songs, others playing dice and others quarreling. One or two were sprawled out dead drunk in the filthy ditch nearby, ignored by their companions who were trying hard to get into the same state of inebriation.

Apart from casting a wary eye over the less drunken soldiers, Talon paid them no attention as he concentrated on his objective. He was walking slowly along the bank across from the walls of the castle looking as unobtrusively as he could at the battlements above them; there was no moat.

The ancient walls were made of rough stone and mortar, the mortar being worn away between the stones, which left nice spaces for fingers to grip. His heart quickened as he realized that these walls at least would not be a problem. What he wanted, however, was a quiet location where people did not come by very often and where there might be dark shadows.

They discovered it after walking for half an hour slowly around the castle base. They had had to dodge the many drunken soldiers that were staggering from one ale house to another. With the English Prince in the town the townspeople were doing a roaring trade in ale, wine and whoring.

They paused at the place where Talon intended to climb. Anwl looked up and said quietly, "Are you sure you can climb this wall, m'lord? It looks both high and dangerous."

"I have climbed much harder in the dark, Anwl. This will be easy by comparison. We will wait near here, and when it's dark enough I shall climb it. Do keep watch, but I shall be gone for several hours, as I have to find the Prince and then get him alone and talk to him, or at least leave a message for him to read in private."

The climb went much as he expected, although on one occasion some drunken soldiers decided to sit at the base of the wall, while he was suspended half way up, and have a drunken argument that led to knives being drawn and much shouting.

One of the sentries further along the way shouted down at the weaving men and they left, shouting back and making obscene gestures at the invisible person on the battlements above. Talon slowly let out his breath when they and the sentry finally moved on. He was tucked into a corner formed by the wall and a buttress, in deep darkness, and his arms and calves ached with the strain of hanging there for so long without movement.

He eased his way up the remainder of the wall and very carefully peered over the battlements to see if there was anyone nearby. He could make out the figure of a man standing about thirty feet away leaning on the battlements looking down at the flickering lights of the town. He was probably wishing that he too could be down there drinking himself insensible with his comrades.

Talon slipped over the edge and disappeared into the dark shadows of the nearby tower where he rested for a while to ease his cramped limbs.

He now had to make his way into the inner keep where the Prince would be dining at this time or even in his own chambers. But first he had to find out what the Prince looked like. He hoped that the Prince would still be dining so that he could see him in the hall, but there was a lack of noise that told him the feasting might be over. It was by now quite late.

He contemplated the rough walls of the towers before him without enthusiasm. Keeping to the shadows, Talon slipped along the inside of the castle outer wall until he came to a large entrance guarded by men at arms. The area was well lit by numerous torches in sconces along the walls. These men wore a triple lion coat of arms on their tunics which Talon assumed belonged to the Prince. He had to get past them and into the inner keep somehow; he faded into the darkness to think about it.

Fortune favored his patience because a group of people attended by servants came walking by. Without waiting Talon seized a torch and joined the group. Their path was lit by torches carried by these and other servants at the front of the group of chattering men and women. At the back Talon drew no attention. People seemed to think he was just another servant in attendance.

As they approached the doorway the guards came to attention and respectfully lifted their pikes to allow the group through. Talon followed, pretending to be attentive to the people around him and ignoring the guards. His interest in the people he accompanied sharpened, these were not ordinary folk.

The group spoke French but they were not of the Languedoc, that much he could ascertain. He assumed they were therefore from Aquitaine, but they kept using words in another language so it was somewhat confusing to listen to them.

Nonetheless they had enabled him to gain entrance and he was just about to leave them when one of the people in the front used the words "My Lord Richard."

Talon froze. This had to be the Prince and a small group of his nobles and ladies. He took off his cowl, which inside the building would have made him conspicuous, and decided to stay with the group to see where they went. He looked about for hounds as these would be the greatest obstacle to his getting close to the prince, but there were none with the party so he walked on with them, hoping he would not encounter any.

In fact the cheerful group wanted warmth and hot wine, which was called for as all of them walked up some wide stone stairs towards the entrance of another low ceilinged chamber that seemed to be private quarters. There were men at arms at this entrance too, but again the party passed through without being challenged.

Talon gave a swift assessment of the room, deposited his torch in a vacant sconce nearby, and left the group for the darkness of the corners. He hid behind some pillars, then waited to see what would happen. In this light he did not think he could be recognized by anyone present, but in his present mode of dress he now stood out as a servant.

He noticed a hound lying in the corner near the fire, but to his relief it showed no interest in him, preferring it seemed to be near the warmth of the fire rather than investigating the dark corners of the room.

There was much banter and laughter from the group at the witticisms of the lead person who now stood by the fire. Clearly the people were pandering to the man's ego as they laughed at almost everything he said, and it was equally clear that he enjoyed the attention. Now Talon could see the features of the man he searched for. At least he assumed it was the Prince.

The man was tall and muscular; his trimmed beard only partially hid strong, angular features and a sensual mouth. His voice was a deep baritone and his laugh infectious. He made an imposing figure dressed in tight silk doublet and fine wool leggings. His long cloak swirled in the torchlight as he turned from one to the other. Talon's assumptions were confirmed when the conversation diverted from jokes to a question put by the same man.

"Has anyone heard tell of Lord Guy at all today?"

"None, my Lord. Was he not due back today from Carcassonne?"

"According to the messenger he sent he was, and his escort was to be Sir Nigel, who has not reported anything amiss, as far as I know it, My Lord Prince." said another.

A log fell with a shower of sparks illuminating the faces of the whole party grouped around the fire. Talon gave a small gasp. Among the gathering of men and women was a face that he would never forget. The same face of the man at the ford who had been shouting orders. He had thought a voice among the crowd had sounded familiar but now there was a face to go with it.

Talon's first instinct was to rush out and denounce the man, but then common sense told him that it might be the last thing he ever did, as there would be an excuse to kill him for supposedly attacking the royal person. Instead he contained his impatience and waited and watched from the darkness.

The mulled wine came and the people drank. More banter was exchanged but it was getting late so, one by one or in pairs, the group of people excused themselves, leaving only the Prince and an older man with a long gray beard talking by the fire. The two sat in large chairs and the old man constantly leaned forward to rub his hands, complaining about the rheumatism in his fingers.

The murderer had left some time ago with a couple of his people. They walked close by Talon, totally unaware of his presence, but he could have reached out and cut the man's throat.

At the far end of the chamber Talon could see a doorway but could not make out its interior. Then a servant came into the main chamber, walked though and carried a torch into the other room. The light of the torch briefly illuminated a bed and drapes.

Talon decided that this must be the royal bed chamber. He must get into it and meet the prince there once the old man had left. But that was not to be for some time as the two men had much to discuss. Again their conversation was hard to follow as, although they used French, they also mixed it with another language.

One advantage this intense conversation provided Talon was that he could make his way unseen to the entrance of the bed chamber, confirm that it was indeed being made ready and then slip into the room without detection.

The servant, a young page in full livery, was busy pulling the blankets on the bed into shape and laying out a nightshirt for the Prince. He looked up at one point, but that was because he felt a slight wind and saw the candle flicker, but he noticed nothing untoward and continued with his work.

Talon guessed that the Prince was sleeping alone this night, as there was no evidence of a woman to be seen in the chamber.

After an interminable period, when the page had fallen asleep at the end of the bed and Talon had almost fallen asleep himself, he heard the outer door of the other chamber open and close and heard footsteps coming towards the room he was in.

Talon heard the Prince call the name of the page, who woke with a muttered apology at the presence of his master. The boy hastened to help the Prince out of his clothes and then fetched the water bowl with a cloth for the Prince to wash with. After some splashing the Prince talked in a very gentle tone to the boy in French who responded in kind. Talon made the realization that this was why there was no woman in the room. The Prince took his pleasure with young boys! Could that be possible, he wondered?

He sat in the dark with his astonishment, wishing he was anywhere but in the Prince's bed chamber.

But it did not come to anything beyond the gentle words this night, much to his relief. Finally the Prince seemed to want to sleep and the boy wanted to join his companions in a dormitory.

The prince got up and went to the *Guard a Robe* in a corner of the chamber and relieved himself noisily, then padded back and clambered back into the bed with a grunt.

Not long after that Talon heard the deep regular breathing of a fit man in a deep sleep. Talon edged out of his hiding place and stood listening to Richard as he slept. This was a man going towards his prime who was already a legend. A young lion, Talon had been told, who was fretting against the chains his father had set about him, wishing for his own kingdom well before the old man died.

Talon decided that he should not wake the Prince but instead leave a longer and more detailed message. He went back into the outer chamber and found a quill, ink and a parchment. The hound, which must have been an old retired dog, looked up at him but appeared to think that he belonged, because apart from thumping its tail on the stone flags it did not come up to investigate him further.

Praying that no one would disturb the Prince, Talon sat close to the light of the fire and wrote a longer and much more detailed account of what had happened and added that he was bound to tell the Prince to his face the information that the Count had given him.

He placed the parchment on the pillow near to the Prince's head and, using the prince's dagger which he found on a nearby table, he drove it silently into the soft material pinning the letter in place within inches of the Prince's sleeping head. The Prince could not possibly fail to notice it when he woke the next day. Talon left as silently as he had come; bypassing the two sleepy sentries at the entrance with ease. Half an hour later he was with Anwl at the base of the castle walls.

No troubled thought at midnight haunts
Of loved ones left behind;
No vision of the morrow's strife
The warrior's dream alarms;
No braying horn, nor screaming fife,
At dawn shall call to arms.
- Theodore O'Hara

Chapter 16

Royal Meeting

After a hurried breakfast of bread and cold milk they left the city the next day at dawn. Although tired from his previous night's exertions Talon wanted to put distance between himself and the city, besides there was a place where he wanted to meet the Prince and talk alone. The monastery was only five miles ride, a short one for the Prince should he wish to follow up on the letter, and a sanctuary for Talon should things go wrong.

They rode up to the large entrance of the stone buildings and Talon banged on the nail-studded wooden door. A monk peered out at them through a grill and asked them politely what they wanted.

"I need to talk to the Abbot; it is very important. The Prince Richard is going to come here today, and he will wish to see the abbey," said Talon as convincingly as he could sound.

The monk gasped with surprise and told them to wait while he hurried off to consult with a higher authority.

A few minutes later the doors creaked open and they were ushered into the courtyard of the spacious building that reminding Talon of Mass Dieu, the Templar building he had visited when he first came to Languedoc.

They were greeted at the entrance to the chapel by a white haired old man in the plain dress of a monk but who carried himself with unmistakable authority.

"Are you the one who is saying that the Prince Richard is coming to visit the monastery?" he asked in a thin, reedy voice.

"Indeed he is coming, my Lord. I am sent ahead to ensure that you are made aware of this. He will want to worship in private in the Chapel. He will not wish to be disturbed while doing so."

"I... I suppose this can be arranged, although it is very unusual," spluttered the Abbot, but he started to issue orders to the monks who began to run about preparing for the royal visit. They completely ignored Talon after this.

He turned to Anwl. "Anwl, go and hide in the forest nearby. Do not be seen by anyone. I don't know how this will go; if he does not believe me the prince could arrest me or even kill me.

"When they, the Prince and his people leave, if I do not come out soon after, do you go back to Carcassonne and tell the Count that I failed in my mission. Tell him all that you know and then go back to my parents and tell of this. Go, my friend!"

Anwl nodded his understanding and trotted his horse out of the courtyard. Talon glimpsed him heading across the fields towards the nearby woods before he tethered Jabbar in the stables at the end of the courtyard. Then he disappeared into the chapel where he hid himself from sight inside the privacy of the choir. None of the monks who came in to pray or tidy up noticed him. His stomach rumbled; they had not eaten very much for breakfast.

His thoughts drifted and went far away as he wondered for the thousandth time what might have happened to Rav'an and Reza while he was in this strange, violent land where life seemed even cheaper than he had known it to be in Persia. He muttered a short prayer for their safe keeping and then remembered Jean the priest, and said one for him too.

Time passed and Talon watched the sunlight moving by the chapel windows outside the choir and wondered if he had been seriously mistaken in all that had transpired. Had the prince seen the letter? He could not have missed it right there on his pillow. Had the prince decided not to come after all?

His worries increased as time went by. It must have been three hours after they had come to the monastery that he heard the muffled sound of iron shod hooves on the stone road in front of the monastery. There was a shout and then the doors creaked open and he heard the sound of several horses entering the courtyard. He heard the murmur of voices dominated by one stronger and more commanding, followed by quiet and then footsteps coming to the chapel entrance.

They paused and Talon could hear the chink of chain mail and the jingle of spurs as a heavy man tramped down the short aisle to come to a stop at the entrance of the choir. There was the unmistakable hiss of a sword being drawn just before the entrance, and the Prince walked forward into the narrow gap between the opposite facing seats within the enclosed space of the choir.

Talon watched the Prince walk in and then stood up slowly from where he had been sitting at the back in the shadows.

The Prince was a large man, and in full chain armor he was imposing; with his sword drawn he was menacing. He leveled the sword at Talon and spoke.

"Are you...!" he began.

But Talon put his fingers to his lips indicating silence and motioned the Prince to a seat while keeping his distance. The prince stood irresolute for a moment then, still holding his sword, sat down hard. But he glared at Talon warily.

"Wh,y you are but a boy! Where is the phantom who placed that letter and knife in my pillow?" he demanded in a hoarse whisper now waving the parchment at Talon.

"That letter was all about treason to my person! Explain it and be quick about it!"

"My Lord, I can explain it..." Talon started.

But the prince interrupted him. "I should have both of you drawn and hung for such a deed. It scared the shit out of me! In fact, I still might do it! How did he get into my bed chamber, for God's sake? The guards say they saw and heard nothing despite a well done thrashing."

"My Lord Prince, it was I who came to you last night," said Talon kneeling, his head bent low.

"You! You are far too young to know such skills. Where did you learn to do this kind of thing? Who taught you? Some devil?"

"Yes, my Prince, in some ways they are like devils. I learned these skills in Persia. But, my Lord, *listen* I beg of you! There is very little time to explain and you are in great danger if we are seen together. I bring a message from the Count of Carcassonne for your ears only."

"Why did you not tell me this to begin with or even last night?" demanded the Prince irritably making a great effort to calm down.

"Because of what happened to Lord Guy, sire. Here I have a sanctuary. How could I know if perhaps what I had witnessed you already knew about, and might even have condoned? Then I would have been in mortal danger," responded Talon.

Prince Richard sat back against the wooden bench; it creaked under his weight. He stared to his left at the simple figure of the Christ suspended in the recess of the apse. Within the confines of the choir it was very quiet.

"I can see that you are not to be underestimated, boy. What has happened to Lord Guy?" he asked in a resigned tone, almost as though he already knew. He placed his sword across his knees.

Talon told him of the ambush and his subsequent flight to Auch. The Prince listened intently, then he asked,

"So boy, you think Lord Guy is probably dead or taken prisoner and the letter is taken; is that what you're saying?" Richard put his hand to his forehead and his other fist clenched as he considered the implications for himself if it found its way to his father.

Then he stirred and spoke quietly but with venom.

"Even if my father obtains this information, my Lord Guy, you will be revenged, and so will you, Sir Nigel, and indeed Sir Bertrand. Good, faithful men who have died to serve me."

"My Prince, there is one man who is very close to you who was there giving commands to the men who killed Sir Bertrand and who chased me through the forest. I... I saw him again last night with you in your outer chambers."

Richard was visibly disturbed. "You were in the room with us last night? How could this be? You must be some kind of phantom. What is this you say? What man? Describe him to me!"

Talon did his best to describe the man and, as he did, he could see Richard pale. He continued, "Sir Bertrand said that Sir Guy was taken by a man with a name something like Cumb'land? I could not understand the name well, but I am sure he said something like that, sir."

The prince sat back as though a ghost had entered the room, his fingers gripping the sides of the wooden seat, his mouth open in surprise.

"God's truth! I cannot believe it! The man you describe as a traitor is my Lord of Cumberland, son of the Count of Westmoreland. How can it be? I have given him all my love!"

Richard was very angry now. His fists were clenching and unclenching as he now paced up and down within the confines of the vestry.

"Yes, I am sure of my man, my Lord, but the Count told me that the letter cannot incriminate you other than it is the normal greetings of one Count to a Prince."

Richard looked surprised and then looked hard at Talon. "Say that again?"

Talon repeated what he had heard from the Count.

"My Lord Raymond is a clever man indeed! Not even my father could find fault with that. I am corresponding with my neighbors and that is called diplomacy in most Christian countries, even in England."

They both heard the door to the chapel being opened and the step of someone entering.

"I left clear orders that I was not to be disturbed for any reason whatever!" roared the prince.

They heard the sound of rapid footsteps leaving and the door slammed shut. There was silence in the chapel, but both men listened for a couple of tense moments then relaxed.

"I am to recite the message from the Count to your ears only, my Lord Prince." said Talon softly.

"Go to then. As you pointed out there is not much time and I am not used to spending it in a chapel. I shall deal with my Lord Cumberland in due course. He is not the only one who understands intrigue. He is for sure working for my father and as such is a viper in my bosom and one I have nursed these many years. But he shall pay for this... the traitor he is, in time... in time. Go on with the numbers from the Count," he commanded.

Talon dutifully recited the men and equipment Richard could expect from the Count when the time came for him to rise up against his father Henry and claim Aquitaine for himself.

Richard listened with great concentration until Talon was sure he had given the prince all the message. There was silence in the choir while Richard digested the information.

Finally he spoke. "The Count was right when he picked you for his messenger, young man. You have excelled in your mission and deserve to be rewarded for your courage. What can I give you for your service?"

Talon knelt in front of the imposing Prince. "I want nothing my Lord, but to serve my new master the Count. This I have done and am content indeed to have met you, sire. Your fame is legend in Languedoc."

Richard grinned at that. "Is it? I am glad of that. Now I have a message you are to take back to the Count. Here too is a bag of gold to pay for your efforts. You have done well. What is your name?"

"It is Talon, my Lord Prince. I am a knight of the Count."

The prince's eyes widened with surprise. "You are a knight, eh? Then Sir Talon, you might be young but you have surpassing courage. Here is the message..." He spoke for a couple of minutes.

He said finally, "There is but one task left for you to perform for me. You know where the Lord Guy my loyal friends died. I need their bodies to be brought back to Auch where they can be buried with honor. Can you wait on the road for a detachment I shall send from the town to meet you, and bring them back to me? Then Cumberland will be confronted and he and his men's heads will grace the gate arch of Auch. Will you do this for me, Sir Talon?"

Indeed I shall, sire. Willingly! I liked Lord Guy; neither he nor Bertrand deserved to die like this."

The Prince clapped Talon on the shoulder.

"Well said, Sir Talon, well said." He took a ring from his pouch, along with a small bag of coins. Talon looked down upon the sack of gold in his hand and the Prince's ring.

"If you are ever within my lands again and need my assistance, young knight, show this to someone in authority and you will be well looked after. You are to show it to the Count, but it is not for him. It is for you. I shall send him a reward in due time for his kind assistance; it will doubtless be in coin. Go now and God protect you along the way.

"The knight in charge whom you are to meet will show you a seal ring with one lion rampant upon it as a sign of my authority."

The Prince strode out of the chapel and slammed the door behind him. There were voices and then the sound of horses leaving the courtyard and finally silence.

Mindful of Anwl waiting in the forest, Talon hastily left the chapel without being noticed. Mounting Jabbar he left before someone remembered to close the main doors of the monastery. In fact one of the monks called after him as he left, but Talon did not want to talk to anyone other than Anwl. He rode in the direction he had last seen his companion take, and was rewarded with the sight of the Welsh bowman walking his horse out of the dense copse where he had been hiding.

"M'lord, I watched them go and was afraid! I thought... I wondered, if you might be harmed," said Anwl with relief as they came together in the middle of a field.

"I am well, Anwl, and Prince Richard is also well, and now he is armed for the treachery about him. There is nothing more we can do for him here.

"He is going to send a detachment of men to join us and we are to take them to the place where Lord Guy disappeared and Bertrand died. We will, God willing, find their bodies still there."

They moved off the road and waited for several hours before they saw a large detachment of mounted men coming along the road from Auch. They were moving rapidly and left a small cloud of dust behind them.

Talon watched them carefully and it was only when the men were almost opposite that he showed himself. Behind him Anwl stood with a bow drawn in case of more treachery.

However the leader of the detachment lifted his hand to halt the band of men behind him and greeted Talon cordially in good French.

"Sir Talon? My name is Sir Harold de Mays. My liege the Prince has told me of your place in this game. Here is the authority he gave me."

He produced a ring for Talon to examine. "Be assured that Lord Cumberland is arrested and in a dungeon at this time. You are safe with us. Your task is to show us where Lord Guy was attacked and where we might find the bodies of my friends Lord Nigel and Sir Bertrand."

Talon gave the ring back to the knight then called out to Anwl that all was well, and after Anwl had shown himself they set off southeast to find the ford.

It was quite dark by the time they came to the scene of the tragedy. The silence of the place was in keeping, Talon thought, as there were new ghosts in the area. They found the field again, and the horses shied at some dark shapes lying in the middle near to a large tree. It was Bertrand, or what remained of him, alongside his horse and several other men whom he had doubtless slain before he himself died.

They settled in for a cold night with no fire. Talon and Anwl were grateful for the hunk of cheese and stale bread that was pressed upon them by Sir Harold, however.

The next morning dawned cold and wet with a light rain. The men huddled in their cloaks and watched as Talon took Sir Harold over the details of the fight near the ford and then back into the field.

Talon stood over the body of Sir Bertrand in silence, Anwl by his side.

"He was a brave man, Anwl; how I misunderstood him!"

"Aye, he was that, m'lord. May God have mercy upon hi' soul!" they crossed themselves in silence.

His thoughts were of the man who he had not trusted simply because of his demeanor, but the man had been a true knight and had served his Prince to the death. Talon hoped that he might one day have the courage to meet his fate with such loyalty as this man. He muttered a prayer for the fallen knight just before the English soldiers came to collect the body and place it alongside the others they had discovered.

The bodies of the other slain men were dumped together in a ditch just out of sight of the road. No attempt to bury them had been made so identification was easy. They had been known to this party.

They found Sir Nigel lying almost where he had fallen off to the side of the road on the northwest side of the ford. His body was like that of the others, mutilated and torn where wild animals had eaten at the exposed flesh.

Sir Harold and his men were deeply angry and there were anguished shouts of rage as the men swore revenge upon the perpetrators of the crimes they were looking at.

The knight, however, composed himself enough to send off men to bring several carts from a nearby village and then addressed Talon.

"There is one curious thing. There is no sign of my Lord Guy. This must mean that they took him prisoner, God protect him. My Prince must find out where before they torture him to death.

"My liege told me that once we were here to let you go. He told me not to ask you where you were going, so all I can do is to wish you God speed and hope you arrive at your destination alive and well, Sir Talon. Go with God," he said.

They clasped hands and parted. Talon waved as they took to the road and headed south into the misty day. Sir Harold did not notice, however. He was engrossed in the gristly business of recovering the corpses of the soldiers.

The two men arrived at Carcassonne late at night and had to talk their way into the city using the Count's name. They were forced to wait outside while the confused sentries went to find a knight who would have the authority to let them in.

Eventually they heard the drawbridge creaking downward to land with a thump on the bank. Men with pikes and torches raised high walked along the bridge to look at the two travel weary men before them.

"What is it that cannot wait until the morning?" asked a man in a truculent tone. Clearly these men had been abed and resented being woken at this time of night.

"I have business with the Count and it cannot wait. His orders were to report to him no matter what time of night or day," answered Talon tiredly.

"God help you if you're lying!" said the same man.

He barked an order and a group of pike men surrounded the two, who were told to dismount and follow them into the town.

It was not a long walk to the castle proper but to a weary Talon it seemed far.

Half an hour later, after much discussion and waiting while a knight was dispatched to see if the Count would see them, Talon was summoned. Leaving Anwl with the horses and the escort, Talon was ushered into the same chamber he had been in before he had started his journey. There was a cheerful fire going in a grate in the middle of the room, the smoke leaving via a hole in the tower roof.

The Count turned when he heard Talon enter and greeted him.

"Well, young knight, you have returned. With good news, I hope?" The Count was dressed in a loose robe as though he had just come from the bed chamber.

Talon knelt in front of the Count and said, "I met with the Prince, my Liege, but the circumstances were much different than those which either you or I had anticipated."

The Count told him to rise. He handed Talon a silver goblet brimful of mulled wine. Talon sipped the hot brew gratefully, warming his hands on the hot cup.

"There is cold food on a tray over there," the Count indicated a table nearby. "You can tell me what I want to hear as you eat."

"My Lord, I think that on balance the news is good, and I have a message for your ears only, my Lord," Talon said between mouthfuls of chicken.

"There is none but us two in this room. Say it and then tell me in your words what transpired."

Talon then recited the message from the Prince. The Prince thanked the Count for his support and generosity for such a gift that Richard would not forget. However due to circumstances he would have to wait for a while, as the spies were so thick on the ground that he could barely tell who was working for his father or for himself. Richard told the Count that he had to tread carefully, as his father was jealous of his kingdom and there was a lot of suspicion about. Therefore it would not hurt to wait a while. He would send word when the time came.

In the meantime the prince complemented the Count upon his messenger and his skill at gaining entrance to a well guarded castle. The Count gave a questioning look at that, but Talon hurried on to tell him of the ambush and the disappearance of Lord Guy, recounting in detail the circumstances surrounding that grim event. He presented the ring and mentioned Richard's words. The Count was aghast at the news of the ambush and presumed capture or death of Lord Guy, but he nodded approval over the ring.

"It was well that I sent you and that the parchment was a diversion and held nothing other than greetings to the Prince. They can do nothing with that to further their ends.

"This ring is proof enough that you met with the prince, Sir Talon. The old king is not about to share his kingdom with any of his sons, so Richard might have to carve out his portion one day, and I think it will be Aquitaine. It does no harm for me to keep on good terms with him should he become my neighbor. If Richard gave you this, then you did him a great service. You must keep it for it is a pass to his lands, and one never knows when it might be needed. Keep it well."

When Talon was done the Count offered him another goblet of wine. Talon declined politely. He was exhausted and just wanted his bed.

"I would keep you near me, Talon, as you have served me well, but I hear that there is a problem of land ownership between your father and your mother's cousin. You must go and help protect your father's interests; and be assured, when the case comes to the court, as surely it will, then your father will be well regarded. When that is over, you will be commanded to attend my court."

On that note Talon realized he was dismissed. He knelt and kissed the hand of his liege Lord and left the room.

Two days later they left for Albi.

All door-ways
Before going forward,
Should be looked to;
For difficult it is to know
Where foes may sit
- Unknown Poet

Chapter 17

Ambush

The journey home was full of good cheer. Although it could be said that most of the men in Sir Philip's entourage, including Talon, had mild hangovers, they were still happy to be going home to the uncomplicated existence at the modest fortress, Fort De Gilles, as it was becoming known. During the ride, Philip leaned over to Talon and told him that he had spent some time with the Count talking about the situation at home.

"The Count told me that he was angered that a man who had fought the good fight in the Holy Land should be treated in this manner, Talon. He told me that his representative would watch the court carefully for any signs of treachery."

"I wonder what that means," Talon responded.

"I don't know for sure, but I was much encouraged all the same."

"Please do not think I doubt the Count's concern, but it would seem that even he has to be careful with the church and its ways."

"He did suggest that we do not seek to engage Sir Guillabert in open conflict while we await the courts to convene."

Talon concurred; they could only lose an all out battle with Guillabert and his mercenaries.

He thought back to the final evening at the court of Carcassonne. Elena had stayed close to him for the remainder of the day, but they had not stayed with the others long that night as she wanted to take him into the gardens. "For a walk," she had said, but his senses told him it might be more than just that.

In fact, she had wanted to walk, and hold him, and talk, too. They had not been alone in the gardens on this warm balmy night. There was muffled laughter and small rustlings and sighs in various dark corners of the gardens.

"You are a strange man, Talon from the Holy Land, a fine and accomplished warrior. My father would have good use for a man of your caliber."

"Why, my Lady, I am flattered. But why do you tell me this?"

"My brother is very impressed with you and asked me to tell you. You should also know that my father is a vassal of the Count of Carcassonne so there would be no conflict there as to loyalty. But also..." She paused, looking down at the ground, hesitating. Then she lifted her head and told him softly. "I, too, have strong feelings for you."

"My lady, you barely know me."

She took his sleeve. "A woman cannot say when and where her love will commence, Talon."

He had been too surprised to answer.

She led the way into a bower of low trees and bushes, and there in the darkness she turned and faced him. Taking hold of both his hands, she said, "I want you to love me as a woman. I am sure that you are as gentle to a female as you are harsh to your opponents on the field. My blood has sung a song for you since the tournament."

He was about to refuse as nicely as he knew how; but, as though anticipating him, she placed his hand on her breast and whispered, "Does your blood not sing too, my warrior from another land?"

Much later they had made their way back to the hall, but their friends were gone and the hour late. Elena kissed him goodbye with tears in her eyes. "I was right... you are gentle. Remember what I asked before, Talon. There is time before you answer. Fare thee well, we will meet again."

The small party stayed the night at one of the fortified villages along the route after a long day. It was a good three days' ride to Albi and they hoped to be able to make it back before sunset on the third day.

Talon was looking forward to the return for another reason. The more he thought about it, the more he liked the idea of seeing Aicelina again. There were twinges of guilt at his behavior at the palace, but also because he knew she had been right about him. His heart was somewhere else in the world, and he did not even know if Rav'an were still alive. He doubted it. The cruel, unforgiving world of Islam would see to that.

They set off early on the third day and made good time along the old Roman road that the main track crossed or followed, whimsically, it seemed. The forest was becoming thicker as they began the slow climb into the slightly higher ground of the foothills of the Cévennes. This was composed of tall oak trees that resembled those around Sir Hughes' land. Mixed in with the oaks were beeches and the occasional stand of fir. The trees were so tall they made the riders seem puny as they rode along under the huge boughs.

By late afternoon Albi itself was only an hour away and that meant they could be home well before the sun set.

It might have been the flicker of light on chain mail that warned Talon of danger, but his reflexive kick to Jabbar's flanks saved his life. As Jabbar skittered sideways the bolt from a crossbow whirred past his side. He shouted his alarm but already Max and Anwl were drawing their swords. Talon stared back horrified at his uncle. Philip was sitting still on his huge horse looking down at a crossbow bolt that protruded from his chest. He looked up at Talon, said nothing, then coughed, and a gout of blood poured out of his half open mouth. Then he slowly slid out of the saddle to fall clumsily at the feet of his horse. Talon ignored the danger and leapt off Jabbar with a shout of anguish.

"No! Uncle! No!" He let Jabbar loose and ran to kneel by his uncle, who was lying on the ground, his hands plucking feebly at the shaft of the bolt in his chest. Philip could say nothing; he was choking to death on his own blood. He simply looked up at Talon, an anguished expression on his face. Then his eyes glazed over and he slumped in Talon's arms.

Talon barely had time to close his uncle's eyes when he was struck a savage blow on the back of his head and the world went black.

He woke trussed up tight, arms tied behind him, his feet firmly bound, lying among leaves and grass in a small clearing in the forest, the peaty smell of the loamy soil in his nostrils. His head was pounding and he was very thirsty. He could feel an area on his head that hurt painfully, and it felt damp. Talon dimly realized that there was someone nearby and turned his head, wincing at the pain, and saw Max in the same condition.

Talon perceived a fire not far off where several men were squatting, talking in low tones. He could not see Anwl anywhere until he heard a scream, followed by raucous laughter. He craned his neck to see where the scream had come from and saw about thirty yards away in the gloom of the surrounding forest several other men standing near to a tree. Hanging off the bonds that held him to the tree was another man who whimpered in agony. Talon realized that it had to be Anwl. They were playing with him and had obviously tortured him for sport.

His anger overrode his own pain and he wriggled closer to Max. "Max, Max, can you hear me?" he whispered hoarsely.

Max lifted his head and Talon saw how badly he had been beaten. His face was bruised and swollen and there was a nasty gash on his shoulder. His hair was matted with blood from a blow to the head. He peered dazedly at Talon from swollen eyes. "I am glad you're alive, young sir. They killed Sir Philip and our groom. God curse them for foul murderers."

"I know, and they intend to kill us after they have finished with Anwl, I am sure of that. How many of them are there, do you know?"

"Maybe six. Two left to bring the 'young Lord,' as they called him. I can guess who that might be."

Talon could, too. "How did they know we would be on this road and at this time?"

"Perhaps it was that man that Anwl saw, Talon. The poor man, they're torturing him." He pointed with his chin.

Talon nodded grimly. "Max, can you move your hands?"

There was silence while Max tried his hands out. "Yes, I can move them, mainly my fingers, but not much."

"Hurry, we do not have much time. There is a knife in my boot. You have to get it out and cut me free. Hurry, Max!" he whispered urgently, wondering if Max was going to fall back into unconsciousness.

He moved his position so that Max could reach down into his right boot leg. There was much fumbling and heavy breathing, but finally Max grunted with satisfaction and lay still, resting for a moment. Talon watched the men at the fire and near Anwl, praying that they would not notice anything, but their attention was on their victim, who was writhing with the pain they had inflicted upon him.

Talon wondered where Jabbar was, hoping he was not too far off. Max, having recovered, rolled over so he was back to back with Talon and then began to saw at the bonds around Talon's arms. The sharp knife made short work of the ropes that fell apart quickly. Talon lay there for a moment, letting the pain of the returning circulation subside, and then moved very slowly to reach down to his feet and cut the ropes there. All the time he watched the men as they worked on Anwl. The men by the fire were too busy watching the sport by the tree to pay any attention to the two prisoners lying on the ground behind them.

He cut the ropes that bound Max's hands and gave him the knife to cut the ropes at his feet. Max handed back the knife when he was finished.

"What do we do now, Talon?" he whispered.

"We leave. Follow me and do as I do."

He slid slowly backward toward the cover of the saplings and trees. Their movements did not attract any attention for the first thirty feet, but then one of the men by the fire glanced up. He noticed that they had gone from where he remembered them to have been. His eyes flicked quickly around and then settled upon the two, many yards away. He let out a yell and pointed. Talon grasped Max by the arm. "Run!"

They scrambled to their feet and dived into the cover nearby. It was none too soon because two bolts from crossbows slapped through the leaves of the bushes nearby.

Talon led the way, hoping he was going toward the road. Ahead he thought he saw a horse trotting through the trees. He could hardly believe his eyes. It was Jabbar, who had been grazing when the noise erupted, and had shied off from the small grassy place he had found. Talon whistled urgently, and Jabbar came trotting back to him, obviously pleased to see him. Jabbar was unsettled and nuzzled Talon as though to ask if everything was all right.

There was no time to lose. Talon seized his bow and arrows from the saddle and handed the reins to Max. "Take him farther off, Max. Find Philip and the other horses. I have something to deal with."

If Max had wanted to argue one look at Talon's tight determined face warned him not to. "Take care; they are many," he said simply as he ran off, holding his wounded arm with Jabbar trotting behind him.

Talon did not even glance at them. He notched an arrow and slipped into the denser undergrowth heading back the way he had come. He saw in the distance first one figure and then another; they were close together, trotting along, looking for a sign of him and Max. They were agitated and didn't seem to care how much noise they made. It was as though they were quite confident they would catch up with them. He hid behind a tree and waited. They were scruffy, tough-looking men who he guessed had been hired by Guillabert or Marcel to kill them. Hired mercenaries abounded in the country; all the wars, including the crusades, had spawned many an unemployed soldier.

They wore quilted jackets with tight-fitting rings across the shoulders and a small breast plate hung by a leather thong. Their helmets were matching, wide-brimmed, and made of thin iron, somehow making them look as though they had huge heads.

He watched them, his bow drawn tight. They were peering about looking for him and striding along the loamy forest floor until they were only twenty yards away. He shot the rear man in the throat. As the arrow whirred past the man in front, he was so startled that he loosed his crossbow wildly, giving a shout of surprise. It was the last thing he did as another arrow took him in the midriff. He sat down abruptly and then fell back with a groan of agony. Talon stepped forward and cut his throat before he could scream and let the rest know what had happened.

He dragged the two corpses out of sight into some denser undergrowth, hiding them with damp leaves. Then, picking up his bow and one of the crossbows, including some bolts, he slipped through the forest to the encampment. He circled around and came upon the encampment from another direction and saw the four remaining men standing by the fire, looking in the general direction that their companions had taken when they left.

He searched for Anwl and found him unexpectedly close. Talon peered through the trees to try to determine if the body hanging on the ropes was alive. There was no motion at all. Talon's anger increased. He would make these men pay for what they had done to Philip and Anwl, and then he would go hunting for Guillabert.

It was getting darker; the sun had set and the forest was becoming gloomy as the light faded. The men at the fire were having a loud argument about what to do next. He could just understand their thick accents as they debated whether to go find out what was keeping their companions, or to stay put and await events. They finally agreed to stay put as one pointed out they were to await the arrival of the Master, although they were very concerned that the prisoners had escaped. It was getting too dark to blunder about, they assured themselves, so they settled down to enjoy the fire.

Talon decided to move over and see if Anwl was alive. He made it to the point where he was right behind his companion. There he whispered to him. "Anwl, do you hear me?" He thought he heard a sigh. "It is Talon. Be patient; I shall get you out of here, but I have to deal with these men first."

There was no answer. Then Talon noticed that one of the men had stood up and was coming directly toward the tree Anwl was tied to. He realized that the man might be coming to finish Anwl off so he made ready. He was right; the man drew his long dagger as he came up, obviously ready to stab the remaining life out of Anwl.

The man got no farther than to start the strike before Talon was there. His dagger was in his left hand as he stepped around the tree and walked into the man's unprotected side. He felt a brief resistance as it slid through the fabric of the quilted jacket and then it was deep into the man' chest. The man gasped with shock and surprise, opened his mouth to scream his agony but Talon's right hand slapped over his wide open mouth, smothering any noise. The man jerked and flailed, but he died. Talon eased him back onto the damp ground and then watched for any sign of alarm from the other three.

He slashed Anwl's bonds, seeing with shock that the man's right hand was missing. He lifted the limp body over his shoulder and stepped out of the light thrown by the fire. Still no sound, so he moved quietly deeper into the woods until he was sure he could lay Anwl down without being detected. He listened for Anwl's breathing and a pulse. It was very low and Anwl barely breathed. Talon noticed many wounds and he noted that the stump of Anwl's forearm was still bleeding. These men had known he was a bowman and had taken his living from him. Talon hastily tore off a strip of his tunic and bound the wound tightly to stop the flow of blood, but it quickly became reddened as the blood continued to seep through. He had no time left.

He had to deal with the others. Before he could move back toward them he heard a shout and realized that they had found their companion. He slipped quietly back around to the other side of the area from where he had released Anwl and found a good vantage point to observe them.

Now they were very agitated. There was fear on their faces as they stared around them at the darkening woods. They had not anticipated this and were now afraid. The dead companion told them that their other companions were probably dead, too. They talked about this and then decided to abandon the fire and head for the road and the dubious safety of the village not too far along toward Albi. One thing was certain, they did not want to stay in these woods a moment longer.

"I will not wait for Master Marcel while there is one of them out killing us," one said loudly. The others obviously agreed.

They hurriedly went toward the fire to pick up their equipment. As they did Talon stepped out in front of them and shot one of them right in front of the fire with the crossbow. The twang of the bow string was loud in the otherwise silent woods. The man fell forward into the fire with a scream, causing a shower of sparks to fly into the air. His grease-stained quilted jacket quickly caught fire and within seconds he was a flaming torch. His screams resounded though the forest, but then choked off as he died.

The other two after the briefest moment turned and ran for their lives. Talon sped after them keeping pace with the terrified men as they fled. He came very close to the rear man, then stopped and calmly took aim. Even in the darkening forest he could see clearly enough to shoot well. The man fell with a shriek, clawing at his back, but Talon's aim had been true. Within a few long seconds that man, too, was dead.

Wasting no time Talon jogged after the last man. It was quiet as he moved silently listening for any sound that might give the direction the man had fled. Too quiet, thought Talon as he slowed. He was right; the man leapt out at him from behind a tree like some dark creature of the night. Talon side stepped the savagely slashing blade of the long dagger and skipped out of range. He drew his own dagger, a much shorter one; his other blades had been confiscated. They were now facing each other in the deepening gloom. It was a bad time to be fighting with blades. It would be too easy to have an accident simply because one could not see clearly.

Talon decided to taunt his opponent. "I did not expect a coward like you to stay around. Now you have made my work easier. Who sent you? Do you realize that you will surely go to hell for the murder of a Knight Templar? He was a man in God's service."

The man grunted, his breath coming out sharply. "The idiot missed you and killed the knight. We did not intend to kill him. Just you."

"Well, you killed my uncle regardless, and you have failed to kill me. Now I am going to send you to join your companions in hell where they are waiting for you," Talon said with a deadly calm. His rage was white hot, but he controlled it with an iron grip.

"Maybe not," the man replied, and with a curse he attacked as Talon had hoped he would, his knife held high. But he was experienced, too. He stopped just before he committed himself, flicked the knife into his left hand and thrust it straight at Talon.

In the dark, Talon could only just parry the blade, but he had underestimated its length; the point slashed through his doublet and cut him across the ribs on his right side. He barely felt the pain; he was concentrating on his own objective. It was easy to slip inside his opponent's guard while they were so close and plunge his own knife deep into the man's midriff and then push up, while blocking the next stab from the long knife. Talon held the man upright for several seconds as he choked on his own blood and died, staring up into Talon's face. Finally, he let the body drop, wiped his blade on the man's jerkin then turned and made his way back to where he had left Anwl.

He was too late. There was no life left in his companion. Talon let his anger wash over him for a long moment as he kneeled by his companion. Then, tears streaming down his face, he stooped and picked up the Welshman. It surprised him how light his burden seemed. He paused at the fire to take one of the bodies and prop it standing against a tree nearby, held up by a long dagger through its chest run deep into the wood of the tree. It would be a gruesome message to whoever came to find them. Then he recovered his sword, along with the other weapons belonging to his friends.

He carried Anwl to the road. He was met by a badly unsettled Max at the edge of the forest where he had been waiting with Jabbar. He had eventually found Philip lying in the ditch with their dead groom. He had also found two horses of the other three. He told Talon that he had heard a scream in the forest; but after that, nothing and had prayed that Talon had survived. As he confessed to Talon, he could not be sure; the odds had been so great.

"Did you kill them all?" he asked incredulously.

Talon merely nodded. "Max, we have to get Philip, the groom, and Anwl back home, but we cannot stay on the road. I heard that Marcel and his men will be along at any time. We shall have to go by the fields. How is your wound?"

"It hurts no mistake, Sir Talon, but I have staunched the blood and I can make it."

It took several tries to get Philip onto his horse. He was a heavy weight but they managed to tie him down, and then they put Anwl on the same horse. It objected to the smell of blood, but Talon was able to calm it so that they could do the gristly work.

They were only just in time. As they left the roadway Talon heard horses coming down the main track in the distance. There seemed to be many. As he and Max were in no condition to put up any kind of a fight, he led the way across a field and into another copse of wood. From there they could remain concealed and then make their way the remaining distance through the night to the fort.

They arrived late that night at the closed gates of the fort to be greeted by Ap-Maddock, who called down in the dark for them to identify themselves or be shot.

Talon called back hoarsely, for he was tired and very thirsty. "Ap-Maddock, it is I, Talon. We need help."

"M'lord Talon! Wait, I shall have the gates open," Ap-Maddock called out.

There was consternation on the walls and men began to rush about. Torches were lit and cast a flickering, smoky light along the battlements.

"Talon," called a voice. He recognized Gareth. "What happened, Bach?"

The gates creaked open and men ran out into the darkness to surround the exhausted men. They gasped with shock at what they found. In the light of the flaming torches that they held high the tragedy was clear to see. They came running up to Talon, all shouting and calling to him at once. He sat still on Jabbar and looked down at Gareth.

"Where is my father, Gareth? I have to tell him."

"I am here, Talon," Sir Hughes said. He came through the gates, belting a sword around his tunic. Then he stopped dead in his tracks. There was no mistaking Philip and Anwl's bodies lying across the horse Talon held.

"Ah, dear God, no!" he groaned. He placed a hand over his eyes as though to blot out the sight and staggered. "What happened, my son?" he asked in a low voice when he had recovered his composure.

The men led the horses into the yard where more people came to witness the tragedy. The flames of the torches cast a reddish light on men and horses, flickering shadows against walls as they moved about.

Talon slid off Jabbar and stood shakily in front of his father and an angry, shocked assembly of men who demanded to know who had done the murders.

"Someone must take care of Max. He is wounded and has lost a lot of blood," Talon said loudly and firmly. After he had seen some men help Max off his horse and take him to the hall to have his wounds dressed, hespoke.

"Father, please find me something to drink and I shall tell you what happened. Gareth, I am sorry about Anwl; I tried to save him but he was too far gone by the time I managed to get to him."

Gareth reached forward and gripped his arm hard; there were tears in his eyes. "Of one thing I am sure, Talon. You have done all you could for him. May his soul go straight to heaven and the Good God forgive his sins."

Men crossed themselves quietly all about. Sir Hughes led the way grimly into the hall after first giving instructions that the bodies were to be laid out and washed that very evening. He called to the womenfolk to perform the work and then to lay them out on tables in the hall for mourning the next day.

His rage and grief was like a huge cloud all around him as he gave Talon a drink of much needed water and sat him down. Marguerite came with Aicelina, their appalled faces showing him that they already knew. His mother embraced Talon, weeping. Aicelina, white-faced, laid a hand on his hunched shoulders and whispered something, and then they were gone to do women's work for the dead.

"Now, Talon, tell me who did this foul deed. I wish to know upon whom I should wreak vengeance for my brother's death," Sir Hughes grated out.

Talon told the assembled company what had happened in brief sentences. He finished with the statement, "I killed the men who murdered Uncle Philip, Father; but before I did I found out who had ordered it. They did not mean to kill him. They wanted to kill me. Nonetheless they did, and for that Sir Guillabert and his son Marcel will die."

There were angry shouts in at least three differing dialects and languages. The Welshmen were incensed at the death of their companion, and along with many others in the hall wanted to rush off immediately and storm the castle of Sir Guillabert. None noticed a dark shadow that slipped out of the hall and, keeping to the shadows, disappeared through the still open gates into the nearby woods. Sir Hughes might have been raging with grief and anger at what had happened to his brother but his characteristic level head prevailed.

"How long ago did you leave the forest, Talon?"

"At least three hours, Father." He knew where his father was taking this. "They will have found the dead men and will have had time to return and prepare for retaliation. We made very slow time back here. I had to avoid the road most of the way."

Sir Hughes nodded his agreement. They thought alike.

"Men!" he roared over the hubbub, "Listen to me! We shall not leave tonight for a fool's errand in the dark and perhaps worse. If they are expecting us then it will be to their advantage, not ours. Go to your beds and rest, we will plan tomorrow what shall be done about this murder. We shall be avenged one way or the other; but on our own terms, not theirs, and not tonight."

The men grumbled, but cooler heads such as Gareth and some among the retainers prevailed. Soon Talon was left alone with his father and Gareth, who he asked to stay.

"Just as I mourn my uncle who was in God's service, so do I mourn your companion and mine, Gareth. We shall be avenged for this cowardly deed—and soon. As God is my witness, it shall be soon."

Gareth gave a broken smile. "I have come to know both you, Talon, and you, Sir Hughes. I trust you as I have few other men. I and my men will be ready when the time comes." They embraced, and then Gareth left them alone.

Then and only then, the two men, father and son, wept for Sir Philip. Talon had never heard his father weep before, but he cried, too. He had been very fond of the big, kindly man who had given him his knighthood. He told his father about the event and Sir Hughes embraced him tearfully.

"I was hoping that something like this might happen." He sniffed, wiping his eyes with his sleeve. "Sir Philip was determined to have you recognized for your part in the battle at sea. God bless his soul. I must have that poor sample of a priest come and say the burial prayers tomorrow."

Talon bade his father goodnight and sought out his bed. He met Guillaume on the way. The boy was cold and frightened. "Have they killed Uncle Philip?" he asked nervously.

Despite his tiredness Talon squatted next to the boy and took him into an embrace. "Yes, little brother, they murdered him."

"Did you kill anyone this time?" Guillaume mumbled into his shoulder.

Talon nodded bleakly; he felt miserable and bone-tired. "Have courage, brother. All will be well again, although we shall miss Uncle Philip very much."

Guillaume nodded as though he understood.

Talon felt a touch on the shoulder. He stood up, still holding onto Guillaume's hand, and turned to find Aicelina standing nearby, her face wet from tears.

"Guillaume, my dear, your brother is very tired. You should go to bed now and we can talk about it in the morning."

Guillaume was going to protest but Talon gave his hand a squeeze and nodded to endorse the command. He hung his head and gave in. Talon stooped and gave his brother a kiss on the head then stood up and watched Guillaume shuffle off to his bed with Aicelina herding him. She glanced over her shoulder at him just before they disappeared.

He collapsed fully clothed on his bed and went to sleep like the dead. He did not hear Aicelina come to him later, holding a candle on high to look down on him, but awakened, startled when she began to pull his boots off. She stepped back at the suddenness of his reaction. He fell back with a groan. He was reminded of the wound he had incurred. He allowed her to pull his boots off then half helped her as she undressed him.

She gasped at the blood all across his stomach and hurried off to get warm water and bandages to repair the slash on his ribs. Despite the sting of the water her gentle ministrations lulled him back to a restless sleep. Before she had finished he was out completely. She shook her head at the nasty bump on his head and placed a cool cloth on the wound.

As Talon slept, Aicelina stood by the door with the candle, listening to him muttering in a tongue she had never heard before and wondered at the strange life he had led. Although she had given herself to him and would again if circumstances permitted, even tonight if he had wished it, she knew intuitively she was not part of his destiny.

How sweet are looks that ladies bend
On whom their favors fall.
For them I'll battle until the end,
To save them from shame and thrall:
- Lord Tennyson

Chapter 18

Bartholomew

Talon woke late and with a heavy heart. His first thought was that he would sorely miss his uncle. Philip had been an anchor to him during his last few months; his cheerful outlook on life and his rough but kindly mentoring had encouraged Talon. Talon realized that it had been no mean feat to have persuaded the Count himself to perform the ceremony of knighting him. Sir Philip must have used a lot of his credit as a Templar returned from the Holy Land to make that happen.

He made his way outside to find Sir Hughes, who was very obviously grieving over the death of Philip, but as was characteristic of him he had thrown himself into the business of preparing for war and was directing activities in the main yard. Gareth and the other Welshmen hurried over to Talon while he was taking breakfast near the kitchens.

They watched him eat, saying nothing. It was as though they wanted to hear from him first. Once again he had to tell the story of the ambush; the men questioned him closely on what had happened. They were angry and frustrated that they could not rush off and deal a deadly blow of their own to the Guillaberts.

Finally, Talon looked across the table at Gareth. "I have to go to Albi tomorrow. Will you and Belth come with me?"

Gareth looked puzzled. "Yes, we will, Talon, Bach. But why?"

"Because I need to take care of something and will need your help to do it, but I must swear you all to silence on the subject," Talon responded enigmatically.

They looked surprised but all nodded and knuckled their foreheads as though to their chief.

Belth nodded and smiled his gap-toothed smile, his freckled face glowing with pleasure. All he wanted to do was to avenge his comrade Anwl and if that meant going to Albi then so be it. The anger in the compound was palpable and Talon wondered if they would contain their rage until he came back.

A man who Talon had not formerly met walked over and sat down at the table next to them. He didn't look like a peasant nor one of the villains belonging to Sir Hughes, but neither did he look like one of the men-at-arms that Talon was familiar with. He wondered if the man might be one of the peddlers who came by infrequently. However, there were telltale stains on his fingers that indicated he could write. He looked at the young man and decided to ask him who he was.

Just as he was about to do so, Sir Hughes came over, carrying a small, rolled parchment with a wax seal attached to it. He dropped it in front of Talon and then, seeing the young man, glanced at Talon.

"Talon, while you were away with your uncle we had this young man as a visitor. Bartholomew, this is my son, Talon. We have also had notification by messenger, from the bishop no less, of the date for the court appearance and where we should plead our case. It is to be three days from today in Albi."

He sat himself down among them and called for food. To Talon he looked weary with worry and grief. There was much gray to his mop of hair.

Talon introduced his archers to Bartholomew who, it turned out, was very distantly related to his mother and had just come from Paris. He was a clean-shaven young man of about twenty years with untidy light brown hair over a high forehead, with intelligent hazel eyes that regarded Talon with interest. Talon for his part was interested in what he might tell him.

"Paris. Tell me, is it a great city?"

The answer was slow in coming. "They tell me that you came back to this land from far away Persia. That you talk of cities that glow in the sunlight from the light off their stone walls. You have told people here of huge caravans of animals called camels—what are those by the way?—that arrive every month to bring even more wealth to these cities."

Talon nodded. "It is true of Isfahan and especially Baghdad; I saw it for myself."

"Then you would be disappointed in Paris, save for one thing."

"What would that be?"

"Why, the church of St Martin, designed and also built in part by the great Abbey Sugar. There is talk that he was inspired by the great Queen Eleanor, but I think it was only God and the use of glass. It is, however, a sight to behold in a city that is otherwise unremarkable despite the Isle de Seine, for in all the surrounding city the streets are like bogs and in winter the wolves roam."

"I thought Paris was the greatest city of this whole realm, second to none, not even Carcassonne," Talon said with real surprise in his voice.

Bartholomew barked a short laugh. "Then you have already seen the greatest city, bar Toulouse, in the whole of the region of Languedoc, Burgundy, and Aquitaine, as well as the feeble kingdom of France. Paris cannot match Toulouse or Carcassonne except in the matter of the Church of St Martin. They are, it is true, building Notre Dame as a cathedral but that will take generations to complete," Bartholomew said, a bit cynically. "The monies they will spend on that will be huge and will beggar the kingdom of France, which barely has enough income to pay for the King as it is."

"What then do you do for a way of life? By your stained fingers I would say you are a scribe of some sort?"

Bartholomew chuckled. "I am more than a scribe, Talon. I was a student and I am now an Advocate by profession, schooled at the University of Montpellier, and then I spent some time in Paris at the new schools of debate. I am here, passing through on my way north again but turned aside to visit my distant aunt, your mother, and Sir Hughes here. I had heard they were back from the Holy Land and wanted to see them before I take up my trade with some lord or other, probably for the Count of Burgundy."

"What is an Advocate? Is that like being a true friend to something?"

"Somewhat. As an Advocate I both advise on and debate the rules and laws of the land and the Church."

"How is this done?" Talon asked.

"We take up a dispute before a lord or a high man of the church and advise him of the law as it should be and ensure that he is not in error."

"Do you advise less exalted men?" Talon asked tartly.

Bartholomew shot him a shrewd glance. "Ah, I take it that you are alluding to the situation of your mother's inheritance?"

Talon nodded. "If you are a man of the law can you not advise and debate our situation before a tribunal?"

Bartholomew looked at Talon. "It is complicated. I have studied Canon Law; there are many kinds, but this dispute is about land and does not directly involve the church. However..." he looked thoughtful. "Before whom do you have to defend your rights?"

Talon turned to his father. "Father, is it not to be before a representative of the Count, perhaps his secretary, and also the Bishop of Albi, and one other local lord?"

His father nodded. "Bartholomew, the bishop is going to weigh in on the side of Guillabert, Talon overheard him talking to our enemies. Tell him, Talon."

For the rest of the morning while the others drifted off Talon told Bartholomew about the plot he had heard. After Bartholomew had gotten over his initial shock at how Talon had obtained the information, he questioned him closely.

Eventually Bartholomew said, "There is little I can use for the court, but it tells me how we should behave when there, which is very useful. We now know exactly how the bishop stands on the case."

Talon plied him with questions about his life in the University of Montpellier and was in turn asked many questions by the inquisitive Bartholomew. By noontime Talon decided he thoroughly liked this astute young man and was convinced that Bartholomew might be at the very least a useful ally.

They were so engrossed in their discussion that they didn't notice Aicelina come up and seat herself at the same table and listen to them. Then Bartholomew hesitated and turned to regard her with undisguised admiration.

"Aicelina. I did not notice, how rude of me. Please forgive me... Talon has beguiled me with tales of his adventures."

She smiled at him warmly and then turned to Talon. "You should have your wound dressed, Talon. It was a nasty cut."

Talon smiled ruefully at Bartholomew. "Aicelina is my nurse, it would seem. Let's talk some more tomorrow. I must submit to her gentle administrations, and then I have things to do this afternoon and evening."

Bartholomew nodded, and with a smile to Aicelina he left. Aicelina made Talon take his shirt off and then changed the bandage around his middle.

His skin tingled at her touch and he wished they were by the pool again. She must have noticed something in his attitude because she began to blush slowly and there was a secret smile on her lips when she had done. "If you are thinking thoughts that are not decent I shall be offended," she said unconvincingly.

"I was thinking that Bartholomew is somewhat taken with you, Aicelina," he teased gently by way of deflecting her.

He was surprised that she looked down briefly. Could it be? he wondered to himself, is Aicelina attracted to this intelligent young man? Did he have a rival? She looked up into his eyes and gave him one of her cool smiles, which he could make nothing of.

He thought about that later that afternoon as he found his way back to the pool. What right did he have to her heart if it was clear in his own mind that he did not intend to stay but rather to leave when he could for the *Outré Mere*? He bathed cautiously because of his wound, but that was not the reason for the visit. Afterward, he went hunting for the small mushrooms that Aicelina had warned him about. They looked like the ones he had learned about so long ago during his training with the Assassins, and what she had told him about them was sufficient to his needs. He plucked several different kinds and put them in two different leather bags he had brought along for the purpose, then found his way back to the busy fort which he entered unobserved except for the sentries.

He was later confronted by his father, who wanted to plan what they could do about the attack on himself and Philip.

"I have talked to Bartholomew, who councils patience, and don't forget, I did get a pledge of help from the Count of Carcassonne. I think we should wait until the court case is done with and then we shall see. To attack them now in full cry would not do our cause any good before the tribunal. Bartholomew is a sensible man; he told me that we should be the ones who appear to bear the pain of persecution and carry it with us when we make our appearance before the bishop and the Count's man. Remember also that the Count promised that he would send someone to watch for a fair trial, Father."

His father, although deeply and visibly angry at the murder of his brother, was still ready to listen to his son. Talon had impressed him since he had been with them, both as a leader and someone with a lot of sense. He shrugged grudgingly. "I would like nothing better than to storm Guillabert's castle and take his head, Talon; but it would be suicide, so I'll curb my rage and that of my people until the time is right to do so."

Talon gripped his father's arm. "Make no mistake, Father, it shall be as you want it, but we should have right on our side when it's done. I grieve for my Uncle Philip, as it was he who brought me here. I miss him badly and like you, I will be avenged."

He went off to find his mother and console her over the death of Philip as he had not had much time to do so before. He found her spinning wool thread and talking with Aicelina. His brother and sister were seated near the herb and vegetable garden in a patch of sunlight. Two of the massive hounds were in attendance upon the children who were playing with the long-suffering animals. He stood still and admired Aicelina's poise before he moved forward.

None of them had heard him come up so they jumped when he coughed and made his presence known.

'Talon!" his mother exclaimed. "I swear the archers are right about you. You're like a ghost. I didn't hear you come."

He kissed his mother and gave Aicelina a smile. She dimpled and looked down as though concentrating on her sewing. He seated himself near them on the grass and Guillaume promptly jumped onto him demanding to hear all about the ambush. He winced from the pain in his side and carefully placed his brother alongside him. The hounds greeted him in a friendly manner and then ambled over to the pond to lie there watching the ducks, relieved of the duty of entertaining his brother.

Talon told them the story simply, as they had not heard it from him. His mother wept when he told her of finding Philip by the side of the road.

They talked about the burial to take place the next day.

Soon it was time to go into the great hall and eat. The sun had set and the evening was cool. The first whispers of autumn were blowing in and the leaves were turning.

Chapter 19

Bishop's Feast

Later that evening, Talon announced that he intended to visit the monastery again and it would be that night. While somewhat surprised, no one remarked upon it; but after the meal he sought out Gareth and told him that he wanted his archers out in the woods again, as Guillabert was not done and could still be up to some mischief.

Gareth told him that he and Max were concentrating on the training of the other villains and then said, "Did you not tell me that you were going to visit Albi, Talon?"

"Yes. That has not changed, and remember I do not want it discussed with anyone at all, but later we will visit the abbey. I go to Albi first."

Gareth shrugged, but he grinned, his blue eyes twinkling, "Do you have an eye on some girl there, then, Bach?"

Talon reached over and cuffed him gently before he could re-act; Gareth laughed.

They left the fort in the dark on horseback and made their way toward the town. Talon had warned the two archers that he had no idea what to expect when they got there—the brawl would still be remembered—but he divulged nothing of the plan he had for when they did get there.

Talon noticed the huntsman Domerc leaning against one of the door pillars, watching them intently as they left. He dismissed the thought that Domerc might suspect where he was going, but somehow it was unsettling and he could feel the huntsman's eyes boring into his back long after they had exited the gates.

Several hours later, they sat their horses on a knoll, watching the town preparing for bed. Nights were longer now and becoming cool. Talon was dressed in rough, dark clothing borrowed from one of the archers so he looked just like the other two. As such he would go un-remarked in a society that dressed for the most part in patched cloth and hand-me-downs. Only the wealthier mer-chants could afford good cloth and therefore good clothes. They could see the lanterns on the masts of the barges anchored or tied up near the bridge. All seemed calm and quiet.

They rode to the walls cautiously and then stopped the horses in a small grove of trees not far from the wooden palisade. Curfew was in effect now, something that Gareth had mentioned to Talon as though he might have forgotten, but Talon had only nodded and ridden on. They were very near the walls but well hidden from pry-ing eyes within the dark shadows of the tall trees. The sentries were unlikely to be very alert, Talon reasoned, as there were no threats about for them to worry about.

He dismounted and handed his reins to Belth. "Keep watch and be very alert. I am going into the town."

There was a muffled exclamation from both men. "Talon, what are you doing, Bach?" Gareth whispered, agitated.

"I am taking care of some business, Gareth. Come with me. Belth, trust me, we shall be back by midnight; and if we are not, then ride to the monastery, ask the abbot if he has found any documents that relate to our case."

Then they were gone. Belth looked around. The two had simply vanished. He dismounted and tethered the horses to a tree and waited. The night was closing in and the bark of a fox a quarter mile away told Belth that the woods were waking up.

Talon and Gareth had moved back into the shadows and then made their way toward the walls. Talon picked a very dark area where the shadows cast by the tall trees darkened the area. He cast a rope with a loop over the spikes and tested its weight; satisfied, he pulled himself up and over the ramparts of the crude wall. He assisted Gareth over the parapet. There was no one to greet them on the walkway, just as he had surmised. The guards were all sitting around a fire down at the other end of the section, warming their backsides, gossiping, their spears stacked against the wall.

The two dark shapes with cowls pulled well over their heads to hide their faces slipped off the ramparts and made their way toward the center of the town. Talon and Gareth used every shadow along the way, moving steadily toward the house that had been pointed out to Talon as the bishop's. He wanted no one to see him that night. It was not hard to avoid the people on the streets; for the most part they were men and most of them were drinking, some were even unconscious, lying against walls and in the streets. The squeaking of rats was loud in some of the corners where there was much filth.

Women rarely ventured out after dark unless they had a purpose, and that was to meet with men in the taverns. Albi certainly didn't seem to lack those, judging by the noise that came from the several candlelit drinking houses they passed. Talon wrinkled his nose at the pungent smells of the streets they crossed along the way. Whenever they came across people walking the streets, their clothes and the cowls covering their heads were enough to persuade people to leave them alone. Talon's main concern was that dogs would bark at him and then follow him, but even they seemed to be hiding from the gathering cold.

The smoke from many smoke holes hung heavy in the night air and assisted them in their efforts to stay out of sight. But for all Talon's care he nearly stumbled onto a group of men gathered around a brazier drinking, talking noisily, and eating roasted meat. One of them spun around, sensing something not quite right, his hand on his dagger. But stare as he might into the darkened recesses of the street he could not see Talon and Gareth, who were hugging the dark shadows, motionless. The man shrugged and turned back to his companions, taking another long swig of wine from a full skin he held.

Finally, they came to the town's main street and could see the activity around the entrance to the house of the bishop clearly. There was no mistaking it; there were burning torches in sconces against the walls and many grooms holding horses standing outside in the street. The grooms were huddled into their thin cloaks, their breath and that of the horses coming out in long streamers. Some of the horses had been well ridden as they were steaming in the cold night air. They fidgeted and stamped their hooves as they waited. The activity indicated that there was some kind of feast in progress, which suited Talon very well. Although there were some guards at the gates to the courtyard, no one would be paying much attention to what went on outside—all attention was going to be concentrated on the feast going on in the main hall.

He nudged Gareth and pointed to the dark entrance of a narrow alley across the street from the bishop's house. They slipped across the main street unnoticed by anyone then hugged the shadows until they were at the entrance of the alleyway. Talon led the way down the dark alley to a point which brought him alongside a low wall, which looked as though it protected the property at the back. There seemed to be a lot of activity going on behind that wall. He motioned Gareth to stay where he was, climbed the rough stones easily, and then slid over the top to land in the shadows among some shrubs.

The back of the bishop's house was a hive of activity. Servants in livery, and common serving men and women, were hurrying about the busy yard, carrying food on trays, and wine and beer in jugs. There was much shouting at sweating cooks to get their work done and give them food to take to hungry guests. The cooks in turn were swearing back at those worthies who were trying to take the food to the guests. There were a couple of cooking pits with a large pig's carcass in one, a sheep in the other. Sparks were flying into the air, threatening the neighboring houses with fire. Talon crouched and watched. He, once again, needed to find someone to change clothes with. Not for the first time he wished he had slain the bishop in Guillabert's castle. Having seen what he wanted, he slipped over the wall again and, crouching in the dark, whispered to Gareth.

"There will be another body coming over the wall; you will need to dispose of it."

Gareth gaped at him in the dark. "What are you going to do, Talon, Bach?"

"You must not ask, Gareth. Simply do as I say."

He felt rather than saw Gareth nod in the dark and gripped his friend's arm. Then he got up and climbed back over the wall.

There was a certain rhythm to the activity in the kitchen. Men came out of the building with empty platters and replenished them at one or other of the trestle tables or fires where the cooks were standing, either carving the meat or dishing out the food. There was a man near them in the bishop's livery, giving orders to one and all.

Talon waited for his victim to walk by.

It was not long before a man in the bright livery of the bishop's retinue strode by, carrying some bread. Talon slipped behind him and had his cord around the man's neck before he could even gasp. The bread fell in a tumble among the bushes and Talon and his victim disappeared. There was a brief struggle, then Talon hit him hard on the top of the head with the pommel of his knife and the body went limp. Talon went through the unpleasant task of changing clothes with the unconscious man and then pushed the half naked body over the wall to a waiting and incredulous Gareth.

"Toss him into someone's garden, Gareth," was the command.

"Yes, m'lord," was the startled reply.

Talon made his way cautiously into the great hall, carrying the retrieved bread in a basket, accompanying several other harassed servants all carrying trays of meat and pies. He gathered himself and looked around.

There was a lot of noise inside the great hall, loud conversation and much laughter that rose to the blackened rafters as people drank the fine wine and mead the bishop provided. The bishop was holding a feast to welcome one of his peers. Talon had heard that he was famous for the feasts he gave. It was almost as though he were Lord of the town, though no one would ever dare to say so. The bishop might be rich from all the Church's land holdings but he could never assume title of "Lord"; he was already one by default.

Talon spied him at the high table with the Bishop of Carcassonne, who was passing through the city of Albi with his retinue. There must have been well over sixty guests crammed together on benches below the high table, dining on the well-prepared food the bishop's famous table provided.

They were a mixed bag of landed knights and their ladies with the occasional rich merchant from that growing group of people who traded with other countries. They were still viewed with much suspicion by the knights, but the few merchants that were there were present because the bishop evidently saw value in cultivating these men. They represented wealth; the knights were, for the most part, barely able to afford their armor, let alone possess any land that was tax and debt free. The two overweight bishops looked magnificent in their clerical robes with silver chains hanging off their shoulders. Ermine collars over soft cloaks of fine English wool held with clasps of silver decorated their chests. Their fingers were bejeweled with rings that flashed in the bright candlelight. Both wore the white felt cap of the clergy that went over their heads and had small flaps that acted as a warmers over their ears.

Bishop Bohemond was wedged comfortably in a throne-like chair of carved oak and his guests to either side of him were equally splendidly seated. An individual servant attended each of the guests at the high table, obsequiously and unobtrusively serving them wine and meats as they brought them in. Then they'd hurry off to obtain more at the guests' request. There was wine aplenty and the conversation was loud and cheerful.

There seemed to have been no expense spared for the huge candles that adorned the tables and the flaming torches along the walls. Their guttering flames flickered and flared in the drafty hall, sending great shadows dancing along the walls, lending the impression that there were many more guests of the phantom kind than there were of mankind. Three minstrels were playing flute and stringed instruments at the back of the hall, their thin music competing poorly with the hubbub of the crowd.

The strong smell of wax mingled with burnt herbs and wood smoke from the huge fire at the end of the hall. Bursts of laughter and loud conversation from the assembled knights and gentry below the high table attested to the fact that the bishop's good wine was doing its work on the guests.

The servants to the people at the high table dispersed to get the next course onto the table before the guests even noticed that their trenchers were gone. Wine servers filled cups and goblets during the interval. Talon followed the man who served the bishop into the darker corridor behind the curtains of the door and before the surprised victim could shout his surprise Talon had pulled him sharply into a darkened alcove well out of the way of the human traffic.

There was a brief scuffle as the man unexpectedly struggled violently. Talon decided that he had to silence him quickly. The man died with a muffled groan. Talon dragged the dead man deep into the darkness under some stairs and left him there. He went to look for the cooks and the next course. As he was moving carefully along the line, a man in the bishop's livery shouted at him from close by, making him jump.

"What the hell are you doing? Have you seen Hubert? Goddamn him. I'll whip that lazy, filthy cur, he is to serve the bishop his next course. Doesn't he know that his lordship hates waiting?" the man shouted loudly. "Here!" He thrust a silver plate laden with succulent-smelling meats and gravy into Talon's hands and pointed back the way he had come.

"Hurry. Take it or I'll flog you as well if you're late with this by even a minute. Don't you dare keep his lordship waiting, you dog's arse."

Talon took the plate and hurried off, head down, looking servile, trying not to attract any attention to himself. He paused in the darkness of the stairway, waited until the other servants had hurried by, then took out one of his leather pouches. He shook it gently and sprinkled the ground-up dust into the gravy. He stirred it with his finger and buried it some more into the meal. Then he all but ran to the hall, following close after the other hurrying figures as they rushed to present the next course to the guests.

The Bishop Bohemond turned away from an animated discussion of the politics of the day with the Bishop of Carcassonne to address the man on his left, Father Eustache, his secretary. Talon ducked his head to avoid Eustache seeing him, and placed the meal in front of the bishop, who turned as he delivered it, saying querulously, "Where is the next course? Why do those lazy servants never bring it when I want it?" He wiped his mouth with a towel he snatched from a nearby attendant. "Ah, about time, too." He waved Talon away. "Father, we have to leave for Burgundy. There is to be a concourse of bishops within two weeks."

"Yes your eminence. I shall make preparations starting tomorrow. When would you want to leave?"

I think by the end of the next week." The bishop turned back to his guest and they continued their discussion.

Talon came back with some more food just in time to hear the bishop say speak.

"Have you notified them? It's time to finish the nonsense with those ploughshare knights."

His ears pricked up at the tone of the bishop's voice but then the priest confirmed his suspicions.

"Yes, your Eminence. I have already sent letters to both parties by horse messengers, including the secretary of the Count of Carcassonne. It's a pity those oafs, Guillabert's sons, bungled their work."

"Why, what work was that?" the bishop asked, gravy dribbling down his chin.

"They tried to ambush the knight's son, Talon, when he and his uncle came back from Carcassonne, Your Eminence."

"Eh. What happened?" He wiped at the gravy with a napkin.

"Somehow they killed the Templar Knight, his uncle, but then Talon proved to be too much for them. He got away after killing several of them."

"The fools! That Guillabert and his sons are very stupid people! I will not countenance the killing of a Templar no matter how I despise them. They are protected by the Pope. That Talon boy is interesting! We have to get him out of the way somehow or other."

"We should proceed with the Tribunal, my Lord. After that we will be able to enforce the law of the Church and have him branded as a heretic."

"If I did not need that odious man Guillabert I would abandon him to the wolves, but just for a while longer and then perhaps we can take care of him as well," the bishop said, taking a long drought of wine.

"Where is that meat? You." He waved at Talon who was hovering unctuously nearby. "Bring more of that meat." He turned back to the priest. "The important thing is to ensure we have the land for the church. The mills and fishing rights will bring in a very useful income."

Neither paid any attention to the servants as they feverishly replaced used platters with fresh ones that contained rich meat and gravy. The bishop ceased talking and turned his attention to the aromatic tenderloin of pork, sprinkled with dried herbs and surrounded with cooked prunes and apple sauce which had been placed carefully under his nose. The guests in the main hall still used trenchers of bread but the high table was honored with silver. The bishop did not stint his important guests.

He beamed delightedly on hearing the notes of a mandolin coming from down in the main area of the hall. The bishop did so like the songs of the troubadours from Languedoc. They were saucy and suggestive and warmed him for the evening to come with the woman he had in his own house. He would of course have to put out a sermon condemning the morality of these same troubadours in the churches of Albi at a later date. For the moment the Bishop Bohemond was a very contented man. Everything was going his way and a ripe plum was about to drop into his out-stretched hand. God was providing.

Talon made his way back toward the yard. To make sure that the irritable man who commanded the kitchens did not see him, he got close to one of the cooks who was garnishing some platters with herbs. Without letting anyone see him Talon sprinkled some dust on the platters and moved off. Next he discovered where the wine was being dispensed to the servants, who carried it into the hallway in earthenware jugs. It was simply a waist high barrel with the top taken off that the harried men dipped their jugs into. He sprinkled more dust into the barrel, stirred it in with a small stick and moved on.

His tour took him all around the yard, stopping here and there to dispense dust in some of the mead jugs or in this or that food tray. Then he made his way back to the hall, carrying another platter which he ensured was placed near to the clerics seated at the same table as the Bishop Bohemond.

It took about half an hour for Talon to be rewarded for his efforts. The first indication that all was not going to go well for the bishop's feast was when a knight staggered to his feet, lurched into the center of the hall and stood there shaking his head as though puzzled, staggering about. Then with a shout he drew his sword and charged the table where a small group of unarmed merchants were seated. He bellowed a curse and brought his sword down hard in a huge arc. His intended victim was just quick enough to slide out of the way along the crowded bench so that the descending blade hammered onto the surface of the thick wooden table. Platters and jugs bounced into the air and some shattered. There was a scream from one of the women nearby.

The sword stuck fast in the wood while the knight slowly leaned over it; releasing the handle to bang his head on the table then slid to the ground senseless.

There was a horrified silence for about two seconds then there was bedlam. The shrieks from the women and shouts of anger and bewilderment from the assembly were a satisfying sound indeed. Men got up but then sat down abruptly with comical expressions on their faces as the effects of the mushroom powder took over.

Others started to laugh and behaved as though they were deranged while the men who had run over to stop the maddened knight found themselves falling over one another giggling and laughing uproariously while tripping over the knight himself, who was quite unconscious.

Talon moved back into the shadows and watched as pandemonium broke loose. The Bishop of Carcassonne tried to stand up, but fell forward and buried his face in a pie, while the priest, Father Eustache, staggered to his feet only to clutch at Bishop Bohemond's cloak and drag it off the sickening man as he fell to his hands and knees, giggling uncontrollably. Bishop Bohemond was choking and holding his throat with one hand with the other pressed against his right side. He looked fearful and very ill, but no one seemed to notice.

Men and women were shrieking with laughter and pointing at one another or falling about the tables and over each other, and falling backward into the rushes of the main floor.

The bewildered servants stared at one another and then smirked, looking down at the assembly with disgust. But they too were not free of the affliction. One of them started to laugh, pointing at the men and women clutching one another in hysterics, and then another, followed by a spastic jerk by another. They had all been drinking the bishop's wine as they served and now they were possessed, too.

Before long Talon was one of the very few still standing in the hall, watching the crazed behavior going on all around him. He quietly made his way out of the hall then made sure he was not observed out in the garden where the servants and cooks were just beginning to succumb to the drug. He slipped over the wall to join Gareth.

"They seem to be having a lot of fun this night, Talon."

"Indeed, Gareth, it is amazing what a few herbs can do when added to a meal," Talon said.

He was satisfied that revenge had been done and that there was a little more balance in place for their trial.

Belth was trying to decide when it might be midnight when he got the shock of his life. Talon touched him on the shoulder and whispered, "You are not very observant, Belth, my friend."

He spun around to see Talon's dark shadow standing right next to him. "*Dieu, Dieu Bachan.* Talon, where in God's name did you come from?" he gasped, his heart in his mouth, visibly shaken by the fact that Talon had come up on him so stealthily.

Gareth chuckled softly at his friend's surprise.

"Now we have to go to the monastery," Talon whispered.

They mounted up and walked the horses around the town which was in the process of going to sleep, and then headed east for the monastery.

Talon and his two companions arrived at the abbey in the early hours of the morning. They stopped the horses on the edge of the clearing that opened onto the area that the fields of the abbey covered. There they slept for the few hours before the cocks began to crow in the yard by the stables. The monks, being early risers, were already up and moving about as the three somewhat disheveled riders came out of the woods, leading their horses, and climbed the hill to the main buildings.

They were greeted by the monks with some surprise, but Talon was made welcome as a friend.

He spent the day with the abbot, who was genuinely pleased to see him, as were Claude, Pierre, and the others. Talon spent a happy and relaxed few hours with the monks, although he had to tell them of the ambush and the death of his uncle. The abbot was appalled and visibly disturbed to hear Talon's description and who was implicated. Talon made no mention of the visit to Albi and had made Gareth and Belth swear to talk to no one about it.

He spent some time with Claude, who mentioned that they had discovered some old parchments in one of the chests in a cell that they were hunting through to see if there was any chance of a document pertaining to the will.

"You cannot rely upon us to save you at the court, I'm afraid," the abbot said unhappily later as they discussed the situation.

"We have an Advocate staying with us who is a distant relative of my mother's."

"An Advocate? One of those young men who have been to the debating colleges in Paris?" asked the abbot with interest.

"I believe he has been to Paris, and after hearing about it I'd like to go to see for myself."

"Ah, you do not find the countryside very stimulating?" the abbot asked gently, amused.

"You might be right, my Lord. I cannot say that it has been lacking in action, but I am surprised to say that I miss the chance to read and to apply my calligraphy."

"Why, then, do you also write in the tongue of the Arab and the Persian, Talon?" asked the abbot with some surprise. It seemingly had not occurred to him that Talon might be literate with the pen as well as with languages.

"I was taught well by many teachers, including my friend, Jean de Loche, who taught me Latin, my Lord Abbot. My 'Uncle' Farj'an insisted that I and my 'Brother' Reza learn both languages and to read and write them well. I shall be forever grateful to him for that."

The abbot beamed and insisted that Claude bring the ink and quills to them and quickly sharpened one with a small knife. "You must show us how they write," he exclaimed.

Talon demonstrated the curling calligraphy of the Arab letters to the enthralled abbot and Claude, who was with them.

They passed many pleasant hours in this fashion until it was noon and time for prayers.

Talon explained that he had to leave as they would be burying his uncle that day. Reluctantly, the abbot bid him goodbye and safe journey. He blessed Talon and told him that he would be praying for the soul of his Uncle Philip, the servant, and Anwl.

Claude told him that they would continue to industriously look for evidence, and God speed.

Hours later, Talon and his two weary friends arrived at the fort. The sentries opened the gates and let them in. Talon was just in time for Philip's funeral. His father looked impatient, but controlled it when he understood why Talon insisted on dressing in his chain mail and wearing his full armor.

The service was held by the same ragged priest from the village who had come into the fort that day at the request of Sir Hughes. He was to be paid a few small coins to perform the simple ceremonies for the dead. Talon stood with head bowed at the head of the grave situated at one corner of the grassy field which surrounded the fort. They placed a rough wooden cross at the head of each of the graves after they had been filled.

When the solemn ceremony was done, Sir Hughes came up to Talon and gave him Philip's shield. They had buried his uncle with his sword in hand and dressed in his Templar tunic. Talon hefted the shield and bowed to his father.

"Your mother has spoken to me of your need to go back to the Holy Land. If that be the case then you will want a good shield," his father said gruffly, as they walked with the crowd toward the gates of the fort.

Talon looked at his father. "I do not wish to leave very soon, Father."

"With winter coming, I should hope not, Talon. Besides we have some unfinished business to take care of before hand. God rot that man, Guillabert," he added savagely.

Chapter 20

The Trial

There was much debate as to who should be present at the dispute to be resolved by the Bishop at Albi and the other judges the following week.

Talon, Max, and Gareth wanted to take only the minimum number of men necessary to get there and back safely while leaving men at the fort to protect it from some treachery from the Guillabert family. They need not have worried; Sir Hughes decided to split his forces and to leave Max and Gareth at the fort with three of the remaining archers and good number of the newly trained villagers while they went to the trial with Drudwas and several of Sir Hughes' mounted men-at-arms. Bartholomew was asked to come along as Talon considered him a potential asset should the trial became a debate.

The two of them had argued back and forth numerous times, trying to build a story that would check the bishop, because Bartholomew was sure he would be the leader of the judges against them and they assumed that Sir Guillabert would not hesitate to lie in front of the assembly.

Bartholomew had grave misgivings, saying that it was a matter of record, quoting many instances where corrupt church leaders of the time had cheated people out of their rightful inheritance and claimed it for the church. While this was not technically the case here, he agreed that it could be the only reason the bishop was involved at all. He nevertheless thought that he could debate in front of the judges, should it come to that, for the sake of reaching the Count's Secretary, another powerful man, and the Lord Theudebert, a landed noble of the region. Talon said nothing.

Gareth and Max were concerned at the few in number who left the fort that day, but Sir Hughes told them that their problems were more likely to occur on the way back from the trial rather than on their way out and they would be prepared. Talon agreed with him.

His mother and Aicelina saw them off at the gates with the remainder of the villagers standing about. Sir Hughes had ordered all his villains and freemen with their families to come into the fortress and await the outcome. The walls were to be manned at all times and the gates locked shut until their party came back.

The group of men rode cautiously along the tracks and paths toward Albi. Drudwas had already taken the road ahead as a scout. Talon had no intention of relaxing his guard even now when they should have been safe. Sir Hughes' huntsman Domerc accompanied them on their journey, as did several churls who ran ahead with Drudwas as scouts.

Talon wondered about the intent looks that Domerc gave him from time to time, but did not remark it too much; his attention was on the road and the surrounding woods and countryside, looking for any signs of treachery. For the most part he and his father rode in silence. Philip's loss had affected them both and Talon knew his father mourned Philip deeply even if he gave little outward sign.

"It was one thing to know my brother was in the Holy Land with all its dangers, and so miss him," he told Talon bitterly. "But it is quite another to know he is dead."

The party arrived at the town of Albi with the sun high in the sky and the bells ringing for noon prayers.

It was clear that the court had been in session as there was a new corpse hanging from a gibbet near the gates. There was also a new head on a spike over the gates, staring sightlessly into the distance through half closed eyes. Flies were circling around the pallid flesh. The men crossed themselves as they went by. The laws of this land were enforced harshly, and it was likely that the victims were only sheep thieves or pocket thieves of some kind.

They were quickly permitted entrance, Sir Hughes having waved the document in the faces of the gate guards. They were then directed toward the center of the town. Puzzled, Sir Hughes asked why not the bishop's house.

"His eminence the bishop has died, sir," the guard captain responded.

There were shocked looks from the group. "What are you telling me, man? He is dead?" asked Sir Hughes incredulously.

"Yes, your honor, died an 'orrible death, too. Like his soul was in torment to the moment he died. May God receive him and his soul rest in peace," the guard intoned piously.

"It was like the whole house was suddenly bewitched. It happened late two nights ago! They all went mad about the same time," another said in a hushed voice.

The men around Sir Hughes crossed themselves, exchanging looks of bewilderment. All of them wondered what this turn of events might mean for Sir Hughes. Domerc gasped and stared at Talon then crossed himself, but no one noticed. They were all crossing themselves.

Hughes said nothing but he exchanged looks with Talon as they turned their horses and trotted along the muddy main street toward the market place.

There was already a crowd of people there. In the middle of the wide town square there was a building that rested upon many thick, wooden pillars. The dispute between the two landlords was common knowledge now and promised to be an event worth watching. One knight clashing with another in a public forum was rare enough. The townspeople were looking for a show.

Talon noticed the Count of Carcassonne's distinctive banner and wondered for a moment if the Count himself would be present. He had assumed that only the Count's secretary would be there. To his astonishment, he saw the Count's son Roger standing on the dais where the judges would be seated. He was talking to someone and did not at first remark the arrival of Sir Hughes' entourage.

Talon and Sir Hughes dismounted and gave their horses to the men and walked forward. Talon noticed that the entire area had been changed from a noisy market place to one of somber dignity. There were men-at-arms posted on all the streets that entered the area and pikemen formed a wide space around the market hall. This was a steeply roofed building with no walls on the ground floor which was supported by many tall pillars of carved wood. This was where normally the merchants would meet during wet weather for some occasion or when merchants and peddlers congregated to show off their wares.

Today it was festooned with banners and colored cloth. There was a raised dais in the large space created under the building by the pillars, and on this had been placed a covered table behind which were three heavy, carved chairs. Talon realized that this was where the court was to be held and the dispute resolved. He wondered if there would be other disputes that day but no one enlightened him.

Sir Hughes went up to a small table set off to the side and presented his parchment to a monk who was writing down details of some sort.

The monk looked up at Sir Hughes, took the paper and glanced at it. "You are to be here within one half hour, Sir Hughes, to stand before the Tribunal and make your case," he rasped. It sounded like he had a cold; his thin nose was red and his eyes watery.

Sir Hughes nodded and stepped back.

As he did so Roger of Carcassonne came over and clapped Talon on the shoulder. "Well, Talon, we meet again." he said by way of greeting. Then he said, as though for the benefit of others nearby, "I did not know you were involved in this dispute."

Talon knew, however, that he must know because of his very presence; but he did not disagree with Roger. "A pleasure to meet with you again, my Lord," he said in a low voice and bowing. "Sire, this is my father, Sir Hughes. It is his land right that is being disputed here."

"An honor, Sir Hughes. Your son has told me much of his travels. I would that I had been party to half of the adventures he tells of."

Sir Hughes bowed. "The honor is all mine, my Lord. We are simply glad that he is back with us. How is your father, the *Compte*? I trust he is well?"

"Well enough, Sir Hughes. But where is Sir Philip, your Templar uncle, Talon? I am surprised he is not with us today."

"He was murdered, Sire," Sir Hughes grated out.

Roger looked shocked.

"We were on our way home from Carcassonne when we were ambushed by mercenaries hired by Sir Guillabert, Sire," Talon said.

"My son barely got away with his life but he managed to obtain a confession from one of the men before one of that scum's sons came back to kill him, too," Sir Hughes growled savagely.

"But I have no witness to this confession, my Lord," Talon said. "Other than Sir Philip's Sergeant, Max, who was with me and escaped with a wound."

Roger looked him in the eye. "This is a serious accusation. Why would they want to kill Sir Philip? He was a Templar Knight, a holy soldier. What could they gain from that?"

"It was an accident, Sire. They meant to kill me. Ever since I came to this land Sir Guillabert's son Marcel has formed an acute dislike for me, and I think he wanted to show his father that he could do his dirty work for him."

He now had all of Roger's attention. The young man's mouth tightened in anger as Talon continued.

Talon went on to recount the incident where he and his band of archers had surprised and killed the men at the burning farm. "I have no doubt that it was revenge for the shame I inflicted upon them at that time, my Lord."

"By God, my father shall hear of this," Roger said angrily. "Sir Hughes, no matter which way this dispute goes today I believe that you should have justice for the loss of your brother. My father does not take kindly to this kind of thing. Especially as he is a patron of the Templars and supports them ardently."

"Thank you, my Lord, for those kind words," Sir Hughes said. "Sire, what of the death of the Bishop Bohemond? What happens to the Tribunal? Who will take his place?"

"Yes, they say it was a horrible death, too, by all accounts. There is talk of witchery as the whole household and the guests themselves went completely mad. The stories I have heard this day about what happened make my hair stand on end. This is mainly why I am here: to witness the burial on behalf of my father. The bishop is to be buried with honors. I have held court all day and your dispute is one of the last, thank God. My Father, God bless him, is determined that I learn the ways of governance, which is why I am here. Then we bury the late bishop tomorrow; he lies in state in his house today."

"What do you mean about the whole household going mad, Sire?" Sir Hughes asked curiously.

"Why, to hear it told, it was the night the bishop was holding a feast for his guest the bishop from Carcassonne. Of a sudden the people there went completely mad, almost as though a devil had come and thrown a spell upon them all. I heard that all went violently insane. Shouting of the devil and calling out that they could see him circling about in the rafters. Others behaved as though they could see something funny that no one else could. Others still were violently ill and a few died, including the bishop."

"Does no one know what happened to make this so, my Lord?" Talon asked carefully.

"I have not heard one word of sense spoken of this strange event all day."

"Are you then one of the Tribunal, my Lord?" Talon asked, changing the subject.

"Not exactly. It is the Priest Eustache, the secretary of the Bishop Bohemond, who is standing in for the bishop; and my father's secretary, as well as my Lord Theudebert, who will hear the arguments. I am here on behalf of my father to see that there is a fair hearing. He did promise that to you."

"We are very grateful, Sire," Sir Hughes said.

As he finished there was a clatter of hooves and rough shouts along the hard-packed street outside the marketplace. Sir Guillabert had arrived with his train.

Talon and Sir Hughes turned to watch while Roger discreetly stood off to the side, watching the arrival of the band of men with Sir Guillabert. Sir Guillabert dismounted and strode toward the court with his two sons Roger and Marcel at his back. He glared at Sir Hughes and Talon before presenting his parchment and saying loudly. "Here is my right to the hearing. I see those scum from my uncle's farm are here early. Who will sit on the tribunal now that the bishop is dead?" he all but shouted.

The monk who was entering the notes in a ledger looked up and timidly stated that Father Eustache, who had been the secretary to the bishop, would be standing in as he had full knowledge of the case and could represent the church.

Sir Guillabert and his leering sons looked pleased at that. Sir Guillabert could not resist striding up to Sir Hughes and standing in front of him with his hands on his hips. "So you are here to claim what is mine. I should have burned you out, Hughes. Were it not for my cousin, I would have."

"I don't think that would have been wise, Sir Guillabert." came a quiet response from the side.

Guillabert turned his head angrily at the interruption, but then he saw who it was. There was no mistaking the livery of the young man standing a few feet away, nor the confident pose.

"Sir Roger de Trenceval. My Lord, I didn't know you were here," he growled uncomfortably.

Both Roger and Marcel, who had been glaring aggressively at Talon, now looked uneasy. Roger's leer stayed on his face, but Marcel shifted and fingered his sword belt awkwardly.

"I am here to see fair play at the court today, Sir Guillabert. But I hear that there has been some foul play elsewhere and I shall investigate. The death of a Templar is an affront to God and will not go well with my father." His voice, though quiet, carried well enough for all around to hear him.

Sir Guillabert blustered. "My Lord, I do not know of whom or what you speak, but for sure I am here to see justice. I expect to regain what was given to me on my uncle's deathbed."

"Then we shall see. The court is about to commence, sirs. I would hear no more of burnings and the like while the court is in session." The young Count's tone brooked no nonsense.

Sir Guillabert and his glowering sons bowed briefly to Sir Roger and moved off to the side across from Sir Hughes and his retinue.

The court was called to order by one of the monks and the crowd told by a sergeant with a loud voice to hush their chatter on the outskirts of the ring of men-at-arms.

They needed no persuasion; this was an unusual case where the dispute was to be settled in court and not on the battlefield, as was still common under feudal law. This, strangely, had been ordered by the Bishop Bohemond himself and was to go forward with respect to his wishes.

A herald walked to the front of the building and shouted, "The court is in session. All that are present are to be respectful of the judges who will preside. Bow to your Lord, Sir Roger de Trenceval, Count Heir to Carcassonne."

The whole crowd quieted and the men in front of the court knelt in respectful silence.

Count Roger took a seat off to the side where he acknowledged the bows of the three judges as they came past him. The three men who were to judge the case walked forward and took their seats behind the cloth-covered table in solemn silence.

One of the monks who had been acting as a scribe stood up and walked to the center of the dais to face the tribunal. "The case to be decided today is one of land ownership, my Lords," he said in a loud voice. "The disputed land is that of the former knight, Sir Rufus d'Albi, who is the uncle of the knight present today, Sir Guillabert, and his only daughter, the wife of Sir Hughes de Gilles, who is also present today. Sir Rufus died of the plague in the year of our Lord 1167 in the month of August."

"What are the claims in this case?" Lord Theudebert asked first.

"The claimant is Sir Guillabert, my Lord, who states that he was bequeathed the land on Sir Rufus's deathbed."

Bartholomew nudged Talon and winked. Talon half smiled uncertainly. Did Bartholomew know something?

"Who contests the will of Sir Rufus?" Father Eustache asked.

"I do, my Lord." Sir Hughes stepped forward.

"My Lord, on behalf of Sir Hughes, I do," Bartholomew said, stepping forward to stand next to Sir Hughes, who looked at him with irritation, not understanding. Bartholomew looked directly at Sir Hughes and said quietly, "I would be honored to speak for you, Sir."

Sir Hughes nodded but remained looking puzzled. He looked back at Talon, who nodded. Sir Hughes shrugged and stood aside.

"Who are you?" demanded Father Eustache irritably.

"I am an Advocate who is representing the family De Gilles in this dispute, My Lord."

"They can speak for themselves, can they not?" the secretary asked, glancing at Roger, who was himself looking interested.

"Indeed they can, My Lords, but they have asked me to present their point of view because of the complexity of this issue," Bartholomew replied quickly.

"Utter rubbish, never heard of this before," Lord Theudebert grumbled, tugging at his moustaches, bristling uncertainly.

"Sir Hughes should stand up for himself in this matter... we should continue," Father Eustache stated dismissively.

"I feel compelled to ask this man his credentials, my Lords," Count Roger put in. "From where do you come that you can presume to be able to dispute this case on behalf of the family de Gilles?" he demanded, a tiny smile on his lips.

"I come from the University of Montpellier and the colleges of Paris with my diplomas in Canon law and estates that entitle me to wear the coat of the Advocate." Bartholomew bowed politely to the Count. He then produced from his brown over cloak parchments bearing impressive seals that he had brought with him for the occasion. He passed them to one of the monks, who in turn passed them to Count Roger, who read them carefully. Sir Roger passed them to the monks, pointing at certain parts of the writing. The two monks squinted at the parchments while he spoke. "These are sufficient evidence of your qualifications, sir," he said. "I am prepared to listen to your learned arguments."

Talon realized that he, along with his father, was gaping and shut his mouth with a click. He had the impression that Roger was enjoying the situation and wanted to see where it would go. Indeed, the monks who had read the parchments carefully seemed impressed. They then presented them to the judges. One of whom, Lord Theudebert, peered at them without comprehension. The secretary and Father Eustace could both read Latin, but it was clear that Lord Theudebert could not, so he pretended to read them and then passed them along.

Neither Father Eustace nor the secretary really wanted to dispute the situation with the young Count so they gave only a cursory glance at the sealed papers and handed them back to the monk.

"Very well," Father Eustache said, "you may represent the De Gilles although I find it very irregular." He glanced pointedly at the Count who ignored him, calmly watching the crowd.

"We shall hear from Sir Guillabert first, as he is clearly the plaintiff in this case," Father Eustache continued in what appeared to Talon an attempt to regain control of the court and take attention away from Bartholomew.

Sir Guillabert came forward and struck a pose in the center of the hall. He was dressed in full chain mail with a russet cloak suspended from his bullish shoulders on a silver chain. The cloak hung almost to the floor. He stood bare-headed with his chain head cowl pushed back off his head and with his hand on the pommel of his sword. He knew he presented a formidable and commanding figure to the crowd behind him.

"I am here to claim what was given to me by my uncle on his deathbed. That is all the lands that commence at the river Tarn and go for forty hectares south and east. I also claim as my right the mills and the fishing rights that are part of the landholding, along with the village and the fort that this usurper Hughes has occupied in defiance of the law. This I was granted by my uncle on his deathbed as his dying wish."

The court was silent as they listened to him speak. Guillabert turned from the judges and pointed to Sir Hughes. "This man came back from the *Outré Mere* and took what is mine without just cause or good reason. I wish him no ill but that he should vacate the land which is not his and leave."

The monks were scribbling furiously at their table while the judges watched Guillabert.

"What proof do you have to support your claim, Sir Guillabert?" the secretary asked.

"What other proof do I need other than the word of a dying man?" demanded Guillabert truculently. "I am a knight. My word is my bond, my Lords," he added smugly. He turned and looked challengingly at Sir Hughes. "All this man has is the word of my cousin, who was in Palestine when my uncle died and, as such, has no rights to the lands."

The judges nodded. They obviously thought this was pretty much the end of the discussion. Talon's heart sank. This was not what he had hoped for at all. Sir Guillabert was taking center stage and winning the battle before it had begun.

"A man is dying and wants to make sure his lands are taken care of. If he has no direct descent and his only daughter is in foreign lands, then it sounds right to me," Lord Theudebert stated with a comfortable shrug of his bony shoulders.

Eustace gave him an approving look and placed both elbows on the table with his hands together in a steepled form in front of his nose and looked pious. To Talon it seemed he obviously thought that the case was almost over.

Bartholomew took a step forward. "My Lords, may I speak?" he asked respectfully of the court.

The three judges looked at him and then each other somewhat taken aback. It was clear that they had not expected and disliked this intrusion by the upstart young man with diplomas. Father Eustache was not keen on the idea at all but the secretary, remembering his place, glanced over to the Count, who nodded.

"Stand forward and speak," said the secretary.

Bartholomew walked toward Sir Guillabert and bowed to him from a discreet distance, then bowed more formally to the judges and Sir Roger.

"Learned Sirs, My Lord. With the indulgence of the court, I would like to ask some questions of Sir Guillabert... just to establish the facts, you will understand."

The three judges looked at one another again and nodded reluctantly.

Bartholomew faced the truculent knight from a distance of about ten feet and with a voice that carried well, he asked, "Have you ever had the plague, sir?"

Sir Guillabert made the sign of the cross. "Would I be here if I had? What kind of question is that? No, thank the Lord, and I never hope to, either."

"So you, like most of us, fear the cursed plague and would avoid it at all costs?"

"I would of course. I am not a fool, churl." He turned to the judges irritably. "My Lords, what is the fool asking of me?"

"I agree with Sir Guillabert, what is the point of these questions, sir?" Father Eustache asked with a frown.

"My Lords, Father, I will demonstrate very shortly where I am going with the questions. I beg your patience for a little longer," Bartholomew responded respectfully.

Lord Theudebert waved his hand as though to tell him to get on with it. Bartholomew turned back to Sir Guillabert. "Sir, how did your uncle inform you of his will?"

Sir Guillabert smirked. "Why like any dying man would, he whispered it on his last breath."

"He whispered it?"

"I was close to him; he whispered it into my ear. I heard him distinctly."

"I beg your pardon, sir, but how close?"

"I had my ear to his face as he whispered. God damn you for a stupid man," Sir Guillabert roared.

Bartholomew nodded. "Had he not written his will and given it to some cleric in readiness of his death?'

"Not that I am aware. He told me that he had not had the chance to do so."

"Did he say anything else at all, other than that the land was to become yours on his death?"

"No, he did not."

"Was there not a priest present to provide the last rites as is normal in these instances?"

"If there was I was not present at the time it was given," Guillabert growled, shifting uneasily.

"But you just stated that he bequeathed you the land with his very last breath. Did you not, sir?"

Guillabert looked irritated. "Yes, I did. Can you not hear? What of it?"

"He did not beg for a priest to come and shrive him?"

"No, he whispered to me that his lands were to be mine on his death," Guillabert said loudly.

Bartholomew turned to the judges. "I am puzzled, my Lords. It is customary for a priest to be present at the death bed of a knight of the stature of Sir Rufus. He was a landowner of not inconsiderable wealth in these parts. Yet Sir Guillabert informs us that there was no priest present at the time of his death. This means that Sir Rufus died unshriven. Sir Guillabert was there to hear Sir Rufus' last wishes delivered without a request for a priest. This is extraordinary, my Lords. A man who is going to face his maker will beg for a chance to be forgiven his sins with his dying breath. I find it hard to believe he would spend his last breath bequeathing his property to even his nephew without asking for a priest."

The judges looked confused. People in the listening crowd were nodding and commenting to one another. Father Eustache, who was beginning to see Sir Guillabert made a fool of, glared at Bartholomew and was about to say something when Lord Theudebert spoke up.

"Young man you make a good argument, but where is all this taking us?"

Bartholomew bowed toward the judges. "My Lords with respect to Sir Guillabert here, I nevertheless find it incredible that in the first instance Sir Rufus had not demanded a priest at his deathbed. Sir Guillabert assures us that there was none; but he, Sir Guillabert, was there nonetheless." He turned back to Sir Guillabert. "Sir, how long were you present with your uncle during this time?"

"Long enough to hear his last words to me," Guillabert snapped, looking annoyed.

"You appear to have spent some time with him discussing the will, is that not so?"

"Yes, we talked, or rather he whispered," Guillabert said with a patronizing smirk. "He was dying, you know."

Bartholomew nodded. "Yes, he was, indeed. How long would you say you spent with the dying man discussing this will, my Lord?"

"How in God's name would I know? Maybe an hour or less?"

Bartholomew paused as though pondering something, and then said, "My Lords, it is common knowledge that Sir Rufus died of the plague."

Father Eustace gave a start. He flushed angrily as he realized the trap that Bartholomew had laid for Guillabert.

"We have heard enough from this man, my Lords," he stated dismissively.

"My Lords, if I might conclude..." Bartholomew said respectfully.

The secretary looked to the young Count who was watching the proceedings with an amused look on his young features. The Count nodded.

"We should let the man complete his arguments," the secretary said firmly.

Father Eustace shrugged irritably. "Then let it be quick; I have heard nothing of interest here so far."

Bartholomew bowed to the judges and then again to the Count. He cleared his throat before continuing. "I should remind the noble assembly that it was the plague that took the life of Sir Rufus along with many, many other people at the time of his death. There was a fear in the land and people fled those areas where it struck so that whole villages were deserted for a time because of the dreadful nature of the disease that passed without effort from one person to another, taking life after life. My Lords, as you will I am sure remember, such was the fear and terror of contracting the disease that not even a priest would visit the dying to administer the last rites. I should also remind the court that Sir Guillabert has stated clearly that he, too, has a deathly fear of the plague. Was that not so?" he asked the red-faced knight in front of him.

Sir Guillabert did not answer, he simply glared, and Bartholomew hurried on.

"How is it, then, that Sir Guillabert could spend so long with his dying uncle—who was dying of the plague, you understand—yet not fear to incur this dread disease? He himself has informed us that he put his head close to the man's lips to hear his last wishes. Did he not fear to die as his uncle was dying in front of him, un-shriven and helpless, convulsing in the final agonies of the Black Death?" He almost shouted the last words.

The people of the crowd listening murmured in fear and many crossed themselves at his words.

Bartholomew stopped dramatically to let the words sink in. Talon listened to the silence as he watched the judges' faces. They looked stunned. It was not as though Bartholomew had provided proof that Guillabert was lying. It was simply that he had sown considerable doubt on the knight's story.

Talon wondered if it were enough.

Bartholomew continued talking to a court that was now prepared to listen to him. The young man had captured everyone's attention who could hear his voice, who were also relaying his words to others in the crowd behind. There were excited murmurs from the people as they began to get the drift of the argument the young man was making.

"My Lords, what I have heard from Sir Guillabert is that he braved the horror of the plague to hear his uncle whisper—into his *ear*, you will also note—and will his land to him. Not only that, but even more remarkably, his uncle disdained the need for forgiveness or to be shriven before he went to his Maker. This I find very hard to believe. However, despite the fearsome nature of the plague, Sir Guillabert is still with us, which means that our Lord was watching over him or..." he let the words hang for a long moment, "Sir Guillabert has fabricated the story and it has no foundation at all!"

There was an audible gasp from the crowd as the words were passed along. Bartholomew bowed to the judges and stepped back. His brown over-smock that denoted his rank as an Advocate swirled as he turned away.

Sir Guillabert yelled in rage. "How dare you accuse me of lying, you cur!" he shouted, his hand going for his sword.

Talon had his own sword halfway out of his scabbard before a shout stopped him.

The young Count was standing now and he was coldly angry. "Enough. Sir Guillabert, if you draw your sword in this court you will be placed in prison. Guards, stand by me."

The retainer knights who were standing nearby strode quickly to his side. Their hands were on their swords and in one case already drawn.

"This court is governed by the Count of Carcassonne and all will show respect," Roger stated loudly. "My Lords judges, you will now adjourn with me and debate this issue in private."

Bartholomew sidled over to Talon, who let his breath out in a long, low sigh. "You are a wordsmith, Bartholomew. If this is what you have learned in the colleges of law and debate, then I would like to go there, too. I also know an abbot who would like to meet you."

Bartholomew shrugged. "Sir Guillabert led himself into the little trap I prepared for him. If he had had an Advocate for himself, it would not have been so easy to ensnare him."

Sir Hughes clapped Bartholomew on the shoulder. "I am still not quite sure what you said, Bartholomew, but you certainly made an impression on the judges and I think you made a fool of Guillabert."

"Yes, Sir Hughes, I am worried about the latter, but the judges are now having to think more about the circumstances than they were prepared to at the onset of the debate. Talon, your enemy in this court is Father Eustace. Are you aware of that?"

"Oh, yes, just as was the bishop," Talon replied.

Bartholomew shot him a sharp look. "The bishop has recently died, and under odd circumstances, would you not agree?"

"If you mean he died suddenly then, yes, I agree, but we don't know how as yet, Bartholomew," Talon said carefully. He was watching the Guillaberts as they stood in a huddle off to the side of the barn-like building, casting malevolent looks in Talon's direction.

Roger had that sneer on his face again and Marcel just looked angry. Sir Guillabert himself seemed to be issuing orders because Roger nodded and then strode away, waving to his groom to bring his horse and then with several of the men-at-arms who attended Sir Guillabert, he rode off down the main street of the town. The crowd let him pass, but there must have been words, for he looked as though he were about to ride down some of the people who shook their fists at him as he rode by. The family of Sir Guillabert was not popular in Albi, it seemed.

Sir Hughes nudged Talon. "Send one of your men after them and find out what they are about."

Talon beckoned to Drudwas, who came over and knuckled his forehead to him and Sir Hughes. "Drudwas, Roger d'Albi, the son of Sir Guillabert, has just ridden off. Do you follow them and find out where they are planning an ambush."

Drudwas gave his gap-toothed grin. "I shall follow them like a shadow, m'lord Talon."

"Be sure you do, Drudwas. I do not want to find you pinned to a tree by their daggers when we take the road home."

Drudwas nodded and then vanished into the crowd.

Bartholomew was watching Talon curiously. "You are a young man, Talon, yet men respect you."

"Talon has known much of life, even for one so young, Bartholomew of Brittany," growled Sir Hughes. "In time you will learn, as I am beginning to, just how much."

"In the meantime, I think the judges are coming back," Talon said, plucking at Bartholomew's sleeve.

They all turned and watched the three appointed judges solemnly tramp down the rough-hewn stairs from the upper story of the building, the Count behind them. The men seated themselves and Father Eustace, who had a face like thunder, motioned one of the monks to announce the commencement of the court again. The young Count seated himself with a satisfied air about him and then watched the proceedings begin.

Father Eustace thrust a paper over the table toward the secretary-monk, who looked askance at it. "Read it, man; get on with it," the priest shouted.

The monk picked up the parchment and began to read. "On this day of the twelfth day of September, in the year eleven seventy-two, in the extraordinary court convened for the purpose of land settlement between Sir Guillabert d'Albi, the plaintiff, and Sir Hughes de Gilles, the defendant, it has been ordered by the court that the lands in dispute shall remain within the possession of Sir Hughes, insufficient evidence having been provided by the side of Sir Guillabert to prove without doubt his claim. The land shall therefore stay with daughter, Marguerite de Gilles, Sir Rufus d'Albi's direct descendent, for all time henceforward. Sir Hughes, because of marriage to the aforesaid person, shall administer the lands on her behalf.

"The court is closed on this issue."

There was a brief stunned silence and then a roar of approval from the crowd behind them. This had been the best entertainment since the last execution, and a very unpopular man had lost. The whole proceeding had been novel to most people. Courts of law and rulings of this type were usually decided in lists where knights fought it out. The winner took all as the loser was generally dead. Everyone was pleased except Sir Guillabert, who was livid.

He stood with Marcel at his side and glared angrily at first the judges and then he turned and shook his fist at Sir Hughes. "I should have challenged you, Hughes. I could have taken it from you then and there. But for the bishop, may his soul rot in hell, I would have the land even now," he raved. His face was mottled with rage and his hand was on his sword. It was clear that he could barely contain his anger at the decision of the court.

The Count Roger ignored the outburst and walked over to Sir Hughes. He smiled at Talon and then addressed the small group. "Sir Hughes, it would seem that you have several talented people within your retinue. However, I feel that you should leave. I do not feel you should tarry for the funeral under the circumstances. I shall send some of my men to your fort after we have taken care of the bishop. I do not trust Guillabert, nor his sons, and the ruling here will not make them pleasant neighbors."

"I wish to thank you for your support, my Lord," Sir Hughes said and bowed deeply to the young Count. "We shall leave immediately."

"I think we'll be all right if Guillabert can be delayed somehow, my Lord," Talon said to Roger.

Roger grinned. "I think that can be arranged. God speed and stay well." He turned away and shouted at Sir Guillabert who was about to depart. "Sir Guillabert, a word with you, sir."

Guillabert had no option but to stride back to the Count, who engaged him in earnest conversation while Sir Hughes' party hurriedly mounted and left through the crowd that was now dispersing. There were many who nonetheless wished them well and called God's blessings over to Sir Hughes, who was known as a fair man.

Chapter 21

Flight

Talon had reason to be thankful that he had sent Drudwas after Roger d'Albi. He was running back toward them as they left the town gates.

The group halted their horses and one of the men-at-arms handed Drudwas the reins of the horse he had been leading. Drudwas pointed down the road as he mounted up. "M'lord, Sir Hughes, Talon, you were right—Roger is waiting for you about a mile down the road where it narrows between two hills. Do you remember the place, Talon? It is dense with thickets there and a bowman could do a lot of killing from cover."

Sir Hughes cursed under his breath. He looked about at the group, then gave a start. "Where is my huntsman? Where is Domerc?" he demanded.

Everyone looked around; no one had noticed that he was not with them when they left as they had had other things on their minds. His absence meant that they were now down to six, not enough men to deal with Roger head on with his superior numbers. He had taken a sizeable number of men with him and Talon had noticed that some of them were crossbowmen.

"We can't go back for him now, Father. We'll find ourselves trapped between Guillabert and Roger soon enough. We must ride round Roger and head for the fort as quickly as we can. I fear that we will have trouble enough as it is when we get back."

Sir Hughes nodded reluctantly. "So be it." He turned to one of the retainers. "Cerdric, you know this country like the palm of your hand. Lead us quickly 'round those scoundrels and back to the fort by the shortest route."

The man grinned. "Aye, I can do that, Sire; it will be a rough ride, but we can do it. Follow me." He turned his horse off the main trail and led the way through the trees for about half a mile then they climbed a steep slope studded with rocks and stunted trees that led up a long ridge.

Talon looked at Bartholomew to see how he was doing. The young man seemed to be enjoying the situation, but Talon was concerned about his ability to fight if it came to that, as it would be every man for himself.

Bartholomew must have sensed the look because he gave Talon a grin. "Do not worry for me. I can ride well and if I have a sword I can use it. Paris as a student is not a life for the weak and trembling."

Talon laughed quietly at that; he was beginning to really like this man. He took off his dagger and handed it to him. "It isn't much for now, but we will provide a good sword when we get home."

It was not long before the town of Albi and the winding river Tarn were laid out below them and from the vantage point of a ridge they paused and saw a group of men leave the town and head rapidly down the road they had just left.

"That will be our friendly neighbor, Sir Guillabert." muttered Sir Hughes. "We have to hurry now as they will soon enough realize that we have slipped them and then they will try for the fort."

The men clapped heels to horses' flanks and rode hard after Cerdric, who was confidently leading the way. They took the hill paths and indirect ways that he knew well; but, even so, it was late in the evening when they found themselves once again on the road to the fort.

Only just in time, too, as Drudwas looked back and pointed. They all turned to see what he was pointing at. There about a mile away coming down a slope at great speed was a band of men. They saw Sir Hughes' group at the same time and gave chase immediately.

"Now we have to make haste! We will fight on our terms, not his!" Sir Hughes shouted.

Talon nodded. They galloped the last mile as fast as the horses could go in the gathering dusk. They went through the deserted village at a flat out gallop and then veered onto the wide, grassy track that would bring them to the gates of the fort.

Gareth had obviously been expecting something of this kind to happen as there was a shout and the gates began to open.

The small party galloped into the fortress' muddy yard just as the men with Roger and Guillabert came boiling out of the village. The gates slammed shut and men raced for the battlements, bows and pikes at the ready.

Talon leapt off Jabbar, leaving a young boy to take the reins and he, too, ran for the battlements followed closely by Drudwas. There was much shouting now as men became aware of the situation and called out to their comrades to man the walls.

Sir Hughes made a more dignified descent from his horse, but he, too, hurried up the stairs to see what was happening.

The band of men with Sir Guillabert was milling around at the edge of the woods near the trail that led to the village, well out of crossbow range.

Gareth and Max came over to Talon and his father as they stood on the ramparts and watched.

"That seemed close. m'lord, Sir Hughes," Max said with a grim smile.

Talon grinned. "They are predictable men, Max. They laid an ambush but we went by it and came by another route."

"Give the word, Sir Hughes, and we can cut their numbers down. They are within range of a long bow," Gareth said eagerly.

"I am sore tempted to let him know our sting, Gareth, but we shall wait and see what he does," Sir Hughes replied, clapping Gareth on the shoulder.

Talon had an idea what Guillabert would do next but said nothing. They watched as two men rode out from the group and came within shouting distance. It was Sir Guillabert and his son Roger. Of Marcel there was no sign.

Sir Guillabert stopped just out of crossbow range and shouted up at them. "Well, Hughes, it would seem that you are trapped. You coward, you flee an open fight and cower in your lair!"

Sir Hughes strode to the edge of the battlements and shouted back, "It is a cowardly thing to lay ambush for innocent travelers, Guillabert, but then you are a liar and a scoundrel as well. I also know your sons to be the murderers of my brother, and one day there will be a reckoning for that, too. You heard the court: the land is not yours, so go home to your pigsty and stay there."

"I shall burn you out of this hovel first," Guillabert shouted. "I'll take what is mine despite the court."

"You would defy the Count of Carcassonne? You are a fool, Guillabert. The Count will not take kindly to what you're doing here. Even now he's sending men to protect my rights."

"They may not arrive in time and the Count can hardly give it to a man who is dead; and you shall be dead when I am finished. Try to leave and you and your heathen whelp will die, as will all who stand with you."

"I think he has laid out his terms clearly enough for us all to understand," Bartholomew, who had joined Talon on the ramparts, remarked.

Shaking his fist at them, Guillabert turned his horse and led the way with Roger at his side back to the group of men gathered at the edge of the woods.

"He will burn the village first," Talon said.

Bartholomew looked at him. "Why would he do that?"

"Why? Because of spite and anger. He has been thwarted at every turn and now wants satisfaction," Sir Hughes answered.

The group of men departed into the gloom of the woods, heading for the village.

Sure enough, it was not long before there was the flicker of light in the darkness and then the men on the ramparts saw tall flames and sparks shoot up into the evening sky.

There were shouts of rage from the village men standing on the walls. They were watching their homes go up in flames and wanted to rush out and attack the enemy.

Sir Hughes called back to Max. "Keep the gates shut, Max, and post reliable men. We will not be rushing about in the dark to be hacked to death by Guillabert's mercenaries. That's what they want."

Max ran quickly down the steps to make sure Sir Hughes' orders were complied with. Then Hughes and Talon posted guards. Gareth elected to stay on the walls for the time being. He and his sharp-eyed countrymen wanted to make sure there was no attempt to scale the walls in the darkness. Despite the fact that all the village population was within the confines of the fort they were still desperately thin on the ground and needed every able man and boy to keep watch.

Talon, his father, and Bartholomew made their way across the crowded yard. There were village folk standing about in the muddy yard in frightened groups, the women holding crying children to them while cattle contained in loosely woven hazel railings lowed loudly for their feed. What sheep and goats the villagers had been able to bring with them were held in noisy herds along the walls in improvised pens. Ducks and geese were trying to settle down where they could near the pond. The house churls and servants hurried about at Marguerite's command, distributing food and what blankets could be found. People were trying to find dry places in the haystacks and barns as night fell. Talon stopped abruptly. "Brother Claude. What are you doing here? Pierre, you, too?"

Brother Claude stood upright from attending to a child with a cut on her hand and pushed against his back.

"Well met, Talon de Gilles, Sir Hughes. We are come to give you news of the inheritance." He looked around. "But I fear that we came too late."

"Although you are always welcome at my father's hearth, you came at a bad moment, my friends. You cannot leave now until this issue has been resolved with Guillabert," Talon said gently.

"What happened to bring this about, Talon?" Pierre asked.

"We went to trial and Bartholomew gave them an exercise in words. Ah, but you should have been there, brothers! The Court awarded my father the land because Bartholomew made them doubt so much what they were hearing from my uncle. But Guillabert would have none of that and has followed us home to try to take it off us or burn us out. To him, I doubt if it matters which."

The two monks looked nervously at one another. "But your grandfather left a document after all, Talon. We have it with us."

"This I must see!" Hughes exclaimed.

Brother Claude took a leather tube out of the folds of his voluminous habit and opened it to pull out a roll of vellum. "It is in Latin, which we use for legal documents."

"I can read it," Bartholomew said, who took the proffered document and unrolled it. He glanced quickly at the vellum. "Remind me again, Sir Hughes, when your father-in-law died?"

"During the summer of eleven sixty-seven. Why?"

"Then your father-in-law was a man who thought ahead, as this document was written the previous autumn and states clearly that the inheritance is to go to his nearest living descendent. In fact, he is specific... it was not to go to Guillabert as he found that man undeserving." He laughed. "I am inclined to agree, Sir Hughes."

Sir Hughes and Talon chuckled dryly at his words.

"Much good this will do us if we cannot defeat the rogue," Sir Hughes said. "He must have known about this, or at least suspected it. I wish to thank you, Brother Claude and Brother Pierre, for taking the trouble to come see us. It is out of the question that you should leave now, though."

"He would not dare to harm two members of the church," Pierre exclaimed.

"Indeed, I think he would," Sir Hughes said.

"At least the men with him would not respect nor protect you. They are thieves and scoundrels, brothers. I could not protect you once you leave these gates."

Brother Claude sighed. "Then, Brother Pierre, we shall stay and offer our services where we can."

"Bartholomew will take you into the Hall, where at least we can feed you. Perhaps you can help should there be wounded?" Talon asked.

Brother Pierre squinted at him. "So you think it will come to a fight, Talon?"

"We are sure of it, brothers, and I would rather you were not in harm's way when it does come," Sir Hughes growled.

Bartholomew led them away while Hughes and Talon continued their inspection. People asked fearfully of Sir Hughes as he strode by what would happen. He tried to reassure them that all would be well and that they would be taken care of but even to Talon's ears his words sounded hollow. Their inspection took them to the ramparts at the rear of the fort where they rested and watched the glow over the dark forest. Even at this distance the flames of the burning village illuminated the roofs and walls of the barns and the main hall in a flickering light.

Then they descended the ramp again, accompanied by several of the hunting hounds that belonged to Sir Hughes and followed them about tirelessly much to his son's annoyance as he found them to stink. They came to the entrance of the hall to find Marguerite and Aicelina standing there, waiting for them.

Both looked pale in the darkening evening but they were putting on a brave face in front of the men. Guillaume was hanging onto Aicelina's hand apprehensively, but his eyes shone when he saw Talon.

Talon knelt and gave his brother a hug and then sent a smile toward Aicelina, who smiled back, albeit nervously. He assumed his sister was in bed.

Sir Hughes stopped in front of his wife. He leaned forward to kiss her cheek and then said, "Your Bartholomew is a remarkable man, Marguerite. He is a wordsmith and although I could not follow all that he was saying, much less where he was going with his dialogue, he surely saved the day."

Marguerite stared back at him, hope in her eyes. He nodded, as did Talon. "Indeed, he cast so much doubt upon the scurrilous story of Guillabert the judges were forced to concede the land to you."

"I think the presence of Roger de Tranceval counted for a great deal of the result as well, Mother." Talon smiled. "Bartholomew achieved with words what other men would have tried with swords. It is now on record that a court awarded the land to our family."

"Talon, it was no great feat to confuse the men at the bench; and as for Guillabert, he walked eagerly into my trap," Bartholomew said with a depreciating laugh as he came out of the dark hall behind the two women.

"In any case it is all bye the bye, as we now have the written proof which the monks brought to us."

Marguerite stared at him in surprise, her eyes wide, then turned to Sir Hughes. "Is this true? There was written proof?"

"The two monks who are with us produced the document and Bartholomew has verified it my dear," Sir Hughes said with a gentle smile for her. "Now all we have to do is to beat Guillabert at his own game."

Marguerite smiled at her menfolk, relief on her face. "With the written proof, will Guillabert not see reason?" she asked hopefully.

"I fear not. He is maddened at the humiliation and will stop at nothing less than our destruction, if he can."

She looked up at him gravely and held onto his arm. "Well, we have some good men with us and surely God will favor our just cause. We shall prevail I am sure, with His help."

Hughes laughed. "There, you see, Talon. We all draw our courage from this woman, your mother, God bless her." He stooped to kiss her, grinning when she flushed bright red.

Bartholomew smiled too, but he was looking at Aicelina.

"No matter what or how, we now have the right to defend the land, and it looks as though we shall have to do that somewhat sooner than I had expected," Sir Hughes said to his wife with a rueful smile.

She placed both her hands on either side of his bearded face. "My knight, my knights and you, Bartholomew of the Words, come and eat and then we shall see what can be done. You must be hungry." She linked arms with Talon and his father and led the way into the smoky hall toward the tables laden with food.

Bartholomew gallantly offered his arm to Aicelina, who shooed Guillaume ahead of her and then placed her hand on his arm.

Chapter 22

Siege

That night Talon joined Gareth and the other men on the parapet nearest to the gates. The cottages still burned in the distant village, casting a reddish glow that illuminated the tense, bearded faces of the men staring in that direction and glimmered off the polished spear heads and the helmets a few of the men wore. Other men, men of the village wearing thick leather caps and clutching pikes or crudely made spears, stood in nervous groups down in the yard.

There was almost no wind so they could clearly hear the crackle of the burning thatch and wood coming from the direction of the village. The smell of smoke was dense in the air. Talon was surprised that the forest had not taken fire. He doubted that Guillabert would care if it meant that fire could come to the fort with less effort.

He and Sir Hughes had spent the last hour ensuring that there was enough water to keep them through a short siege. They at least had a well, although Talon doubted that it held enough water to sustain them over a week with all the extra people they now had inside.

Gareth, Max, and Feremundus had accompanied his father as he walked the perimeter of the fort along the battlements and posted their most reliable men on the corners in the makeshift towers and in the center of the walls. There were few enough men, Talon thought glumly. He had looked at the huddled villagers and the old men down in the yard and almost despaired. They would be lucky if they could hold off Guillabert and his men in the first rush—which he was quite sure would come with the dawn.

In spite of his nerves and the fear gnawing at him he drew much comfort from his father's calm. Sir Hughes seemed unperturbed and continued to walk around briskly, barking orders and, although he must have been concerned, he did not show it. His father was putting his extensive soldiering experience gained in Palestine to work for him now.

The four of them had worked with the archers, and set a couple of the men-at-arms who served Sir Hughes to take stock of their weapons and any other deterrents they might have at their disposal. Apart from a few long-shafted pikes and of course the bows, they possessed only a meager amount of heavy armament.

Feremundus, who had gone off to stoke his fires, had rejoined them and quickly agreed to work all night if necessary to produce some more spearheads and arrowheads. He went off again with one of the archers to get to work. It had not been long before they heard his hammer beating on the red-hot metal.

"We don't even have enough rocks to throw at them," Talon exclaimed irritably to Max and Gareth, who grinned.

"We have enough cattle to make dung balls for the tossing at them," Max said with an attempt to raise their spirits. They chuckled, it relieved the stress.

"I take comfort from the amusement you two great warriors find in our situation!" Talon said tartly.

Max and Gareth looked at one another and burst out laughing. Talon had no choice; he joined in. There was nothing else to do. People around them stared at the three men laughing in the middle of the yard and decided they were mad. Was not their situation dire? But these three men from other parts were laughing nonetheless.

"We could use fire again. Remember the galleys, Talon," Gareth said, wiping his eyes.

"They won't be sailing in to fight us, Gareth."

"I doubt that Guillabert knows how to sail a galley anyway," Max said lugubriously.

This set the three of them off again.

"But you're right, we should at least have hot coals to pour onto them if they try to climb the walls. I shall talk to my mother and ask her to prepare something we could use in the morning. They will come with the dawn," Talon said, still chuckling.

"If they use ladders, we should have long poles to push them off with," Max said.

"Yes, and if they try to ram the gates, we should pour pitch or boiling slops onto them. Do we have any at all?"

They went and asked Sir Hughes if he might know. "What did you and your companions find so funny about our situation, Talon?" he growled.

"Father, Max, and Gareth are madmen and just wanted to cheer me up," Talon said, glancing at his still grinning companions.

"It would seem they succeeded," Hughes said with a dry smile. "I think there is some, but I shall send off one of the servants to see if there is any. We usually have some for the torches."

There was to be little sleep for the men in the fort that night. Sir Hughes insisted that men were rotated onto and off the walls and that the off-duty ones got some sleep, but those who stood down only ate a little and then napped restlessly huddled in their cloaks. The noises of the yard didn't allow for a peaceful rest; the animals, unused to being herded together so tightly, bleated and bellowed continuously.

The harsh sound of the grinding stone on steel added to the general din as the men sharpened their weapons. The Welsh archers attended to their arrows and their bows, waxing strings and testing for flawed arrows. Gareth had made sure there was a good supply for this eventuality. There were several fires in the compound around which some of the villagers and men-at-arms still stood, nervously anticipating the day to come.

Talon turned to Gareth. "Go and get some sleep. I'll stay here a while longer."

He saw Gareth nod in the flickering light, then he laid his hand on Talon's arm. "You should get some sleep as well. It will be a long day tomorrow."

"You're right, I shall. But I need to spend some time up here before I do. Goodnight."

In truth he was too tense to sleep. He realized that men looked to him for leadership and he wondered if he were up to the task. His father was an old hand at fighting, having earned his spurs in the Kingdom of Jerusalem. Sir Hughes was every bit the leader and very much in charge at present. Talon drew some comfort from that fact and resolved to emulate his father in every way. Even if it meant that he should die, he would not display fear in the face of the enemy. His resolve deepened when he considered the consequences of failure, the very extinction of his family.

After Gareth had gone, Talon walked alone along the parapet deep in thought. It was probable that the enemy was watching them from the edge of the forest even now, too alert to be surprised. What he had in mind would have to wait until the next day, even the following night, if they survived.

His father stamped up the wooden steps, shaking them as he came. He walked to Talon, a dark bulky form in the night. He, like Talon, was fully armed, wearing his chain hauberk over which he had a plain, unadorned surcoat. His helmet was firmly planted on his head. His mail clinked as he moved.

"Talon is that you?" he growled.

"Yes, sir, it is."

"I have to say that I am almost glad it has finally come to this, my boy. I have had to endure the gibes and insults from Guillabert for far too long. Were it not for your mother's sake I would have challenged him long ago."

Talon nodded in the dark. "You are a wise man, Father. They would never have met you in fair fight. Witness Marcel's behavior, and I would not trust Roger as far as I could throw a spear."

"Guillabert has sired a couple of dogs, that's for sure, a pity he also has a daughter who is quite a nice girl from all accounts. Marguerite thinks no ill of her."

Talon was silent, remembering the night in the castle.

"I think they'll try for the gates tomorrow," his father said. Hughes turned and moodily contemplated the crowded space below inside the fort. "We have a lot of people, but few who can fight. I am glad that Max and Philip managed to train some of them before this came about. Dear God, but I wish he were here now."

Talon stared down at the young men and boys of their makeshift army who huddled together around the fires in the yard. Some were wearing the captured hauberks taken from the men killed during the forest ambush. A hauberk was so large on one of them it looked ridiculous on the skinny lad. He sighed.

"I, too, Father. The very presence of Philip in his Templar uniform would have been a deterrent to even these scum. The two remained silent for a while, each in his own thoughts. Then Talon said, "I think the Welsh are going to be the key to this fight tomorrow. We might tip the odds somewhat with their longer bow range."

"If we can keep the pikes in the front to protect the bowmen, we have a chance. I wish I knew where Domerc was. Not like him to be absent like that. I wonder if the Count really did send men to help. Lord save us, but we could do with them now."

Talon wondered, too. Domerc had not been very friendly since the first day and it struck him that the man had shown little respect for Philip, either. It was as though he resented them all for some reason. He was also puzzled by the lack of promised help. It did not seem like Roger to promise him help and then not keep his word.

"Strange about the bishop dying the way he did, almost as though he was struck down by some witchery," Sir Hughes mused. "I don't doubt but that he deserved it, though, with his evil thoughts against Guillaume. Did you indeed go to the abbey that night?"

Talon sensed that his father was looking at him in the darkness. He evaded the question. "It would seem that he ate something that disagreed with him, Father. I for one am relieved that the trial is over. We'll find a way to deal with Guillabert."

"Hmm, I am sure we will. There is still much that I would know about your life in Persia, my son," Sir Hughes said meaningfully.

Talon was aware that his father was staring at him, but said nothing; instead he turned and looked out toward the woods. Nothing stirred.

"You have shown me that you are a well grown man since you came back to us," his father said gruffly. "But I know, too, that you are young and that you might not have faced odds of this kind before. It will go hard for us, as we do not have sufficient men to fight them on even terms, nor even from behind these walls, for very long. But we must if we are to survive. The men will look to you and me for courage and leadership in a time like this. I have no fear that your courage will fail you, as that is strong within and clear to all. You will do well and if anything should happen to me, I want you to know that I am proud of you. Very proud."

It was a long speech for his father and Talon was almost overcome with emotion. He said nothing. Instead, he embraced his father hard and then they held one another at arm's length, looking one another in the eye.

"Let us show them all who the de Gilles are tomorrow!" growled Sir Hughes.

Talon nodded. "Thank you, Father. I am proud to be a de Gilles this day."

They parted soon after to get some sleep.

Chapter 23

Assault

The men of the fort moved quietly into their positions at the first hint of dawn. Apart from the chink of mail and the occasional loud creak of a board this was accomplished without incident. Max and Talon were especially busy taking men and boys to the very place where they were to fight. The day dawned gray and overcast and a sharp breeze started up from the northwest.

Gareth and Talon stood together with Sir Hughes on the ramparts near the gates.

Gareth sniffed the air. "This is the beginning of the autumn. We can only hope that Guillabert and his sons don't burn what crops that remain to be harvested."

The men with weapons were standing in groups all around the fort walls; everyone was tense and keyed up. Max had been put in charge of the rear of the fort, with him was Bartholomew and two of the archers, Devonalt and Ap-Maddock.

Sir Hughes had made it his business to defend the gates and Talon wanted to fight by his side. Feremundus and a couple of other men were on the ground near the gates, prepared to defend them if they should be broken into. Talon felt comfortable having that big man there with his axe in hand and the round shield on his left arm. His habitual scowl was more intense than ever.

Talon stared off toward the entrance to the forest that led to the village and noticed some activity. He nudged Gareth. "Let's see if we can surprise them with some well aimed arrows before they get too close."

Gareth nodded and then spoke to Belth and Drudwas in their language. The other two grinned and tested their strings. The three of them took out arrows, checked their feathers, smoothing them with careful, calloused fingers and made ready.

"They only have to come within sight and we can take them down. The distance is not that far."

It was true; the distance was only about one hundred and fifty yards to the woods. If the enemy ventured within a hundred and twenty they became vulnerable.

Talon hefted his own bow. He did not have the range but he could inflict a lot of damage when they came within eighty yards.

"Remember; kill the crossbowmen while we are out of range of their bolts. Let the rest come on. We'll deal with them when we're finished with the bowmen," Sir Hughes ordered.

Talon noticed more activity and even signs of horsemen moving among the trees. Sir Hughes had noticed, too. "Stand by, men. They're moving into position to attack," he called out.

He hoisted his triangular shield onto his left arm and drew his sword. The silence grew as the people on the walls waited tensely. Even the sheep and cows seemed to have stopped their noise down in the yard.

There were about twelve able-bodied men with Talon and Sir Hughes on the walls facing the approaches to the village; there were another ten on the rear walls. Even if one counted the older boys and one or two old men who were armed with spears that were positioned as lookouts on the flanks, they numbered very few. Talon knew that Gareth would be watching to see if there might be a surprise attack from another quarter, but he worried nonetheless. The tension grew and men's breathing became short as they waited for the attack that must surely come.

Suddenly the enemy came boiling out of the protection of the trees. They were well armed and wore chain-mail vests. They came at a run and roared their battle cries as they started out. Talon noticed that it was easy to distinguish the crossbowmen from the others—they were not running as fast and of course they carried their bulky weapons in front of them at the ready. There was one horseman who Talon took to be Roger, but when he looked hard he saw that it was Marcel. He felt uneasy about that, but could not for the moment think why and had to pay attention as the large group of men was running hard toward their gates.

There were answering shouts from the men on the walls as much in defiance as to warn the people in the fort that the engagement had begun.

"Loose your arrows when ready, Gareth!" Hughes called.

The three Welsh bowmen pulled, aimed, and shot their arrows in one swift motion. Arrows flew and struck. Three of the crossbowmen fell, their surprised screams choked off as they died. One even discharged his bow into the back of a man in front of him as he fell. Their bodies lay like limp rags on the trampled grass.

The men running near them swerved aside in surprise and slowed. As they slowed they bunched-up, and they were only sixty yards away. Three more arrows found their mark and more bodies littered the field. The men on the ground began to mill about. Some even stopped and, crouching, hid behind their shields. There was angry shouting from two of the men who seemed to be leaders as they harangued their men to continue. One even beat the crouching men with the flat of his sword angrily, shouting at them to get up and continue. They were finally successful as the men began to run toward the gates again. They carried ladders and the long trunk of a tree with a sharpened end that six of them carried clumsily with ropes while the others tried to protect them with their shields.

Talon noticed that other horsemen had emerged from the woods, galloping up to the men on the ground almost as though herding them toward the gates. Talon took aim at Marcel, but as his arrow left his bow. Marcel's horse swerved and the arrow embedded itself in another man behind, who went down with a scream.

Gareth and his fellow Welshmen were shooting arrows into the group as fast as they could as the enemy came in a rush toward the gates. The mob of men managed to hammer the tree trunk once into the gates with a crash that shook the gates and the walls that held them. The men on the ramparts could do nothing but look down on them and wish for things to toss down onto their heads. They had nothing so they shouted abuse and the archers continued to shoot. But the crossbowmen were well within range now and they were firing steadily enough to force people to keep their heads down. The men on the walls were only twelve feet above the enemy.

A ladder appeared against the wall next to Sir Hughes, who roared for his pike man to come and help push it off. Men at the base were struggling to get onto the ladder while a couple of crossbowmen were firing their bolts up at the defenders. It only needed one bolt to go home with a sickening thump into the chest of one of the defenders, for the others to seek cover. Hughes bellowed at them to get to their feet and prepare to repel the assault.

Gareth felled the crossbowman but another took aim at him and nearly got him with a bolt that hummed past his ear.

Talon peered cautiously over the edge of the wall to see men on the ladder moving up slowly on the swaying frame. He seized the pike from the nervous man next to him and locked it into the top of the ladder. "Here, help me push!" he commanded the man.

Together they heaved at the pike and the ladder left the side of the wall. They pushed hard and had the satisfaction of hearing the fearful shouts from the men outside as they realized that they were going to have a nasty fall. They pushed back with one last heave of the pike and they stood back. Just in time, as several bolts thudded into the wall nearby and one whispered past Talon's face.

There was another noisy crash that shook the gates again as the men below rushed in again.

Sir Hughes turned to Talon. "I doubt if the gates will hold much longer with this kind of thing. I shall go down to greet them if they get in. You see if you can't dissuade them from up here."

Just as he left some women came puffing up the steps carrying a big metal pot with its handle looped over a thick stick. Aicelina was leading them, holding onto another one of the pots with cloths wrapped around the handle.

"We have coals, Talon!" she called.

Talon seized the pot from her and, using the cloths to protect his hands from the heat, he quickly leaned over the parapet and poured the red hot coals onto the milling mass of men below.

He was rewarded by shouts of pain and rage as the coals fell onto their shoulders and in some cases, bare heads. The smell of burning hair wafted up to the defenders. One of the other men took another pot and tossed the contents over the wall. Another stream of coals fell onto the already badly burned men. Talon peering carefully over the edge of the wall and saw a horse whinny in pain and bolt. He thought it might be Marcel and laughed.

Then he looked up and caught Aicelina's eye. She looked frightened, but was calm.

"How can you laugh at a time like this?" she exclaimed.

"I think we just poured hot coals onto Marcel. His horse bolted." She flashed a grin at that.

"Thank you Aicelina, we need more coals. Go down quickly—it's not safe here—and bring us some more boiling water, or coals, or pitch, if you have it."

She gave a quick nod and was gone with the other two women. He turned back to see what was happening. It had gone quiet for the moment. The shouts of rage and pain were temporarily silenced. He saw why: the men and other horsemen were running back to the woods, dodging and weaving as the archers on the parapet followed them with arrows to speed them along.

The defenders jeered the retreating men loudly, offering lewd gestures as they did so. One of the village youths went so far as to drop his hose and show off his genitals to the retreating men. His action was greeted with hoots of laughter from his relieved comrades.

But then Talon heard shouts and the clash of steel behind him. He turned around and his heart sank as he saw men fighting on the walls on the other side of the fort. He muttered a curse, told Gareth to stay on the wall and shoot anyone who was rash enough to come near, and he set off at a run with his sword drawn, calling on a couple of pike men to help.

He had to sprint across the muddy yard, followed by two of the huge hounds, Rolland and Beatrice; they raced up the crude steps that led to the platform. There were men locked in combat twenty feet away and just as he reached the top he saw Bartholomew go down, clubbed from the side by a man who had clambered over the wall. The man had not yet noticed Talon. He was about to deliver a fatal blow to Bartholomew, who was unconscious at his feet. He never finished his work as Talon was on him and had thrust his sword into his side. The man gave a choked gasp and fell over the edge of the parapet.

Talon heard the hounds drive past him to charge into the mêlée of men fighting farther down the ramparts; they set upon one man, snarling and growling, and drove him down, screaming. Whirling, Talon almost beheaded another man who was trying to get over the wall. The man fell back out of sight without a sound. He heard two pike men pounding up behind him to join the fray. Looking up, he saw one of them stop near the point where the ladder was against the wall, he shouted and stabbed downward with his pike.

Turning back to see what else was happening Talon saw that Max was engaged in a furious fight with a burly looking man in mail. They were hacking wildly at one another, while the two archers were facing off against another man, also in mail. Behind the archers there was a fight going on between some of their spearmen and several of the chain-mailed enemy. He saw at least three bodies lying wounded or dead along the narrow way. The two hounds were still worrying the man on the floor, who was now covered in blood and had stopped screaming.

It was no time for niceties, Talon decided, and seized an axe that was lying on the floor; he stepped forward and hammered the blade onto the top of Max's opponent's head. The man fell forward in a spray of blood almost into Max's arms. The surprised Max nodded at Talon and let the man fall to his feet.

"Take care of that other one, Max. I'll deal with any more that try to come up."

The pike men sidled past Talon and joined in the battle, helping Max.

Talon picked up a pike lying next to one of his father's men and again hooked it onto the top rung of the ladder. He heaved with all his strength at the frame but it barely budged. There were heavy men on it and they were shaking it furiously as they struggled up. He was still trying when another person joined in to push at it from behind. It was Feremundus. Between the two of them they managed to push the ladder over its center of gravity and it began to fall away. Several heavily clad men clutched it, shouting their anger while another let go and fell with a cry to the ground. Talon could have sworn that one of the men was Roger.

Talon picked up the axe again and turned quickly to find himself staring at a very groggy-looking Bartholomew. There was a livid bruise on his temple and some blood trickled down his chin from his nose.

"Thanks for the help," Talon said to Feremundus.

"I think we should be thanking you, Talon," Bartholomew mumbled. "You arrived in the nick of time. Dear Lord, but my head aches."

"Stay here, Bartholomew; I have to help clear the parapet of these vermin," Talon said. "Feremundus, stay you here with Bartholomew and stop them from trying again. Thank you for your help."

Feremundus grinned as he watched Talon stride off toward the others. "That man is a fighter." he said to Bartholomew, who nodded emphatically in agreement, then clutched his head as though to keep it from falling off.

The fight had not yet gone out of the men left behind, however. One of them was lying in a pool of blood but the other three were fighting savagely against the overwhelming odds against them. One decided to take his chances and leapt down from the wall to land badly on the outside. The remaining two were finally driven into a corner where they had to reluctantly surrender their weapons to a gleeful group of spearmen.

Max came toward Talon. "You and Feremundus came at the right moment; it helped tip the balance here. I thank you."

"I half suspected that they would try this when I didn't see Roger at the gates. He is not a coward. Can you hold for a while longer? I shall leave the two pike men with you, although I have no idea how useful they will be. I am sure that Roger will attempt to get up again. I need to have Feremundus near the gates; they will try again for that target."

"I think so, but if the Welshmen can pick off a few more of them and make the thought of pillage less appetizing, they might reconsider. Hey, Devonalt, Ap-Maddock, start shooting at them, we need to cut their numbers down," Max shouted to the two bowmen.

The Welshmen were filthy and covered in blood, some of it their own, but they nodded and grinned cheerfully. They hefted their long bows, leaned over the wall, and began their work. The screams from below were testament to their deadly aim. The man who had jumped off the battlements was killed while trying to crawl away.

Talon looked down at the men below, who were beginning to run in all directions, trying to get away from the arrows. They abandoned the ladders and began to run for the forest. A couple of arrows took two more down before they made the cover of the woods. At the edge, another man turned and stared back balefully for a long moment before he, too, went for cover as another arrow whispered past his cheek to thud into a tree nearby.

Talon took one last look at the woods, then turned and made his way back to the gate side of the fort. The hounds bounded to him and followed at his heels.

The women and old men called out his name and blessed him as he walked through the crowded yard. They had witnessed the end of the fight on the walls. He nodded to them and continued to his father, who greeted him with a hand on the shoulder.

"You are indeed a warrior. Philip was right when he told me of your ability," Sir Hughes said as he came up to him.

"I think we may need all our collective skills this day and night. I can't see Guillabert giving up so easily, and certainly not Roger. He came close to succeeding back there."

He felt a hand on his arm. Turning he looked into Aicelina's eyes. There was concern, but also pride. She held up a leather cup full of water. He drank the cool water and realized how thirsty he was.

"Thank you, Aicelina, that was good. Bartholomew got a nasty blow to the head; could you perhaps help him?"

She nodded and hurried off. It wrenched him to see the look of alarm in her eyes. She seemed to care for Bartholomew in more than just the ordinary way.

Talon made his way back up to the battlements and joined Gareth. His friend pointed to the bodies lying in the grass at the foot of the walls. "They have lost almost ten men killed and more still wounded, but I fear they have more where those came from. We lose two men and it hurts us. Guillabert must have a lot of money to be able to hire that many mercenaries."

"We lost more men on the other walls and it will hurt us even more."

"They'll be back."

"Yes, and we must hold until the night."

"That's when we strike, Gareth. Get some rest whenever you can and make sure you and the other archers are fresh for the night. They'll be back soon enough," Talon said with tightness in his chest.

Although they could not see the sun because of the overcast sky it was clearly well past noon. How had time flown by so fast?

His father tramped up the ramp onto the battlements and looked out over the field. He called for a roll of dead and wounded and then shook his head, saying in a low voice to Talon, "We have lost five of our own and the more wounded. We can't sustain these losses for much longer before they come over the wall and we have to fight them inside." Then he smiled at Talon. "Calm as ever, Talon. Nothing seems to unnerve you, my boy. Well, we made a good account of ourselves this time. Curse that man, I suppose he will be back. They've gone to lick their wounds for now."

But even as he spoke there was another concerted charge for the gates. The fighting was bitter and men fell on both sides. Talon was amazed that the gates could hold up under the savagery of the attacks. Each blow from the ram crashed noisily and shook the gates and even the walls that held them. He kept a wary eye open to their rear even as they fought off two attempts to storm the gates that left the defenders exhausted and bleeding. There were more dead and wounded from the bolts that flew despite the deadly fire from the Welshmen.

Talon ached from stabbing and lunging at hard, determined men who tried again and again to scale the ladders and gain a foothold on the parapet. He and Feremundus had joined Max, and again repelled a very determined assault on the rear of the fort. He was sure it had been led by Roger, but that man stayed out of the way of the arrows. To the weary defenders it seemed that Sir Guillabert had an endless supply of men.

The womenfolk led by Aicelina helped with pans of red-hot coals again and again. A bolt struck one of the women in the side just as she and Aicelina arrived at the parapet. The woman screamed and fell, letting go her end, spilling hot coals out of the pan they were carrying, creating a small fire that distracted the defenders as they tried to put it out.

Guillabert's men took advantage of this and launched a determined attack with ladders farther along the wall and almost gained a foothold. A fierce counterattack led by Sir Hughes threw the attackers off the walls. More of his men had been wounded and two more had died.

Despite the danger, Aicelina had continued to bring coals as often as she could, thus earning the admiration of the men. During the lulls between fighting she and other womenfolk brought water for the thirsty men on the parapets. Exhausted men and boys gulped gratefully from the leather cups and blessed them.

Late that afternoon the enemy seemed to have had enough. Sir Hughes strode over to Talon, his face streaked with sweat, blood, and grime. "I think they've had enough for now," he growled through parched lips.

They stood together and surveyed their sadly depleted force. Talon could sense the despair beginning to grow within the fort. He himself was beginning to have doubts that they could possibly survive another determined attack, but he knew they must. He tried to keep a brave face on things but within his heart he was becoming unsure. There was still no sign of the extra men that Roger was supposed to have sent. He resolved to take the battle to Guillabert that night.

Almost as though he could read Talon's mind Sir Hughes said, "Guillabert must be betting everything on winning this before the Count can send reinforcements. He must know that he can't fight the Count, so he needs to win this very soon. He can't have enough coin to pay all the men he seems to have. We must hold them just a little longer. There's no alternative."

Talon nodded agreement. "Tonight when it's dark—there will be no moon—they will come again. That way they can make their way right up to us without us knowing they're there, if they are quiet. They will try one last time, I am sure of it."

"We should prepare torches to throw down on them when they come."

"I agree, but I shall be going out of the fort tonight."

His father stared at him. Somehow Hughes seemed to be unsurprised at the statement. "What do you intend to do?" he asked as though he had expected something of this kind.

"Guillabert has done enough harm to us. If I can put a stop to it, I shall."

"I suppose it would not do any good to ask you not to go?"

Despite himself Talon had to smile. "No Father, this is something I can and must do. Eventually he or Roger will overwhelm us, and that I do not wish to happen. I hope to even the odds somewhat."

They spent the rest of the late afternoon and early evening in tense, watchful silence. The woods gave nothing away to the defenders who, in spite of their exhaustion, were kept busy by their leaders making sure torches were made. Boiling water as well as coals were prepared to toss down on anyone who came. A quick sortie by some men retrieved as many arrows as they could, but they were chased back by Guillabert's horsemen, who charged out of the woods and came close to cutting down one or two of the running men but for some well-aimed arrows from the walls that wounded one of the horsemen and brought down a horse. Everyone retreated to their respective corners to lick their wounds and consider the next move.

Marguerite, Aicelina, and the other women dressed the men's wounds and fed them. Pierre and Claude said prayers over the dead and helped to comfort the village womenfolk. The dead were laid out in a row, the enemy among them, in one corner of the fort. Sir Hughes supervised the retrieval of the two scaling ladders which were hoisted over the walls, and brought into the yard. Then Sir Hughes took Talon and Gareth with him when he interrogated the captured men.

They were both tough-looking men who obviously lived by their skill at weapons and were paid to do so. They gave nothing away other than to sneer at Sir Hughes and to tell him that there were many more to whom Guillabert had promised silver. Hughes regarded them with obvious distaste; they were filthy, and they stank of old beer and rancid sweat.

To Talon, watching them, they looked as though they carried vermin on them and had lank, filthy hair that he was sure was full of lice. He was revolted by the thought that these men might win this battle and then pillage what was left and rape the surviving women. He became more determined than ever to reach Guillabert before he could do more damage.

As though he had thought the same Sir Hughes decided to hang them. "There are not enough of us to keep watch over them and they are cunning enough for sure to get loose during the fighting later if we leave them in the charge of these village simpletons." he remarked. Talon agreed.

The execution was summary and quick. Although they protested loudly at first, they went to their deaths stoically enough in the end, Talon thought. The men were hung from the gates. The bodies were displayed near the front gate in full view of the impassive forest.

Talon could not help but notice that Bartholomew stayed away from the executions: he was not surprised. The man was unused to the grimmer aspects of warfare. Talon had no quarrel with his ability to fight, however. In spite of his sore head, Bartholomew had taken his place at the rear of the fort alongside Max and fought valiantly the rest of the day.

Later when there was a respite he found Bartholomew sitting near to Aicelina, his head still bandaged .He seemed to be enjoying her attentions. Talon shrugged mentally; his fate was tied to some other place. He watched the women and children moving about in the yard, cleaning and looking after animals and considered his life. This was not what he was going to be, he decided. The life he was used to, far to the east of this land, was so different. If he survived he would go back to Palestine even though it was an unknown quantity.

Chapter 24

Assassin

The people of the fort made ready as darkness fell. Exhausted men went quietly to the walls and stood watch. The archers stacked arrows and men piled such rocks as the boys could find for tossing onto the enemy. Fires were fed more logs to ensure coals and Talon at last smelt the bitter stink of pitch being melted.

Talon and Belth would leave by way of one of the side walls when it was really dark. He hoped that they would be able to get to Guillabert before they decided to attack again.

Shedding their armor and taking only knives and one long bow, they went down by rope with a whispered good luck from Gareth, who had wanted to come, but Talon had told him to protect Sir Hughes.

The two men inched toward the woods, crawling on their bellies.

It was just as well that they took so much care—they heard men talking when they were within yards of the cover of the woods. Roger, no fool, had posted sentries, who were quietly talking to one another. Talon looked back over his shoulder and could barely make out the darkness of the fort, so he realized that it was very likely they had not been detected.

Now they had to deal with the enemy in the darkness ahead. He inched on his belly into the ground cover of bracken and long grass, careful not to disturb any dry twigs or leaves. He slid over to Belth when they were within the darkness of the forest and well concealed and whispered. "Stay here; I shall deal with them." Belth gave a sigh, but said no more.

Talon slid along the ground feeling his way in the dark inch by inch, the voices of the two men guiding him. When he was within a few feet he stood up carefully and took out his knife. The killing was swift, and noiseless. When it was done, he whistled softly to Belth who came up to him.

Talon gave Belth one of the helmets taken off the dead men. "This will help us move more freely, they will think we are archers; I have to find where Guillabert is."

They donned the wide-brimmed iron helmets which were of the type that crossbowmen used. They also took the quilted jackets from the dead men, although they were wet with their blood. Talon also picked up one of the crossbows, cocked it, and placed a bolt in its slot.

Now they moved quietly toward the village where Talon assumed that Guillabert would have set up camp.

His guess proved correct; when they came to the edge of the woods near the village, they saw the fires in the street. Not all the houses had been burned down and there were some horses tethered near one of the larger thatched houses. Talon thought that this might be where Guillabert was bivouacked. They walked quietly through the forest until they were behind that cottage.

"Belth, you should stay here and keep your bow ready. I am going to pay Sir Guillabert a visit. I may need your help to get away," he whispered to his companion.

They could see the groups of men around the fires through the gaps in the huts and cottages. There did not seem to be any sentries posted; but they seemed to be preparing for action. There were ladders nearby, but their use did not look immediate, so he guessed that they were waiting until later to make their attack.

He crept carefully toward the back of the larger cottage, stepping noiselessly, listening to the activity going on in the village street, his former training coming to his assistance now. Taking great care not to make any sound, he moved slowly right up to the back wall of the cottage and listened at the opening of a window. The shutters were closed but candlelight showed through the rough wooden slats.

There was the murmur of voices inside. He lifted his head to peer into the room through the slits. Roger was inside, standing by a fire, still dressed in his hauberk of chain. The man dominated the room to the extent that Marcel seemed small by comparison. There was the bulk of another man seated with his back to Talon whom he could not see clearly. They were arguing.

"We will wait until it is late and they are tired before we go in," said the man with his back to Talon. He realized that it was Guillabert.

"The longer we wait the more prepared they become, Father," Roger snapped.

"I agree with Father, we should wait, Roger. Their cursed long bowmen will not be able to see in the dark and we can get close more safely."

"It was your hasty retreat today that cost us, brother. If you had had the courage to stay just a little longer at the gates the last time, we would have had them. Have you no stomach for this fight? Are they too much for you?" Roger jeered.

"Enough of this bickering, both of you. We might have lost the first round, but tonight they'll be ours and I can let the mercenaries loose upon the place in lieu of payment. They are getting nasty; none expected the resistance we've seen and I don't have the money to pay them all. The Devil's curse upon those bowmen of Hughes. After I've seen Hughes and that cursed son of his dead the whole place can burn to the ground and all in it," Guillabert said loudly.

"Roger, go you and get the men ready, we'll leave within the hour. Make sure the ladders are ready and have more than two this time. We will assault the gate, but at the same time you'll attack the rear again, and this time make it at the same time we attack. Marcel, go with him. I am not done with my supper. Come and tell me when you're ready." He drank deeply from his goblet as his two sullen sons shuffled out of the house.

Talon realized that he would have to go in through the door—to crash through the shutter would give Guillabert a chance to shout the alarm. He stood up and walked as casually as he could around to the front of the cottage. Its low front was lit by the fires in the street but there was no sentry at the door. He hefted the cocked crossbow onto his shoulder and strolled to the door. He had pulled the wide helmet down over his eyes and slouched as he walked. He came to the door and still no one gave any sign that they were concerned about his presence. The men were drinking and some were even laughing as they stood by the fires. No doubt boasting of what they would do to the luckless victims of the fort when they sacked it. Men were beginning to buckle on weapons and pick up shields as Roger and Marcel shouted orders from down the street.

Talon estimated that there were about thirty men in the area and ten horses saddled. His heart sank, they could only muster fifteen fighting men in the fort; this was lot of men to fight off. He slipped in without being accosted, but almost ran into someone at the entrance. It was one of the mercenaries. He was a rough-looking man in chain mail who was holding a chunk of bread that he was gnawing as he walked. He shoved Talon aside as he went by with a curse.

"Out of my way, you! Goddamned bowman."

Talon mumbled something back by way of apology and slunk into the main room. There were only two rooms in the cottage and Guillabert was seated in the larger.

Inside the low chamber Talon could see the flames of the well-fed fire merrily flickering in the fireplace. The fire and one candle were the only light in the room and they cast moving shadows against the walls. Talon saw Guillabert the moment he came to the entrance to the room, he was noisily engaged in eating a meal at a low table, seated on a stool sideways to the door. He was unaware of Talon standing at the entrance.

Slowly Talon raised the crossbow and pointed it directly at Guillabert. Guillabert looked up at the last second and saw his assassin about to kill him. He got out a shout of terror that stopped abruptly as the crossbow twanged and a bolt shot into his eye, penetrating deep into his skull. His body jerked sideways and fell with a crash in a tangle of arms and legs to the earthen floor.

Talon did not wait; he ran to the window, opened the shutters and dived out onto the rough ground below the window. Then he scuttled into the woods to where Belth was waiting.

As he made the darkness of the forest there was a shout of alarm and a figure appeared at the window illuminated by the fire behind. Belth was waiting and sent an arrow in that direction. The man at the window must have sensed something as, with a shout of alarm, he ducked and the arrow hammered into the holding beam inside the cottage.

By now men were yelling and raising the alarm to the others in the street. Talon and Belth wasted no time. They ran as fast as they could through the woods back the way they had come. It quickly became clear that there was some kind of pursuit by the noise behind them, which only made them run faster. They had a wide swath of grass to cover and a wall to climb.

They came to the edge of the woods and began to sprint as fast as they could toward the walls, calling out as they ran to alert the men waiting.

Ropes were thrown down and the two frantically hauled themselves up the wood frame with men above calling encouragement. Their pursuers were shouting angrily and running toward them in the dark. Some bolts from crossbows thumped into the wood near them, further encouraging them to climb faster.

Their luck held until they were just about to climb over the top of the walls then a bolt hit Belth. He gave an agonized grunt and fell forward into the arms of the waiting men on the platform.

Talon scrambled quickly over the top of the wall just as men on the platform threw torches down onto the ground below.

The guttering pitch balls illuminated the dodging figures below enough for a couple of the Welshmen to fire arrows at them. They were rewarded with a yell and curse as one was hit and then the noise of men running off into the darkness. The men on the walls listened; silence. It seemed the enemy wanted none of the archers' medicine. Belth was groaning as he lay on the floor, so Talon snatched a torch from one of the men and held it over his friend.

The bolt had pierced his shoulder; it stuck out of the flesh between his neck and his shoulder blade. Talon cursed quietly to himself, they needed all the bowmen they had and now Belth was definitely out of action. Gareth was there, he knelt and swiftly got his knife out and cut the short shaft with the metal point then with Belth gritting his teeth, drew the bolt out the way it had come.

Gareth leaned over him. "You were lucky, Belth Bach; it could have gotten you in the neck." He turned to look up at Talon in the flickering light of the torch and asked. "Did you succeed, Talon?"

"We only partially succeeded, Guillabert is dead. But Roger will not give up so we must prepare for an assault from both sides; they intend to come at the same time."

They took Belth down to the hall to join the other wounded and where the women were waiting to take care of him.

Talon snatched a quick bite of cold mutton from one of the men who handed it to him and discussed the situation with Gareth, Max, and his father. "They will bring more ladders and try from both sides. It's too dark to see them until they're up to the walls and then it will be too late to stop them from placing the ladders. We have to throw torches as far out as we can to allow the archers a chance to kill them as they come."

"I hope they are somewhat demoralized by your actions," Sir Hughes growled.

"Marcel might be, but Roger will be enraged and will certainly try his luck tonight. He'll seek vengeance. I had hoped to kill him, too."

They walked toward the hall where Talon and Sir Hughes were going to try to get some supper. Talon wanted to know how Bartholomew was; he had not seen him on the battlements.

They went into the hall and were met by the warmth of the great fire and the noise of people talking within. There was a lot of light thrown against the walls by the huge fire in the middle of the hall and the warmth it threw off was welcoming.

Talon realized that he was cold. The evenings were becoming chilly, but with all the activity he had not really felt it up until now. He also realized that he was hungry and was glad to see Aicelina bringing him and Sir Hughes a platter of meat and bread. The two men thanked her, Talon smiling his thanks and receiving one in return.

They ate standing and looking about. Marguerite had turned the hall into a hospital. She was presiding over the care of the wounded and making sure that food was taken out to the men on the walls. Several huge pots of copper were hanging over the fire that bubbled and stank. Talon sniffed and gathered that it was the pitch. He was glad; they would have need of it this night.

Sir Hughes was going to say something when there was a shout outside. Talon and his father dropped what they had in their hands and rushed out into the darkness. Men were running toward the battlements.

Talon heard a crash from the gate and realized that the enemy had managed to get close enough to ram the gates with something substantial. Gareth came up to him and shouted down that they had used horses this time. Somehow they had managed to create a sling and then galloped horses down the lane in front of the gate, holding a beam that they had driven into the gates.

In the torchlight Talon saw that one of the bars that held the gates shut was broken and the left hand gate was hanging partially open.

"Gareth, place your men onto the ramps and throw torches as far out as you can. They'll be coming any minute; shoot them down as they come. We will be at the gates," he shouted back.

Gareth ran off.

Talon and Sir Hughes were fully armed and both ran toward the gate, calling on their pike men and the other few men-at-arms to close with them. Talon hefted the axe he now carried with him at all times. The he saw Feremundus running toward the gate and felt somewhat better. With that man laying about him with his axe the intruders might be more intimidated.

We're going to have to do well tonight or it's all over, he thought grimly.

They got to the gates at almost the same time as a mob of screaming men came barging in from the outside. He knew that the Welshmen were giving a good account of themselves, but also that once inside, friend could not be distinguished from foe and thus they would have to watch helpless.

Talon, his father and Feremundus, bellowing his war cry, made a tight group with four other men clad in chain and charged into the mob that was trying to get through the gap in the gates. Talon hacked and struck at anyone who came close. He heard his father roar out his battle cry and the fight was joined. In the semi-dark the men in chain-mail armor and their six pike men strove determinedly to beat back the equally determined group of men who were trying to push through the half open gate. Some men from the village were trying to push it shut even as the fight took place.

A spear came out of the dark and rammed into Talon's side but did not penetrate his fine chain. It winded him enough to make him stagger, but he whirled his axe at the arm that held it and struck it off. A man shrieked in agony and the pike disappeared. Another man pushed his way in and made a wicked slash at Talon's head with a sword. He ducked behind his shield just in time and then rammed the haft of the ax into the man's nosepiece. The man dropped his guard for an instant and Talon hammered the axe down onto his iron-clad head. His opponent fell without a sound beneath the feet of the stamping, struggling men. He heard the sound of steel on steel as his father fought next to him but felt that they were being pushed back inexorably.

He stepped back and shouted up at Gareth. "Come down and stand behind me with your bowmen, Gareth! Hurry!"

He did not wait for a reply but stepped forward and hacked down at another man's shoulder as he separated himself from the others. The man's shield came up fast and then his sword flickered out and smacked hard onto Talon's shield, it was the one his uncle had left him. Its stout frame withstood the blow easily. All the same the blow was forceful and he realized that he had a strong opponent to deal with. He stepped back another pace and became aware of Gareth just behind.

"Shoot into the mob at the gate, Gareth; they are all the enemy."

Talon stepped back another pace again, almost falling over a body lying in the mud. His father was next to him and shouted for the pike men to rally to him. With a quick word here and there he had them spaced just in front of the bowmen.

"Stand your ground and strike at anyone who tries for the bowmen," Sir Hughes ordered.

Still they were being forced back even farther and now the gate seemed to be in enemy hands. There were yells from the mercenaries as they sensed victory. They hacked down the remaining villagers who had stayed to hold the gate. There was no mercy for them; they were butchered before the watching men standing with Talon and Sir Hughes.

The men shifted uneasily, the fight was going hard against them and there seemed to be so many of the enemy.

"Hold together," Hughes shouted. "There is no hope if we separate."

A volley of arrows sped past Talon's side and several of the men clustered in the gateway fell forward. Others tried to step over them but were again shot down as the Welshmen fired their arrows at close range. Hughes whirled back at Talon just after piercing a quilt-and-plate-armored man through the chest.

"Fall back with me, Feremundus, and guard the flanks of the pike men and then we move forward as one," he called.

His eyes gleamed from behind the nosepiece of his helmet. He was savagely intent upon winning this fight. Another volley struck the men at the gate, more men fell with shrieks and groans and Talon had the faint hope that they were weakening.

His father noticed, too, and shouted, "Keep shooting as fast as you can, Gareth! We must win back the gate."

Talon watched with sinking heart as the barn nearest the gate was set afire by the yelling mercenaries and watched as the village women and children who had been trapped in that area, fled the battle area screaming, stumbling through the churned-up mud of the yard toward the doubtful safety of the hall. The flames took and became an inferno.

He licked his lips with a dry tongue. They were being burned out.

Despite the devastation inflicted by the arrows more men managed to get inside and came charging toward the small group of defenders waiting near the entrance to the hall. Talon stepped forward only to be confronted by the big man in mail who had lunged at him earlier.

"Where do you think you are going, heathen?" the man yelled as he swung a ball-and-chain at Talon's head.

Talon only just had time to duck as the spiked ball whistled past his head and then brought his shield up. He knew it was Roger and he realized that, no matter how the battle went, this fight was now just between the two of them.

He became aware that there was a small space forming around them even as the arrows continued to speed and the fighting intensified for possession of the area in front of the gates. Vaguely he heard his father call out encouragement to his men as he drove forward, trying to take possession.

Then, as though from a distance, Talon heard more yells, then some other men stampeded past him through the mud to crash into the struggling mass of men at the gate. He realized that Max had come to his father's aid.

But Roger was coming at him again, the hideous ball-and-chain whirling around his head once more. Talon dragged his shield up and took the full blow on his left arm. He felt the numbing force and heard the crash of the ball on the metal-encased wooden shield at the same time. He responded with a slash at Roger's exposed head with his axe but Roger was too quick and brought his shield up in time. The axe glanced off the top of the shield and because its handle was slick with blood, it flew out of Talon's hand like a missile.

"Is that the best you can do? You heathen pig! You will pay for murdering my father with all your lives, you first!" Roger yelled at him as he started to whirl the ball again.

Talon drew his sword and waited. He would have to endure one more beating in order to make his move. The ball came hissing down again and smashed into his upheld shield. Again the force of the blow numbed his arm and drove him to a kneeling position. He was almost sitting on the back of a man who was face down in the mud behind him.

Roger swung his shield around and slammed it into Talon's body, driving him back onto his heels. He was now kneeling and groggy with the pain in his left arm and his bruised side. Roger stood over him, his face almost hidden by the wide nose piece of his helmet. Roaring his victory, Roger raised the ball-and-chain high in the air above him for the final blow. Talon was numb from his neck down to his left hand but he knew that unless he moved he was going to die.

He forced himself to ignore the pain and drove himself off his kneeling position in close to Roger, knocking aside the shield with his blade. In one fluid move, Talon stabbed his sword into the un-covered region just under Roger's armpit. His finely tempered blade even flexed as he drove it through the thick leather and then into the ribs, deep into Roger's chest. Talon forced himself to his feet and drove the blade in even deeper.

Roger gasped, groaned in agony, then tried to pull away. His shield arm seemed to lose all its strength and his right arm fell to his side, loosing the deadly ball that flew off into the darkness. His hand went to the entrance of the wound but it was too weak to do anything but clutch feebly at the steel of Talon's sword. His face was close to Talon's, his eyes wide with agony and despair as he realized he was a dead man. Talon held the blade in relentlessly, pushing it deeper into his victim. Roger fell to his knees and coughed; a gout of blood poured out of his mouth and he fell forward onto his side. Talon quickly tugged his blade free and looked around.

He noticed that the gates were shut and in the torchlight men were standing watching him. He stared around him in the silence that followed, hardly daring to believe what he was seeing. There were many bodies strewn about nearby, both the enemy and his father's men. The fire still raged, but it was now the only sound in the yard other than the occasional groan from a wounded man.

His father came striding over to him, calling for light. He was covered in blood. A torch was produced and men gathered round Talon, looking down on Roger's corpse.

"Father, what of the enemy? We need to be ready for more attacks," Talon gasped, leaning on his battered shield.

His father placed a mailed hand on his shoulder. "They saw you slay him, Talon. They lost interest in the fight and gave up after they saw him fall; and, with Max to help us with his reinforcements, we took the gates from them." Sir Hughes sounded weary.

Max was standing nearby, his face and tunic filthy with sweat and gore, but he wore a happy grin on his face.

"Thank you, Max, you saved the day," Talon said wearily.

Gareth called from the parapet. "Sir Hughes! They seem to be gone, my Lord... at least for the moment."

There was a muted cheer from the darkness, which was taken up by others, and the next thing Talon knew men were crowding around, slapping him on the back, unaware of the pain they were inflicting and cheering for all they were worth. His father took his helmet off and grinned tiredly at him. Sir Hughes was red with his and other men's blood. His shield, too, was dented; but it was a relieved smile he gave Talon.

"Now we must put out the fire or we'll have lost all we fought for," Sir Hughes shouted. "Get water! We have to put the fire out!"

Instantly, men were galvanized and ran to throw water with anything that came to hand on the flames.

Talon looked around him, bemused. All about were filthy, bloody men shouting jubilantly at one another and some were even dancing a jig, even as they attacked the fire. He saw Max grinning at him in the crowd and called to him. "Did they come, Max? Did they come on your side, too?"

Max walked over and with him was Bartholomew, they were laughing excitedly.

"They came, Talon, with two ladders, but we were expecting them and poured pitch and coals onto them. The Welshmen did their work well, too. The scoundrels lost heart very quickly after we had driven them back twice. Then I left Bartholomew to keep watch and came over here; it looked a bit too close for comfort," Max reported cheerfully.

The two of them were bloody and filthy and looked as though they had had a stiff fight of it. Time enough to find out how it had really gone, he thought.

The flames of the barn were finally extinguished and reduced to a smoldering pile. Boys were posted to watch in case the flames flared up again. Exhausted men sat or stood around in the early hours. Few had any energy left to rejoice at their hard-won victory. Most were wounded and needed attention.

Despite the reprieve, neither Talon nor Sir Hughes were going to take any chances. They posted guards at every point and admonished the tired men to be vigilant. Another attack like the last one could carry the day for the enemy if they were determined enough. In his mind though, Talon was almost sure that there would be no further attacks. Marcel was now the sole leader and for sure lacked the will to take further action— if indeed he could even rally the mercenaries he commanded. He lacked the strength of will that his brother had possessed, and most probably the respect needed to lead this type of men.

Nonetheless, bone weary as he was, he worked with his father to ensure that they were not vulnerable. The gates were shored up and repaired as far as possible. Heavy beams were stuck in the mud and wedged against the shattered wood to hold it in place.

Exhausted men stayed at their posts and were relieved with water and food brought by the village children and women. The wounded were carried or helped to the hall and their injuries bound by Marguerite and Aicelina, assisted by the other women, with Claude and Pierre in attendance.

Hughes oversaw the gristly work of cutting off Roger's head and sticking it on a pike at the main gate.

"This will serve as a warning to them in the morning should they be contemplating another attack." he said grimly to Talon. "I don't want to deal with this scum again for any reason."

Talon spent the hours before dawn with his companions the Welshmen on the battlements. They talked in low tones about the battle and what the following morning might bring. None knew what to expect, but they all hoped the mercenaries would have had enough. The price was high to take this fort; perhaps they would go elsewhere for easier pickings.

As the light of dawn streaked the eastern sky they forced themselves to their feet and stared with red and gritty eyes at the forest, alert once more, waiting for any sign of attack. Weary men—knight, man-at-arms, and villager alike—their clothes damp from dew, with weapons tight in their hands, waited fearfully and stared toward the woods in the direction of the village. A light drizzle began to fall, chilling the men who huddled into their cloaks, wishing they had a warm fire to stand in front of, better still a warm bed; none had been near a bed for two days now.

There was only silence from the forest's edge. No sound from the village or any sign of movement. Still they waited.

Sir Hughes stood with Talon on the ramparts and stared with the rest of them as the day dawned overcast and wet. He shook the drops of rain from his shoulders like an irritated bear and then said, "We should send out a sortie party to find out what's going on, Talon."

"I agree. Will you let me lead it? I'll take a bowman and Max if that's all right with you."

His father nodded, staring reflectively at the grisly sight of Roger's grinning bloody head and the bodies hanging nearby. "If they're gone, I'll ensure he is buried well. If not, they can see what their fate is should they wish to continue."

Talon and Max rode out with Gareth for company. They made their way cautiously on their horses until they were close to the forest edge at the opening that led to the village. They could smell wood smoke coming from that direction but there was no sign of life. They rode their horses along the wide path toward the village, finally coming out onto the end of the main road where the huts and cottages commenced.

Apart from the tendrils of smoke coming from the remains of a fire in the middle of the street, there was nothing to be seen. Some crows lifted off, cawing loudly to flap away over the trees leaving behind an eerie silence. The ground was littered with discarded equipment, some ladders, and even meat and bread, as though the mercenaries had left in a hurry.

Max and Talon dismounted at the spot near the cottage where Talon had killed Guillabert. They hefted their swords and advanced cautiously. Talon led the way toward the entrance of the cottage. They came to the doorway; the door was hanging by one leather hinge, and went inside.

They found Marcel lying on his back in a large puddle of blood near the cold body of his father. Talon stooped over Marcel's corpse and saw there were many wounds in his chest and front. He turned the body over and found even more. Although it was dark in the room, it was clear there had been a fight; the table was broken and the stool was smashed, and Talon thought he knew why.

"It would seem the mercenaries wanted their money; they had no stomach for more, is my guess."

Max nodded. "Marcel was a fool to argue with the likes of them; they simply took it for themselves anyway."

"I doubt he had enough to give them. In any case, he was no better than they, after what he did to Philip. I would have taken care of him if they had not," Talon said grimly.

The walked carefully around the village to ensure there was no one else about and then rode back to the fort.

After they had dismounted, Talon told his father what he had found. "There is the chance that the mercenaries did not find all the money that they expected in the village and went back to the castle. We should perhaps go and investigate, as Petrona will be there and they will not treat her well."

Sir Hughes nodded. "We should go as even now it might be too late. Are you able to come?"

Talon nodded wearily. "Yes, I should go, too. We must make sure she's at least safe."

"There is more than that. I mean to have that castle for myself. We've earned it and I shall have it—and no one else!"

Talon looked hard at his father, observing the red-rimmed, bloodshot eyes and the determined look on his filthy, unshaven face. He nodded agreement. Sir Hughes was right—the castle was a part of the spoils of war.

Soon Sir Hughes left the fort at the head of as many men as he could mount. They left Max in charge of the fort and galloped as fast as the horses could take them in the direction of Guillabert's castle.

The rode down the wide path before the castle a few hours later and saw smoke rising from the inside the walls.

Sir Hughes grunted. "I fear we're too late."

As they galloped up to the castle they could see the drawbridge was down and the gates open. They could hear drunken shouts and laughter, and the sound of breaking furniture came to the mounted men as they approached.

"We should just go right in and take all before us," Sir Hughes declared loudly. "Follow me."

They swept across the drawbridge with a noisy clatter of hooves on the wood and then they were into the yard. There were only a handful of men there and most were lying drunk against walls or staggering about, holding skins of beer. There were bodies of both men and women lying at odd angles, indicating that the mercenaries had all but sacked the castle.

Sir Hughes' followers dispatched the men in the yard, chasing them down without mercy, knowing them to be scum who would not have scrupled to do the same to them. There was a loud crash inside the keep and a scream that told them some more had just managed to knock down Petrona's chamber door and had found her or some women in hiding.

Talon and Gareth rushed up the stone stairs, almost tripping over a drunken man lying in their way. As he came into the ante-room where he had listened to the conversation with the bishop, Talon heard Petrona crying and a struggle going on in her chamber. There was raucous laughter from more than one man.

Gareth and Talon approached the chamber in silence; there was a low moan from Petrona and some heavy breathing. They slipped into the room. One of the men had Petrona held down on the bed, her dresses up around her waist, while another was preparing to rape her.

Talon's sword ripped into his back before the man even noticed that he was there. The blade protruded out the front and the man fell forward so that his face landed on Petrona's belly. She screamed with fright and horror struggling frantically to push the body off her, screaming all the while. Talon wrenched the blade free and turned.

The other man had just time to let go of Petrona, when Gareth's dagger went into his throat. He fell with a gurgle to the floor.

Talon hastily covered the still screaming Petrona with a large blanket and held her until she had calmed down enough to recognize him. Then she fell to weeping, great racking sobs that shook her frame. She babbled his name over and over as they left the room.

They left the bodies where they were and took her down the stairs. Men were still hunting the remnants of the mercenaries, some of whom were fighting with the desperation of cornered rats, but the fight was all but over and Sir Hughes was still sitting on his horse, watching and directing events. There would be no prisoners taken today. He intended that the victory be complete and uncomplicated.

The smoke they had seen billowing into the air from the castle came from a fire that had been started in the stables. They were now a blazing ruin. As Talon and Gareth came out of the keep, the beams fell inward with a crash and a shower of sparks rose into the air.

Sir Hughes watched the fire grimly. "Let it burn; we'll be coming back to claim this place later, the fire will not damage the keep nor the walls." When he saw Talon carrying Petrona, he grunted. "Did you get there in time? Is she alive?"

"Just in time; she is alive."

"Then we should take her back to the fort." He turned to one of his mounted men. "Cedric, go fast and take down Roger's head, make sure the body and the head are placed together. Go, man!"

Chapter 25

Aftermath

Talon woke feeling bruised all over. In particular his left arm and shoulder ached badly. He groaned, rolled off his pallet and stood up shakily, wondering what time it might be. He checked himself over and found that, besides his bad arm, he had numerous other bruises, welts, and cuts about his body. The sounds from outside were muted by the thick wooden walls of the hall, but it was clear that the fort was awake.

There seemed to be the usual bustle of a normal day going on outside and he wondered for a moment if the previous few days had been some kind of nightmare, but his left arm and shoulder reminded him of the unpleasant fact that it had been all too real.

He walked slowly along the short corridor, holding an arm that he could barely lift, into the hall where he saw some of the more seriously wounded still lying on straw beds. The several who were awake called out his name. He waved at them with his good hand and smiled, then continued on out into the bright autumn sunshine. The rain had left the ground smelling clean and fresh to be dried by a light wind from the northwest that rustled the leaves of the tall trees. He could see clouds over the low hills that looked as though they held some rain.

He seated himself gingerly on a bench by the door and looked about him. It was still early morning but most of the villagers had left already. He surmised that they had a lot of work to do on their houses and barns, and there were the remains of the harvest to bring in now that it was safe to do so. He realized what had struck him as different this morning; it was the lack of bleating sheep and goats or bellowing cattle. Only the stock belonging directly to Sir Hughes was still there, quietly munching their fodder or turned out onto the field to graze alongside the detritus of the battle that was still strewn about.

The yard in front of the gates, which were still prudently closed, was churned up and muddy where the fighting had occurred. He noticed with wry amusement that the battered and dented shield he had used during the fight with his cousin was now suspended from one of the poles of the gatehouse. Also that the corpses of the two mercenaries they'd hanged were now gone.

A hand touched him on the left shoulder; he winced and turned his head to see Aicelina standing just behind him, looking concerned. He returned her smile with a rueful grimace and rubbed his left shoulder gingerly.

She was immediately concerned. "Are you hurt?"

"I am, my lady. My left shoulder and arm feel as though a giant battered it all night and the rest of me is little better this morning."

She opened his shirt to expose the arm, without a word and quite unabashed. It was swollen and bruised from the shoulder down to the wrist. The late Roger had been a big man with enormous strength. Aicelina hissed at the sight and told him to sit still while she brought food for him and some salve for the arm and his other superficial wounds.

Talon complied willingly. He let the watery sun soak into his skin; he shut his eyes, enjoying the moment. One of the female hounds, Beatrice, slouched up to him; the huge animal's head was almost up to his chest as he sat. She nudged him with her nose, wanting a scratch. He absentmindedly rubbed her neck and head.

He reflected upon the situation as he saw it now that Guillabert and his sons were dead. Technically, the castle still belonged to Petrona, but she could not be expected to run the place on her own. Sir Hughes, having won the dispute by right of arms, could assume the ownership of the castle. Bartholomew had informed them of that last night; it was part of old feudal law. Petrona would become Sir Hughes' ward or he could marry her off and hope that her husband would be more amenable to living as a good neighbor. Talon doubted that his father would take the latter course. Where did this leave him, Talon?

He knew his destiny lay not in this land. Lush, green, and fertile it might be compared to his previous world, but in his heart he knew he wanted to return to the land that had become his home, the land that was in his blood. Not only that, he had vengeance to take for Rav'an, who he was sure must now be dead.

He could not imagine her surviving the wrath of her brother once he discovered she was pregnant. Once again his heart ached as he raged against his impotence to do anything to save her. Yet there was a tiny hope still within him that this might not be true and that she still lived.

He thought of Aicelina. He liked her very much. She was open and intelligent, a young woman with a mind of her own. It didn't matter one bit that she was not of the common faith. Her adherence to this new faith known as Cathar, which the abbot had told him was the other name for these people, was of no importance to him at all. After all, what was he now, a Christian or a Muslim? He could do far worse should he stay.

But then there was Bartholomew, who was making sheep's eyes at her, and to Talon's mind she had not been disinterested. He knew that to be his fault as she had divined where his heart lay and then told him it lay elsewhere. He could not stand in her way should she decide to take a good man like Bartholomew. Finally there was Petrona. He should watch out for that; that situation could get complicated. He saw Claude and Pierre preparing to leave and got up to bid them goodbye.

They clasped hands firmly. The two men wished him well and thanked him for taking care of them.

"You will always be welcome at the abbey, Talon. We know there is still much for you to tell us about your time in Persia. Be sure to come when all the harvesting is done and there is time to sit by a fire and talk. God protect you."

"I would welcome that, my brothers, and God protect you, too. But it is we who owe thanks to you for having produced the real proof so that my father and mother can live peacefully now without looking over their shoulders." The two men smiled and then walked out of the gates with a wave of farewell.

Talon went to sit back on the bench and rubbed his sore arm while he resumed thinking of the future. He decided that when the spring came and the ships began to sail the middle sea again, he would take his leave. His peace was not to last for long. He was prodded on his right side by an impatient hand pushing at him. He looked up and then down. The hound had left and in its stead was Guillaume, standing there looking at him, hero worship in his eyes, but a determined look, too.

"Brother Talon, I want to know all about the battle you had with cousin, Roger," he said in his five-year-old voice.

Talon smiled tiredly at his young brother. If he left for the far lands Guillaume would one day inherit all of this, and if his perky stride and attitude were anything to go by he would be the right man to fill his father's boots. Talon sat up and placed a hand on his brother's shoulder. "I shall tell you all, Guillaume, but today I am tired and need some rest. Will you be good and wait a while? We can go swimming and I shall tell you then... when you are cleaner."

Guillaume looked alarmed and uncertain. There was a light laugh behind them both. Aicelina had returned with a chunk of bread with some cheese on top.

"In that case, I doubt you will have the chance to tell Guillaume, Talon. He fears water more than a barn cat does." She began to apply some of the salve to Talon's swollen arm, kneading it with gentle fingers. He winced at the pain, but her fingers were gentle and soothing.

"I'm not afraid of water," said Guillaume defensively.

"Oh, yes, you are, you young scamp," Aicelina replied, laughing.

Talon smiled, too. "Are you as courageous as a de Gilles should be? There is more to being a knight than just slaying all your enemies, little brother."

"Such as?" Guillaume asked doubtfully.

"Reading, and Latin, writing, counting, and things like that. Being clean, too. The womenfolk prefer it. A lice-ridden knight who stinks like a pig's sty is a poor bedfellow."

"Yuck! I won't bother with girls when I am a knight. I shall be far too busy slaying all our enemies and conquering new lands for the Count of Carcassonne."

Talon and Aicelina laughed together at his screwed up face.

"I am sure you will," Talon said dryly, "but for the tale of my battle you must have a bath; that is the condition."

"Are you going to have one?"

"I am a man used to making sacrifices. Of course I am. We can bathe together and Aicelina can wash our backs."

"Away with you, Talon." His mother was standing at the doorway, her arms crossed over her bosom, listening with amusement. "I am sure Aicelina has better things to do than to watch you and your brother playing about in hot water."

Talon smiled at his mother and glanced up at Aicelina, who was staring off at the barn, pretending she had not heard, but he caught sight of a dimpled smile on her cheek. *Hmm... I wonder*, he thought.

"Hello, Mother, I hope you are well?"

"I am. Aicelina has told me of the bruised arm. I see what she means. We'll dress it again when you've had a bath. I am sure I cannot remember the last time Guillaume had one, so this should be interesting."

Guillaume was looking trapped but Talon gave him reassuring pat on the shoulder as he bit into the bread and cheese.

The four of them walked to Marguerite's small garden and spent a pleasant hour talking about the recent events and speculating about the future. Talon was careful not to mention his intent to leave one day for the *Outré Mere*. It was not the time or the place. He asked about Sir Hughes and Petrona. His mother told him that Sir Hughes had risen early and taken Max and some men to look the castle over and make sure it was secure from marauders and looters. He intended to leave some men there to guard the property until they decided what to do with it.

Petrona was still in bed, the previous day's experiences were still too fresh in her mind. She was well aware of the fight that had taken place here, and the deaths of her father and brothers, although not the circumstances of their deaths.

Talon and Aicelina stayed in the garden after his mother went off to order the hot water prepared. Guillaume was forced to go with her, protesting vehemently all the way back to the Hall.

"So you would not want to join me in the bath?" he enquired.

"I would have no scruple there, Talon, but I fear that you will be sharing the water with more than just your brother," she said with a grin.

He knew what she meant. Guillaume was most probably covered with ticks and lice passed on by the hounds that were infested, and these little bodies would be floating all about as they bathed. He laughed a bit uncomfortably and then told her of his experience in the Assassin castle when he was forced to bathe for the first time in months and then had his head shaved to clean him completely. He told her of the kindly but firm woman who had made him wash and then looked after him many times after. She smiled with him at the memories, but she looked pensive.

"You are looking serious, Aicelina. Surely this is a day to rejoice; we have overcome poor odds and survived."

"I think of you and your restless soul. You know so little of that which others of us call peace, and I know that one day you'll leave us for those lands again."

Talon was too surprised to say anything.

She continued. "I would that you would stay, but I know in my heart it is not to be. So I ask that you release me from any bonds we might have formed as I would be free to make a choice."

Talon looked into her eyes and saw them filled with tears. He knew exactly what she was talking about.

"Has the learned Bartholomew of Brittany taken your heart then, Aicelina?" he asked her gently.

She blushed for the first time since he had met her.

"Truly, I do not know where my heart is at this moment, but I do know one thing." She looked directly into his eyes. "Although we have loved and it was a good loving... Indeed, I would have had more if it and willingly become betrothed to you," she gave that dimple of a smile, "it is not to be. Bartholomew is making eyes at me and... well, he is not an ignorant nor unhandsome man."

"You would have a fine husband there, Aicelina. I will not stand in the way of that. You're right of course, about me, although I would wish it were not the case. You're a fine woman by any standards and would make a wife for a man to be proud of, but I would only cause hurt to you."

She put a hasty finger on his lips. "I do not think you could willingly hurt me; you are not that kind of man. I would trust you with my soul. Will you bless me and wish me joy if Bartholomew should ask to take me for his wife?"

"Has it come to this so quickly, Aicelina?"

She blushed again. "While I was dressing his head wound, he told me he was in love and asked for my hand."

"The man moves fast, despite his wound," Talon said stiffly.

"Nay, Talon, I told him not to jest, but he replied that he had been sure from the day he had arrived and was deadly serious."

"What was your reply?"

"I told him that I was the ward of Sir Hughes and Lady Marguerite and that he had to make his suit to them first and then if they agreed we would see. But I came to you to ask for your blessing, too. You have become close to me and I do love you... but, despite our physical mating, I feel more that you are my brother whom I never had." She gave a short giggle as though she saw how complicated it had become.

Talon gave a rueful laugh. Then despite the pain in his left arm, he seized her around her waist and lifted her off her feet so that her face was inches from his. He gave her a kiss on the lips that she returned. "That shall be the last passionate kiss I shall give you, my lovely sister. For now you are to be married to a good and clever man who had the sense to love you the moment he met you. Of course I shall bless the union."

Aicelina gave a delighted laugh that warmed him and threw her arms about his neck and gave him another kiss on the cheek. "Truly, Talon, I do love you for your kindness and understanding. Now it is time for your bath—perhaps if your mother can be distracted I shall wash your back after all."

They went off toward the Hall, arm-in-arm.

Later that day, the men came back from the d'Albi castle. Bartholomew and Max told Talon of the day's happenings.

Bartholomew and the Welshmen had accompanied Sir Hughes and Max to inspect the place. They had found it undisturbed but there had been a lot of work to do to clean up the corpses and a burial party had been pressed into work from the town.

Sir Hughes had told the people of the village to pass the word. He was henceforth the lord of the castle until the Count made a ruling. He would be fair and just, but any treachery would be rewarded by harsh justice. Apparently, the villagers were joyful about the news, as it was common knowledge that Guillabert had been a tyrant. They worked willingly with the men on the castle and then, when told to go and work on the harvest and bring it all without a tithe for this year, they had cheered and then vanished to go to work in their fields.

Bartholomew, having helped tell the tale of the day's events, immediately set off to look for Aicelina and when he did accost her in the yard Talon could see him talking to her earnestly. He seemed to be very happy about something and after a while they walked off to the garden. Talon assumed that Bartholomew might have asked his father for Aicelina in marriage. He enquired tactfully as to how his father felt about the man during their inspection of the yard together.

Sir Hughes did not need much prompting; he told Talon that Bartholomew had asked for Aicelina's hand. He looked sideways at Talon as he said this. "I have to confess I was somewhat surprised at the speed with which he has made this proposal, Talon. I had thought that there might have been something between you and Aicelina."

"We are close friends, but a bit like sister and brother, you understand?"

"Harrumph... well, all right then, I can pass the news onto your mother without fear of contradiction?"

"None, Father. I am truly happy for both of them. He is a very bright young man with a good future in the law, and she would make the perfect wife. You should try to keep him here with you as your advisor. He will make you rich."

Sir Hughes looked uncomfortable. "I am in agreement with you there. I certainly do not have a head for the accounts. While we are on the subject of wives... have you no maiden you would care to marry? There is after all Petrona, and the dowry she brings is not insignificant."

Talon felt the prickle of sweat around his neck. "The answer is 'not as yet,' although there was a lady at Carcassonne who caught my fancy while I was there with Uncle Philip," he lied.

"Ah, you never mentioned it."

"It is a delicate subject at best, and you have to admit we have been somewhat busy for the last few days."

"True, and had it not been for you, we might not be talking as we are today. I owe you a debt of thanks that cannot be repaid."

Talon stopped and took his father's arm. "Father, I have done what any son would do and there are no thanks to be given for that. You led us to victory and I, along with everyone here, owe you much for that! Everyone fought hard and we prevailed with much help from God, I am sure. I only ask that we make a decision about the Guillabert castle that will stand the test of time. I do not want vengeance to raise its ugly head a generation along from ours should Petrona marry another man and take possession of the castle as hers by right. It is yours by right of arms now, and we should petition the Count appropriately."

"Yes, we should consider this situation carefully. Perhaps Bartholomew can be of help there," Sir Hughes said, thankful they were off the subject of women and marriage.

"Is Petrona not of an age as yet where she is able to inherit?"

"That is true. I could adopt her and then we'd have the castle in the family. I wish to take possession of the castle as it would provide me with both lands and prevent the avaricious priest in Albi from claiming it for the church."

"I am in agreement. I also think that it is yours by right of arms in any case," Talon said firmly.

"I feel that it's mine by right of arms, too. We should write to the Count and petition him. He or at least his son, Roger, is well aware of the bad blood that existed, and will not be surprised at the news when it comes. "By the way," he said almost as an afterthought, "the whole problem would be solved very cleanly should you decide to marry her, Talon."

Talon said nothing but resolved never to underestimate his father.

They walked toward the hall where people were beginning to congregate. There was an expectant air about them. They would feast this night to celebrate a victory well won.

Talon was joined by the archers, who all greeted him enthusiastically as a friend. Even Belth was there with his arm in a sling, cheerfully greeting him. There was now a bond between them that was stronger than that of master and servant. Max soon joined them and amid much banter and laughter, the group joined the villagers and other men-at-arms.

As the Welshmen trooped into the hall there were shouted welcomes and greetings to these men who had once been strangers but were now considered one with the people of the village. They were also greeted by the smell of cooking meat and the sweet scent of pies baking by the roaring fire in the center of the Hall.

Sir Hughes presided over a joyful feast that night. His lady Marguerite, Aicelina, and now a pale and tired-looking Petrona sat to his left while in the place of honor to his right he placed Talon, and on Talon's right sat Max. Talon had asked that Gareth be placed at the high table, to which his father had willingly agreed. Gareth sat next to Bartholomew with a bemused expression.

The evening was soon lively and noisy as relieved men drank too much wine and celebrated their deliverance. All concentrated on eating and drinking while recounting their deeds of the day and night before. The deeds of the men who had defended the walls were talked about with pride by all there. Many a toast was shouted toward the high table.

Talon had not spoken to Petrona since he had carried her into the hall the day before, so he was curious as to how she would behave given that the victory was against her blood kin. She was silent for the most part, and only ate a few morsels of meat and bread. She retired with Aicelina as the evening advanced, who made the excuse that she had to put Guillaume to bed.

Talon and Bartholomew, as if by mutual consent, skirted the issue of Aicelina for the time being and concentrated on Petrona.

After some thought, Bartholomew said, "There are few options open to her in this day and age, Talon. However, she is actually well off with a guardian such as your father who would always deal fairly with her, even to ensuring that she had a good dowry when she married."

"Neither I nor my father could ever countenance that she would have the lands and castle of her father after all that had happened, Bartholomew."

"That I can quite understand, Talon. I agree with you, too. It is a harsh decision, but I can see clearly what it is founded upon. There is the de Gilles' survival to consider. But for some good fortune, and a lot of help from God, this family would not be here today if Guillabert had had his way. I think we can persuade the Count to allow the land and castle to pass into Sir Hughes' hands. All the Count really cares about is his taxes and tithes. Who would have been better to provide this kind of stability and hence the better tithes, your father or Guillabert?"

"I see what you mean. Will you help us to prepare the letter to the Count?"

"Of course. Now I have something I want to tell you. Aicelina and I are to be betrothed. Your father gave permission this afternoon and your mother approves. I am now asking for your blessing as you are my friend... no, you are my brother. Not only that, you saved my life and I wish to thank you."

Talon pretended surprise. "Why, Bartholomew, I believe life as a student has made you a man who is quick to make decisions. You barely know her."

Bartholomew leaned toward Talon, his voice slurred with the wine. "From the very moment I saw her, I fell in love. Do you know what I am saying? It was like a bolt of lightning and it struck me right here." He thumped his chest.

Talon nodded silently. "Yes, I do know of what you speak." He paused. "Will you be kind to her? Promise you will treat her well."

Bartholomew drew himself up and looked directly at Talon. "I swear to you that I shall defend her with my life, and cherish her as no other can. I could see immediately that she is a rare woman. I also knew that if I did not make haste, someone like you would take her and I would be the loser."

Talon grinned at Bartholomew. "No fear of that, my man. She is like a sister to me." He called over to Max and Gareth next to them. "Drink, my friends, this is a night to celebrate our victory, but also the betrothal of Bartholomew here to Aicelina."

That was it, the news was out and there had to be toasts from all and sundry.

Bartholomew stood up holding his leather goblet in the air toward Sir Hughes and Lady Marguerite and shouted over the noise in the hall. "I give you the finest knight and lady in this land. May God bless them and give them long life. I also give praise to their kin, Talon, my brother, and to Aicelina, to whom I have proposed. May God bless them with his everlasting kindness."

The crowd roared and every man and woman in the hall shouted their thanks to their good fortune and wished Bartholomew well. It was a long night.

The next day everyone had a hangover, including Talon, and he was glad to note his father also had a thick head. All the same, Sir Hughes behaved as though a great weight had been taken off his shoulders.

At breakfast the group of archers, men-at-arms, Max, and Talon sat nursing their heads in company with Sir Hughes. Later, Talon threw cold water over his head and brought himself back into a better state in preparation for the day to come.

Talon was soon to discover that even if they were very happy to have survived the battle there was the winter to survive as well. His experiences in the mountains of the Alborz gave him a good understanding of the urgency that now took everyone's attention.

The harvest was brought in despite the small rain squalls that came sweeping in from the west. Hay was stacked with the help of every man, woman, and child in the village and the fort. The village children and older girls plied the hedges and hedgerows, looking for berries of many kinds that Talon was not familiar with. There were raspberries, blackberries, and gooseberries, and others in a succulent array that his mother took charge of and made into preserves in earthenware jars.

Sir Hughes' responsibilities now also extended to the village near to the old castle of Guillabert. He spent long hours in the saddle with Talon in attendance while the other men, including the Welshmen, were pressed into helping with the cutting and stacking of the hay and the corn. The slaughter of the excess animals commenced and the terrified squeals of pigs going to their slaughter filled the air.

News of another, more somber kind, arrived a week after the battle. A farmer came across the bodies of some soldiers lying just inside the woods near the road to Albi. He came rushing into the fort breathless from running and blurted out the bad news. Sir Hughes and Talon, accompanied by Max and Gareth, immediately set out to see what had happened. They discovered that the men were indeed those of the Count of Carcassonne and had clearly been ambushed while on their way to help with the siege. A grim Sir Hughes ordered the men to be buried back on the land near the fort and sent a messenger to the Count informing him of the discovery. It was a sober group of men that rode back that day.

Bartholomew wrote a letter describing the circumstances of the fight and the outcome, making it clear that Guillabert and his men had provoked the war.

Before long the wild geese were flying overhead, honking as they sought warmer climes. The geese in the yard with their wings clipped honked back and tried in vain to take off while the ducks huddled in the barns out of the rain.

Then the sky cleared, the first real frost came and the ground became hard while the fields in the morning were white with hoar. Men rubbed their hands together and huddled under their cloaks in the early hours of dawn as they gathered to go out and complete the preparations for winter.

With the onset of the colder weather, Gareth and Talon talked seriously about their parting. They would not discuss these things in front of others. Instead they would go off hunting and while out in the forests they would talk.

"We should be on our way home before the end of autumn, Talon, or we will not be in Wales before the snows come."

"Then you should be going any day now. It is colder and I expect that long before Christmas we will have some snow even here in Languedoc."

"There will be much more snow in Britain and we still have to find a boat willing to cross the troubled seas to get there. It will be difficult in a few weeks if we do not go."

"Then you must leave, my friend, and God go with you. Without you and your companions we would not be having this conversation. I am more than grateful to you and deeply in your debt."

Gareth put a calloused hand on his shoulder. "Talon, my friend, we have been brothers at arms and we have prevailed. I would that one day perhaps if the Good Lord is kind to you that you come to visit us in our home in Wales. We shall speak of you in our Halls and make your name known to our people."

Talon resolved to make good on his payment to these men and send them on their way as soon as possible. He brought them all together in the privacy of one of the hay barns. It was raining gently outside and becoming colder by the day. The Welshmen stood around him with drops of water on their cloaks and glistening in their hoods and beards waiting for him to speak.

Talon drew out a small bag of gold from his belt and gave it to Gareth. "These are your wages, Gareth."

Gareth felt the weight of the bag and his eyes widened in the gloom of the barn. He opened the bag and poured some of the contents into his hand. The other men clustered around. They all exclaimed at the stream of gold. Gareth lifted his head and stared at Talon. "Talon, m-m-m'lord. This is far and away above any wages we have earned."

The others were muttering in Welch and staring at him as though they did not believe what they were seeing.

Talon held up his hand. "Listen, my friends. We have become brothers, it is true, but this is small payment for what you have helped me and my family do. Besides, you went to the Holy Land to get rich, did you not? You just had to take bit of a detour to do so," he said with a grin.

That broke the awkward silence. The men chuckled and then Gareth put the strange gold coins back into the bag and said simply. "You honor us, Talon, and we shall not forget." He stepped over to Talon and embraced him hard with tears in his eyes. "Aye, Bach. We are rich men. This will buy us all much land and cattle when we come home to our people."

One by one the men embraced Talon who called each by name. They shook his hand murmuring their thanks and swearing their loyalty to him as a brother.

They were to leave within a couple of days before the weather started to get much colder. There was still a long and dangerous path to take before they came to their home.

Chapter 26

Witchcraft

Talon had been avoiding Petrona for some time now. He saw her in the hall it was true, but apart from the occasional exchange of greetings they had not had time to spend together. Talon wanted it to stay that way for a while longer but he knew it could not be put off for much longer.

They met outside the linen house the day after his farewell speech to the Welshmen. After the polite greetings she looked him in the eye. "Talon, I can tell you are avoiding me. Have I offended you that you ignore me and do not pay me any attention?"

He mumbled something to the effect that he had been busy, but she would have none of it and, linking arms with him, insisted that they walk to the garden as that provided the most privacy. Petrona was still very subdued, quite unlike the girl he had met on the road to Albi the first time. He felt some sympathy for her: her world was now turned on its head and her future uncertain. She sat down and waved a hand toward the bench, indicating that he should be seated, too.

"I owe my life to you, Talon. Had you not come to my help those brutes would have taken me and then no doubt killed me."

Talon nodded. He would not deny this. "But we managed to bring you safely here. You should not dwell on that time. You will be welcomed here and my father and mother will take good care of you from now on."

He dreaded the direction this conversation might take but before she could respond there was a disturbance at the gate and men started hurrying toward the entrance to the fort.

There was a shout from outside and Max and Sir Hughes came out of the Hall. They climbed the stairs to the platform and looked out.

Talon quickly took Petrona by the hand and led her to the hall. "We should talk again, Petrona," he said with barely disguised relief. Then he hurried off to the stairs leading up to the platform where his father stood, leaving her staring after him.

Talon made it to the top just as his father called down to the people below. Talon looked down and saw the priest, Father Eustache, mounted on a fine horse, but what made him start were the men with him. The priest was accompanied by six well-mounted men-at-arms carrying spears, who sported the deceased bishop's livery—and with them was the long-lost huntsman, Domerc.

Sir Hughes saw Domerc and called down. "Where have you been, Domerc? Did you not know we had troubles? Have you forgotten that you work for me?"

Father Eustache called up to him. "Sir Hughes, I wish to talk to you of important matters. Domerc works for the bishop's office now."

"God's truth, he does? You dog, Domerc. When did this happen that I was not informed?" Sir Hughes called back, beginning to look angry.

The priest's whole demeanor changed when he saw Talon. "Sir Hughes, open the gates. I come in the name of the bishop's office to arrest that man." He pointed directly at Talon.

There was a stunned silence. Sir Hughes called down angrily. "Be careful, priest. You come here and expect a welcome when you wish to arrest my son. On what charge?"

"On the charge of witchcraft," the priest shouted back. "Open the gates that I can take him back with me to stand trial for witchcraft."

Sir Hughes stood still for a moment in stunned disbelief and then visibly collected himself. "Who is the scoundrel who would accuse my son of such a thing?"

The priest indicated Domerc next to him. "This man."

"You, Domerc? You filthy dog! You desert my office and most probably have stolen my revenues for the benefit of Guillabert and then you dare to accuse my son? You shall die for this!" Sir Hughes shouted, by now thoroughly enraged.

He shook his fist at the priest. "You shall not dare to come into this place to arrest my son on the word of a thief and a deserter."

"I have a warrant that carries the bishop's seal. I have the right to pronounce excommunication upon all in this place should you resist the order, Sir Hughes. Do not defy the power of the Church. You do so at the peril of your soul and put in jeopardy the souls of all within."

"Curse you, priest, and damn you to hell, Domerc," Sir Hughes yelled down at the man. He turned to Talon with an anguished look in his eyes. "I do not know what to do Talon. He carries the ultimate power with him."

"I shall go with him. To resist him would be to put you all in real danger that not even the Count can prevent. You could lose all you have gained." All around him men growled angrily at this but Talon held up his hand. "The priest has no proof and the word of his man Domerc can be easily denounced. Bartholomew"—he turned to Bartholomew who had joined them—"do you not think so?"

Oddly, Bartholomew looked unsure. "Why would they accuse you of witchcraft, Talon? That part confuses me." He leaned over the battlements and shouted down. "What is this charge of witchcraft based upon?"

Domerc leaned back in his saddle and called back.

"It is I, Domerc, who accuses him. I followed your son to Albi the night the bishop died. I saw him fly over the walls of the town. His wings were black and he spat fire. Later I saw him fly back over the walls and again he was spitting fire. That same night the bishop died, calling out to God in his agony, calling for mercy while dying of the horrible fires of hell. It was he, Talon, the infidel, who placed the curse of the Devil upon the poor soul of the bishop."

He crossed himself piously and so did the other men in the priest's entourage. Some men on the walls did so, too, and there were fearful glances at Talon, who stood as still as stone. His thoughts were in turmoil. They had been followed to the town of Albi the night he had killed the bishop. The only man who knew positively was Gareth but he would not tell a soul. He realized that he was lost, but he determined that it would not take his father down with him.

"Let the priest in. I shall go with him and stand trial. He has no proof. Domerc is lying."

"This charge is very serious," Bartholomew exclaimed nervously.

"That is clear, but to have excommunication is worse, as they can confiscate all that my father has fought for. I will not have that, Bartholomew."

Sir Hughes looked at his son in anguish. "I would rather cut off my right hand than lose you to this vindictive man. The charge of witchcraft is trumped up, but they do not need much proof other than the word of one man to condemn you."

"We cannot stop them, but I need talk to Max and the Welshmen before they take me."

His father nodded mutely. "Go down and talk to them. I will stall this priest."

Talon clasped his father's arm and then embraced Bartholomew. "Take good care of my parents, Bartholomew, your wisdom and skill will be needed. Give my love to Aicelina."

Bartholomew nodded but said, "Do not give up hope. We will have the Count in this and stop the priest."

Talon did not think that Bartholomew fully understood. He knew he would be lucky if he made it to Albi alive.

Max and Gareth followed Talon down the steps and walked with him to the end of the yard. There he turned and said to them, "It is clear that Domerc followed us to Albi, Gareth. That makes me a condemned man."

Max was staring at him and Gareth. "What do you mean? He followed you to Albi? I did not know that you went; I thought you went to the abbey."

"You were not meant to know, nor anyone else other than my brother, Gareth, here. I slew the bishop because of what I heard in Guillabert's castle. He promised my father's land to Guillabert and told them to kill Guillaume. That made him guilty of a great evil. I merely killed him."

Max stared at both of them wide-eyed as though re-evaluating Talon. Then he seemed to come to a decision. "We have come through much together. Although you did commit a grievous sin, Talon, I will not allow the priest who was party to his plotting to take you. What do you suggest?"

"I hear that the Templars do not ask questions of men who come to them wishing to fight in the Holy Land."

Max considered this thoughtfully. Then he said, "They are six and well-armed. How can we defeat them on the road?"

Talon nodded to Gareth, who grinned. "Do not worry about that, Max. Be prepared to flee with him when it is done," Gareth said.

They spent a few more minutes talking and discussing the plan, then Talon made off to find his mother and bid her goodbye. He saw the Welshmen equally hurriedly preparing to leave. They would not be coming back, either. He stalled as long as he could saying goodbye to everyone, most of whom were tearful. All the while he was noting the activity going on at the back of the fort and finally he saw the Welshmen, laden with their meager belongings and their bows slipping over the back walls with the help of some of the men-at-arms, who were their friends.

The priest was finally allowed in but stayed mounted, he and his men were surrounded by a baleful group of angry men who would as soon have dragged Domerc down off his horse and killed him then and there as let them do more than sit their horses, waiting.

The farewell was hard. Marguerite was stunned and could not believe this was happening, nor could Aicelina. They both clung to him, crying his name, begging him not to go. Both women believed in their hearts that it would be the last time they would ever see him.

Guillaume, not fully understanding the situation, did realize however that his brother was leaving him and sensed that something was very wrong. He, too, began to cry until Talon crouched near him and lifted his chin with a gentle finger. "You are a Gilles, Guillaume. We do not cry. We are fighters and we prevail. I expect to come back one day and find you a grown man who has looked after our mother and father in their old age and all the women and protected our heritage. Honor and obey our father in all things, and become a good knight."

His brother wiped the tears from his eyes and nodded but when they embraced he was weeping again. Ermessenda was not to be found so they had to forgo bidding goodbye to her.

Talon finally turned to face his father. "Forgive me if I have dishonored you, sir. I feel that there was no other way. I shall write to you."

Sir Hughes looked devastated. "God has seen fit to give me barely a glimpse of you before taking you from me again, Talon. No father could have asked for more from a son. You have honored the family and will be named in our roles. We will take this case to the Count and we will win you back, have no fear."

They embraced for a long moment and then at last they separated. There were tears in all eyes as Talon placed his cloak around his shoulders and mounted the ready Jabbar. The whole party wheeled and rode slowly out through the gates of the fort.

When they had left the gates the men closed in around Talon and he knew then that he was right, he would be lucky if he reached Albi alive.

He looked back once to see his father standing with Bartholo-mew and his mother and Aicelina on the parapet above the gates. He waved, and then faced forward. He hoped that the Welshmen and Max would succeed in their endeavor.

For thy sake yielding all I love and prize;
And O, how mighty must that influence be,
That steals me thus from all my cherished joys.
Here, ready, then, myself surrendering,
Prepared to serve thee, I submit; and ne'er
To one so faithful could I service bring,
So kind a master, so beloved and dear.
Thibaut Of Champagne, King Of Navarre

Chapter 27

Templar

The small party of men with Talon in their midst and accompanied by Domerc and the priest Father Eustache rode slowly through the village where the people had gathered in small knots. Some of the bolder villagers called out to Talon, wishing him courage. Word had spread fast and had already arrived at the village. The people were frightened and angry. Some shook their fists at the priest and damned him but others made the sign of the cross for protection from evil as the accusation was of witchcraft. They saw Talon as doomed; no one survived an accusation of this kind. The church saw to that.

As the party rode out of the village toward the fields, Talon took care to not seem too curious about what might lie ahead. But inside he felt numb and his stomach was knotted up. He had not anticipated this to happen—the bishop had won after all, reaching out from his grave to seize Talon and take him down.

Now his life was in danger of the most awful kind and he had only one hope. If the Welshmen failed he would go to a prison from which there was no chance of release other than the long walk to either the scaffold or the pile of faggots around a pole. He recalled with a cold chill the bishop's words when he had been listening in Guillabert's former castle. That would be his death and his funeral pyre at the same time. He kept his head down and hunched into his cloak as though cold; he was, somewhat, from the turn of events.

Once they were out of sight of the castle and the neighboring village, the priest rode closer to Talon and demanded his attention.

"Well, Talon de Gilles, you young heathen, you are about to get your just deserts. You may have outwitted the others and murdered the Guillaberts, but the charges you now face will take more than even the Count's power to get you off."

Talon said nothing. He was watching the track which was now narrower and led between tall trees on either side. They were entering a denser part of the forest with much undergrowth along the side of the road.

The priest continued. "I can say it with impunity now, but you thwarted the church in many ways by slaying the Guillaberts. You deprived us of important revenue which I shall see we get in the end despite your efforts. The death of the bishop can easily be placed upon your head as we can accuse you of being not only a heathen but also to have used witchery to send him and others of his household to their maker."

Talon turned on the priest. "You are wrong about the possession; the abbot found the will of my mother's father and we now have absolute proof that Guillabert was lying. I also suspect that 'his maker' will have some questions of his own to ask the bishop when he presents himself."

He did not expect Father Eustache to react the way he did.

"You heathen pig, how dare you blaspheme in his name?" He slashed his whip savagely across Talon's back.

It made him gasp but before the priest could raise the whip again Talon shot his hand out and seized Eustache's wrist, then held it in a vise-like grip. His eyes bored into the priest's. "Be glad, priest, that I did not come for you. I know of your lusts and your appetites, especially for Petrona. I saw you that one night when you tried to get into her chamber."

The shock on Father Eustache's face would have been comical had the circumstances been different, but Talon was not able to hold the man's arm for long. One of the men riding next to him brought down the shaft of his spear on his back, followed by a curse.

Talon had to release his hand to ward off another blow. Domerc laughed nastily and rode his horse hard into Jabbar, then gave Talon a heavy blow with his fist on the side of the face. Talon was unable to defend himself from the blows that now came from all around, all he could do was to hunch down in the saddle and hope to avoid the worst that were aimed at his head. Before he could do anything he found the reins snatched from him by one of the men at arm and his arms bound behind him.

The party was thus engaged when there was a loud shout forward along the path that led through the forest's edge.

Every man looked up. There, standing in the middle of the road were two men in long cloaks with hoods concealing their faces. Talon instantly recognized Gareth and Drudwas; they had their bows at the ready with an arrow notched.

"Priest!" Gareth shouted. "Halt your men and come forward. I would speak with you."

Father Eustache looked shocked and went pale. "What do you want? Are you robbers? We are on church business. We have no coin. Get out of the way!" he shouted back.

The men in his troop were now tensely pointing their spears at Gareth and Drudwas as though getting ready to charge them. Before any of them could put into motion the idea of running the two men down, an arrow whispered out of the forest and buried itself deep in Domerc's chest with an audible thump. He gasped, clutched his chest, then fell off his horse, making a surprised choking sound as he landed. He rolled over onto his back and died without another word.

There was a stunned silence for a couple of moments. This example of bowman's skill should have stopped the men but someone shouted. "Charge through the scum! They can't kill us all, some can escape."

This seemed to cause a general panic and the men-at-arms jammed spurs into their horses' sides. The horses leapt at the two men in the middle of the road.

Talon was dragged along for a moment, but then the reins went slack as the man tugging at his horse took an arrow in the throat and toppled off his horse. Jabbar was dancing about nervously with Talon still trying to stay on, but unable to control him other than to talk to him to try to calm him.

All about was not calm, however. The other men who rode for the priest had taken their chances and failed. Only one got past the hail of arrows that were sent at them by both Gareth and Drudwas and the other Welshmen hidden in the forest. The two men in the roadway had jumped aside when the horsemen charged them but not before discharging their arrows with deadly effect. The one survivor galloped frantically off down the trail, leaving his fallen comrades behind.

The only people left on the road who were still mounted were Talon and the priest, who seemed paralyzed with fear. His horse was prancing about, snorting at the smell of blood, unnerved by the screams that filled the air from the couple of wounded men.

A man with a hood over his head, Belth, came running out of the undergrowth, seized Talon's reins then tugged him urgently behind him into the forest. As he went Talon looked back and saw Father Eustace look about fearfully. There was no one other than the groaning wounded or dead on the ground. He glanced down at them indifferently and then he clapped spurs to his horse and galloped off down the road in the direction of Albi as fast as he could go.

The Welshmen surrounded Talon and Jabbar, babbling to one another in their tongue and then as Gareth strode up someone cut his bonds free. Talon shook himself and took back the reins. He looked down on his friends clustered about and grinned through the blood on his lips and the bruises on his face.

"That was close, my brothers. I am again in your debt. I think they were getting set to finish the work before we even got to Albi."

"Indeed we thought so, too, Talon Bach. But there is no time to waste. You have to head south for a mile where Max is waiting for you with your belongings. He is going to take you to Mas-Dieu."

Talon looked at them in surprise. "Max is taking me? All I wanted him to do was to bring my equipment."

"He thinks you mean to go to Mas-Dieu alone and will not have it that you should go alone," Gareth said.

They all walked deeper into the forest to where there were several horses tied to trees.

"We too must leave, m'lord Talon. The winter comes and we would be home before the snows come down hard."

"You will be hunted men, Gareth. Do you go quickly and get into Aquitaine where the law of this church will not have such an easy time. I shall miss you sorely my brothers, truly."

Once again they clasped hands but wordlessly this time. In virtual silence Talon turned Jabbar and headed in the direction they had told him. He looked back once and saw only shadows. The Welshmen were gone.

Talon found Max at the place the Welshmen had described. Max came out of the copse of trees when he saw Talon riding down the path toward him. He looked surprised when he saw the bruises on Talon's face.

"It would seem that the Welshmen got to you just in time, Master Talon," he said dryly.

Talon nodded and took a long drink from the water skin Max handed to him. He washed his face with some of the water and dried it on the edge of his cloak. "They told me that you were taking me to Mas-Dieu, Max. There is no need, I can find the way."

"Your uncle, Sir Philip, may God have mercy on his soul, once told me that if I should survive him then I was to help you in any way I could."

"He did?"

"Yes. He knew that you would one day go back to the land where you were born and where you really belong. I have a wish to accompany you back to Palestine. I am a Sergeant in the Order of the Templars and as such I am bound to go back to my order now that my duty to Sir Philip is done. I find it too close here and I long for the wide spaces. If you will have me as your Sergeant, Talon?"

"Have you, Max? Are you mad? Of course I would have you with me, no one could ask for a better companion, but as a friend, not as a servant. A Sergeant you will stay and a better companion a man could not want for."

"Then it is settled. You are now a hunted man and if I am not mistaken the priest—if he can be called that—will start a manhunt as soon as he is back in Albi. We have probably three hours on him and we must use the time well."

Without further ado they took the road southwest. Max had brought all his possessions, including one of the two remaining sacks of gold. Talon had instructed him to leave the other in the care of his mother, who he knew would make it known to his father in due time.

It was a mark of his trust for Max that he could have asked this of him as the money, being gold in a land where it was scarce, would have made Max a very rich man. Max had handed the possessions over without comment and then concentrated on their next move.

They slept that night in the hills deep in a forest where the only company they had were the animals of the woods, and they left them alone. They did hear the lonely cry of a wolf far away and it made Talon remember another time and another world where wolves were part of his life. His thoughts were confused and, although he had Max with him, the long night was his alone. For the first time in many months he thought of that faraway place where he had grown up, and then the remark made by Aicelina came to mind. Would he ever know the meaning of the word peace? He slept, finally, still thinking on that.

They made their way as fast as they could, but also with great caution, along the roads west and over the same mountains that they had traversed when they had first come to Albi. Max did not think that it would occur to the priest that they would head for a Templar fort. Talon was a fugitive. Nonetheless whenever they saw horsemen in front or behind them they would prudently leave the path and watch them from the cover of the woods as they went by.

Talon rode without caring for the first few days, his shoulders hunched and his thoughts bleak. The life he had known at his parent's hearth was not one that he could have lived willingly for too long, but it had been a wrench to be taken away from it so brutally and so soon. His thoughts lingered on the people he knew he was unlikely to ever see again and he brooded on what fate had handed him.

Max kept pace with Talon, watchful for danger, but gave him space and his silent companionship, aware of the desolate state of his friend's mind.

It took a week of living in the woods and hedgerows before they came within a day's ride of Mas-Dieu. Talon's mood had improved and he was taking more interest in the world around him. The days had become cold and the nights were freezing. It began to rain as they walked their horses down the rutted cart track that passed as a road toward the collection of buildings that comprised the Preceptory. It was sleeting by the time they came within sight of the stronghold. The sleet settled onto their thick cloaks and the horse's mains and tails, giving them a ghostly effect.

They rode up to the great wooden doors with the Templar seal carved into the stone above, depicting two knights on one horse. Max pulled on the rope hanging down from the archway. The bell inside clanged loudly in the still of the late evening. They waited, listening, until they heard the crunch of boots on the stones inside and a voice demanded their business.

Max called out, "Max von Bauersdorf, Sergeant of Templars, on urgent business with My Lord Sir Greves."

There was a muttered comment and then they heard the huge wood bars being drawn and the right hand gate swung open. They walked the horses between the three guards on the other side and on into the courtyard, hearing the door crash shut behind them.

A man came over to them carrying a flaming torch held high over his head. "You can put your horses in those stables over there," he said gruffly, and pointed in the general direction of some low buildings against the walls. "Then come into the Great Hall. The knights are at dinner."

They complied with his instructions, finding two unoccupied stalls where they were able to untack their animals, and then found feed to place in front of them. It was hard to see in the gloom of the darkened stables but Talon was fairly sure Jabbar was fine for the night. He made sure he went through the little ritual that he knew Jabbar loved of rubbing his face with a blanket before leaving.

They carried their few belongings with them toward the doorway at the other end of the yard from which there came light and the low murmur of many voices. The tantalizing smell of cooking meat and vegetables came to them as they walked. Talon realized that he was very hungry.

They were met at the door by a servant who told them to leave their baggage in the hall where it would be safe and then showed them the way toward the Great Hall.

"We're safe here," Max murmured as they walked down the corridor. "We are with the Templars now, your new family."

Talon said nothing. His eyes were drawn to the men he saw seated on benches at long tables, eating. There were servants moving about, providing them with wine and bread and salt when called for. The hubbub of a large hall full of eating and talking men was somehow reassuring to the two men who were used to sleeping rough and eating whatever they could trap, fish, or buy in passing.

Talon saw that there was a high table, not unlike the one at the abbey. Here, though, instead of men of peace, there were hard-faced, bearded men who wore uniforms and the insignia of war.

The servant who had brought them to the entrance told them to wait and went into the hall, wending his way to the high table where he came up to a man who looked quite senior and, bending over, whispered into his ear.

The man glanced up at Talon and Max, and then nodded. The servant left him and came back to them. Talon thought he had seen Sir Greves at the head of the great table but was not sure. The candlelight was not sufficient to see clearly who sat at that table. The candles cast huge shadows on the walls as they guttered in the drafts but failed to light the whole room well.

The servant approached them and told them to find a place among the knights and eat supper. The Knight Master would talk to them in the morning after Lauds.

"What are Lauds?" Talon asked Max.

"They are the morning prayers; now they are oft-times called *matins*. We shall have to educate you in the ways of the knights, Talon."

They settled in among some younger men who were, it seemed to Talon, almost as new as he was to the whole brotherhood of the Templars. These men maintained a silence of a sort even as they regarded the two travel-stained men with curiosity. Both Talon and Max were tired and not inclined to answer questions so they ate the simple fare of bread and stew and then left for the cells that the servant provided.

Talon woke to the sound of a bell and realized that he was probably late for the prayers called matins. He got up and dressed in his filthy clothes. He longed for a bath but knew that this would not be available here. The men he had sat next to at supper were so smelly that he had almost gagged. He wondered why they abhorred cleanliness. Long ago the doctor who had been his mentor had mentioned that filth and wounds did not go well together. These men were warriors and so wounds would be part of their lives. He shook his head with resignation; but if this order of warrior monks took him back to Palestine he would put up with it.

Max was waiting impatiently for him out in the courtyard. "We're somewhat late, I fear," he said tactfully as they hurried toward the chapel that Talon remembered from his last visit here.

The audience with Sir Greves was brief but significant. When they knelt before him he addressed Max. "You are Max von Bauersdorf. Sergeant to Sir Philip de Gilles, are you not? Where then is Sir Philip?"

"He is dead. Slain by a coward in ambush, God rest his soul. I am here with his nephew Sir Talon de Gilles, who would join the Templars."

The old man with the very long beard looked down at them. "Arise, gentlemen; I would see your faces."

They both stood and were subjected to a close inspection by the master of the lodge. His eyesight was obviously going because he squinted as he looked at Talon's face. Talon submitted meekly to the inspection as he stared at the huge silver clasp that held his cloak about his shoulders. The Templar seal showing the outline of a temple topped with a cross on a rounded roof supported by pillars within a ring of words *De Templo Cristi.*

He had seen the other side of that crest above the gate: two knights on a single horse, illustrating the humble beginnings of the Knights of the Temple; the words ringing that crest were *Sigillum Militum.*

"Ah, now I have it, you are Sir Philip's nephew, Talon. You are the one with the languages. Is that not right? Are you then knighted? I heard the sergeant call you Sir Talon de Gilles."

"I am, my Lord. His highness the Count of Carcassonne knighted me in the presence of my uncle and the master of the Templar lodge in Carcassonne."

"Come to join us, eh?" said the old man. "Then we shall make you welcome, Sir Talon de Gilles. A man of your experience in the Holy Land will be valuable to us." He turned to one of the men who had been hovering nearby. "See to it that Sir Talon de Gilles is entered into the roles of the order of the Templars and ensure that he is educated in our customs and rules, Sir Martin."

The interview was over and Talon bowed deeply, as did Max, then they followed Sir Martin out into the yard. He was a thin man who looked as though he would be better off with a pen in his hand rather than acting as the secretary for this warrior monk order.

"You have to train with the newcomers who have already been here for several weeks, Sir Talon. I fear that they will have the advantage of you." His voice was a high-pitched.

"I shall apply myself, Sir Martin. I am sure I will make good on the training."

Max coughed respectfully. "I can vouch for Sir Talon. I think he will catch up quite quickly."

"We shall see," sniffed the knight. "You, sergeant, can work with him to teach him the customs, our ceremonies, and our prayers. I trust you still remember them after all your travels abroad?"

"Indeed, sir, I do. I shall be pleased to help as much as I can," Max replied, his neck becoming red.

"The first thing you must do then is to move into one of the rooms for the knights and obtain the clothing and equipment needed. Did you bring any of your own equipment? The order is not made of money, you know. It is helpful when 'knights' bring at least something of their own."

"I have my armor and my weapons, sir," Talon said stiffly.

"He has his own horse, too, Sir Martin. However, it is not a Destriere."

Sir Martin sighed and seemed to be mentally tallying up the cost of a Destriere in his quartermaster-like mind. "Then we shall have to arrange for one. You both should draw blankets and clothing from the storeroom today; and sergeant, find him a place to sleep with the others. You should report to the training field when this is done. I am relying upon you, sergeant, to ensure that he attends all the prayer times. If I am not mistaken you were both late this morning." Sir Martin turned on his heels and left.

Max bowed his response to the departing back. He turned back to Talon and winked. "This is going to be somewhat new for you, master Talon. But I am sure that you will manage well. Let us go and obtain the necessary items and find a bed for you."

Talon nodded unhappily. It seemed to him that he was losing a lot of freedoms in return for the safety and the privilege of belonging to this elite group of men. He hoped it was worth it.

The next few days were a flurry of activity for him. Although he was by now a relatively experienced soldier and fighter he still found that he had a lot to learn about the methods and ways of this stern order, particularly the strict regimen of prayer and work. No more lying in bed waiting for the sun to come up, nor enjoying idle time with gossip.

One day, after a meager lunch, he confided in Max that his opinion of the food was very low as it seemed the cooks held to one recipe at all times with no thought to variation.

"I truly miss the food we ate at my father's hearth."

Max chuckled. "I too had become too well used to the food that your good mother caused to be made for us, God bless her. What I would not give for the taste of a good hare stew or some duck, hmmm." He shut his eyes and pretended that he was elsewhere.

Talon chuckled. "Max, I do believe that the Templars nearly lost you because of my mother's cooking. For shame!"

Max laughed and clapped him on the shoulder. "I shall deny that on my deathbed, but you know a winter of hunting and eating would not have gone amiss before I would have had to come back to this."

They were interrupted by a shout from the yard.

"Sir Talon de Gilles, if you would do us the honor of your company we are about to work in lines." Sir Martin was sitting on his palfrey with a disapproving frown on his face. Around him the other mounted recruits prepared their Destrieres for the afternoon exercises.

Talon was assisted hurriedly by Max to get his Destriere out of the stable and he mounted the huge animal under the impatient eye of another instructor, who then led the way out of the yard toward the practice fields where the knights carried out their training.

To Talon this was very new. He had never seen the line-abreast maneuver that the knights learned as a basic tactic for going into battle.

The sergeants went around pushing or pulling the recruits and their huge horses into a rough semblance of a line. Eventually, there were about twenty men on horses, stirrup to stirrup, at one end of the huge field. The field was still white in places from the previous night's frost and the breath from the horses' nostrils created a cloud of steam in front of the assembled men. Talon felt the cold seep through his clothing as they waited.

Then the sergeants shouted at the mounted men to get their shields up level with their eyes. This Talon and the others found hard to do as they were so close that they bumped each other in their clumsiness and in some cases there were curses and muttered threats made by nervous and irritated men. They might have been recruits for the Order but some of these men were hardened fighters and didn't like to be jostled.

The man next to Talon had a scar running across his forehead and down his cheek, making him look sinister and someone not to be trifled with. He glared at Talon when the tail of Talon's shield bumped his knee.

"Watch what you are doing, you poor excuse for a man!" he snarled before Talon could apologize.

"No talking in the ranks of the knights!" bellowed a sergeant nearby who had overheard.

The men now had their shields up and were then told to bring their spears to point downfield as though they were going to charge. Again there was some confusion because of the proximity of their neighbors, but it was finally done without mishap. Now all the men were deep in their high saddles, waiting for a command to move.

"Walk the line forward!" shouted one of the sergeants.

The line of knights moved their massive horses forward and immediately the line began to waver and disintegrate as some of the more eager men put spurs to their mounts while others reined theirs in.

The sergeants, many of them grizzled veterans of Palestinian wars, bellowed for the men to stop their horses, and after ten minutes of confusion and shoving, the process was repeated all over again.

Talon was beginning to see that there might be some point to all this when, during yet another realignment phase, his unpleasant neighbor rammed his horse sideways into his, which slammed his knee.

Talon looked into the man's face which was very close and muttered, "Do you know how to control that animal, sir?"

"I know to take you down a peg or two if you don't watch who you're talking to, you babe in arms," the man sneered. He was a big man with a florid face covered in whiskers; his huge shoulders made him look like a troll, Talon thought, trying not to grin.

They could not continue the conversation as Max had come up and asked challengingly of them both if there was anything wrong. His look to Talon told him that he knew there was but needed Talon to say so.

Talon shook his head and glanced sideways at the man with the scar and said politely, "We were just discussing the art of riding, Sergeant."

Max nodded. "There should be no talking during this work, sirs," he said politely but firmly and moved off.

The man next to Talon grunted and then said out of the corner of his mouth, "We will settle this later."

The recruits were worked hard that afternoon and finally they were able to walk their hot and eager Destrieres along the length of the field in one long line. It was clear that the sergeants, who had worked tirelessly, had hoped for better, but it was dusk and time for them to prepare for the prayers so they were sent back to the barracks.

Talon overheard a sergeant mutter to his companion. "They all start off like this. It is a betting matter as to when they actually get it and ride the line all the way down. I won't give you much for this lot."

Max joined Talon as he rode back. "What was the problem back there, Master Talon? It looked as though there was a quarrel brewing."

"Perhaps, Max. He is somewhat short-tempered, it seems."

Suddenly the man was at their elbow. "You." He pointed his grubby finger at Talon. "You need a lesson in manners, boy."

"The knights are not allowed to fight each other, sir," Max said quickly. "We are to fight the infidel in God's name, not our own kind."

"This pup insulted me and I will have the satisfaction of putting him in his place."

"What did he say that was so insulting, sir?" Max asked politely.

"He called into question my skill with a horse. A mere boy should not open his mouth without permission."

Talon turned to Max. "It seems that we have to deal with this one way or the other, Sergeant," He turned back to the man on his right. "If you are not afraid, sir, we can fight with sticks and this way no one can draw serious blood. If you think you can teach me a lesson, that is."

"I should talk to the master about this," Max said. "He would not approve, but we do allow men to train with sticks. Perhaps we can put you two together tomorrow morning after prayers, for the stick training. Will that suffice to settle your issue with Sir Talon, Sir Montague?"

"It will do. I shall see you in the training yard tomorrow, young whelp. Bring bandages; you will need them." He rode off, smirking, leaving them to watch him leave.

"I should report him and have him disciplined, Talon. The order does not put up with this kind of thing. We cannot afford to have knight fighting knight when we are all God's soldiers training for the fight in the Holy Land."

"Why does the Order accept men like that, Max?"

"We should not, in fact. But if the truth be known the Order is always short of experienced men. We need men who know how to fight and these days we are ready to even accept some who have questionable histories. I do not know of his, but I know he is from Normandy. We take men who are from all over Europe; for many this is the last place that will take them; some face the gallows or worse back at their home towns."

Talon realized with a start that now he, too, had come to the last place that would have him without questioning his past. It was an uncomfortable thought. "Well, tomorrow we shall see if he knows how to fight with sticks as well as his mouth."

"I saw your fight with the knife and stick in Montfort, Talon. I think sir Montague is in for a surprise."

The evening passed without incident but it was clear to Talon that the word was out that there was a grudge fight to be witnessed in the courtyard the next morning. His companions, some of them as young as he, were eying him speculatively and some even came up to him and asked him of the pending fight. His calm impressed them, but inside he was in turmoil, reliving a fight he had had in Palestine nearly eight months ago with knives and sticks which had ended with his opponent dead and he in chains.

The knight then had been the one who had captured him and refused to allow him to leave the castle to go and find Rav'an. The same knight had challenged him to sticks and knives. Talon had been so angry that he had taken his revenge on the man.

He observed Sir Montague with some of his friends at table and noticed that he seemed in good spirits. They were watching Talon and seemed amused at the prospect of the fight the next day. Montague even came over later after prayers when they were all making ready for bed. "Young Talon, I shall not be too hard on you tomorrow, but you understand that we have to settle an issue of honor in public, do you not?"

"If you say so, Sir Montague," Talon said meekly, remembering the many training classes he'd had in Samiran with Reza and the other boys who'd become *fida'i*.

The man clapped him on the shoulder, laughed, then left him to get ready for bed.

The next day dawned bright and with a brisk cold wind sweeping in from the north. Autumn was becoming winter in earnest and the men in the barracks woke up cold to find the water in the buckets outside covered with a thin layer of ice.

Max had spoken to the other sergeants about the grudge fight and they arranged for the students to start the day off in the sword yard, but they were to be paired off and to train with poles. This was done as though the students were meant to start the day in this manner so that Sir Martin would not be aware of the event until it had taken place, as surely he would have forbidden it then and there.

Sure enough, Talon was paired with Sir Montague. They eyed one another; both were dressed in wool breeches and leggings, leather sandals and linen undershirts, a light quilted jacket for the cold, and a leather cap that sat close on their heads.

Both held a pole six feet long and two inches in diameter that they would spar with. The other men were paired off in two rough lines, waiting for the word from the sergeant in charge.

At the shouted command the men set to, trying to trip or hit their opponents with their poles.

Montague wasted no time. He charged in with his stick high with the intent to smack Talon a heavy blow on the head or shoulders. Talon waited just long enough for the blow to start, tapped it aside with the end of his own stick, slid in sideways, backed in low, and rammed the end of his pole hard into his opponent's midriff. Montague gave a gasp and doubled over, whereupon Talon smacked him briskly on the side of his head and stepped back out of the way.

Montague was on one knee, holding his ear where he had been struck. He squealed with pain as Talon had not struck gently. Then he stood up and came in again. This time he was more cautious and whirled his stick in an arc as he came to confuse before he changed its direction and struck at Talon's legs. Talon blocked the savage swing hard and then equally swiftly he reversed his stick and rammed the side of the other end onto Montague's other ear. It stopped the man in his tracks and Talon was just about to deliver a hard poke at Montague's face when the man stepped hurriedly out of the way.

Then they went at it hard. Montague was no novice at the game of poles and once or twice he got in very hard blow to keep Talon from getting too confident.

By this time the other trainees had abandoned their own sparring to watch this fight. A loose circle had formed around the two combatants which the other sergeants did nothing to stop. Everyone knew that these two men had to settle a grudge and the fight suddenly looked like it was not going to be an easy one for Montague. Talon could hear the comments being made by his companions who were clearly glad that he was able to punish his opponent.

He felt loose and comfortable facing the big man before him. Montague's anger and the pain Talon had inflicted early on to his ears was getting in the way of his judgment. Talon was relying on his speed and the skill he had learned long ago in the mountains of the Assassins to keep his opponent off balance. He allowed Montague to make the attacks with the purpose of tiring the man and it was beginning to work. Once again Montague rushed in, his stick whirling about his head, trying for a weak point; although he feinted and struck for another target, Talon blocked his stick with a loud click and deflected; then before he could think of another move, Talon reversed again and delivered a nasty blow to his opponent's knuckles. The crowd were taking sides and cheering now. Talon danced out of the way and in a circle, with the angry Montague following him, jeering at him to stop and face him.

Talon nodded then and stepped in to deliver a lightning-fast poke to the face that landed on Montague's chin, drawing blood. The man yelled in rage, paused to glaring at Talon, then spat out a tooth onto the dirt.

But he surprised Talon because he grinned in spite of that and shouted, "You are a worthy opponent, Sir Talon. By the time we are done you will be on your back, begging for mercy." Then he rushed in and delivered some very fast blows up and down and from all sides. Talon was forced to retreat and block as many as he could but the sheer force of the attacks drove him back. The crowd of men was shouting like madmen now as they knew they were witnessing the closure of the fight.

Talon suddenly found that his back was against a wall and his opponent's bloodied face was floating in front of him looking dangerously confident. It was time to take the fight to Montague. He ducked a wicked swing that hit the wall and dislodged a few chips of masonry then dodged under Montague's guard to whack his opponent hard on the knee. Montague swore and stumbled back, holding his stick up with one hand while he rubbed his knee. Talon gave him no respite but followed his opponent as he fell back, striking and stabbing with his stick at Montague's face and other exposed parts.

He felt a small flame of anger rising in him and knew that he should finish it soon or his more bulky opponent could overwhelm him. He struck hard at Montague's guard and began to drive him back. Montague tried to regain the initiative but Talon was intent upon denying him any openings. With three more vicious and well aimed blows, Talon brought Montague to his knees. They were both tired and panting hard but it was clear to the crowd that Talon had the upper hand now and they were yelling at him to finish his opponent off.

He knew he could, but something stopped him. Montague had fought well and without too much malice. Instead of knocking his man to the ground Talon stopped and let his stick fall to the ground. He took a step toward his opponent, who was still kneeling, looking dazed and offered his hand instead.

Montague looked up, his scarred and battered face covered in blood and saw the hand in front of him. He looked at it for a long moment in the absolute silence now surrounding the two. Then with a crooked smile he took it, dropping his own stick at the same time. Talon pulled him to his feet where he stood shakily still clasping hands.

"Can we be comrades, instead, Sir Montague? Is honor satisfied? I would be your friend."

Montague spat some blood through his split lips onto the ground and looked blearily at Talon. "You are a fighter, young pup. We should be friends, by God. I have never had to fight with sticks like this before."

The men who heard this applauded their approval. They laughed and cheered the two gladiators and came to surround them. They now had their arms around each other. Talon felt like he needed to support Montague somewhat as the big man was still shaky on his feet.

The crowd was suddenly split; men moved back to get out of the way of someone and the severe face of Sir Martin appeared in front of the two men. He looked very annoyed. "This is a time for training, not for games." he said loudly. "Get back to your work, all of you. Sergeants, where are you that these men are behaving as though they are at a celebration?"

Max appeared looking apologetic. "Sire, the students were a bit over enthusiastic and..."

"I fell on my face, sir," Montague said loudly.

Sir Martin looked at him, taking in the battered face and the blood-streaked hair. He was no fool and he understood what was going on, so he said, "See to it that you improve your balance in future, sir. We have to fight the Saracen, not be falling about all over the place getting wounded unnecessarily before then." He looked hard at Talon as though sizing him up. He turned on his heel and left.

Everyone was quiet as he left the scene. Then slowly men went off, talking among themselves about the fight and its unexpected outcome.

Montague turned to Talon. "I was wrong to goad you the other day, Sir Talon. Will you accept my hand on that?"

"Willingly," Talon said and they clasped hands while the other students recommenced their training with sticks.

Max strode back to the two men. "I think you two have had enough training for the day. Go and clean up, you look as though you need it."

Montague said to Talon, "Where did you learn to fight like that?"

Max answered for Talon. "He learned to fight like that in the Holy Land. You're lucky you did not fight with knives or it would have gone very badly for you, Sir Montague. I have watched him kill a man much older who thought he could win against Sir Talon. He is far better to have as a friend than an enemy."

"I shall remember that in the future, Sergeant. I would like to hear of your life in the Holy Land, Talon. We will all be going there one day and I know nothing of it."

Later, Max sidled up to Talon. "I am glad that you won, Master Talon. I bet a lot on you." He jingled some coins in his pouch. "The other sergeants thought you were finished when Montague challenged you."

Talon laughed. "For shame, Max. Aren't the Templars forbidden to gamble?"

Max grinned. "There are times when the opportunity cannot be missed. You as a knight have to hold to higher standards, so you may not. I, on the other hand, a lowly servant, must make my money where I can."

Talon laughed. He knew perfectly well that Max had no need of money. If he had, then the gold he brought to Talon would have vanished long ago. His affection for the battle-scarred sergeant grew.

The training continued day after day in an endless series of drills on horse and off. The tactics used on horseback became clear to Talon as they progressed. It was a few weeks later that with Montague at his left stirrup and another man close to his right that the new recruits managed to charge in a straight line for the length of the long field. The thunder of the huge, eager Destriers in a wide, level line and the battle cry of *"Dius Lo Volte!"* as they charged was enough to heat the blood and give every man in the line the feeling of invincibility.

The sergeants and several of the older knights who had been in battle explained that the shock of the Templar charge had often as not so fractured the enemy armies that it was only needed once and then it was a matter of dealing with the foe as they ran from the battlefield. They explained that as long as the line was level and every man was protected on his right side by his comrade's shield they were almost impossible to stop. Coupled with the huge horses they rode which often towered over those of the enemy, it was a brave or foolish Saracen army that confronted the Templar charge.

It became common knowledge that Talon had lived in the Holy Land, and many came to him to ask him to tell them of the country and what they might expect there. It was sometimes awkward for him as he could tell them almost nothing of the Templars in Palestine, never having been associated with them until just before he left for France. So he would point them to Max and tell them that he was really the person they should ask about their future lives.

The Master Sir Greves called him in to discuss the people and cultures, as that man was keenly interested in knowing his enemy better. Max informed Talon somewhat scathingly that he was impressed by the Master of Mas-Dieu; he had found it rare that a senior officer of that order was in any manner interested in the habits of the other side.

"We have been badly led in the past by several of the most senior men in the Holy Land, Talon."

"How is that, Max?"

"These men came to grief because they had offended God with their arrogance, thinking themselves and their men invincible. They die trying to prove it, charging into not hundreds of the enemy but thousands with only a couple of hundred knights."

"That sounds foolish. The Turks are not fearful men, and some are very great warriors."

"I know that, but these men knew little and cared less of the mettle of the enemy, so they would be swallowed into the dense packed ranks of the Saracen to disappear from sight as they were cut down. They only reappeared as their heads were carried off on the enemy spears for display in Baghdad or Damascus."

Talon discussed this with Max often. Max had spent many years with Philip fighting up and down the kingdom of Jerusalem and counted himself lucky that he had not been led by these arrogant hot heads.

He shook his head. "We are the holy monk warriors of the Christian lands, Talon. But I fear that we are only human and not often well led. The Saracen might not amount to much when alone or in small numbers, but in large armies they can be formidable. They also have the ability to replenish their losses faster than we ever can."

Talon remembered the great cities and the endless lands to the east of Palestine and the vast number of Muslims who could, if united, flock to a single banner. He knew Max was right and he prayed that this might never happen, for if it did, then Palestine was lost.

The days passed in a blur of more training and more drills, so that it became automatic for Talon and his companions to assemble quickly and move into a straight line, then on a shouted command to charge the whole distance of the hard, white fields and crush to pieces the straw figures aligned against them at the farthest end.

He became used to the thick air warmed by many bodies that constituted the heating for the bare, barrack-like rooms, and the constant stink of unwashed bodies. He slept in a stone chamber with a low ceiling and rounded arches that dripped with moisture at night, with twelve other men. They slept under thin patched blankets with an oil lamp burning in the center of the room all night long, shedding a dim light on every bed. This, he was told, was to prevent any man from sinning during the night.

He got used to the routine of getting up in the early dawn with his companions to dress hurriedly and cross the windswept cobbled yard to prayers in the muted light of the morning. He would break the ice in a bucket so that he could at least dash some water over his face. He longed for a hot bath but an amused Max had told him that this one thing he would not be granted while here in Mass Dieu so he had better get used to being filthy for a while.

"The training will be over before long, Master Talon, and then we can take ship to the Holy Land."

"It had better be soon. The winter storms will put a stop to that if we do not take ship soon."

"You're right. I hear that they are assembling a squadron of Templar ships that is due to sail within the week. It will be the last one from these lands this year."

"Where did you hear this?"

Max put a finger to the side of his nose. "We sergeants get to know things, young sir. While you are busy training to be a great Templar warrior, we are listening to the rumors and talking about what is really going on."

Talon laughed at the mild sarcasm aimed more at the system than at anyone in particular. "So we will be on the ships... soon?"

"That depends upon the officers like Sir Martin, Master Talon."

Max rode onto the field leading Jabbar three days later in the afternoon of an overcast day while the students were out on the training fields. He was dressed for travel and Jabbar had bags hanging off his empty saddle. Max was in a hurry. He rode over to the senior sergeant and spoke urgently with him, leaning down from his saddle so only the man he spoke could hear what he said.

The sergeant nodded and Max rode directly over to Talon; he looked strained. "Dismount, Talon. We have to leave at once." He did not elaborate.

Surprised, Talon leaned down from his huge Destriere. "What is it, Max?" he asked in a low tone.

Max said urgently, "We have to leave at once. I shall tell you while we are on the road, Master Talon."

Talon turned to Montague and tossed the reins of his Destriere to him, saying, "I have to leave Montague. Go with God."

There was not even time to say goodbye to his newfound comrades. He looked back at their puzzled faces and lifted his hand in parting, but then they were riding off in one direction while the sergeants were shouting orders at the rest, who wheeled and headed back to the other end of the field.

Talon was impatient to find out what was going on but he left it to Max to tell him when he was ready. They had put a good mile or two between themselves and the Templar stronghold when Max turned in the saddle and said to him, "Word has reached the Master of the Templars here that you are a hunted man, Talon. I heard the news only a few minutes after the messenger left. The Master then called me into his offices and told me to get you away from here as fast as possible and onto a ship, if we can reach the port."

"Who could have known I was here?" Talon asked.

"The Church has many ears and spies, just as we do. I think that the Master Sir Greves must have decided to get you away before there was any embarrassment. Even though we enjoy the direct protection of the Pope it is not a good idea to have unnecessary confrontations with the bishops and priests over an issue of witchcraft. I even had the help of Sir Martin to get everything ready. That man seems to have taken a shine to you."

Talon nodded. He realized that he was protected by the brotherhood of the Templars, but even they did not want to run afoul of the Church over something as serious as a charge of heresy and witchcraft. He sighed. "So we are to go to sea again. Once again I am to take ship and flee; this time I hope not in chains, but still a fugitive."

Suddenly Max turned in the saddle and lifted his hand for silence. They heard the pounding of hooves in the distance and before they could make off they saw Sir Montague and two of their erstwhile companions riding hard toward them. Montague was leading Talon's Destrier by the reins.

Montague reined hard as they came up to the two men. "Talon, you forgot your horse." He grinned. "There is a man and several others, perhaps eight of them, riding after us. They have gotten wind of your route. We came to help."

"Montague, Gerard, Jeffrey, you are all mad. What will Sir Martin say?" Talon asked.

"To hell with Sir Martin," Montague said. "We can't have a mob of bad men chasing after our friends."

"But you don't..." He got no further.

Max had caught the sound of others on the road. "Time for that later, sirs. You are welcome company; but now we have to ride hard, for we are pursued and we have a ship to catch or we'll not be able to leave the country. Hurry! We fly to Aigues Mortes where there are ships of the Temple ready to sail and where we can find safety."

They rode hard for Aigues Mortes all that day and then on into the evening. Talon changed horses and led Jabbar to spare him although he was fit enough and ready to take his master where he would. Max rode a good, strong-boned animal that did not tire easily either. The three other knights who were now part of their group rode good, big horses themselves. All were silent and somber as they rode. Talon and Max in particular felt hunted again and nervously watched their backs.

It was soon clear that they would not shake off pursuit in time to make it to the port.

"How many men did you say there were behind us, Montague?" Talon asked as they rode.

"I counted eight men-at-arms and another who seemed to be their leader."

"Max, we are five and all armed, but we can't outride them to the town..."

"You mean we have to deal with this now?" Montague asked. His face glowed with excitement under his beard.

"Then we must take them by surprise, but we lack much time to do so," Max answered.

They had been cantering along a wide track that might have once been a Roman road, but it was in a sorry state of disrepair with breaks in the slabs and hedges of hazel and thorn very close to the actual track.

"See that dark space over there?" Jeffrey asked. He pointed to a narrowing of the track with thick bushes on either side.

The others saw it clearly. They could turn and face their enemy without fear of anyone getting past and coming in from behind. They galloped up to the narrow space and turned their horses to face their pursuers.

They did not have long to wait. They were warned by the thud of hooves on the hard ground and the jingle of bits and metal as men on horses came into sight about a hundred yards back along the road.

"Halt where you are," Montague bellowed. He looked huge and menacing on his tall horse with his helmet pushed down over his forehead, his lance lowered, as were those of his companions facing the oncoming men.

It was quickly clear to Talon that their pursuers were not as well horsed nor armed as were the Templars. "We could charge them just as we have been trained, and they would be dispersed easily."

There were chuckles of surprised agreement from his companions.

"Time perhaps to put your training to good effect, Sirs," Max muttered out of the corner of his mouth.

In the few seconds that the men ahead of them were milling about the Templars moved quietly into a short, solid line; knee to knee, shields up, and lances down.

A man who appeared to be the leader of the group ahead rode forward and shouted. "You have a criminal named Talon de Gilles with you. Hand him over and no harm will come to you. We want only him."

"By what authority do you wish to arrest him?" Gerard shouted.

"By the authority of the Church of Albi. He is a heretic and is to be tried in that town."

There were surprised grunts from Talon's companions. "Is that true, Talon? This is serious indeed."

"It is not true, Sirs. I was there. My companion and Talon's uncle, Sir Philip, as true a Templar as ever rode, was murdered, partly because of the greed of the Bishop of Albi, who would have stolen his brother's land," Max said vehemently.

"None of us are here because we're saints," Montague growled. "Talon, Max, we are your sworn companions, but you should tell us of this when we are done here."

"They killed a Knights Templar," Gerard said softly. "I do not see why we should hand Talon over to these men."

The others muttered their agreement. The tension grew.

Finally, Gerard, who seemed to have some education, shouted, "You are out of your jurisdiction. We will not abandon our comrade this day."

"Then you are also party to his crime and will be punished for it. Hand him over or we will take him by force," the same man shouted back.

"I think the time for talking is over, my friends," Montague said, with a look at Talon. "We have not enough time to waste as it is."

He stood in his stirrups and shouted at the men to their front, "Go back and leave us, as you cannot win this fight."

There were derisive jeers and the men in front began to raise their shields and prepare for battle.

Montague, who had taken the lead, simply shouted, "Charge them now, my friends, before they get ready." He clapped his spurs into the side of the Destrier and led the small group at a sharp, powerful gallop straight at their opponents. Shouting, "Deus lo Volte!" as they had been trained, the four men galloped as though locked together at the knees straight at the larger mass of men facing them.

The charge was so sudden that the Templars crashed into their opponents as a solid mass that was irresistible. Each lance took a man in the chest or shield and in each case unhorsed the man, who crashed to the earth with a sickening thump. Talon felt the wooden lance of the man he was aiming at splinter on his shield, but his own found its mark in the man's chest.

The Templars were through and turned almost as one to face the tangle of horses and men they had just cut through. There were groans and screams from the downed men and one horse was lying in its own blood, its pitiful screaming adding to the chaos.

"One more charge and they are finished," Jeffrey shouted.

The four men lowered their lances and again rode straight back at their surprised opponents with their great shout.

As they charged Talon could see that three of the men were down completely, while another was crawling about on hands and knees. The other four were milling about trying to recover and face the oncoming knights. They had no chance to defend themselves. The solid mass of the Templars smashed into their milling ranks and took them down. Horses and men were tumbled in an untidy, struggling mass about the grass verge and the road.

"They are finished," Montague shouted.

"And we must leave at once," Talon called, who had said nothing up until now. "We have a ship to catch tomorrow night or we'll miss the sailing."

They continued to gallop up to Max, who held Jabbar.

They rode into Aigues Mortes late the following night, tired and hungry. They were challenged at the gates to the port town but were admitted without any questions when the sentries saw their garb. They rode slowly along the narrow streets that led down to the harbor, exiting onto the wide wooden quay through the gates on the seaward side of the walled city.

Talon could smell the sea and the rank odors that come with a large port. The quays were busy regardless of the late hour. He heard the creak of timbers as wooden boats thumped against pilings in the choppy water of the harbor basin and the occasional cry of a sea bird not yet gone to sleep. He could hear the calls of seamen; the port seemed very active. The sounds of work being done on decks and the splash of slops being thrown overboard all seemed to him as though the ships were very awake. The sky was overcast and it was cold, with a sharp breeze coming off the water.

Ahead he could see the dark shapes of a squadron of huge ships in the harbor, most looked well filled as they rode low in the water; it was as though they were only waiting for a signal to leave. In the late evening light, Talon could just see a forest of masts and spars crowded on each other from the ships in the basin. Ships were tied to ships and also along the wharf side.

There were many men milling about on the quayside, many were carrying heavy sacks up planks to be carefully positioned into the waiting holds of the ships alongside the quays. Torches placed at regular intervals on the walls opposite the wharf gave off a hellish light that reflected off the bare, sweating backs of the common laborers and the chain mail of the supervising soldiers. Men were busy winching sacks of grain and other provisions onto the nearby ships.

Max stopped and dismounted. He tossed the reins to Talon. "Stay here, sirs. Talon, I shall find the man who is in charge." He headed off to the groups of men gathered on the quayside, quickly becoming indistinguishable from the dark figures moving about.

Talon and the other three men waited with the patient horses for what seemed an hour. His thoughts went back to his father and mother in Albi. He wondered if they were safe from the predations of the vindictive priest. He shivered, but for the Welshmen and Max he would be in a prison destined for a fire. This was not the way he would have wanted it, but there was now no going back. The gold would help his father rebuild the castle and establish himself as a well-to-do knight in the region. His brother would inherit and do well, he was sure of that.

He was lost in his own thoughts when Max reappeared. He looked up at the companions on their horses. "We have a ship, sirs, but we must hurry. They're about to cast off to anchor out in the broads and we need to load the horses and ourselves." He led the way hurriedly down to the quay itself and then along the heavily boarded wharf. The horses' hooves sounded loud on the boards despite the shouts and cries of the working men. The whole place was lit by flaming torches placed here and there to shed some light upon their activities.

They were greeted by a shout from a high-sided ship tied to the pillars along the wharf. "Hey, hurry up, you men on those horses, or we'll cast off without you. We have a tide to catch and it waits for no man."

Talon dismounted quickly and led the nervous Jabbar toward the man standing on the quayside.

"Are you the Templars to be shipped?" the man asked querulously.

"Yes," Max said shortly.

The man turned and shouted some commands and several men stirred on the deck of the ship. "Get these horses loaded within the half hour or you shall feel my whip on your backs," he shouted at them. He turned back to Talon and his companions. "Take your baggage and saddles off them and then, when the men take them, get aboard. Keep out of the way; we have done this a thousand times and don't need your damned help."

Rough men took the horses off Talon and the others, who hefted their saddles and bags and then walked carefully up the slippery plank that passed for a gangway to the deck of the ship. It was a big vessel, much larger than the one Talon had arrived in from the Holy Land. It was already loaded with other horses and men, seemingly ready to make for the sea.

They were shown to a cramped upper deck at the back of the boat and pointed to a corner where they were told they could stow their things. Pallets would be provided when they were underway. Dumping their bags in a space they went back on deck to watch the unhappy horses being loaded by the skilled seamen into the hold where there were stalls.

They climbed up a short flight of steps at the rear of the huge ship to a much smaller, shorter deck, where they could see out over the wharfs toward the darkened town. Looking out to sea, Talon could make out ten other ships of the same size as this one that were standing off shore anchored in the tidal river. They all gave the appearance of being ready to sail; all were low in the water with their cargoes of supplies for the Templars in the Holy Land.

Their ship cast off once the last horse was loaded and not too soon. As they used long oars to help drive the ship out to join the other ships in the main harbor, Talon noticed men on horses galloping along the roads that led to the wharf. Men dismounted and he could hear distant shouting from the men on the quayside.

Men waved their arms at one another and pointed toward the ships in the middle of the harbor. It was clear that their pursuers were frustrated, as no one could help them with information. Their ship was now hidden among the many others in the basin of the harbor. Talon and his newfound friends made sure that they were not seen and watched the events taking place from the shelter of the ship's lower deck.

Montague turned to Talon, "We should have finished them off on the road. They do not look dangerous to me."

"You're probably right, but I don't think they can do much now. We're safe on a ship bound for the Holy land."

"You're right, Master Talon," Max said. "These are all ships of the Templar fleet. They would have to go to the Pope to gain permission to search them. These ships are well manned and well armed. No pirates would ever dare to attack us. We should have a safe journey."

Max was standing next to him, staring at the distant figures on the dock that were now mounting up and preparing to leave.

They were all tired so after they had checked on the horses on the lower deck and made sure they were fed they went below and made themselves as comfortable as it was possible in among the cordage and sacks that littered the after deck. Talon went to sleep almost immediately and only woke when he felt the motion of the ship change.

He went back on deck to find that the cold light of dawn was illuminating the walls of the town. The ship had quietly pulled up its anchor and was following several other ships as they now sailed with the morning tide. The broad, round bow of the huge ship dipped and rose in the tidal waters that were taking them down the wide, shallow estuary and out to sea. A light spray flew past the bow and wet his face.

He was glad of his quilted jerkin but even so he wrapped his cloak tighter about him as he stood on the poop deck and gazed back at the receding land. The fortified city fading into the distance seemed to stand alone in the endlessly flat, marshy country-side. The distant stands of trees they passed on their way out to sea were bare of leaves. The world looked gray and colorless in this cold, wet dawn. The gulls wheeled and cried as they glided in the wake of the ships, hoping for scraps to be tossed overboard.

He looked up at the huge sails that were full bellied in the following wind, the rigging taut and humming. Men were busy on the deck below, making fast and preparing for the full swell of the sea that they would encounter later in the morning. There was a brisk cold breeze blowing in from the north. Talon shivered.

Max came on deck. Rubbing his eyes, he saw Talon, and grinned. "We're on our way back to the Holy Land, Master Talon. Are you pleased?"

"In so many ways I am sorry to be leaving this country, Max. It is the home of my father's father and I shall miss my family sorely. But still... I feel like I am finally going home."

James Boschert grew up in the then colony of Malaya in the early fifties. He learned first hand about terrorism while there as the Communist insurgency was in full swing. His school was burnt down and the family while traveling, narrowly survived an ambush, saved by a Gurkha patrol, which drove off the insurgents.

He went on to join the British army serving in remote places like Borneo and Oman. Later he spent five years in Iran before the revolution, where he played polo with the Iranian Army, developed a passion for the remote Assassin castles found in the high mountains to the north, and learned to understand and speak the Farsi language.

Escaping Iran during the revolution, he went on to become an engineer and now lives in Arizona on a small ranch with his family and animals.

Assassination

in

Al Qahira

James Boschert

Talon, a young Knight of the Order of Templars is finally returning to the Holy Land to search for his lost friend, but Fate as other plans for him.

He and his companions find themselves shipwrecked on Egypt's shore. In that hostile land they face the constant threat of imprisonment, slavery and execution.

When Talon thwarts an attempted murder, he finds out that a good deed can lead to even greater danger. Soon Talon becomes a pawn in a political game within a society that is seething with old enmities, intrigues and treachery at the highest levels. To save the lives of two children and a beautiful widow he is now oath-sworn to protect he must call upon all of his skills as an assassin.

A page turner that you will not be able to put down. It grips you from the very beginning

Review:

I was completely unfamiliar with this period and found it fascinating once I got started. I have gone on to read all of the books in the series (that have been written) and find them exciting interesting, very well crafted, informative and difficult to put down.

So thank you James Boschert for writing such an amazing book. I am extremely glad I found and extremely glad you have such a passion for the period and such creative flare.

I highly recommend this book and the rest in the series.

From a reviewer on Amazon

PENMORE PRESS
www.penmorepress.com

Historical fiction and nonfiction
Paperback available for order on line
and as Ebook with all major distributers

GREEK FIRE
BY
JAMES BOSCHERT

In the fourth book of Talon, James Boschert delivers fast-paced adventures, packed with violent confrontations and intrepid heroes up against hard odds.

Imprisoned for brawling in Acre, a coastal city in the Kingdom of Jerusalem, Talon and his longtime friend Max are freed by an old mentor from the Order of the Templars and offered a new mission in the fabled city of Constantinople. There Talon makes new friendships, but winning the Emperor's favor obligates him to follow Manuel to war in a willful expedition to free Byzantine lands from the Seljuk Turks. And beneath the pageantry of the great city, seditious plans are being fomented by disaffected aristocrats who have made a reckless deal to sell the one weapon the Byzantine Empire has to defend itself, *Greek fire*, to an implacable enemy bent upon the Empire's destruction.

Talon and Max find themselves sailing into perilous battles, and in the labyrinthine back streets of Constantinople Talon must outwit his own kind - assassins - in the pay of a treacherous alliance.

PENMORE PRESS
www.penmorepress.com

Historical fiction and nonfiction
Paperback available for order on line
and as Ebook with all major distributers

A Falcon Flies

by

James Boschert

Talon has returned to Acre, the Crusader port, a rich man after more than a y
in Byzantium. But riches bring enemies, and Talon's past is about to catch
with him: accusations of witchcraft have followed him from Langued
Everything is changed, however, when Talon travels to a small fort with Sir (
de Veres, his Templar mentor, and learns stunning news about Rav'an.

Before he can act, the kingdom of Baldwin IV is threatened by none other th
the Sultan of Egypt, Salah Ed Din, who is bringing a vast army through Sinai
retake Jerusalem from the Christians. Talon must take part in the ferocious ba
at Montgisard before he can set out to rejoin Rav'an and honor his promise ma
six years ago.

The 'Assassins of Rashid Ed Din, the 'Old Man of the Mountain', have targe
Talon for death for obstructed their plans once too often. He is forced to tak
circuitous route through the loneliest reaches of the southern deserts on his v
to Persia to avoid them, but even so he faces betrayal, imprisonment, and
threat of execution.

His sole objective is to find Rav'an, but she is not where he had expected her
be.

PENMORE PRESS
www.penmorepress.com

Historical fiction and nonfiction
Paperback available for order on line
and as Ebook with all major distributers

Penmore Press

Challenging, Intriguing, Adventurous , Historical and Imaginative

www.penmorepress.com

www.ingramcontent.com/pod-product-compliance
Lightning Source LLC
Chambersburg PA
CBHW070337170726
48291CB00001B/81